SPACE THRONE

Also by Brian Corley
Ghost Bully

SPACE THRONE

BRIAN CORLEY

ISBN (e-book edition): 978-0-578-70594-1
ISBN (Paperback edition): 978-0-578-70595-8

Library of Congress Control Number: 2020910326

Cover image from istockphoto.com
Cover and Interior design by Jessica Reed

Printed and bound in the USA
First printing 2020

Published by Electric Fern in 2020
www.brian-corley.com

To my sister, who is the best.

CHAPTER 1

Parr drummed his fingers along the arm of the captain's chair of his Fano-class cruiser, the *Aurora*. For the first time in years, he'd tried to reenter the gates of Bilena Epso Ach—tried and failed, and now he hovered alone in space like jettisoned cargo. He'd have to come up with another tactic in order to get back home.

Not that he particularly wanted to go back.

The comm link pulsed yellow, which seemed curious.

Parr squinted at the signal and ran a hand through his scruffy brown locks.

The guards at the gate hadn't exactly been polite, but their communication had come to an end. They wouldn't follow up with a warning signal just for loitering.

Parr pulled up his nav and leaned forward. The ship that hailed him was positioned in the opposite direction from the guard's tower. Whoever wanted to talk had the *Aurora* locked in their sights. Parr absentmindedly twirled a tiny crimson gem linked to a golden chain around his finger while he searched his monitor for more information on the source of the hail.

Norfung Gortn. It was worse than he'd thought. The notorious bounty hunter had a reputation throughout the Twelve as a brute—recalcitrant, unfeeling, but more likely to bring in his quarry alive than dead, which wasn't always as nice as it sounded.

Parr brought the nav full-screen like a windshield across the bow side of the cabin. The Dreadnet, a handsomely sleek spacecraft full of jagged angles, just like its pilot, faced down the *Aurora* with its weapons system hot. Both ships floated just outside the gate to Bilena Epso Ach, a two-planet system and the capital of the intergalactic kingdom known as the Twelve. A gate Parr desperately wanted to find himself on the other side of at that moment, and not just because he was in the sights of one of the most dangerous ships in the galaxy, piloted by its most famous recoverist.

Parr took a moment to collect himself and, after a forceful exhale, kicked a foot up on the dash and leaned back in his chair before activating the comm.

"You got Parr," he said. "Go."

"Glogs and borlongs!" Norfung said. "Of course I have you; it's what I do." His voice boomed through the bridge of the *Aurora* like an explosion at a sand and gravel outpost. The bounty hunter had tracked him down once again.

But how, Parr thought—*and more important, why?*

Parr perused the cabin of his ship as though the answer might be on one of its dingy walls. The blue, green, and orange lights of the ship's panel blinked their familiar, comforting rhythm, while the oxygen unit whirred with a soothing hum.

"Norfung, buddy," Parr said. "It's been too long. What can I do for you?"

"I'm not your friend," he replied. "Prepare to be boarded."

"Boarded in open space? Not on a Fano-class, pal." Parr leaned closer to his monitor as the *Aurora*'s computer scanned Norfung's ship. "Yeah, says here you're flying a Hawv-class. No way we're docking out here, I don't care what kind of makeshift adapter you think you have."

Norfung grunted under his breath, and Parr could hear him fumbling with the controls of his ship. "Hold on, don't go anywhere." The comm link was muted.

Parr grinned and, with just the slightest of touches to the manual control, discreetly maneuvered the *Aurora* around to face the Dreadnet.

He knew how difficult it was to focus a Hawv-class's dual cannon configuration on a target at that range—especially if it was moving toward you.

His old flight instructors had compared it to how your eyes crossed whenever something got too close to the middle of your face. Another teacher had said "nose," but Parr thought that was a bad example since not every creature had one, or at least one at the center of their face.

Parr eased the *Aurora* forward.

The comm link clicked. "Stop right there, Parr, I mean it."

"Sorry, Norfung, I can't help it." Parr pounded his fist against the arm of his chair in mock frustration. "The stasis mount is on the fritz again."

The warning lights in the cabin began to glow red. Norfung wasn't buying it.

"Alright, alright, take it easy, Norf," Parr said. "I'll manually stabilize." He grinned again and pulsed the ship sideways…just out of the twin cannons' reach due to the close proximity.

"If you don't stop that ship, I'll blast you out of the sky!"

"We're not in the sky, Norfung; we're in space—"

"Don't correct me."

"Look," Parr said. "What do you want to do here? You're clearly after something. Why don't we set down on the nearest inhabitable and talk this out?"

Norfung seemed to consider Parr's suggestion for a moment. "Good. Open the gate, and we'll go through to Walo Station."

Walo Station, once a beacon of hope from the old world to the new, had become a different type of freestanding station over the years since the wall went up. Traders, pilots, and creatures with reputations just this side of respectable could do business at the free-floating outpost without going too far into the core of the system.

Unfortunately for Parr, his reputation was too far shy of the respectable mark for him to enter the gates without a verified and desirable commodity, and he didn't have anything that the kingdom wanted at the moment.

"Sorry, Norf, can't get in. Wish I could." Parr sucked a breath in through his teeth. "Say, you wouldn't happen to have a clearance, would you?"

Norfung grunted again and made what sounded to Parr like a dozen disconnected excuses under his breath. Parr was surprised to find that even the galaxy's most feared bounty hunter couldn't get access to the core cluster of the Twelve.

Wow, they're really cracking down these days, Parr thought. *Still, it was worth a shot.*

"Welp," Parr said, "why don't we cruise the rifts until we find a spot worth landing in?"

He didn't always use them, but the rifts were the quickest way of getting from one spot to another in the galaxy. Plenty were mapped out, even more were not—and he'd been warned by his instructors time and again to never take one that wasn't mapped. Nothing worse than slipping blind and ending up on the inside of a black hole when all you really wanted was a couple of good games of blocca and a place to sleep for the night.

"Fine, have it your way," Norfung said.

Parr smirked. "Alright, follow me," he said before Norfung could object. "I know this system like the back of my hand." He activated the ship's boosters, checked a few instruments on the panel above him, and pushed the *Aurora*'s throttle forward.

The sprightly ship came to life and skimmed along the edge of the galactic shield Parr's forefathers had put up generations ago to protect the core two-planet system and its eight moons. It was a beautiful sight to behold, even from a distance, and the grand, spherical shield seemed to emphasize the core's majesty. Like the snow globes they sold for souvenirs at Versit Station.

Someday, this will all be mine.

He remembered, when he was much younger, beholding Palace City from the observation deck of the Tower Royal. Prince Parrtec, as he was known back then, was terrified at the thought of ruling such a vast empire. He didn't care for the fame, the fortune, or the responsibility. He was happy in the small spaces, like in his room or below the control panel of a cruiser as he played with his toys on trips to the outer reaches. All he really wanted was anonymity, freedom.

"Glogs and borlongs," Norfung said. "While we're alive, Parr."

Parr grinned as he pushed the *Aurora* forward a little faster and began to put some distance between himself and Norfung—but not too much. He couldn't risk alerting the bounty hunter to the fact that he was trying to skip. The *Aurora* was fast, but not fast enough to outrun cannon fire, at least not at that range.

As they cleared the protective bubble of the two-planet system, Parr opened up the channel to scan the rifts and was hit with a flood of ads. *Slip to Mecclee's, hottest brool in the Sixteen Systems.*

Sixteen Systems? Parr thought. *I've been in the outer reaches too long.* It used to be twelve. *Malista must have made additional alliances and acquisitions.* Parr knew his sister was thoughtful and strategic, but four additional planets in a couple of years? "Overachiever," he said under his breath.

Try Moma Shando's Delicious Food! another ad said.

Terrible copy, Parr thought. *I can't believe they spent good buldoons on that.*

Parr checked his nav as well the bow display and eased the *Aurora* just inside the gravitational pull of one of the smaller, uninhabitable planets outside the system's shield. He did his best to look as though he were flying casual. However, he was employing an old trick he'd learned long ago when a cocky, up-and-coming pilot showed him how to use a planet's gravity to help sling his ship further and faster without signaling any additional acceleration from its engines. There were always several different angles and approaches one could take, as well as several nav programs to use, but Parr always seemed to have a knack for finding just the right trajectory.

Norfung kept pace. "Nice try, Parr, but I've used the ol' grav slip a time or two myself. Do it again, and I'll turn your ship to dust."

Parr's hands began to sweat. He hadn't expected to break away on the first sling, but he hadn't anticipated that Norfung would be able to identify the maneuver so quickly and adjust on the fly. Most recoverists weren't big on nuance, but apparently, Norfung was more than a one-dimensional gun for hire, and that made Parr nervous.

"Sorry, Norf, old habits," Parr said. He made a point of smiling as he talked, even though Norfung couldn't see him on the other side. It was a trick he'd picked up somewhere along the way in the outer reaches. Apparently, creatures heard a friendlier tone when you spoke that way. "This used to be part of my trade route." Parr fidgeted with a few different switches and checked a few gauges. "I know there's a rift around one of these planets that's perfect for us. I just can't remember which. Don't worry. I'll know it when I see it." Parr let out one long exhale. "That sounded believable, right?" he said under his breath to his ship.

It didn't answer back; it was a Fano-class, after all.

There was no way under the five suns that Parr would voluntarily meet up with Norfung. He'd be a goner if the bounty hunter ever caught up with him. Thankfully, he had the upper hand since he'd learned how to fly in this system. Parr had no intention of setting his ship down anywhere near Norfung or the *Dreadnet,* and if he played his cards right, he'd soon be out of the bounty hunter's reach.

The *Aurora* was on target and just shy of the beginning of Parr's favorite route for building speed. Good flying was more than just powerful thrusters and a fast ship. It was about using the surroundings to your advantage. It was a basic lesson his father had taught him years ago—or at least his father's best pilot had taught him.

There were three planets and five moons between him and freedom. He'd use their gravity to pull and sling him to gain more speed than his thrusters could ever produce on their own. It was a tricky maneuver even for those familiar with the layout, and it would be practically impossible to pull off for even the most skilled pilot if they'd never done it before, especially at full speed.

Parr slung the *Aurora* around the first moon, and the cabin's red emergency lights began to pulse.

The comm clicked, and Norfung growled, "What did I just say?"

"Take it easy," Parr said. "The rift has got to be around here somewhere."

"What was wrong with Moma Shando's?"

"What was wrong with Moma Shando's?" Parr asked. "Did you see that ad? Everything. Everything was wrong with it. Relax, I'll find us a spot."

Parr could hear Norfung grumble a series of curses on the other side of the comm, but the connection began to fuzz out as he eased the throttle forward and whipped around another little moon. "Come on, Aurrie," Parr said, and tapped the console of his cruiser. "Now's your time, girl."

The emergency lights strobed faster, and the comm buzzed with a distorted message from the *Dreadnet.* Parr was still within range, but

Norfung was going to have to follow his exact path now in order to have any hope of keeping up with him. Parr spun the crimson jewel around his finger one last time before he gripped the throttle and eased it forward.

Through the next grav slip, the *Aurora* once again proved her reputation as one of the fastest—if not the fastest—ships around. She poured on speed and started to put real distance between the two ships. The comm link blinked a dark orange.

"That's not good," Parr said under his breath. "Come on, you got this, girl."

Parr frantically evaluated the rifts and scrolled through them almost as fast as Aurrie moved between moons.

Red warning lights pulsed through the cabin as the third sling almost put the *Dreadnet* out of range. The bridge's klaxon joined the pulsing lights as Norfung fired on Parr.

Parr glanced at the monitor and was relieved to find that Norfung had launched a nonlethal burst meant to arrest movement rather than destroy. Parr deployed two projectiles behind him with the same tracking identifiers as the *Aurora* in the hope that they would distract whatever modules Norfung had fired.

It's now or never, he thought. Parr hammered the throttle forward as they headed toward the last sling.

CHAPTER 2

Parr desperately searched through the names of the rifts down the right side of the cabin's largest monitor. He had to choose while his ship was still outside the *Dreadnet*'s range on the far side of the endmost moon.

Finally, a wash of symbols that wouldn't have meant much to anyone who hadn't spent much time in the outer reaches popped up on the monitor. Fortunately for Parr, he'd spent enough time in the outer reaches to know the symbols indicated that the rift led to Lobrow, an outland planet just shy of respectable. A place where Parr felt most at home. Not Lobrow, specifically, just planets like it. And stations. Anywhere he could find a cold snack, a strong drink, and a good game of blocca.

He eased the *Aurora* into the final sling with one hand on the stick control while punching in his destination with the other. He grasped the tiny crimson jewel in his hand and kissed it for luck as he finessed the final keystroke and jammed the throttle forward.

Once again, he'd chosen the perfect trajectory for the grav sling, and the *Aurora* left the *Dreadnet* behind. Norfung lost visuals, and Parr slipped the rift.

A tube of blue light encapsulated the Fano-class cruiser. Even after all this time, he still marveled at the effect. Parr breathed a sigh of relief and wiped his sweaty palms across his pants before he stood up out of his chair to get a better view. No ship, missile, or projectile was faster than another inside the rift—it was like a crease between places.

He took a few moments to stroll around the bridge and admire the swirling mists of the prismatic blue through the viewscreens.

Another close call, he thought. Why was Norfung even after him? His mind raced through the various creatures that would have loved to put a bounty on his head. He chuckled to himself and ran a hand through his scruffy brown locks. There were too many to count. But who could afford to hire Norfung Gortn?

Hopefully, it wouldn't matter soon. If he could just figure out a way to get inside the gates to Bilena, it would all be over.

The console chirped a notification, and Parr slumped back in his captain's chair with one leg slung over the arm. He brought up the broad view on his monitor and made some adjustments to the instrument panel as the *Aurora* exited the rift.

Parr never got used to the sensation. Even though the *Aurora* burst through at the same thermal-tile-melting speed it had maintained in the rift, it seemed like nothing compared to the velocity inside the swirling tube.

He couldn't recall if that was a trick of the mind or actual physics. It had been a while since Parr had taken that class, and given the subject matter, he probably hadn't been paying quite as much attention as he should have been. He had always been more concerned with the practical aspects of how to get in and out rather than the mechanics of how it all worked.

He pulled up an additional nav screen and scrolled for information on nearby ships, but nothing came. No *Dreadnet*, no Norfung. Parr chuckled to himself, gripped the tiny crimson gem in his hand tightly, and pounded it against the armrest of the captain's chair. He'd done it again.

"Nice work, girl," he said with a soothing pat to the control panel. "I knew you had it in you."

Parr double-checked his coordinates and guided the *Aurora* toward a tiny red planet.

⌃

The docking process was more relaxed than Parr had anticipated. Apparently, the outpost at Lobrow was more interested in helping ships dock than keeping them away and accepted a very light information package.

Parr suspected he could have even fudged his name if he'd wanted to, which technically he did whenever he docked. No one could know they were hosting the long-dead Prince Parrtec.

However, in this case, he was pretty sure he could have told them he was Moma Shando, and they would have believed him.

Parr left the cockpit of the cruiser and milled about in the somewhat grimy but well-kept living quarters to check out the gallery of trinkets he'd collected from various markets across the galaxy. He stalled for a quick perusal before he punched in the code to the case. The keypad chirruped, and the top of the display slid open.

He reached in carefully and picked up a tiny figure he'd acquired on Bostrap to remind him of a fortuitous shipment of kalchoes—his first big-ticket haul. He'd had no idea how much those would be worth when he'd arranged the deal, and luckily for him, neither had that dumb hick trader. It had felt good to close his first big deal, and thanks to the little curio, he'd never forget it.

The figurine was rustically carved from a locally sourced root, and the artisan had topped the tiny creature with a shiny golden hat. He'd spotted it on his way to the meeting and promised himself he'd pick it up on the way back as a reward if he got a good deal … and did he ever.

Hopefully, he'd find something just as rare on this scrappy little rust ball of a planet. Something that would gain him access to Bilena's core system through the agricultural gate. If they weren't going to let him in based on the falsified credentials he'd acquired, maybe they'd let him in if he had something they needed.

Parr returned the tiny figurine to the display case and locked it back up before heading down to the hangar.

⋀

The place was semi-modern, with tubular lighting strung horizontally along the walls. The metal ceiling was dimly lit, highlighted by a dull glow reflected from its cream enameled arches. The deck of the hangar was crawling with life, and a team of dull brown, chitin-encrusted creatures chirped and skittered all over the *Aurora*. One of them held a clipboard and scuttled over. He was half Parr's size, and all edges and points.

"Welcome, sir," he said between a series of clicks and hisses. "My team is checking your vessel for chips, scratches, and whatnot that ships accumulate via the various debris and whatnot one encounters while traveling through space and whatnot. It's a free service—free to you anyway; your insurance will cover it—"

"That's OK. I'm good," Parr said.

There was an operation like this at almost all the ports these days. The crews tried to scare creatures into thinking that the small scratches and cracks would turn into something worse and suck them out into the vacuum of space. Parr could see a hustle coming from a farlong away and didn't have time for their foolishness.

A tall, bipedal figure with gray, bark-like skin that Parr recognized as a firdug approached down the midway. He carried a binder and moved slow and flowy, as though he were strolling through deep water. His dark green uniform indicated that he worked for the dock, so Parr marched forward to close the distance and hurry up the interaction.

"This your ship?" the firdug said with all the speed of a thol on a lazy afternoon.

"Yep, she's mine," Parr said.

The firdug licked a long, spindly finger and sorted through a few pages. The bark-like flesh above one of his eyes raised before he looked back up at Parr. "The *Aurora*. I've heard of this ship."

Parr stared at the creature, and the creature stared back. He was waiting for more from the firdug, but nothing came.

"Yeah," Parr said. "She's probably everything you've heard about and a few things you haven't."

Parr was impressed with himself and waited for a response from the firdug, something like a smile or a laugh, but instead, he got more of the same, which was to say, nothing. He'd heard of firdugs before but had never met one in person. They were said to be good-natured, wise, and some of the warmest creatures you could ever hope to meet.

Maybe this one was a dud.

"We received your payment, thank you," the firdug said. "Now, let me talk to you about the extra services we provide."

Not this guy too, Parr thought. *Everybody's got a hustle these days.*

"Yeah, yeah," Parr said. "Clean and refuel, just like I sent in the transmission—and don't skimp on the SDUS."

Places like this always skimped on the SDUS.

"Right away, sir," the firdug said, and waved to the control booth like he was inside a particularly slow time warp.

"Thanks, take care of my girl," Parr said, and started toward the exit. The bustling port housed many and varied types and classes of vehicles. There were a couple of larger ones, but mostly the small-to-medium-sized sort one would expect on this type of planet. Plucky transport that was easy to get in and out of a place unnoticed by a lot of monitoring systems—most, even, if you really knew how to fly a ship.

Parr scanned the shadows around the door to the main exit and found a gang of furry numblers scurrying around on the edges of the light—just what he was counting on. *They'd probably know a place,* he thought, and he made his way toward them.

"Hey," Parr said to one as it flitted his way. "You know of a good market around here?"

"Oh, I don't know," it said in a high-pitched voice. "Maybe I do for, say—a half buldoon."

Parr chuckled and tossed him a quarter buldoon. Creatures in the shadows almost always dealt in hard currency. The numbler rolled it over in its little hands, inspected it with a critical eye, and gave it a long sniff. It seemed to clear inspection because the little creature passed it off to an even tinier numbler that scurried off into the deeper shadows.

"Yeah, I know a place," he said with an easy smile. "Tap me."

Parr never trusted an easy smile, but he still bumped his wrist nav to the numbler's outstretched paw and heard the chime that indicated a location had been received. Numblers had a good eye for baubles and trinkets and knew where to get the best, so he'd be sure to check that market out after he finished up with the larger business for the day. "Thanks," Parr said, and strode out from the corridor and into the glow of the planet's tiny sun.

While it had clearly once been a desert planet, Lobrow had been developed quite nicely over time. The architecture was modern steel with a nod to its rock and clay predecessors. No building stood more than a few stories high.

Parr scanned the area for signs to the main expo and began to follow the route.

He was going to need to exchange his cargo of Varulean napedes for something else if he wanted to have any hope of getting through the gates of Bilena Epso Ach. The officials he'd talked to earlier would have directed him to the agricultural gates if they'd needed them, no matter how fuzzy the credentials.

He wished he remembered their names. Parr wasn't exactly the vindictive type, but he sure would enjoy a reunion with them after his ascendency.

"Hot snack, cold snack—both types," a squat, roly-poly vendor shouted. The creature wore a strangely folded paper hat, and the sleeves of his uniform bunched at his four elbows.

Parr was famished but pushed his hunger aside for the moment. The street was crowded with various types of transport cruising on the ground as well as one level flying through the air. Modern silver and bronze vehicles mixed with the outdated dusty roses and drab greens.

Merchants hawked their wares on the sidewalks, and creatures milled about at food stations with their heads down in bowls or checking their personal comp systems.

Even though it appeared as though everyone was minding their own business, there were usually more than a few predatory eyes on waystations like this. And as with most predator/prey scenarios, it usually behooved one to travel in a crowd.

A group of respectable-looking creatures in dark blue suits with darker blue buttons made their way down the street. Parr was thankful he'd never had to wear those, either as a royal or now. It wasn't that he didn't enjoy the look; it was that he felt like those who wore it were rarely authentic to the way they presented themselves.

Still, given their attire, Parr guessed they were headed to the expo as well, and since there was safety in numbers in a place like this, he slipped in just behind them as though he were a part of the group. Even though Parr knew how to handle himself in a street fight, he preferred an advantage when he could get one.

It took a moment for his translator to kick in, as the business-creatures in the group did not care to be understood. Their clicks and bellows soon translated into a boorish conversation about the correlation between their hard work and hard play cycles.

Parr rolled his eyes.

The expo was within sight, but instead of heading toward its entry gates, the group beelined into the purple light of a nearby brool. *Typical,* Parr thought.

Parr had to hand it to the proprietors of the brool; it wasn't obvious at first glance. The place looked respectable enough and was well positioned, given its proximity to the expo. There was no doubt they catered to a higher-end clientele based on the façade, but the purple light and telltale music that spilled into the street were a dead giveaway. The business-creatures congratulated themselves on their discovery and were warmly greeted by the staff.

Parr hurried past and slipped into the queue for the expo, trading the relative safety of the small group for a massive crowd. The crowd's sheer numbers didn't mean he was safe, however.

He hated queues. He always worried someone would recognize him and he wouldn't be able to break away. Either because too many people would block his path of escape, or because he'd be next in line and too stubborn to leave after a long wait. There were too many variables that could make such an encounter go wrong and only a few that could make it go right.

Maybe in the best-case scenario, someone would recognize him as Prince Parrtec and escort him back to the two-planet system and directly to his throne to begin his reign—but probably, especially on a place like Lobrow, someone would relish the opportunity to ransom Prince Parrtec.

Wait, he thought. *Ransom a prince who everyone already believes to be dead? Not likely.* Which was way worse. A guaranteed death sentence since there wasn't much use for a worthless prince on the open market.

Of course, there was always the very real possibility that someone would recognize him as the guy who'd gotten the better of them in a deal or the guy who may have exaggerated or downplayed facts to get the upper hand. The guy who'd swooped in and taken everyone's buldoons after a round of improbable good luck at the blocca table.

Two security guards began to eye him once he was next in line for entry.

"Parr!" a voice bellowed from behind him.

The voice set every nerve ending in his body on edge, and he did everything he could to face forward as though nothing were happening. *Why now?* he thought. *I'm almost inside.* He ignored the voice and tried to convince himself it was calling for someone else with a similar name.

"Parr," the voice bellowed again. "Don't act like you can't hear me, I saw your head start to turn when I said it before."

Parr cursed under his breath and continued to act casual.

"Parr, you skrill-backed son of a grebulox!"

The security guards' hands moved to their blasters like languid skurks stalking their prey, silent, smooth, and barely noticeable to the untrained eye.

Why? Parr thought. *Why can't I just have a normal day at the expo like everyone else?*

"Parr, you scruffy-looking, white-eyed shank of a dolker," the voice continued to yell. "It's me, Manc! I traded your ship to you?"

Manc Yelray was a round ball of creative curses and big ideas that didn't always pan out. He was an outlander who'd risen high in the ranks of the Corpulon Valvente and then, like many, left the highly regimented fleet behind for a life of privateering. He'd traded in his uniform for a three-quarter-length fur cloak that was almost indistinguishable from his mane of unruly dark hair. He wore a wide leather belt full of brass buckles, loops, and bric-a-brac that jingled as he wobbled forward.

He was also the trader responsible for the transaction that had dealt Parr the Aurora. Parr still couldn't believe he got her for that clunky pile of armada surplus garbage he'd offered the old pirate.

Manc cut the line and clapped a hand on Parr's shoulder.

"Still can't believe you traded me straight up for a badged, official vehicle, you airy-brained, silver-tinged plonk," Manc said as he rubbed his hands together and cheerfully nodded a greeting to the security guards, both of whom cast a questioning look back at Parr.

"It's OK," Parr said unenthusiastically. "The old man's with me."

"I'm not that much older," Manc said to the guards with a wink. He really wasn't that much older than Parr, to be fair. More like a young uncle, or someone who would pretend to show a young pilot the ropes of a station only to position a trade when the time was right.

The guards shook their heads in unison and waved them both through. The creatures in the queue behind them all grumbled their disapproval, and some even went as far as to make a few rude gestures in Parr and Manc's direction. Even in an outland station like this, cutting the line was frowned upon.

Parr kicked himself for failing to consider the scenario that someone would recognize him, turn half the market against him, and potentially slow his progress before he stepped foot into the expo. However, he made a mental note to add that to the list for future reference.

"Hi, Manc, so good to see you," Parr said.

He didn't mean it.

"Thanks for letting me through," Manc said. "I hate lines; never know who might recognize you or for why."

"Yeah," Parr said. "I get that."

"Course you do, you steaming pile of croker droppings!"

"Yeah, well, I have cargo to move, so … ," Parr said. He meant it as a polite way to part company, but the old pirate didn't, or more likely wouldn't, take the hint.

"So, I'll come with you," Manc said. "I have some time to kill anyway. Besides, safety in numbers in this type of place. Don't want people to think they can make a deal, then take you out when you leave by yourself."

He had a point, Parr thought.

"Fine," Parr said. "Let's go."

The expo hall was much larger than Parr had expected for a planet of this size and caliber. Business-creatures mixed with the typical rogue's gallery of traders, legitimate captains, and smugglers. The structure itself was a mix of natural and manufactured elements. It appeared as though its origin was a large cave, from which it had expanded over time. As a result, one side had a darkness to it, while the other was well lit through a combination of both artificial and natural light. Parr was impressed by the beautifully crafted steel, enamel, and glass design, as opposed to the hodgepodge of parts he was used to seeing on some of the stations in the outer reaches. The updated portion was even lit with Xanderian crystal chandeliers, clusters of thin, round tubes.

Parr decided to head toward the cave area, which seemed a little more clandestine. The booths that greeted the customers at the grand entrance of floor-to-ceiling windows were great and all, but they didn't seem the type to sell what he was looking for.

Larger booths were typically operated by companies or traders with a solid reputation to uphold and usually dealt in commodity-type fare. Given the size of the *Aurora,* however, he would need something small, unique, and valuable if he had any hope of getting past the gates back into his home system. The ship wasn't exactly tiny, but the *Aurora's* cargo bay couldn't haul bulk commodity foodstuffs—at least not enough for them to open up the agricultural gates back at Bilena Epso Ach.

Smaller booths were usually hit-or-miss. They were most often occupied by either merchants trying to get their business off the ground or burnouts going through the motions until their businesses finally spiraled down to their sad and uninteresting ends.

Every once in a while, however, there was a tweener. Someone in the shadows who stood back and waited for just the right customer to come to them. That was Parr's bread and butter.

Sure enough, Parr spotted his target. A slime-covered, corpulent mosp stood behind a table at his booth. The mosp was on the green side of the slime scale, which meant he ate regularly. Hungry mosps were on the redder side of the range, which meant a different advantage at a different time, but for now, green suited Parr just fine.

"Greetings," Parr said.

"Yep," the mosp said. His head was down as he stared at his comp device, and he wouldn't even look up to greet Parr.

It was just as Parr had hoped. The kid was disengaged and more interested in what was going on somewhere other than the expo. Parr had half a mind to bet Manc that the guy was the owner's kid or a friend of a friend. Presented with all the variables, the other half of Parr's mind took over and convinced him to keep his gambling money safe and to focus on the event at hand.

"Mind if I take a look?" Parr asked.

The mosp grunted and nodded his head.

Manc leaned in, and Parr nudged him out of the way with his elbow. He wasn't about to let the old pirate get the first look.

Parr pulled up the inventory list on the table's monitor and scrolled through the commodities until he got down to some of the stranger, more exotic items. He did some mental math on weight-to-thrust ratios and pulled up his own charts on the scarcity of some of the items.

Finally, he decided to make an offer on the rarest item—the Gorlem slak. There was no way the mosp would go for the first offer, so he thought he'd shoot for the moon. He'd gladly settle for a shipment of Walpez pepperbalm on a second or third offer.

"So," Parr said. "Got a skonk of Varulean napedes I'd like to trade."

He had the mosp's attention. "Varulean, you say?"

"Best napedes in the Twelve—Sixteen, I mean."

"No doubt, no doubt," said the mosp. "How much would you like for them, or are you looking to trade?"

The direction of the conversation was better than Parr could have ever hoped for. He hadn't expected the vendor to ask buying questions right off the bat. He figured he was going to have to lead the entire exchange.

"How about the skonk of Varulean napedes for your grint of Gorlem slak?"

"Hmm, a skonk of napedes for a grint of the slak … ," the mosp said.

"Varulean," Parr reminded him.

"Varulean," the mosp repeated with a finger tapping at his lips.

He was going to do it; Parr couldn't believe it. He was as good as a purple-scaled welper basking on the shores of the Tirelean Sea, as good as—

"Ha! What a terrible deal, you mushy-witted pisloot," Manc said.

Manc's outburst caught the attention of all who were passing by as well as a few neighboring vendors. Parr shot a look like a dart out of the corner of his eye at Manc, who returned his look with a wink.

"You're a wily one, Parr," Manc continued. "You smooth-talking chadorak!"

"Um, well," the mosp said. "Let me consult the trades—one moment."

Parr knitted his eyebrows together before mouthing, *What are you doing?* at Manc.

Manc held his hands up and mouthed back, *Sorry, I thought the deal was done.*

"According to my research, I would need three skonk of the napedes for the one grint of slak. Add that to the ledger, and we have a deal."

It was a fair assessment, even at wholesale, but Parr needed cargo that would guarantee his entrance, and one-third of a grint of slak wasn't going to do it. Moreover, now that Manc had brought the mosp to full attention, his odds of negotiating a good deal had been significantly reduced.

"Sorry, just have the one skonk," Parr said. "Have a good day."

Parr bumped Manc out of the way as he marched down the aisle of vendors. He was going to have to put some distance between the mosp's booth and whoever his next target would be.

"You ruined my deal," Parr said.

"Sorry, pal, I feel like a real grooq-fisted shamdook."

"Manc, I don't understand half of what you say. What in the five suns is a shamdook?"

"You never seen a shamdook?"

Parr shook his head.

"Big ball of meat and fat that floats in the water off the coast of Rofilda. You telling me you never heard of them?"

Parr shook his head again.

"Terrible eating, but cute as a fogvorn. Still, people keep raising them on farms inland on a couple of systems now. Just a shame. Enough to put a fellow off meat for a while."

"You a vegetarian, Manc?"

"No, not quite, I'm afraid. I keep trying, but I just can't do without a good ol' shank of benixton here and there."

"I hear that," Parr said.

A shadowy figure in one of the smaller booths caught Parr's attention. The figure was tall, with a large purple-domed head, and wore a jacket of muted colors that changed in a distinctly unextravagant manner whenever the light hit it at a different angle. In fact, almost everything about the vendor was eye-catchingly unremarkable.

Just the type of creature he was hoping to see.

"Wait here," Parr said under his breath to Manc. The old pirate gave a mock half salute and rocked on his heels as he watched Parr follow the vendor into the shadows.

"Greetings," the vendor said.

Parr hadn't seen anything like the creature before. Her features seemed to shift whenever she moved her head to a different angle, which was constantly.

"Greetings," Parr said in his normal tone of voice. Which was by no means full throated but still seemed too loud for the vendor's comfort. She folded her arms across her body as though she were hugging herself, but Parr knew that she was covering her ears. Her skin flushed momentarily, as though she'd just revealed a secret. "Sorry," Parr said in a softer voice. "Is this better?"

The vendor nodded her head and, without taking her eyes off the rest of the room, reached into her long, multicolored jacket; pulled out a small ledger; and offered it to Parr as though the tablet were a twig for bandolet—the outland child's game.

He took the tablet and discovered a veritable treasure trove of rare items, most of which were only found in the deep outer reaches, if at all. Nearly any of them would be of value inside the gate to his old home system.

"Are you looking to buy, sell, or trade?" the vendor asked in a voice just above a whisper. She lifted Parr to look behind him, then set him back into place.

"Trade or sell," Parr replied, and did his best to look as though he weren't unnerved that the creature had just picked him up off the ground like a trinket lifted for dusting.

"OK then, what do you have?" the vendor asked.

"Got a skonk of Varulean napedes," Parr replied.

"Varulean, eh?"

"That's right, only the best."

"It would not be wise to try and pass Wiblong napedes off as Varulean," she said with a sideways look and an arched brow. "We had someone try it at another expo, and it did not go well for them."

"Nope," Parr said. "These are authentic Varulean. On my honor."

"Your honor?" She gave him a long look before her neck started to make a series of clicking noises. "OK, what do you want for your honorable napedes?"

Parr scanned the abundance of riches in the ledger until his eyes began to settle toward the bottom. He was pleased to see that she knew where he was looking and didn't seem to flinch.

"How about two grint of the Binalen apdos?" Parr asked.

"One grint," she countered.

This is too good to be true, Parr thought. *Should I ask for a grint and a half? No, I don't need it. I just need the grint to get back home. Just strike the deal.*

But before Parr could seal the deal, a commotion arose from a nearby booth. The vendor's eyes snapped to the source of the disturbance. She didn't look pleased as she undoubtedly did not enjoy the undue attention on her area of the expo.

Parr looked back to find three heavily muscled creatures with large tusks jutting from their lower jaw surrounding Manc. Either their body temperature ran hot, or they felt very comfortable in their own skin, because they wore very little clothing outside of some strategically placed leather.

One thing was for sure: they looked like trouble.

CHAPTER 4

"Aren't you the guy that cut the line outside?" one of the tusk-jawed creatures asked.

"Me? No. I just got here," Manc said.

"Liar. You're the guy—and there's the guy that let him in," another said, pointing at Parr. "I still remember his name—Parr. You called him a white-eyed shank of a dolker."

"Yeah, that was kind of rude," said the third tusk-jawed creature.

The vendor nervously covered her face with one sleeve and then another. "Take your friend and get out of here," she whispered.

"Let's just seal the deal," Parr said. "C'mon, a skonk of Varulean for the grint—"

"Go!"

Parr cursed underneath his breath.

One of the tusk-jawed creatures pushed Manc's shoulder and said without a hint of irony, "I don't like rude creatures."

Manc put his hands in his pockets and grinned wide.

To most passersby, it was a friendly smile, but for those involved, it was almost certainly more. The move risked putting Manc off balance, but to the trained eye, it indicated he had weapons hidden inside his jacket—and someone who'd smuggled weapons into the expo was a very dangerous someone, indeed.

Apparently the tusk-jawed creatures had just such trained eyes, and each backed off a step.

"C'mon," Parr said, trying to monitor the unfolding scene as well as the vendor. "Nine-tenths of a grint, I doubt they'll even look, I can probably pass it off as a full—"

"Leave before I call security," the vendor replied.

"Fine," Parr said, holding up his hands. "I'll go." It wasn't that he was afraid of the security so much as he was worried about the attention. No one would want to deal with someone who'd had security called on them; it didn't matter if it was here in this expo or anywhere else on the little rust-ball planet.

"Yeah, and take your friend with you," one of the tusk-jawed creatures said. "All the way out."

"You got it," Parr said. "Let's go, Manc."

"Goodbye, friends, until next time," Manc said with a deep, floor-scuffing bow. He added, as soon as they were out of earshot, "You filthy blor-bitten sons of grebuloxes."

"Why did you put your hands in your pockets like that?" Parr asked. "You sneak a weapon in here?"

"*A* weapon?" Manc replied with a wink. "No."

"Stop winking at me, it's weird. So, multiple weapons then?"

"Maybe."

"Whatever, Manc," Parr said. "You skorked both of my deals; this has been a total waste of time."

"Oh, I don't know about that," Manc said, and slowed to a stop. He gently pulled at the hem of Parr's jacket to stop him as well.

"I do," Parr said, and rounded on the trader. "Look, I have someplace to be and don't have time to keep finding expos to offload cargo."

"Well," Manc said, "it just so happens I know a place that buys Varulean napedes at multiple times the market rate because no one ever travels out that far."

Parr stopped in his tracks. "Really? How far out?"

Manc barked out a full-belly laugh. "I'm not telling you, you squirmy little bindalooth!"

"OK, so ..."

"Parr, you dunderheaded coocaroo, *I'll* trade you for the napedes," Manc said, then pulled him in closer to whisper, "They're actually Varulean, right? The folks I have lined up can tell the difference."

"They're Varulean."

"Outstanding," Manc said, and clapped him on the shoulder. "How 'bout I trade you half a grint of Gorlem slak?"

"You son of a—" Parr said. "You intentionally skorked my deal back there."

"Ha!" Manc exclaimed, and held his hands out in front of him. "Now, Parr, it's just business."

"Just business, huh?" Parr said, and jutted a hand inside his pocket. "Well, look here, Manc. I don't think you have weapons in your pockets. But I do. And I don't appreciate it when people get between me and my business."

"Hang on now, lad, let's talk this out," Manc said.

"Two grint," Parr said.

"One grint, final offer," Manc replied.

Parr pulled up the inventory on his nav and selected the napedes while Manc brought the slak up on his. Each seemed to want to move before the other could change his mind. They bumped wrists to seal the transaction and set a process in motion far away from the expo center.

Unseen but secure, the dock crews would move the cargo from one ship to another. The whole process was safer than passing an item back and forth between two creatures at the expo because it at least guaranteed the payload would be on the ship whenever the trader returned.

There weren't a lot of things one could count on in the galaxy, but that was one of them.

Pleased with their transaction, the two shared a few jokes on the way out. They exited the expo center through the same spot where they'd entered since it had entrance and egress doors right next to one another.

Red lights pulsed, and a loud beeping pattern blared from rue scanners that indicated a weapon or weapons had just passed through.

He wasn't sure about Manc, but the method Parr used to conceal his weapons was always good for at least one pass through security, but never more than two or three. He wondered why it worked that way, but it rarely let him down.

Security at the entrance sprang into action and apprehended the creatures they were scanning as Parr and Manc strolled toward Lobrow's main thoroughfare. They did their best to stifle their laughter as they parted ways.

⌃

After scoring a shipment that was sure to guarantee him entrée into his home system, Parr decided to indulge in one last celebration. He checked his nav and pulled up the coordinates to the other marketplace the numbler had told him about back on the dock.

He searched inside his pocket for the gem on the chain and gripped it for luck. Parr made sure to keep it concealed—too many creatures around that liked shiny objects, and many more that enjoyed the challenge of unburdening travelers of their possessions. He could certainly appreciate both sentiments to a degree.

He looked forward to one last scavenge—whatever he found at the marketplace would symbolize his last days as an ordinary denizen of the galaxy and forever remind him of his final moments of freedom before he took on the responsibility of the crown. He would need to find something truly exceptional to mark the occasion.

The nav pulsed, and Parr followed the little arrow until he came to a large, clay-walled structure. Its entrance, shaded by a rug on stilts, indicated that it might be the exact type of marketplace he was hoping to find. It was guarded by two heavily robed and hooded creatures that didn't seem to be paying much attention to anything in particular until Parr approached.

"Two buldoons," one of the hooded creatures said without shifting its focus.

"Three if you want snacks," the other added, looking straight ahead, seeming more concerned with the activity on the street than the customer in front of him.

"Sure," Parr said, and bumped his wrist for the transaction. "Three buldoons sounds OK. I am a little peckish, after all."

"Keep that weapon holstered," one of the figures said.

"And have a good time," said the other.

Parr arched an eyebrow, but still, both guards barely gave him a glance. They'd easily detected Parr's smuggled blaster with a cursory look, while both he and Manc had slipped through the state-of-the-art expo security without a hiccup.

He loved places like this.

Parr walked inside the shadowy entrance, through what appeared to be a simple pottery shop. He admired a variety of hand-fired clay pieces on his way to an adjoining room that was filled with all types of metallic bric-a-brac. He was tempted to start perusing objects then and there but figured something much better might await. An attendant saw him and pulled a giant red carpet away from the stone wall, revealing a carved-out opening.

He trundled down a set of stairs chiseled from natural rock that led to a dimly lit tunnel, which, after a few minutes' walk, opened up into a large, open space within a natural cavern. The sounds of the busy market reached his ears before he saw it. The lazy music wormed its way through the tunnel alongside the chitters and chatters of negotiations, curses of protest, and laughter at the punch lines of dozens of jokes—well told and otherwise.

He took a moment to soak in the scene once he was through and wondered if the grand expo he'd just left had looked like this originally: a mishmash of tents and portable buildings—the type you'd see in settlements or in the wilderness of barely inhabitable moons.

A small, purply-red creature in loose-fitting clothes scampered up to him holding a tray high above his head.

Parr signaled to him with a twist of the wrist to indicate that he'd bought the snack-inclusive package.

"Snacks," the creature said, stretching out as tall as he could. "Cold or hot—which will it be?"

"Hmm," Parr said. "I think I'll take the cold."

Cold was always a safe bet in places like this. Heat attracted all sorts of microscopic life, and you could never be sure how long something had been sitting out on a platter. Cold snacks, however, had to be kept cold, and therefore were usually fresh.

The creature scurried along to find someone else in need of snacks, and Parr scanned the area for a good place to start. The tiny makeshift booths all looked equally promising, so he decided to follow the path closest to him and entered a tented sea of textiles, banter, and strange music.

These types of places were usually laid out in such a way that most of the good stuff was in the middle, so you had to travel past all the more mundane vendors and items. Rare weapons, armor, and information were all strategically placed in the center. However, on this occasion, Parr didn't need any of those things. He would find what he was looking for somewhere between the entrance layer and the middle. More than likely in the outer middle, full of tents that harbored the things people pawned, sold, or traded to get the weapons, armor, and information further in.

Parr stopped to look at a few shiny items laid out on a table and was immediately greeted by a droopy-eyed creature that appeared as though he'd just been roused from a nap.

"You can put your leaf in that," the creature said, holding up a small pipe. "Fiiive buldooons, and she's all yours, shebbie."

Five buldoons for this hunk of glass? Parr thought.

"Half a buldoon," Parr said.

"Half a buldoon? Look again … that's high-quality work. Creature crafted, non-manufactured, shebbie."

Parr turned it over in his hands and looked back at the vendor with a neutral mask. "Yeah, no, I don't see it."

"C'mon … three buldoons."

"One and a half buldoons and not a puri more," Parr said.

"Fine, shebbie, take it."

Parr bumped the vendor and pocketed the pipe. He didn't even smoke leaf but wanted to warm up his haggling skills. Other vendors usually had their eyes peeled in a market like this, and it was good to let folks know you were there to buy.

Creatures called out from stalls, barkers shouted in the crosshatching of paths, and music spilled from an open tent toward the middle of the market. *Music, of course,* he thought. Maybe a rare instrument was just what Parr needed to remember his life of grand adventures. Something he could use to write songs for himself. Songs written on the instrument he procured in this very marketplace during his last day of freedom. It was a fine idea, maybe one of his better ones.

He usually tried not to get his hopes up when walking up to a booth—it was bad business—but he couldn't help himself. The idea was too perfect—he had to leave this rock with some sort of an instrument. Didn't even have to be that collectible as long as it was unique and played well.

A bulky-limbed rimiker leaned against the counter, using it as a vantage point to watch both customer and merchandise. Two front teeth gently protruded from its upper lip, and a crown of long, silvery hair rounded its sleek head.

"Let me know if you see anything you like," the rimiker said with a slight lateral lisp.

"Will do, thanks," Parr said.

The walls displayed a gallery of generic stuff that could be found almost anywhere—tiled morindas, fluted lonluns, and a variety of pounders—all new and overpriced.

He needed something with more character—an instrument that was well loved and showed the signs of it. One could always tell if a used instrument played well by the wear and tear. A bad-sounding piece of gear usually wasn't played often and rarely showed marks in all the right places.

"You know, we got a lot of good stuff in this morning," the rimiker said. "Had a guy come in earlier and offload a bunch of stuff before heading out for the booths in the middle. A lot of it is still in a pile over there."

It didn't take long for Parr to see the Skelly in the pile of stuff on the floor. It was painted in a black-to-green burst pattern and had signs of wear just above the receptors and right where it sat in the stand—exactly the type of musical instrument Parr was looking for. He wondered if the rimiker even knew what he had. Surely if he did, the Skelly would already have been polished and exhibited in a more prominent place.

Parr casually sorted through the pile and acted as though he hadn't noticed the prize. He picked up a large black disc. It was a Djalean mroob, bouncy and almost unbreakable. The instrument was used as a drum and seemed rigid until you hit it with something; then it gave you a nice little bounce. It made a pleasant bass sound that used to strike fear into the hearts of the Djaleans' enemies but now provided a decent rhythm for most of the popular music in the galaxy.

"How much for the mroob?" Parr asked.

"Hundred buldoons," the rimiker said.

Not a bad price if it were actually crafted on Djalea, Parr thought. However, it was hard to tell what was made on- or off-world these days, and Parr was far from a mroob expert. It would have been a nice souvenir if he were sure it was Djalean, but he wasn't, so he moved on. He asked for prices on a couple of decent items that he wasn't interested in to further gauge the vendor's ability to mark the items appropriately.

The rimiker was hit-or-miss with them—he knew a lot about most of the newer models of the name-brand stuff but not much about the more esoteric pieces. Parr had half a mind to pick some of those up as well, but time was running short, and he'd rather travel light back to the *Aurora*.

Finally, he got around to asking about the Skelly. Parr picked the instrument up by the neck and supported the body with his other hand. He fought the urge to whistle as he turned it over—it was almost too perfect. Sure, it had a busted tuning knob, but that was an aesthetic knock that was an easy fix for creatures that knew what they were doing—and Parr was one of those creatures.

"What do you want for this green one with the busted knob?" Parr asked.

"It has a busted knob?" the rimiker asked, and came around from behind the counter to look. He put a hand to his chin and made a tutting sound. "It sure does. Well, I'll be a—I guess I just got overwhelmed by the celebrity; I didn't even notice."

Celebrity, huh? Parr thought. *Add that to the profit column—or at least to the collectibility.* Not that he had any intention of ever selling it, but Parr loved a good deal.

"Happens to the best of us," Parr said. "So, how much do you want for this?"

"With the broken knob? I guess I'd say about fifty buldoons."

Parr could tell the rimiker thought he was pulling one over on him. He didn't know what he had and didn't understand how easy the fix was. The Skelly was worth at least ten times that, maybe more depending on the celebrity who'd previously owned it.

"Fifty buldoons for a busted instrument like this?" Parr said. "I'll give you ten."

The rimiker shook his head. "I could probably get sixty based on who sold it to me alone. No, you're getting a good deal, I couldn't let it go for less than forty-five."

It was perfect. A great deal for a Skelly he could play for the rest of his life. Rare and beautiful, an instrument that would look at home in both the *Aurora* and the palace.

"Deal," Parr said, and bumped the vendor for the transaction. "Now, who was the celebrity who sold this to you?"

The rimiker pursed his lips and, in keeping with the tradition of his kind, nodded his head in three directions before pointing.

"Glogs and borlongs!" a voice shouted from across the marketplace.

Parr felt like his blood had turned to ice.

Norfung Gortn? No, it couldn't be.

CHAPTER 5

"Him," the rimiker said. "Norfung Gortn, greatest bounty hunter in the Sixteen and beyond. Nice guy, even wrote my nephew a note." The rimiker leaned close and whispered, "I don't even have a nephew; I was just too embarrassed to ask for myself."

Maybe it's just a coincidence, Parr thought. *Maybe he's not here for me.*

"Parr!" Norfung exclaimed. "There you are. Rarely do I find such a slippery bounty so easy to track."

It wasn't a coincidence.

Parr white-knuckle gripped the Skelly and turned around to face the bounty hunter. A numbler bumped wrists with Norfung, then scurried back to the middle of the market.

Those double-crossing little … , Parr thought, but he didn't have time to waste thinking about the tiny, opportunistic creatures.

Parr had heard of Norfung Gortn long before he'd ever faced him—well, "faced" may not be the appropriate word. "Confronted"? They'd met in space twice now but only communicated over comms. This was the first time the two were able to size each other up in the flesh.

Norfung stood head and shoulders above everyone in the market-place, which made him a formidable figure. Parr couldn't help but wonder how that affected his travel. Most interstellar vessels weren't meant for creatures that tall. Still, he struck a majestic profile, Parr thought. His muscular build stretched fabric in all the right places, and Parr could see why the bounty hunter had become such a presence throughout the galaxy and beyond.

Norfung's dusty-burgundy face, however, was pockmarked and scarred like an interstellar map of moons and outposts you'd never want to visit.

He wore dark-colored, custom-modded military-surplus fatigues with extra pockets crudely sewn in to hold the various and sundry items a good bounty hunter needed—and Norfung was a great bounty hunter, so he probably required more than most. Over the surplus fatigues, he wore two slings filled with various tools of the trade along with a thick belt around his middle with even more pockets, holsters, and a handful of blast canisters.

Parr took a deep breath and composed himself. "Yeah, hey, Norfung. Saw you missed the rift back there, good to see you."

"Ha!" Norfung said instead of actually laughing. "I think not. If you're like most, you're probably shivering in your long boots about now." He looked around a small, gathering crowd for support but instead was met with only a few awkward smiles and a couple of forced laughs. Even though everyone knew who he was there for, his presence made them all uncomfortable. It was more than likely that several vendors and customers at this layer of the market had some sort of price on their head.

"Ah, but I'm not like most, Norf," Parr said. "I know your reputation. You're a bounty hunter but also a business-creature."

"Glogs and borlongs! Don't insult me, my word is my bond. My business of bounty rests on my reputation. I'm afraid I can't go back once a deal is struck," Norfung said. "Now hold still."

"Yeah, sure," Parr said while looking around for anything that could aid in his escape. Something to throw, a table to hide behind, an escape route—preferably one that wasn't obvious, but he'd take what he could get. "You just take your time."

Norfung unholstered a few weapons, activated them, aimed them at Parr, then holstered them again. "Sorry, I don't often use non-incendiary devices."

Non-incendiary? Parr thought. *On the one hand, it's good to know he's not trying to kill me, but on the other—why does someone want me alive?*

"No problem," Parr said. He decided to leave his blaster holstered to keep things nonlethal and scanned the area for something to use. More than likely, Norfung would use some sort of net to capture and haul him in, but he'd probably use a pulser to immobilize Parr first.

Parr thought of the Djalean mroob in the pile behind him. Tough but flexible, it might just bounce back whatever Norfung shot in his direction.

He took a slow step back and checked to make sure Norfung didn't notice as the bounty hunter examined and inspected his gear. Parr was almost there when the bounty hunter finally found what he was looking for.

"Aha!" Norfung said.

If only Parr had a few more seconds; the mroob was just a few steps out of reach.

"Now ... where's the canister?" Norfung searched his slings and pockets while those who had gathered either leaned forward in anticipation or started to slip away while his attention was focused elsewhere.

Parr wondered if the bounty hunter was used to capturing his prey on board his ship in open space as he made the few remaining steps back and felt behind him for the disc.

"Aha, there it is." Norfung found the cartridge he was looking for and clicked it into place. The weapon whirred to life as he brought the muzzle up to point at Parr.

Parr snatched the disc and tried to look cool and calm while he frantically searched for an escape route, but all the pathways through the market looked the same.

"Nothing personal, kid, just hold still a few more seconds," Norfung said.

Parr's survival instinct kicked in, and he seemed to feel the click before he heard the report of the weapon. He pulled the mroob up to dead center on his chest, hoping it was the spot the bounty hunter had aimed for.

It was.

The pulser round bounced off the mroob and hit an unsuspecting bystander. It was just the distraction Parr needed to slide under the flap of a merchant's tent, sprint through its back flap, and run back toward the way he'd come in.

"Glogs and borlongs!" he heard from behind him.

Parr couldn't fight the grin that stretched out across his face as he dashed toward the rough-hewn corridor. He tightened the strap of the Skelly across his back and let part of his mind wander to the song he'd write about this encounter.

Maybe he'd use a rhythm track similar to the squeaking sound he heard just in front of him … what was that squeaking sound? Then there were more; the uniform call-and-response seemed familiar.

Of course, he thought. It was the numblers. Whatever deal they'd struck with Norfung must have included an escape contingency.

Parr could hear Norfung's roar through the crowded marketplace. He stole a look back as he sprinted toward the door and saw tents being dragged down while creatures dashed off in different directions.

Furry numblers emerged from the shadows to try to stop Parr, but they were too small to arrest his movement. He swerved, hopped, and danced around the tiny creatures as they threw themselves in front of him. Parr wasn't sure what the bounty hunter had paid the cadre of creatures, but it must have been pretty rich for them to venture out into broad daylight.

Parr racked his brain as he sprinted away. What could possibly make the bounty hunter go out of his way like this? Surely there were larger bounties to be had out there in the galaxy—weren't there? Did he know about Parr's royal pedigree? That would certainly fetch a bounty worthy of the trouble Norfung was going to in order to apprehend him.

A pulser round whizzed by Parr's ear and hit a numbler a few yards ahead. The numbler froze in its tracks before toppling to the ground. Parr could see the corridor just in front of him but worried he'd be too easy a target within the confines of the walls.

He'd need another distraction if he was going to make it out. Parr snatched an item off one of the last remaining tables before the barren stretch between the tents and the exit and winged it back at Norfung.

"Ayy, shebbie," the vendor cried out as his merchandise flew toward the bounty hunter. He heard an almost inaudible plink of breaking glass before Norfung spouted a litany of boisterous curses.

Parr knew it wasn't enough to slow him down. Norfung wasn't far behind, and Parr would have to think of something better if he wanted to escape.

A numbler stepped in front of Parr and aimed a pocket-sized weapon at him. Without thinking, Parr grabbed the tiny creature on the run. The numbler squeaked in protest before Parr tossed him in a lazy arc behind him.

It was kind of rude to use a creature like that, but if Norfung was going to do what Parr thought he was going to do, he'd need something living to avoid it. Besides, those little jerks had sold him out and had it coming.

Sure enough, the report of a net gun sounded and whipped itself around the numbler behind him.

Parr grabbed the poles of the final two tents and pulled hard enough to collapse them both across the pathway. Merchandise flew and panicked vendors rushed to protect their wares.

He ducked into the shadows of the corridor and heard a different kind of sound from behind him. Instead of the report of the pulsor, it was higher and tinnier.

What is that?

Something buzzed at him at fantastic speed.

A dart punctured Parr's boot just above his ankle. His leg buckled and he slid forward into the clodded clay and gravel. Parr fought to control himself as his heart beat like a thousand mroobs. He grabbed at his ankle, twisted, pulled, and removed the foreign object from his leg, but kept it in hand in case he needed something sharp in the not-too-distant future.

A dart? Parr thought. *How many weapons does that guy carry?*

He limped along as fast as he could manage, back through the pottery display in the false-fronted business and out into the street, where the two guards remained.

"Nice Skelly," one of the guards said, and pointed to the instrument on Parr's back.

"Find everything you're looking for?" asked the other.

"And more," Parr said as he held up the dart for the guards to see. "Norfung Gortn is in there shooting up the place. I thought you ran a decent establishment … well, safe anyway." Parr thought about what he'd said, then added: "Safe from immediate violence, I mean."

Parr felt like a whiny brat telling on a sibling, but in his pain, he felt like whining, and he could use any advantage he could get. If the guards were discerning enough to detect his weapons based on a visual, maybe they had other skills as well.

"Norfung Gortn?" they said at once. They seemed alert for the first time. One of them stood up and uncovered an upside-down basket to reveal a big red button. The guard slammed his foot down and one of the most subtle but off-putting alarms Parr had ever heard rang out.

"I'm refunding your buldoons," one of the guards said. "Hope you'll come back."

"Did you get the cold or hot snack?" the other guard asked.

"Cold," Parr said.

"Good call," the guard replied. "Never know about the hot ones."

CHAPTER 6

The entrance to the port wasn't far, and Parr hobbled toward it as fast as he could with an injured leg. He pulled up a systems report for the *Aurora* on his wrist nav. The cargo from his deal with Manc was in place, and the fuel system was fully green. There was a passive-aggressive note attached from the ground team about how it had cost them more to plug in the *Aurora* than what they'd charged in fuel and that Parr should always let crews know if he'd just filled up at the previous port.

That's not going to get you a bigger tip, Parr thought.

It seemed like more and more crews were sending those types of notes lately, but Parr hadn't fueled up in a while, so he wasn't quite sure what they were on about.

The wound in his leg pulsed with pain as the adrenaline from his encounter with Norfung started to wear off. His pace was slowing, but he needed to get out as quickly as he could. He put the *Aurora* through an automated prelaunch check so she'd be ready for him when he arrived and sent a note to the control tower of the port. He'd want to kick off as soon as he could.

"Glogs and borlongs!" he heard from afar.

Parr's pulse quickened, and he wondered if the dart was tracking him. He tossed it into the bin of a passing garbage vehicle and limped off toward the port. A disturbance clattered behind him—presumably the marketplace guards tangling with the bounty hunter. He hadn't forgotten how impressed he was with the guards at the rustic marketplace, how easily they'd ascertained he was carrying a weapon. Parr winced once again from the pain and hoped the guards' combat skills were as well honed as their powers of observation.

At the pace he was hobbling, he was going to need every advantage he could get.

Parr stepped across the hangar's shadowy threshold. The same numbler from that morning was poised in the shadow of the corridor, perusing the traffic for a potential mark.

"Hey!" Parr barked as he stumbled toward the tiny creature. "How much did he pay you?"

The numbler looked less brave as he tried to catch the eye of some passersby, hopeful that he would find a sympathetic creature. "I don't know what you're talking about."

"Too late for 'I don't know what you're talking about.' Your friends back there already intervened."

"Two thousand, and you were never here," the shifty-eyed numbler said.

"Two thousand, huh?" Parr replied. "I doubt I could throw you that far, but let's see."

"No, I meant two thousand buldoons—"

He snatched the creature by the scruff of his fuzzy little neck and tossed him high and long, just like he used to with the battenball back in the day. He'd had one of the best arms in the Twelve back then, but now he probably only threw the creature a few hundred feet—far less than the two thousand he'd intentionally misunderstood, but still pretty far.

The numbler landed with a crash off in the distance. A satisfying (to Parr at least) roar of disapproval rose from an unseen ground crew, who were clearly unhappy with tiny projectile's arrival.

Parr glared into the shadows, and the rest of the numblers scattered. He didn't appreciate being taken advantage of and wanted to make sure the rest of the little creatures had learned their lesson.

Parr tapped his nav and followed it toward his cruiser, which was tucked away among the other vessels preparing for takeoff. The yellow blinking light indicated he didn't have much time to board if he was going to make the launch window for the next batch.

His leg was practically screaming by now, and he couldn't wait to get to the med kit on board his ship.

"Glogs and borlongs! Get off of me, you persistent tordostrangs! No, you can't have a picture!"

Norfung was in the hangar.

How is he still following me? Parr thought.

Blood trickled from the wound down Parr's ankle, and he noticed the trail of blood he'd left along his route.

Oh. That's probably it.

Parr pushed his hobble as close to a sprint as he could muster. He'd be a goner if he missed the next launch window.

"I see you, Parr!" Norfung crowed. "You won't escape me."

Parr responded with a rude gesture he thought was sure to infuriate the bounty hunter, and judging by Norfung's roar of unintelligible insults, it did.

Just a few more steps until he could fling himself onto the *Aurora*'s lift and up to safety. The yellow light on his wrist blinked faster, indicating that the batch the *Aurora* was assigned to was about to take off. A projectile whizzed past his head and bounced off the ship closest to Parr. He cursed under his breath as he turned the final corner toward his escape.

Norfung was closing in.

Red lights strobed overhead to indicate a disturbance in the hangar. Parr cursed louder this time. Red-light alerts sometimes shut down a port until they were resolved. The clang of boots against the metal catwalk got louder as the bounty hunter closed the distance between them.

Parr mustered every last bit of resolve he had left in him to sprint toward the lowered platform of his cruiser.

"Glogs and borlongs!"

The voice was loud and clear; Norfung must've been right behind him. Parr leaped to make the final few feet between him and freedom. The *Aurora's* platform began to recede as he tripped the proximity sensor and crashed inside. The lift carried him steadily up toward the main compartment as projectiles pinged against the metal around him. Parr stayed flat against the floor of the platform and hoped for the best.

The lift hissed to a stop, and Parr heard the comforting clank of locks that meant he was safely inside. Norfung was dangerous, but he didn't have the equipment to put a hole in a Fano-class on his person—probably.

Norfung would need his ship now if he wanted to have any hope of stopping Parr, and he wasn't going to be able to get to the *Dreadnet* before the next batch launched. Parr panicked as he pulled himself away from his immediate victory to see the yellow light was blinking faster than he'd seen it blink before. It was more strobe than blink at that point, and it began to have an effect on his eyes. He was going to have to get to his chair and manually respond before they'd let him jump with the rest of the group.

Stupid regulations, he thought. There was no reason it couldn't be done automatically, but they still wanted creature-made decisions in the loop … and rules were rules.

Parr didn't think he could stand on his leg, and by now, he'd noticed a bit of a numbing effect creeping its way through his lower torso. There was something on that dart, and it was spreading through his system.

He bit his lip almost as a way to give his mind a different kind of pain to focus on as he crawled through the cabin. The Skelly on his back bumped into the display case, and the jarring motion sent waves of agony through Parr's body. He did his best to push the pain away and keep going, but in the back of his mind, he hoped he hadn't dinged the instrument too badly.

He pulled himself across the floor as quickly as he could, bumping the Skelly on a chair, a stand, and so many other things that he lost track. His head started to spin. He wasn't sure how much longer he could hold out.

Finally, he turned the corner to the bridge; he could see his captain's chair almost within reach. Once he was at the foot of it, he could pull up his comms and blast through with the rest of the group. If they were still allowing ships to launch.

He was exhausted.

Parr's comm buzzed. The control tower was hailing him.

Just a few more feet, he thought. *One hand over the other.*

He was almost there.

Parr cried out and threw himself toward his chair. He miscalculated and bounced his head off of the footrest. He'd feel that later for sure … not that he didn't feel it entirely at the moment. The Skelly dug into his back as he rolled on the floor.

The comm buzzed again. He was running out of time.

He reached deep within and pulled himself up from the ground. He twisted his body so that it fell roughly but effectively into his chair. The Skelly pressed hard against his back, and he worried that he was damaging both the instrument and his beloved captain's chair.

The yellow pulse on his wrist turned orange.

Was he too late?

Parr tapped his comm and tried to compose himself. He may have been injured and out of breath, but he was a captain and needed to sound like one.

"You got Parr, go," he said.

"Thank you, *Aurora,*" the voice from the tower said. "You're approved for launch. Align yourself with the group and wait for the signal."

The comm cut off, and Parr laughed.

Not because anything was funny, but in relief. He couldn't believe he was getting out.

He traced a pattern into his nav, and his ship hummed to life and gracefully eased forward. He called up the ship's med bay and pulled up a kit to be delivered to his chair. The *Aurora* shuddered, and the overhead lights flickered and cut out.

Parr clicked the button for the med bay again … then again. *Did that short the system?* he thought. He kept clicking. He knew it never helped, but he did it anyway. There was always the hope that if two clicks shorted the system, maybe ten would bring it back.

His comm blinked.

Parr stared at the device before he accepted the hail; he knew who it would be before he ever heard the voice.

"Shame about your power, Parr," Norfung's voice boomed through the speakers. "I'll be up in a minute."

CHAPTER 7

Parr finally had clearance from the port, but now he'd lost power. He wasn't sure what Norfung had done, but whatever it was, he'd effectively stranded Parr on this rusty backwater planet with the bounty hunter. Norfung would either wait for Parr to go outside to survey the damage or position the *Dreadnet* to launch alongside the *Aurora*. Either way, Parr was a sitting duck.

Parr pulled his favorite trinket from his pocket and spun the little gem around his finger as he thought of a plan. After a few rotations, the overhead lights flickered back to life, and the *Aurora* began to hum as its systems came back online.

Normally he'd have wondered if it was more than luck, but there wasn't much time for introspection when you were on the run from one of the most dangerous creatures in the galaxy.

"Glogs and borlongs!" Norfung exclaimed through the comm. "How?"

Parr kissed the gem wrapped around his finger and pulled up the preflight list. Everything was still green, and his group was about to launch. Norfung spewed an unintelligible string of curses through the open comm.

Parr thought about cutting off the transmission, but the bounty hunter's audible dissatisfaction was too entertaining to miss, and he decided to leave the comm open until his voice faded away after launch.

The thruster engines of the ships around him came to life all at once with a beautiful blue light before the vessels took off as one synchronized unit. The ships' navs all synced with the tower control to avoid any collisions.

Parr slumped back in his chair. He was thankful for the automation and took a moment to enjoy the view from the monitor as the *Aurora* sped away from the hangar with the rest of the ships in the pattern. They traveled in tight auto-formation as they left Lobrow's atmosphere, then split to the far corners of the galaxy to do their business.

Parr reprogrammed his trajectory and brought up a list of available rifts to search for the most direct route back to Bilena Epso Ach. He wasn't sure how Norfung was finding him, but it was quite possible that he was paying off various station agents.

The usual ads popped up, including *Try Moma Shando's Delicious Food!*

Parr shook his head; he still couldn't believe they were spending good buldoons on that dumb advertisement. He ignored the other commercials until he found the quickest path to Bilena's agricultural gate and set a course for it.

Won't be long now, he thought.

With his direction locked, Parr set his mind to more pressing matters. He mashed the button for the med kit again but was met with a squelching sound. He banged the arm of his chair before mashing the button again, with the same result—just the bonk of a jammed mechanism.

Perfect, just what I need.

He grimaced as he crawled over to the galley. His lower leg throbbed with pain at the site of the puncture from Norfung's dart. He was grateful to be back home in the *Aurora,* with its blinking lights, the climate set just so, and the med kit placed just where he liked it. Not where some stupid Corpulon regulations mandated.

He pulled himself up into one of the chairs around the galley's small table and slid off his boots. Sure, he only needed to take off one, but he didn't know what he may have been tracking in from the station.

He usually removed his footwear around the hatch but hadn't had time given the whole life-in-danger bit from before.

Parr pulled up the cleaning options from a monitor close by and selected the option for a quick vac and mop. Two devices whirred into motion, a circular vac droid and a rectangular scrubber, which chirruped to alert him to their presence so he didn't step on one again.

Parr didn't mind a slight patina to his ship's interior, but he couldn't stand a dirty floor.

Parr winced as he gingerly rolled up his pant leg and examined the wound with his fingertips. It looked clean enough, but he needed to be sure, so he opened the kit and unclipped the scanner. After a few passes, everything checked out. No tracers, life-forms of concern, or significant damage. Parr spray-cleaned the wound and foamed some cells into it for a quick bubble and patch. He flexed his foot up and down. His body felt cool as the medicine's nanos tracked down whatever the dart had introduced to his system, and before long, he was feeling back to his old self.

He sighed and perused the monitor for drink options.

⌄

With Norfung behind him, his course set, and his cargo safely stored, Parr could turn his attention back to the Skelly. Parr padded barefoot back to the bridge to give the instrument a once-over. His escape had added a couple of dings to it, but no big deal; they'd just be more souvenirs of the whole adventure.

He turned the instrument over and admired the aged finish. He felt the scuffs of use in all the right places that indicated it was a fine-sounding instrument. The paint always dulled on the neck where you moved your hand back and forth across the board. Instruments that played well showed that kind of wear. A player wanted to play something that sounded great over and over, while other instruments found themselves in a storage compartment gathering dust. Sure, the older—sometimes more valuable—Skellys looked pristine in a display case, but they rarely sounded right to a knowledgeable ear.

Parr pulled the busted knob off and examined it. Nothing seemed broken on the connecting end. He looked back at the instrument itself and found a small metal washer stuck down around the base of the pin. It took a couple of pulls, but on the third try, Parr was able to extricate the little metal ring. He squinted at the tiny little disc.

"What were you doing there?"

The disc didn't answer.

So, Parr tossed it. He tested the fit without the washer, and the knob found its purchase on the pin. An easy fix and a stroke of good fortune—things were looking up for Parr.

"Just need to get you in tune now. Let's see what you sound like."

He rummaged around and found an old automatic peg winder and started to restring the instrument. The winder had a mind of its own and spun out of control, pulling the string too tight too fast and busting it. Luckily, Parr had plenty of replacement strings in a kit. Parr was a bit of a Skelly enthusiast, and although he hadn't had one on hand in quite some time, he'd gotten a good deal on a repair kit a while back.

He strung the Skelly by hand, strummed a few chords, and started to hum a tune. After he found a melody, he began to put words to it.

Parr spent the next hour or so trying to write a song about his exploits but never really got past the first couple of lines. He wasn't sure if it was because he was coming down off an adrenaline rush or if he just wasn't that good of a writer, but he was leaning toward the excuse of physical exhaustion.

The good news was that the Skelly was in perfect working order, sounded great, and would be a fun topic of conversation whenever someone toured his personal quarters after his coronation as king.

He looked at his nav and saw that he had about a half hour before he arrived at the gate, so he set the instrument back on its stand and decided to pick up a little around the *Aurora* before he arrived. He couldn't have his future staff witness a mess in His Highness's personal vehicle.

He reached down and grabbed a shirt that was more rag than apparel and stopped for a moment to recall the concert where he'd bought it. Parr's favorite band, Electric Fern, had been in port; he'd seen them a few times on the sly back in his days as prince and even a few times in disguise with Jessaba. It was only fitting that it would be his first concert as a free man in the outer reaches—he'd never forget his first taste of freedom. No one escorting him to his seat away from everyone else. No one telling him who to speak to, when to speak, and for how long. No constant attention from doe-eyed admirers looking up at him from below—*OK*, he thought, *maybe I liked that part*. He clutched the shirt to his chest before he put it away to be cleaned in the auto-cycler. He'd probably wear that under a robe or two someday in the future.

Parr used his toes to kick up a pair of ill-fitting orange pants. He'd always regretted buying them but had never thrown them away for some reason. They were the first pants he'd ever bought on his own, and he liked the way they looked even though they weren't quite the right size—especially after a couple of cleanings. He remembered he'd quickly acquired another pair after merciless mockings at various trade stops from creatures asking if he'd just arrived from a high-water planet.

He held them out away from his body for a moment before tossing them into the trash.

There was still time for a quick self-cleaning, so he jumped into the little compartment to start the process—nothing like a hot cleaning, no matter who you were. Unless you were some sort of tonshula, and Parr was no tonshula. Besides, a tonshula wouldn't be caught dead around water, anyway.

I might even miss this little stall, he thought. The palace's cleaning facilities were vast and staffed with a cadre of assistants to make sure he had the proper amount of cleaning supplies and fresh, fluffy towels. *Looking forward to those towels,* he thought, *even if it is weird to have a bunch of people just standing around while you're naked.*

A few minutes later, he popped out and put on his most fashionable garb—unwrinkled black leather pants and woolly blazer. He wanted to emerge from the *Aurora* as a hero of the realm—a dashing explorer the people could look up to. He gazed into the mirror as he smoothed the collar on his jacket and confirmed the idea to himself in the mirror.

Yeah, he thought, *the shaggy hair makes the look. I'm not even going to shave. Everyone will love it.*

Parr strode back to the bridge of the ship and slumped into his chair. He raised one leg over its armrest and practiced his best steely gaze. *No,* he thought. *That's trying too hard. How else could I look?*

Parr thought about a visual comm conversation even though they were highly frowned upon. A lot of gate agents these days worked from their domiciles and didn't always have their uniforms on. It was bad form to expose them, and besides, most traders were in a constant state of dishevelment in their lonely lives aboard a ship, so a professional etiquette of voice and text communications suited everyone just fine.

So Parr scrapped the visual-comm idea. He'd let the cameras back at the palace capture everything for the first time—that would be more exciting anyway. The whole of the Sixteen, seeing him step out of the sleek and dangerous-looking Fano-class cruiser and wave to an adoring public. It would be perfect.

The queue to the gate was long, and he'd been in line for hours. Parr was having a tough go passing the time and twirled the little jewel around his finger as he nervously paced around the bridge. The gem always seemed to bring his thoughts into focus—the lights seemed a little brighter, the engines seemed to hum a little cleaner. Still, he was restless.

He was one of the next in line, and soon he'd be on his way through.

He wandered into his little trophy room to look at the baubles he'd picked up along the way and wondered if he'd be allowed to keep any of them. Sure, he'd be the king, but there were protocols to follow, and some of the figurines wouldn't be appropriate in the palace. He chuckled to himself as he pictured the foreign minister perusing his collection and stumbling across the set of grinklebons he'd picked up on Merkalian-9.

His comm blinked, and he headed back to the bridge to take the call.

"Greetings, *Aurora,*" the voice from the agricultural gate said. "State your business."

"Greetings," Parr replied. "I've come to Bilena with a full grint of Gorlem slak."

"Hold, please," the voice said. They would, of course, have to check to see if there was a need within the system for the slak. The good thing about premium stuff was that it was almost always in need—except for Varulean napedes, apparently.

"Good news," the voice said. "We are in need of that product. Please send a sample to confirm, and we'll pass you through."

"Stand by." Parr punched up the cargo and sent a bot out to the gate to confirm the goods. *Won't be long now,* he thought. He couldn't wait to sleep in his own bed. He wondered if they'd kept his room the way he'd left it, then wondered if it was still his room at all. What if his parents couldn't bear to look at it? What if Malista had erased every last trace of him?

The comm buzzed.

"Greetings, gate," Parr said. "Everything in order?"

"I'm afraid we have a problem, *Aurora*," the voice replied.

A problem? There couldn't be a problem. Everything was in order.

"You said Gorlem slak?" the voice said.

"That's right, a grint," Parr replied.

"Your bot says it's Grolen slak."

"What?" Parr struggled to control the timbre of his voice. "Grolen? No—no. There must be some mistake." Grolen slak was easy to grow—it needed very little light and very little water, and as a result yielded very little taste. Grolen was about as common as dust in any of the lesser quadrants.

Parr pulled up his inventory, and sure enough, it said Grolen. *Manc definitely said Gorlem*, he thought. He'd said it with such conviction that it must have tricked Parr's eyes into seeing that instead of "Grolen." Parr slammed a fist down on his armrest. He'd have his revenge on that no-good pirate if it was the last thing he did.

"Unfortunately," the voice from the gate said, "Bilena has zero tolerance for misrepresentation of goods, and you are now banned for life. Have a nice day."

What? Parr thought. *A lifetime ban for a simple mistake?*

Parr jammed his thumb down on the comm. "But you can't ban me, I'm your king!"

It was too late; the comm was dead, and a tug beam pushed the *Aurora* out of the queue and into space.

CHAPTER 8

Valk, valk, emeffing valk! Parr thought as the *Aurora* floated listlessly away from the queue and Bilena Epso Ach.

Away from his triumphant return, away from his people … away from his destiny. Parr punched the air once, and then again. He threw a series of his deadliest punches and kicks into the ether until he got tired, which didn't take long.

He slumped into his chair and whirled the gem with one hand while drumming the fingers of the other along the armrest. *What now?* he thought. *How do I get in?*

He gazed at the blinking lights of the instrument panel as if the answer were in the pattern. Nothing came. He had a grint of Grolen slak, a highly collectible Skelly, and a dwindling cash reserve.

He remembered something one of his teachers had said about business: "Don't waste your time trying the same thing over and over. When you fail, fail fast and move on to the next tactic."

May as well get rid of this cargo until I come up with something better, Parr thought. More than likely, he'd need cash for his next approach, and it never hurt to have as many buldoons on hand as possible.

Grolen slak was a commodity that sold at floating prices on the open market. There usually wasn't a haggle involved in its trade, so he just needed to match with a supplier. Parr typed his cargo into a query that returned a list of destinations with red, orange, and yellow dots next to their names. He scrolled through pages of vendors on a multitude of planets and outposts until he finally found his first solid green.

Far away in the outer reaches—it would take weeks to get there, even with the *Aurora*'s speed. No wonder they were in need of the basics.

Parr zoomed in on the station—Weblin-9. He'd traded there before; it wasn't so bad. In fact, on second thought, he was surprised they were in need of Grolen slak. Sure, it was farlongs away from any civilized system, but it was a hidden gem of an outpost if he remembered correctly.

He jammed his thumb down to lock in the order before they changed their mind or another trader got there first.

Accepted, the screen read, and coordinates were sent to Parr's nav.

"Looks like we got at least a couple more runs in us after all, Aurrie," Parr said as he tapped the console. "Get us there as fast as you can, girl." He transferred the coordinates from his nav to the ship's guidance unit, and the engines roared to life.

Two weeks, Parr thought. *What am I going to do for two weeks?*

⋀

The answer was, not much. He attempted to write songs of his adventures on the Skelly, but given his unfortunate outcome, they all ended up more depressing than fulfilling. He spent a lot of time brainstorming ways to get back into Bilena Epso Ach, without landing on any good ideas. So eventually, he turned his attention to the screen he had mounted in his dingy, spartan living quarters. There was just enough room for a bed and an oversized closet where the other bed or bunk would have been if someone had ordered the small crew package on the Fano-class cruiser instead of the single-pilot.

He caught up on old plays, mostly comedies, and a few think pieces on modern society and whether a monarchy still suited the Sixteen. He sifted through a list of documentaries. He'd been waiting for one in particular about Agrofor Telfo, the infamous pirate king, but it wasn't available yet.

Another doc, however, caught his attention. It was called *The People's Voice*. The film focused on Malista's rise to power and how she was able to expand the empire so quickly. The documentary was thorough but didn't exactly paint the best picture of his sister.

It was well reviewed and had received a lot of media attention before the documentarian tragically threw himself out of a window to his death shortly after its release. *Shame,* Parr thought. *That creature was talented.*

The show made Parr reflect on the state of the empire. The galaxy's economy was strong and had just enjoyed the highest year over year growth in its history. Most of the success was attributed to his sister, who seemed to keep herself out of the news as much as possible.

Parr wondered if she was still insecure about her appearance.

Malista had been born with deformed hands, and she'd never quite bonded to her artificial replacements. That made her appear clumsy; she was always dropping things at inopportune times. It was the only part of Malista's life that didn't operate with precision. Sometimes their father would jokingly describe her as "his little watch." She hated it and always told him so, but still, he persisted.

His father could be a real jonapor's behind. Parr felt his skin flush as he recalled the memory, and decided to think about something else instead.

His thoughts landed on his parents' accident.

Five suns, why did I jump to that? Parr wondered.

From what he knew, his family had been enjoying a diplomatic tour among some of the less frequently traveled planets and stopped off to see the volcanic islands of Gallas. It was possible that it was just a tremor from an active volcano that had sent their parents over the edge of the observation deck, but didn't anyone think it was strange that Malista was the only one who'd managed to hang on given her disability?

The more Parr thought about it, the more it seemed that a lot of Malista's political foes had met an untimely end. She'd been ruthless and plotting for as long as he'd known her and never hesitated to take an advantage once it was presented … but was she evil enough to have murdered their parents?

Surely not.

Parr took an absentminded bite of a protein stick and looked up at the ceiling as he chewed. He wondered if that singe mark had always been there and dwelled on the thought until he'd consumed the entire stick.

He licked his fingers and returned his thoughts to his family.

Their parents hadn't been the most present mother and father, but both Prince Parrtec and Princess Malista had been provided everything they could ever dream of growing up—the finest clothes, a veritable feast of the most nutritious foods for every meal, and an unparalleled education. They had both followed the basic core curriculum; Malista had excelled, of course, and Parr—well, Parr had passed. Outside the core curriculum, they were encouraged to seek the tutelage of the greatest minds of any field they were interested in.

Parr had chosen music and acting, and of course had learned how to pilot spacecraft. He'd excelled in two of the three and had picked up a little more than acting from a few of his tutors in that arena.

One of his teachers was Jessaba (no middle or last name), one of the Twelve's brightest stars.

Jessaba, Parr thought.

He felt a small smile spread across his face at the thought of her.

She had dark features, beautiful hair, and captivating eyes. Jessaba had a sultry way of moving and was one of the few creatures he'd ever seen properly pull off the head scarf as a look.

There were some who said she had designs on a higher station and may have positioned herself to be Parrtec's queen. He was used to creatures' coming at him with an angle, though, so if that had been her intention, it was nothing new.

He wondered if that was why he always kept creatures at arm's length, never fully able to trust anyone.

He chewed on the inside of his lip for a moment. *Whatever*, he thought.

He'd loved his lessons with her. She'd come from humble beginnings in one of the smaller inhabitable moons in the system and clawed her way up from practically nothing. Parr had learned more about the mechanics of a business deal from her than from any of his economics professors, as they'd often sneak away from the palace to haggle in the marketplace.

On those outings, she tried to teach Parr how to inhabit a character—become another person entirely. One that would allow him to blend with the masses and obscure one of the most recognizable faces in all the Twelve.

He'd always remember one particular night with her. She distracted a merchant with a fluttering flourish of her fingers in one hand while she pocketed the desired item with the other. Normally, his eyes would have followed the gesture just like the merchant. But he'd grown distracted during the transaction and was only half paying attention. Which, as it turned out, was how he was able to track the maneuver. It was a sleight-of-hand trick he'd never forget.

Parr could feel his pulse quicken as he recalled the maneuver.

He'd waited until they were far enough away from the marketplace before confronting her, and rather than defend herself, she softened, put a hand on his shoulder, and asked him what he thought. He told her he thought she was quite clever and would like to learn more if she would teach him.

She would, and she did. Night after night, they'd slip away to the marketplace in disguise and work one vendor after another, never crossing the same creature twice. Parr had a rough go of it at first, but she was also a skillful escape artist, and after a few attempts, he began to get the hang of it. Before long, he was just as good as she was, and maybe just as charming.

Parr chuckled to himself. No, he wasn't.

Unfortunately for Jessaba and the young Parr, she'd become a little too sticky-fingered at the palace and got caught nicking an old family something-or-other, which had led to her untimely demise.

Parr's hands began to sweat, and he batted at the protein crumbs that had fallen on his shirt.

Stealing from the crown was a capital offense, regardless of whether the item was something that they valued, used, or even cared about.

It was the last thing she'd ever teach him, and a lesson he'd never forget.

CHAPTER 9

Parr crumpled up the wrapper from the protein stick and tossed it into the refuse bin in the galley. The floor was cool to the touch, even through his socks as he slid across the small galley and searched its cabinets for something else to munch on. He squinted at cereal, jellied preserves, and a half-empty box of protein sticks. None of the options particularly appealed to him, so he pivoted to the fresher.

Frigid air met his face as he leaned inside the appliance to look around. His stomach groaned for the food of his former life. The fresh fruits and vegetables. The meats and cheeses. All he had was a full supply of milk, a half dozen hand fruits, and an open box of powder that was supposed to keep the inside of the appliance smelling fresh if you changed it regularly. Which Parr never did.

He shut the door and grabbed a bag of water and another protein stick from the cabinet before padding back to his quarters. Although he may have missed the food and drink of his former life, the narrow passageway felt as welcoming as a weighted blanket around him. He didn't miss the cold, broad corridors and massive arches of the palace.

Parr slumped back down on his bed, dropped the protein bar on his chest, and tossed the bag of water off to the side. He'd set the screen to autoplay something an algorithm thought he might like, and maybe he would, but his mind was elsewhere. Parr couldn't shake the image the documentary had presented of his sister.

He wondered if he'd missed something. He put the wrapper of the protein bar between his teeth, ripped it open, and took a bite. He decided he needed to watch it again to make sure he'd interpreted it correctly.

But he barely got through the low, bowed tones of the intro music and opening credits before his mind wandered elsewhere.

Parr and his sister had always had a complicated relationship, which wasn't to say it was bad—just, well, complicated. He and Malista had played together from time to time when she was younger. Parr would entertain her at the breakfast table with an array of cutlery tricks while none of the staff were looking, which usually ended with Malista's being disciplined for laughing too loudly at the table. Something she felt was unfair since her older brother was the one who'd instigated the disturbance in the first place, but their mother always said something about a princess's discretion.

Parr couldn't help but chuckle a little at the thought; all those years later, it still felt just as exciting to get away with something.

He and Malista grew apart over the years, with Parr gaining the love and adoration of the kingdom while she accrued a vast array of allies among powerful people within the government. Parr thought she would make an excellent minister of state and never saw anyone but her for the role during his tenure as ruler. He told her as much, and she thanked him, the way she often did when he'd talk about his plans for the future—with gritted teeth and a tight smile.

For her tutors and mentors, Malista sought out the minister of the interior as well as the foreign minister. She dined with the minister of defense and used his connections to meet the military's top vendors so that she could take lessons in physics and chemistry from their most talented designers. It wasn't enough for her just to understand the current technology; she needed to know where it was going and how she could use it to the kingdom's advantage—or, more directly, her advantage.

She grew obsessed with power, both political and as an actual resource. According to the ministry's projections, the current trajectory of the kingdom's growth would consume their entire energy reserve within both her and Parr's lifetime. A new discovery was needed—either an alternative fuel or a means to consume their current supply more efficiently.

Malista decided both strategies were equally good and dedicated much of her time and the palace's resources toward them.

Their father, however, seemed to show very little interest in the concerns of his daughter as well as the Ministry of the Interior, and instead became more and more impressed with his son's piloting skills. Parr always felt a little guilty about that.

The king did everything he could to arrange lessons for Parr on a variety of craft. Nav systems had advanced to the point where most creatures could find some sort of aircraft to fly—they practically flew themselves in those days—but some craft required more expertise than others.

The right pilot could find the right advantage at just the right time to make all the difference in a race or dogfight, and Parr trained with most of those pilots. Over time, he began to realize that he could even become one of them if his station didn't prevent him from veering into the more dangerous parts of the galaxy.

Their mother did everything she could to teach Malista the subtle arts of hospitality, but despite her efforts, Malista just wasn't interested. She could barely tell the difference between a peelo and a percut, or at least that was what she'd say before storming off. Parr always got a kick out of those displays. It was a successful tactic, she told him once. She'd noticed that their mother didn't like a big scene, so she'd let Malista go. The queen wasn't much of a disciplinarian outside of cutting looks and snide remarks … and there wasn't a cutting look sharp enough to penetrate a teenage girl's slamming bedroom door.

The queen didn't understand her daughter's interest in economics, sociology, technology, and science. Parr remembered their mother doing everything she could to steer Malista toward a life of luxury and relaxation, but to no avail.

Malista wasn't interested in projecting images of herself to the kingdom in various states of repose on windblown sandy beaches in front of crystal-clear water. Instead, she much preferred to be tucked away inside a library or lab. She even went as far as to refuse to pose for pictures when she won awards. Neither Parrtec nor his father ever understood that last bit. She was so talented, let the kingdom see, they'd say. She'd usually seem as though she was thinking about it, catch sight of her hands, then hold them behind her back as she shook her head and walked away. Award announcements always looked better in printed words rather than pictures, she'd say.

As time went on, the freedom of their youth progressed to the responsibility of their future. Parrtec's time was no longer his own but doled out in portions by his handlers. They steered him to meetings he had no interest in and classes that bored him. Like lectures on leadership. Parr never understood those—leaders were born, not made, he thought. He did, however, find one lesson from an economics class particularly interesting.

The instructor, eager to break Parr free from his boredom, and probably in a lapse of his better judgment, showed Parr how one could move funds from a legitimate bank account through a network of shell accounts until the money's source was no longer recognizable.

Parr couldn't believe his ears and scanned the area to see if anyone else was around to hear what this paragon of the Twelve's wealthy elite was telling him. No one was paying any attention but him. The tutor, encouraged by Parrtec's rapt attention, would take long drags of his smoker for dramatic pauses during the lesson. Parr requested more private sessions with that one.

He saw less and less of his parents and his sister. His parents were always off to one planet or the other on a goodwill tour, and she was … well, she was off doing her own thing. She didn't have the pressures that he did—the burden of being a future king.

Whenever he was around, his father grew impatient with his progress on his coursework. Why couldn't he be more like his sister? Why couldn't he grasp basic concepts of leadership or macroeconomics? He was substandard at almost everything but piloting, the arts, and that one less-than-ethical microeconomics tutorial. Malista seemed to lurk in the shadows of many of their conversations, both literally and figuratively. If her performance wasn't being held over his head, he'd see her in the wings, just out of the corner of his eye, as he was dismissed from his father's presence. Such dismissals usually led to his storming off—not to his room or someplace like the battenball court to blow off steam, but wherever his handler led him to next.

It was a claustrophobic life for Parr, one he would have done anything to escape. Days, weeks, and months on end forced to learn things he had no interest in learning. It went against his personal belief system—to do whatever it was he wanted whenever he wanted to do it. Moreover, his new lifestyle wouldn't get any easier. He could see it, even in the cold eyes of both his father and mother; they were almost like prisoners to their duties. Even if their prison had jewel-encrusted thrones, beautifully appointed furnishings, and uniforms made from the most luxurious materials in the galaxy.

He remembered the day his father refused to toss the battenball around with him for the first time. The king had been called to receive an ambassador, but he'd put those types of appointments on hold before. Parr could see the change in his demeanor, and if he could have seen inside the king's head, he probably would have seen a minor war raging between father and mantle.

Instead of the usual response he received from his father, young Parrtec was told it was time to put childish things away and become a man.

Parr remembered thinking he would never put the things he enjoyed as a child away just because he grew older. He would like whatever he liked for as long as he lived. The more he thought about it, the more it made sense. Once down that road, how would you decide what you actually enjoyed versus what you thought you were supposed to enjoy? How long would it take before you lost yourself? Maybe that was why his father was the way he was.

It was at that moment he knew he had to break away on his own. If only he could come up with a plan.

And then, one day, an opportunity presented itself.

He was on a tour of a facility that transformed and multiplied matter for food to supply the basic needs of the less fortunate of the inhabitables. The machines replicated cells, for the most part, to provide sustenance for the masses. The steaks looked like steaks, felt like steaks, but didn't quite taste right. They never could work that out, although everything seemed correct on a cellular level. Of course, if you didn't know what a real steak tasted like, then you wouldn't know the difference, and that was the saving grace of the machine.

Parr's pulse quickened as a thought suddenly crossed his mind. What if he could replicate himself in one of those machines? Seemed easy enough; he'd seen the process. They hired the lowest-skilled workers to operate the machines—literally anyone off the street could walk in and do it if they had access. And he had access. The prince had access to just about anything in the Twelve if he wanted it.

A fleeting thought transformed into a plan during the next stop of the day.

One of the armada's top brass wanted to show off a new shipment of spacecraft and took the prince on a tour of the armada's facility. Parr observed a fleet of aging spacecraft loading into a hangar just off the entrance. The general mentioned something about decommissioning aged vehicles.

That's when the inspiration hit. The hangar was a holding pen before they de-badged the vessel (a term for delisting the vessel's identification for access to and from the various galactic gates as well as its visual markers). At this point in the process, the general explained, they'd already been accounted for on the ledger and no longer existed on the armada's inventory.

His hands began to sweat. There was an expectation of stoicism on these royal inspections, and he fought to keep a smile from breaking through.

If Parr could use the machines from the factory to craft a perfect cellular replica of himself, he could fake his own death by throwing it off the highest tower in the palace.

But that wasn't enough, he'd have to alert the media—or at least his favorite trashy tabloid show. *Sordid Universal Celebrity Stories,* or SUCS, loved a juicy piece of gossip, no matter how morose. He couldn't rely on the closed circuit footage from the palace—they'd never release that on their own. No, cameras from an independent source needed to be involved, and one that wouldn't spike the story.

While everyone was distracted, he'd then wire funds to an untraceable account. Normally, such a transfer might catch the eye of someone in the treasury. After he had the funds in place, he'd escape using one of the spacecraft below, and lead a life of freedom without the burden of the monarchy constantly crushing him.

Later that day, he employed his well-honed skill of misdirection to give his handlers the slip; procured a streetcraft to take him back to the factory, where he was able to create a cellular-perfect (but non-sentient) replica of himself; and set his plan into motion. Parr took a moment to examine the copy. *Handsome,* he thought. *Although, my triceps could probably use some work.*

Smuggling a huge duffle with body shaped contours into the palace was easier than one would imagine. Parr took a back entrance with little to no cameras, while guards and staff were forbidden from looking at the prince directly.

With his doppleganger stowed away in his room, Parr just needed an impetus for the event, some sort of conflict to help sell the desperate act—the ultimate form of misdirection. An argument should work. Something minor he could turn into something major as an excuse to storm off and cloister himself inside his quarters.

Fortuitously, his parents were at home for a private family dinner that night. Parr waited patiently for an opportunity to present itself, but the conversation trended on the lighter side that night. His parents were droning on and on about their goodwill tour to Gallas and its beautiful volcanoes.

Parr would need to spur things along if they were ever going to find a contentious subject, so he butted in about his day, which, of course, reminded his father that his son had slipped his handlers at some point after a tour of the armada facilities.

His father gave him the usual talk about a king's role and responsibilities in overseeing a kingdom and asked what he had been thinking and where had he gone.

Neither question was out of bounds, and ultimately, the king was right in what he said, but young Prince Parrtec had youthful rage and general immaturity in his toolkit and wasted no time starting the row to end all rows. For him anyway.

More misdirection.

He railed on about how he wasn't ready for the responsibility, how his father was right, he wasn't fit to lead. Malista would make a better ruler, and they should just give her the queenship. She perked up as soon as she heard that but had a strange look on her face. Like she knew there was something different about the disagreement.

Which, of course, there was.

His father, of course, had the usual response about birthrights and heirs going back millennia, and Parr responded with something petulant about not wanting to live anymore before he stormed off to his room.

Parr remembered Malista's raising a hand to stop him, but instead she spilled her drink onto the floor and quickly withdrew into herself, as she usually did whenever she managed to do something physically clumsy.

His heart sank. Who would take care of his sister when he was gone? Most creatures, even he, didn't think that she needed much from anyone. But in their own way, they were always there for one another. At least he was there for her.

He wanted to pick the cup up off the floor, put a hand on her shoulder, and tell her everything would be OK, but he couldn't. It would mean breaking character, and he couldn't do that now.

Parr hated himself for it. It seemed like something his father would do—stick to a plan no matter who it hurt.

Although he believed his parents to be genuinely cold and dispassionate people, Malista had probably adopted those traits as her protection against the world. More of a useful façade than her true character.

No, she'd be better off without him in the picture, he told himself. At least for a few years while he worked out who he wanted to be. His parents would probably be embarrassed by his death for a short time but then go back to their tours of the Twelve. Perhaps they'd even spend more time touring their precious Gallas.

What a dumb planet, Parr remembered thinking. *Who likes volcanoes, anyway?*

Still, it was a little disheartening that no one followed him to his room. He'd been hoping to slam his door in at least one person's face. To be fair to his parents, it was against royal protocol to succumb to threats of any kind, and they probably thought he was just venting steam.

Parr wondered if they were just as surprised as the rest of the galaxy when they later saw Parrtec's limp body fall past the enormous window to the ground below.

The next bit was easy; it all fell back to the lesson he'd learned that fateful night in the marketplace—misdirection. With the entire planet focused on Parrtec's dead body on the grounds of the palace, he slipped away in a vehicle set for debadging, off the books but with all its keys still live. He transferred funds through a series of shell accounts and made his way past the gates of the system and on to his new life.

⋀

Wow, did I just space out for that entire movie?

In all his time in the outer reaches, he'd never put much thought into how his passing may have affected his family—or the kingdom. Even now, he wondered if his parents had cared more about losing a son or losing an heir. He wondered if Malista was sad to lose a brother or pleased to gain a queenship.

He'd probably never know for sure.

The credits of *The People's Voice* ended, and a prompt popped up that recommended other titles, like *Why the Queen Is Always Right, Our Great Leader's Search for New Energy,* and *Seek Facts Before Jumping to Your Conclusion.*

What a long title, Parr thought. *"Jumping to Your Conclusion."* Also, what a coincidence that his parents and Malista's political enemies had all met similar fates.

Parr's wrist buzzed with a proximity alert letting him know that after two weeks of travel, the *Aurora* was approaching its destination. Parr looked down at the state of his attire and decided he should probably jump into the facilities for a cleaning and a change of clothes before interacting with creatures again. He smelled the inside of his shirt and winced. Regardless of which creatures inhabited this post in the far-flung outer reaches, he was overly ripe for any type of business transaction.

CHAPTER 10

Parr swaggered away from the *Aurora* and made his way to the stark, unadorned, bare-metal central loading area to ensure his cargo was hauled away and buldoons were assigned to his account. The place smelled like a mix of oil and cleaning supplies, which Parr was thankful for. He had been expecting something much worse.

"Hey! We need to show you something on your ship and whatnot," one of the brown-chitined creatures from the grounds crew shouted as he walked by.

Are these guys seriously at every port now? he thought. Parr waved a hand over his head, replied, "Eh," and kept walking. He knew it was rude, but he had business to attend to, and he wasn't about to let the skittery grounds crew slow him down.

The dock wasn't quite desolate but certainly wasn't a bustling hub like the one on the rusty little planet he'd just left. Parr was able to identify the exchange booth needed to validate his transaction easily. He strode up to the quilted-metal structure and tapped the large yellow button next to the window. An older-style comm speaker jutted out of the middle of the console.

C'mon, Parr thought.

He tapped the yellow button a few more times for emphasis.

Parr heard a buzz on the other side of the metal enclosure as well as the sounds of someone bumping around behind the glass-and-metal barrier. He might have even heard a grunt or two followed by what sounded like a minor disturbance.

Parr banged the button with the back of his fist and held it down. The disturbance transformed into muffled cries as a metal divider opened on the other side of the glass to reveal a dual-headed tordaver. The tordaver was pasty white with a sweaty pink sheen and wore an audacious silken robe of vibrant yellows and reds streaked across a sea of blue.

The left-hand head, perched on a long neck, blinked at Parr with watery black eyes while tufts of gossamer pink hair ruffled in the soft wind of the atmospheric conditioning inside. The eyebrows of the right-hand head rose high above a blindfold and reissued muffled pleas for help behind a gagged mouth.

"Don't mind 'im," the left head said through the staticky old speaker. "We 'ad a bit of a disagreement."

"Sure, whatever," Parr said.

The tordaver spoke with an accent, which meant it wasn't using a communicator. Parr was always impressed by creatures that naturally spoke other languages, but he'd never understood why they wouldn't just use the technology available to them. It wasn't that expensive.

It was illegal for one head of a tordaver to restrain another, but stations like these in the outer reaches had their own code, and Parr had inventory to move. So he decided it wasn't the time to cite case law from the Sixteen. For all Parr knew, the right head may have deserved it.

"Vis one 'ere, 'ee got a liddle familiah wif va missus a few years ago. Needed to be taught some mannuhs, see?"

Tordaver relationships were tricky, and it was really none of Parr's business. He just wanted to get in and out of this deal as quickly as possible. "Yeah, OK, makes sense."

The other head shook in wild protest and tried to give his side of the story behind the gag, but Parr couldn't understand a word. The left head looked at the right and then back to Parr before chuckling to himself.

"Vis much for a grint-a Grolen?" the head asked. "Vas 'ighway robb'ry, it is." He arched an eyebrow at Parr.

Parr just raised his eyebrows and rocked on his heels. "What can I say?"

"Mus' be your lucky day, kid."

Parr's wrist buzzed, and the transaction completed. "Mind pointing me to the expo?" Parr asked. He'd need to load up on something else to make a few buldoons to help keep him afloat until he came up with a better plan to get back inside Bilena Epso Ach.

The left head hawked up a phlegmy, guttural chortle. "Expo? Haw haw! Where you fink you landed, son?" He knocked the right head with the back of his clammy hand. "You 'ear 'at? Expo, 'e says. Lawh dee valking dawh, Ya 'ighness! Haw haw!"

Parr squinted and laughed uncomfortably along with the tordaver but wasn't quite sure if he was being condescended to or if the station agent actually knew something about him.

The right head nodded in agreement, hoping to curry some favor from his partner-in-torso, but instead, the left head peered down at his comm and pulled himself away from the frivolities. "Marketplace is vat way, kid. Wahtch yaself … ah, who'm I talkin' to," the tordaver chuckled, and hooked a thumb at Parr. "Va kid who got vat price for a grint-a Grolen."

"Thanks," Parr said, and turned to leave.

"Oh, and drop vat blastah into the canistah on yer way out. No guns 'lowed in the market, son. Tah." The right head screamed one last muffled protest as the metal barrier clanked to a close behind the glass.

Parr marveled at how much better the security was in places like this than it was in the more civilized and advanced parts of the Sixteen. Nothing beat a sharp wit and a keen eye, he thought.

"You got it," Parr said. "I always forget."

He never forgot.

He dropped his blaster in the canister, which he fit into an airtight tunnel that shot it immediately back to the *Aurora*.

Parr made his way in the direction the tordaver had pointed to and tried to stop imagining what the right head may have done to "the missus" to have ended up that way for so many years. Tordaver courtships were notoriously tricky since it involved at least four personalities (tordavers were also found in three- and four-headed varieties as well) instead of the traditional two, and taking one out of the mix was practically unheard of. Ah, but there he went with outdated thinking. It was a new dawn in the Sixteen, and maybe the tordaver had found love with another species. Parr wished them the best as he made a visual with the marketplace.

He wasn't sure what he was looking for, but he whatever it was, he knew he'd probably find it toward the middle.

CHAPTER 11

Parr stepped out of the hangar and into a gentle creature-made breeze. An artificial orange glow, made to mimic light from a sun, bathed the cool, open air of the backwater station.

Places like this in the outer reaches never seemed to get the settings quite right, and the light always looked too orange. He wondered if the creatures that ran these places had ever even lived on a proper inhabitable. *Oh well,* he thought. It was a necessity out here; too much time without sunlight left some creatures in a real bad mood.

What lay before him wasn't exactly a marketplace, but it was close enough. Rounded domes with manufactured elements mixed with temporary wood structures and tents. Parr couldn't decide if he liked it or not, but he'd just spent a few weeks cooped up in a ship, and he felt like stretching his legs.

"Hot snacks, cold snacks, got 'em all," a tiny hooded creature squeaked as it rolled up to Parr on a one-wheeled transport so small that he could barely see the tread of the tire sticking out from under the hem of his robe.

Parr eyed the little guy up and down, trying to identify what sort of creature hid behind the hood. No luck.

"Hey, mister," the creature prodded. "I asked you if you wanted snacks."

Parr wasn't particularly hungry, but these little vendors were sometimes good for more than food. "Sure," Parr said. "How about something cold?"

"Two buldoons, please."

"Two buldoons, are you out of your mind? Cold are going for a handful of puri back in Lobrow," Parr said. It wasn't true, but Parr wanted to show the market, or at least whoever might be listening, that he knew the value of a deal from the jump.

"This ain't Bilena, pal," the tiny hooded creature said.

He had a point. This place wasn't Bilena, and Parr was about ready to get back to the paved streets of his home system.

"Fair enough," Parr said. "One buldoon, and you show me where to find the best stuff in this joint."

"Right-o. Two buldoons and I'll show you to the best spot," the creature said. "And you'll take a hot snack."

A hot snack, Parr thought. *Why'd he say it like that?* Maybe it would be worth the two buldoons not to piss the creature off.

"Fine," Parr said. "Two buldoons. Deal?"

"Deal," the creature said, and hopped up to tap the transaction into effect. "Follow me," he said, and sped off into the market, kicking up a cloud of dust and gravel behind him.

It was apparent from the way the creature moved that time was money to him. Parr almost broke a sweat keeping up with the little guy and found himself huffing and puffing as he caught up to the creature outside a tent adorned with exotic silks and strands of beads.

What is this? Parr thought. *This can't be the place.*

"This is the place," the tiny vendor said. "And here's your snack." Parr couldn't see inside the hood, but if he had to guess, he'd have said the little creature inside was smiling—and not in a pleasant way. Probably one of those smiles with rows and rows of pointy little teeth.

"Just a minute," Parr said while trying to catch his breath. The air on this station was thin, and he wasn't used to moving as fast as his guide was doing now. "I just—need—a minute."

"Don't have a minute, take snack."

Parr was thankful he couldn't see what was under the hood as he took the hot snack from the outstretched hand and waited until the creature wheeled out of sight before tossing it into a nearby trash bin.

"Welcome, traveler," said a sultry voice as smooth as the surface of a lake on a holiday morning.

Startled, Parr turned around to identify its source. She was beautiful. Dark features and a dimpled grin. She reminded him of Jessaba, his acting tutor (and much more) from all those years ago in Bilena. The galaxy seemed to screech to a halt for a moment, and everything stood still. Except for his heart, which pumped like a cruiser's engine right before launch.

Parr ran a hand through his scruffy hair and searched his mind for something clever to say, but nothing came, so instead, he tried on his high-beam smile.

Not that big of a smile, Parr, you're blowing it.

"Good idea to bin the hot snack," she said. "Never know how long they've been out or what's growing on them."

"I know what you mean," Parr said. He tried to play it cool and stay focused. He was there for a reason.

"Plus," she said, "I'd never trust anything that little grifter handed me. He's good for business, but just barely. Makes me pay him to bring people my way, but he does the same for most out here. I think we're all afraid of what he'd do if we didn't pay up. That crooked-toothed smile looking—" She shivered as though shaking loose the thought before extending her hand. "Anyway, I'm Katherine."

Parr shook her hand. *What a strange name*, he thought.

"But my friends call me Ren," she said.

"Then what should I call you?" Parr teased.

"Oh," she said with a sarcastic flourish of her hand. "You must be some sort of comedian. Please, regale me with your jokes and hilarious stories."

Parr almost blushed. Almost. "Sorry, Ren, I'm Parr. Nice to meet you."

She looked him up and down. Her tongue did that clicking thing at the top of the mouth that creatures sometimes did while processing information. Her eyes flashed. "Parr? Not Parr of the *Aurora,* Parr?"

So she'd heard of him, he thought. Parr's chest swelled with pride, and he tried to hold back the dumb smile that wanted to shoot across his mug. "Yep, that's me."

"The Parr who came out of nowhere to breeze through the time trials on Zebulon Quarto?"

"You got it," Parr said. It felt good that his reputation seemed to be catching on out there in the outer reaches. Moments like these made all that time and effort building a brand worth it.

"The same Parr who earned the top spot in the Corpulon Valvente, only to leave it to pirate about the outer reaches?"

"Uh, more like an independent merchant, but yeah," he said. He was starting to get uneasy; how could she know this much about him?

"You mean to tell me you're the Parr—the very same Parr—who keeps slipping the clutches of the great Norfung Gortn all over the galaxy?" She asked in such a way that it didn't seem like a question at all. More like a promise or a threat, and he wasn't quite sure which. One thing was certain—she was well informed. Maybe his two-buldoon investment would pay off after all if he played his cards right.

"Eh," Parr said. "Norfung's not that great. Anyway, that's right, Ren, that's all me. Look, you sure do seem to know a lot about a lot … this your tent?" He hooked a thumb toward the collapsible habitat.

A dimple creased her cheek. Stars and fathers, Parr couldn't get over how much she reminded him of Jessaba. "That's right," she said.

"And what do you sell?"

"Information." Her eyes sprang to life. She flourished her hand in such a way as to invite him inside the tent, and with one last look around the market, he accepted her invitation.

The interior of the tent was draped in more silks and lit by oil lamps. Their smell evoked a sense of the past. The lamps' warm, waxy scent mixed with the smoke of a musky incense that added a layer of exotic mysticism to the cozy space. Multicolored beads dangled from the entrance to the tent and seemed to drape from every weaving hung around the room, including the tablecloth covering the small round table in the center of the space. Music from another time and place poured out of the cone of a device meant to look older than it was. The device was lit in a golden hue by four diode tubes that jutted up from its base.

Ren invited him to sit across from her at the table. Parr did his best to swagger the step or two it took to get to his chair and slumped himself down.

"To most," Ren said, "I'm a fortune-teller or medium who connects creatures to souls from their past lives. Would you like a reading?"

Parr squinted at her.

"No," she said. "Of course not. Not the great smuggler Parr. Follower of the rogue's path, am I right?"

"I don't know," Parr replied, and scratched the back of his head while flashing her his most winning smile. "I guess some could call it that."

"Ah," she said. "There's the life that's led by the well-adjusted type with a firm family system. I'm sure you keep in constant contact with your parents and siblings … or is it 'sibling'?"

Parr dropped the winning smile. She was starting to make him uncomfortable. It took all of his extensive training and education not to look affected by the comment. However, he still found himself squirming in his seat.

"Where are you going with this?" Parr asked, trying to take back control of the conversation.

"Nowhere," she said with a lazy wave of her hand. "Just making small talk." She sat up straight and folded her hands in front of her. "Now, as I said, my trade is information. By this point, I trust I've demonstrated my abilities to a satisfactory degree, yes?"

Parr nodded.

"Good. Now let's talk business."

A lopsided grin broke out on Parr's face. "Not so fast," he said. Now it was time for him to show *his* powers of deduction. He pulled the tiny gem out of his pocket and twirled it back and forth around his finger while leaning back in his chair.

Ren's eyes darted to the trinket and back to meet Parr's. She cast a flirtatious grin, and her head quirked like she was giving a toast.

"See," Parr said. "You already tipped your hand about that little racket you set up with the creature up front."

"Please, continue," Ren said.

"Your … *décor* here is another tell. For eons, fortune-tellers have pre-researched their marks before they ever walk through the door."

"Tent flap."

"Of course, my apologies, through the tent flap. May I continue?"

"Be my guest, this is such an exciting way to pass the time," she said in a flat tone.

"This port isn't busy, and it wouldn't be too much work to check the ships' manifests and do a little digging on the crews before they walk past your tent in the marketplace … because of course they will, what else is there to do on this tiny floating chunk of nothing?"

Her cheeks flushed as she leaned back in her chair, surveying Parr like he was contraband tech smuggled in at a ridiculously low price. "I'm not sure how to feel about your characterization of my home … but, how do they say? The digging is what you're paying for—and I'm, like, the Oro Stanto of digging."

Parr chuckled. "Wow. Oro Stanto is my favorite battenball player … you are good."

"The best," she said. Her dark hair fell to frame her face as she leaned forward. "Now, tell me what it is that you want."

CHAPTER 12

Parr stared at the gentle lights of the music device in the corner of the tent and let his mind start to put some pieces together. He'd been through plenty of scrapes in his time and had rarely found himself at a disadvantage. Maybe because most of those scrapes had happened when he was behind the control panel of the *Aurora,* where he felt the most at home, where his piloting skills and the sheer speed of his ship could unjam the stickiest of situations.

But now he felt exposed, on his own, in a less-than-reputable spaceport on the edge of nowhere, dealing with a seasoned professional who traded in secrets. There was no telling the information he could gather from her for the right amount of buldoons, and just about everything had a price out here.

That was what worried him.

How much would information that the rightful heir to the Sixteen Systems was floating free, on his own, in the outer reaches be worth? Of course, it was entirely possible that the information was already out there. Why else would Norfung Gortn be so hot on his trail, refusing to use lethal means to drag Parr's scruffy scalp in?

For the first time, Parr was starting to feel there was an expiration date on his freedom. Maybe now he needed to claim his throne not just for the good of the kingdom but to save his own skin.

"So," Ren said, her voice as smooth as a velvet-footed murr on a lofted plain. "Are we going to do business or what?"

Parr studied her face one last time. Was this a simple transaction to her or something more? Was she trying to win his confidence or just close a deal? Did they share a connection? Because it felt to him as though they had a connection—

"Parr," she said. "At the risk of sounding rude—have you ever heard the expression 'while we're still breathing'?"

"I need to get inside Bilena Epso Ach."

"So? That's not so hard. Find cargo they need. That will be fifty buldoons. *Next!*"

Parr exhaled a quiet chuckle and held his hands out across the table. "Yeah, well, it's not as easy as that."

"No?"

"No. See, I've been banned for life."

"What? You didn't do something dumb like misrepresent your cargo, did you?"

"Something like that," he said, and twirled the gem back and forth around his fingers. The lights on the musical device in the corner seemed to glow a little brighter, from a golden hue to a lighter white, and even the music itself seemed to resonate cleaner. Things always seemed to jump into sharper focus whenever he had the gem in hand. A totem of comfort—his good luck charm.

Ren's eyes darted toward the trinket, then back to meet Parr's gaze as though she were hiding a secret. "Oh—I see," she said. "Something like that. You didn't try to pass Grolen slak off as Gorlem slak and then offload your cargo here. OK."

Parr looked at her with a slack-jawed expression as tumblers of comprehension locked into place. Had she arranged this whole thing? How could she know? No one was that good.

"What?" she asked. "Why are you looking at me like that? Have you not been paying attention this entire time? Now, let's get down to it. You want to get back to Bilena Epso Ach, and I can help you."

"I want to get *inside* the gates of Bilena Epso Ach," Parr said, and held up a finger to clarify.

The dimple creased her cheek again. "You don't think you can trust me; that's OK. I appreciate a well-structured deal. I can get you inside Bilena Epso Ach . . . for the right price."

"Name it," Parr said, and immediately regretted it. His eagerness had given away his negotiating power.

"Forty thousand," she said.

Forty thousand? That was almost everything he had. If he spent all that in one go, he wouldn't be able to reprovision. Maybe if he cut out snacks and scaled back to two meals a day, he could get by with the rations on board the *Aurora* for the next couple of weeks, and it would be worth it.

Still, there was a principle in play. He couldn't just take the first offer, and he'd rather not starve himself before his triumphant return.

"Twenty thousand," he said.

"Forty thousand."

"Fifteen thousand."

"Fifty thousand."

The deal was spinning out of control. She knew she had him, but he couldn't let her know that he knew.

But she knew.

"Twenty-five thousand," he said, and spun the gem a little more casually.

"How about I just trade you for that stupid little trinket you seem so preoccupied with?"

"What, this old thing?" Par replied. "It helps me focus. Besides, it's not worth much." But her interest made him wonder. He remembered how much the vendor he'd stolen it from said it was worth. Orders of magnitude more, a king's ransom—or at least a prince's. Even at that ridiculous price, the vendor wouldn't sell it. Said he was holding it for someone. *That valking guy,* Parr thought. *What an abosamper.*

Besides, he'd grown attached to it, and it would always be a reminder of his past whenever he reclaimed his throne … along with the Skelly, of course . . . and the *Aurora.*

"It would be worth it for me to have it out of my sight," she said. "So annoying with the back and forth and back and forth. Either trade it or put it away, it's distracting."

Parr grinned and continued to spin the gem. A good distraction might just help him with the negotiation. "I'm sure, but it's not up for trade, and I'll do what I like, thank you. Twenty-five thousand."

She arched an eyebrow. "Thirty-five thousand."

"Twenty-seven thousand."

"Thirty and done." She spat in her palm and extended her hand.

He would've been skeeved out in other circumstances. In fact, he'd walked away from a deal like that before. Of course, that had been another time, a phlegmier hork, and the creature hadn't really been his type. No, in this case, he was too excited to have a path back home to dwell on the off-putting custom and eagerly gripped her hand to strike the accord. Their wrists beeped, and Parr flinched. He tilted Ren a curious look and checked his account to make sure she hadn't taken more than they'd agreed upon.

Thirty thousand buldoons exactly.

She must've had it loaded up before he ever arrived. Normally, he'd have been upset, but he couldn't help but find himself impressed by the well-thought-out plan and execution. Had he been a mark since the gate at Bilena or before? Just how good was she?

"Good," she said. She raised an eyebrow and shifted her balance in the chair. Maybe she was a mind reader too—Parr would have believed almost anything at this point. Which was good, because he'd invested half of everything he had left in her expertise. He had full confidence that she was the one to get him home; nothing could stop him now.

A commotion suddenly arose from outside the tent.

"Glogs and borlongs!"

CHAPTER 13

Ren's eyes grew wide. "Go," she said. "I can't be seen with you."

Parr took note but wasn't surprised that she recognized Norfung Gortn's voice. It was probably nothing more than the fact that he was the galaxy's most notorious bounty hunter and she was a professional courier of intel, but he couldn't be sure.

"Probably too late for that," Parr said. "Besides, we have a deal." He pointed at her. "You owe me." He enjoyed seeing Ren on her back foot for the first time, so much so that he was willing to push his impending doom at the hands of the galaxy's most notorious bounty hunter to the back of his mind for a few moments.

"Glogs and borlongs, Parr," Norfung shouted. "Get out here and face me before someone gets hurt."

It was an empty threat.

Probably.

Norfung Gortn had a reputation as a merciless creature who always bagged his quarry, but he also lived by a code. He wouldn't hurt anyone that he hadn't been hired to hurt, but those he did hurt, he hurt spectacularly. Besides, Parr wouldn't just give away his position. There were hundreds of tents out there, and he wasn't about to let Norfung know which one he was in.

"Ren Shando," Norfung bellowed. "I know he's in your tent. Disarm your system and come out with your hands up."

OK, Parr thought. *He knows where we are—that's bad. But he's afraid of Ren's defenses—that's good.* But how did he know who Ren was, and how was he able to track them down?

"That no-good little swindler," Ren said. "If I get my hands on that little hooded neck . . . ."

Of course, Parr thought. The little snack grifter from the entrance to the market.

"So, you got a way out besides the front flap?" Parr asked.

She arched an eyebrow. "Of course." She reached under the table and pulled a lever. The table popped up to reveal a shallow tunnel underneath. Ren kicked a spot on the ground, and a soft amber light pulsed to life below.

"After you," she said.

"No, no," Parr said. "Beauty before wisdom."

Her jaw clenched, and she rolled her eyes. "Crooks before looks."

"Femmes before hims."

"Dirt before the broom."

"I'm out of idioms," Parr said.

"Look," Ren said. "Just get down there and follow the lights, I have to reset the table and arm this place."

Parr crawled down below and scrambled along the lit corridor, hunched over uncomfortably to keep from hitting his head on the smooth clay roof. He looked back to find Ren wrenching a wheel into place to seal the hatch above her.

"Go," she said, speeding toward him. "What are you waiting for?"

Parr turned and made his way down the tunnel as quickly as he could and soon found Ren pushing him along from behind for good measure. He noticed the corridor slanted down as they traveled a hundred yards or so away. He wondered where the tunnel went, and whether there was a secret underworld to the place or if it would take them outside the market to the small city beyond.

His thoughts were interrupted by the sound and tremor of an explosion overhead.

"Sounded worse than it was," Ren said. "I confined the blast radius to specifically harm whoever was trying to get into the tunnel, which is now impossible."

Parr looked back past her to a rain of dirt and debris. The explosion had caved in the immediate area below the tent and bought them more time to escape.

"Now go," she said. "Move!"

They hurried down the length of the corridor until they reached its end. A rickety ladder led up to a round hatch with a wheel attached just below it. Ren pushed past Parr and climbed the ladder to the top. She released the wheel and mashed a hidden button embedded in the manufactured rock that opened the hatch. She waved for Parr to climb before she scrambled up another ladder and out of the tunnel.

Parr tested the ladder. It was made from industrial scraps and held together by pieces of animal hide. Thankfully, it wasn't a long climb to the top, which meant it wouldn't be that far of a fall if the thing fell apart. Just enough to break an ankle or leg if he fell wrong. No problem.

He put his boot on the first rung, and it collapsed into two pieces and fell to the dusty floor. Parr looked up with knitted eyebrows as though to admonish Ren, but she wasn't looking down. He gave himself a pep talk and hauled himself up as quickly as he could.

Parr pulled himself up onto the dusty ground of the marketplace and took one last look below. He watched, without surprise, as the ladder collapsed and fell in various pieces to the floor of the tunnel.

He dusted himself off and shot a wink at Ren, who was reclining on her side a couple of yards away. It appeared as though his luck was changing.

Or maybe not.

There was a muffled popping sound, and before he knew it, Parr was on the ground constricted in a tightly woven net, buzzing with electrical pulses. He recognized the tiny robed creature before him through the webbing. A scaly beak protruded through the hood, displaying layers of pointy little teeth.

Not this guy again.

"Delivered, as promised," the hooded creature said, and tossed a hot snack up in the air behind him. "With my compliments."

Norfung Gortn holstered the netter and flashed the winning smile that had helped elevate him from run-of-the-mill bounty hunter to galactic celebrity. He snatched the sketchy food item out of the air and gave it a sniff before bringing it to rest down at his side. It was apparent he didn't want to eat it but had the good manners to wait until the creature sped off before tossing it away.

The tiny creature's scaly beak flitted to Ren before he returned his gaze to Norfung. Parr imagined the little creature's beady eyes blinking up in anticipation from underneath the hood. Norfung stared at Parr with a broken-toothed grin. On most creatures it might have seemed off-putting, but Norfung had a way of pulling it off.

"Finally," he said. "I have you."

Parr, as subtly and quickly as he could, scanned the area for an escape route or a distraction but couldn't find anything he could use to his advantage within reach. He knew he was getting a little ahead of himself, but it wasn't the first time he'd found himself tangled in one of these, and he knew a way out. There was a release point in the octagonal wad that launched the net and powered the pulse. The right pinch would set a creature free if they could put up with a few seconds of intense electrical shock. It was an easy trade, really. A moment or two of unimaginable pain versus whatever future awaited him with Norfung.

"System after system," Norfung said. "Planet after planet, station after station."

That's right, you handsome old gasbag. Just keep talking while I figure out where the release is. Stars and fathers, what does he put in his hair to make it so shiny?

The tiny robed creature remained, hands clutched together in front of his chest, and looked up at Norfung as though he were witness to a deity's glory. "My wife baked that, you know."

Norfung glanced down at the creature.

There it is, Parr thought. His fingers lightly gripped the edges of the release. *Now, if I can just get some sort of distraction.* He strained against the netting to try to get Ren's attention, but she would not return his gaze. She seemed to be coolly taking in the scene, but Parr guessed she'd already worked out a dozen different ways to extricate herself from the situation.

Norfung blinked. The tiny creature had arrested his train of thought, and he lost the thread of whatever it was he was going to say. He cleared his throat. "She did, did she?" He turned the hot snack over, viewing it from a few different angles. "Well, I look forward to tasting her handiwork." He gave a soft smile and a thumbs-up before he returned his gaze to Parr. "Like I was saying—"

"She worked many hours over a hot stove crafting the hot snack," the creature said.

Norfung shot a guilty look out of the corner of his eye. "Yes, I'm sure she did. It smells delicious." The bounty hunter reached down to one of his many belts and unrolled a length of rope. "Now, hold still, Parr. This—"

"It would mean a lot to both of us if you tried it," the tiny creature continued. "It would bring our family much honor." The hood fell away to reveal two imploring brown eyes as big as saucers, which were almost watery as he beheld his hero. It would practically be an insult at this point not to at least sample the morsel.

"He's going to do it, I can't believe it," Ren said under her breath. "He's really going to eat it."

Norfung shifted his weight on his heels before working up the courage to pop the whole treat into his mouth. His countenance vacillated between grimace and smile with each grinding chew. Anyone who'd stepped foot into a strange port more than once knew better than to ever eat the hot snack, and Norfung was a seasoned vet. He swallowed and licked his fingers as a sign of respect.

The tiny creature snapped a picture of the occasion and profusely thanked his hero before turning to shrug at Ren. "Sorry, Ren. Just business," he said. "Good trap back there, you almost got me."

Ren shot him a glance that could have peeled mold off a terrabo. "Better luck next time, I guess."

"You'll be lucky if there is a next time," the creature said, and replaced his hood before speeding away to make his next buldoon.

Norfung blinked hard and raised his eyebrows before suppressing a burp. He shook his head before returning his attention to Parr. "Now, just hold still, and let's get this over with."

To most onlookers, Ren casually shifted her weight and fussed over a chip in a painted nail, but to Parr's trained eye, she was poising like a coiled spring looking for a place to bounce. At least, that's what he hoped he saw.

She nodded in one direction, which Parr understood as her signaling an escape route. All he needed now was the distraction. If only he could reach his blaster, the whole thing would be so much easier.

A glint of metal caught Parr's attention; apparently, Ren had been working through a similar line of thinking. She slowly extricated a small blaster from her sleeve.

There was the walloping sound of a discharge, and a blue goo instantly hardened in place over Ren's hand. Norfung had noticed her move too, and now she was stuck.

That was fast, Parr thought. He hadn't even seen a gacker on Norfung's belt before he drew it. The bounty hunter was quick on the draw.

Norfung guffawed, "Easy there, Ren, ain't got no problems with you. Just need to take this one in—*braaaap.*"

The bounty hunter was caught off guard by the eruption of a terrible rattling belch. He covered his mouth with a fist. "Sorry about that," he said, and placed the gacker back into his belt and buckled it into place.

Parr was in trouble and running out of options. Norfung was going to capture him and take him back to whoever had put the price on his head. Once he was identified as Prince Parrtec, his fate would be sealed. Outside the Sixteen, Malista could easily pay the price to have him removed from her life for good. Of course, it was possible that no one would believe he was Prince Parrtec and they'd refuse to pay any type of ransom at all—resulting in a similar end. No way to bring in a princely sum if no one believes you have a prince.

Of course, someone might try to use him as a pawn. The rightful, true king of the Sixteen, theirs to control in a coup. Parr cringed at the idea of becoming someone's puppet—he wouldn't do it, which also meant certain death.

His only hope was that his sister would be so overwhelmed with joy to learn that her brother was still alive that she would pay the ransom, cede her throne, and welcome him back with open arms.

Yeah, that doesn't sound like Malista.

So it was that he looked through the webbing of a nonlethal device, only to see death staring back at him with a gruesome smile.

"Let's wrap this up then," Norfung bellowed.

"Don't start using puns now, please," Parr said.

"What?" Norfung asked. "Ha! That's good, can I use that?"

"Yeah, sure," Parr said, then mumbled under his breath, "you're the one who said it."

"Alright," Norfung hollered. "Everyone out of the way unless you want a free ride on the *Dreadnet* too."

"Ooh, did he say free?" a denizen of the marketplace asked before his friend's hand slapped across his chest to keep him from continuing forward.

Norfung sneered at the creature before turning his attention back to Parr. "Nothing personal here, kid," he said before his expression changed to reveal a new line of thought. "Naw, to tell you the truth, Parr, with all the trouble you've caused me, I am going to enjoy this a little mooore—"

He was cut off by a spasming heave. The bounty hunter's hands went to his knees as he doubled over and retched his guts out on the ground below. Hundreds of tubelike life-forms inched away in all directions from the pool of sick issued forth by the great Norfung Gortn, and parts of the gathered crowd either ran away from them or stomped the ground around them before the creatures could climb up their boots.

It was more than Parr could have hoped for and just the distraction he needed. He pressed the octagonal device and convulsed at the shock that channeled through every nerve in his body.

Thankfully, the pain was only temporary, and Norfung was down on one knee with other things on his mind. Parr kicked off the dusty ground and sprinted in the direction of Ren's earlier nod. The report of a netting gun sounded just after a loud, disgusting belch. Parr felt the edge of the net whiz by his ear and into the wall behind him.

"Glogs and borlongs!" he heard behind him as he darted toward the shadowy tunnel of the hangar.

"Never eat the hot snack," Ren quipped as she caught up with him in the tunnel. "Which one is yours?"

Parr shot her a look.

"OK, OK," she said. "I know which one it is. Go!"

"Hey!" one of the brown-chitined grounds crew called out to Parr. "Glad you're here. We need to show you something on your ship and whatnot."

"No time, thanks," Parr said, and remotely punched up the pre-check system for the ship while sending the boarding sled down. He was halfway up the return before he realized it wasn't just him huffing and puffing; Ren stood next to him.

"Where are you going?" he asked. He was surprised she was still with him. Glad even, but he did his best to hide it. Not every creature honored their deals with money in hand and the opportunity to escape.

"We still have business, remember?" Ren said.

"I don't have enough provisions to get us both back to the gates—not without starving ourselves out."

"We're not going to the gates yet," she said. The sled came to a stop with a slight bounce, and the airlocks clanked into place. "Here, let me see what you got, give me access."

Parr glanced at her sideways. "Yeah, no, I don't think so. No-no-no-no-no."

The *Aurora* rocked back and forth.

Parr's comm blinked. It was Norfung. Of course it was Norfung. He must have hit the ship with something. Parr knew the bounty hunter probably couldn't carry anything large enough to do real damage to a Fano-class cruiser while on foot, but whatever he had had been enough to power her down for a bit back at Lobrow.

Maybe that's what the grounds crew was trying to tell him? Parr cursed under his breath at the one time the grounds crew could have actually provided a valuable service.

"Look," Ren said. "You're going to have to trust me. Not just for our deal, but if we're going to make it out of here at all."

Trust, he thought. *Like it's just that easy.*

Parr's comm buzzed again. Someone else was hailing him—it was the station agent. What could the tordaver want? Aside from stopping an enraged bounty hunter from shooting up his hangar, of course. Parr clicked to ignore the hail.

He had to think fast; it wasn't going to take Norfung long to get to the *Dreadnet.* Even taking into account stops for heaving up the remnants of the hot snack.

You really never knew what could grow on those things.

"Fine," Parr said, and slid access over to Ren. "But this doesn't mean I trust you."

She rolled her eyes, pulled up the ship's manifest, and started scrolling through it. She looked up and counted on her fingers as she did some quick mental math. "Yeah, we have plenty to get there."

"Where?" Parr asked.

"You'll see, I'm sliding you the coordinates," Ren said. Her hand ran across her nav, and Parr's wrist immediately buzzed.

Versit Station? he thought. *I haven't been there in a long time.*

"Now," Ren said. "Let's see what the fabled *Aurora* can do."

They scrambled to the bridge, and Parr took his place in the captain's chair. He glanced over at Ren. "Uh, hold on to something … just got the one seat."

The *Aurora* hummed as Parr brought the engines up and angled her toward the hangar's exit. Which was closing.

Why is the exit closing? Parr thought.

Ren's comm buzzed. "Where ya fink yer goin'?" the tordaver's voice crackled.

CHAPTER 14

The *Aurora* shook with another blast.

Ren tapped wildly on her panel, then swiped a transaction through. "It's all there," she said. "See for yourself. Forty thousand."

"For'ee fousand?" the tordaver said. "All of it? How'd you get ya hands on—'old on. I fink yeh forgot about me int'rest."

"That includes a compounded thirty percent stake," she said.

"Not 'at int'rest, missus, my … int'rest. Y'know—pewsonahl-like."

Did he just call Ren the missus?

"I'm flattered, really," she said. "But a deal is a deal. Freedom is mine, bought and paid for. Fair is fair."

A tumbling commotion bled through the transmission, followed by muffled screams of protest from the tordaver's other head. "I'll deal wif yous la'uh, you softhearted, biscuit ea'n brummah."

Parr must have lost something in the crackly transmission and wondered what a biscuit-eating brummer could be. A brummer that ate biscuits was his best guess.

Ren flew across the cabin as the *Aurora* violently shook. The overhead lights blinked red, and the ship's klaxon blared a warning. Parr brought up a panel and checked his systems. There was no damage to the hull, but the ship's energy resources were draining. Norfung had hit him with something similar in their last encounter, but it hadn't rocked the ship like that.

Parr brought up his remote monitor and saw the *Dreadnet* approaching from the back of the hangar.

"That was fast," Parr said while frantically turning knobs and flipping switches.

"What was?" Ren asked.

"He's already in his ship."

"Yeah," Ren said. "There were like five in here to begin with."

The tordaver spewed forth the most eloquent and filthy string of curses Parr had ever heard. Ren cocked an eyebrow and nodded out of respect.

"Wha' kina idiot fiahs 'is cannon inside a wohkin' hangah?"

Parr nervously plucked out his favorite trinket, kissed it for luck, and began to spin it around his finger. He needed to focus and think fast. He was stuck in a hangar with a failing ship and was taking fire from a relentless foe. At least said foe had just hacked off the station agent by firing his cannon indoors—bad form.

Lucky for Parr, it wasn't long before the *Aurora* stabilized on her own. His comm buzzed with messages like a swarm of honey flies—one from the station agent, and a couple from Norfung.

Parr chose the one from the station agent first. He opened the text line to find he'd been cleared to go, but there was an additional message attached. He double-tapped to open it.

You haven't heard the last of this. You're taking something precious from me, and I'll never forget that. I have half a mind to let that maniac take the both of you out, but rules are rules, and I have no legal reason to keep you in dock.

I'd tell you to watch yourself, but I hope you don't. I'll catch you at your first lapse in judgment, Parr. I will have my revenge.

Toodles.

PS: Good luck finding a place to dock your overrated piece of space debris, you feckless little wump. Consider yourself blacklisted.

Parr exhaled and leaned back in his chair as the agent's threat washed over him. The hangar's doors began to open slowly. The station agent may have had a vendetta against Parr now, but he still had to comply with dock protocol if he wanted to remain in business.

That didn't mean he had to comply quickly, though, and Parr noticed the doors were moving slower than gloth through hardened reeple butter.

"Not going to miss him," Ren said before she flew across the bridge. The *Aurora* rocked from the force of a blast once again. She landed hard on the other side of the control room, cursed, and checked her mouth for blood with the back of her hand. "Doesn't this thing have shields?"

"Of course it does. Oh, right," Parr said, and brought up a series of energy shields.

The ship's comm squawked to life.

"Glogs and boooorrrrrrr—" a sickly, heaving Norfung's voice crackled through.

Despite the threat to their lives, Parr and Ren couldn't help but share a laugh at the bounty hunter's expense as they waited for the hangar door to open up enough to squeeze the *Aurora* through. It was one thing to learn about the hot snacks academically, but it was quite another to hear the lesson play out over the comms.

Parr eased the *Aurora* forward manually. He hoped she was fast enough to get into a rift before the *Dreadnet* could catch up. *Come on, Aurrie. I know you got this, girl.*

Norfung's voice boomed over the comms once more as he found a way to pull himself together. "Glogs and boooooorrrr—oh the seven lords, why?"

No, apparently he wasn't done.

Stars and fathers, that door was taking forever. Once again, Norfung recovered enough to talk.

"Don't—*blehp*—don't even—*merp*. Don't even think about taking your ship out that door, Parr. I'll shoot you oooooooooout—"

Parr was shaking with laughter. It was a terrifying situation, the bounty hunter had him dead to rights, but he'd never been threatened in such a hilarious manner before. He'd also never been more thankful to be in the civilized age of audio and text interfaces. The sound of Norfung's predicament was bad enough; he couldn't imagine an earlier time where visual communications had been forced upon creatures.

"Glogs and booorr—nope. Not saying that again. Set 'er down, Parr, or—"

The door to the hangar was about as open as Parr needed it to be. It would be a tight fit, but he needed every advantage he could get, and the bulky *Dreadnet* stood a little taller than the sleek and trim *Aurora*.

The lights on the bridge blinked red.

"He's targeting you," Ren said. "In the hangar?"

"I know, right?" Parr replied. "You'd think he could hit us manually as close as he is."

"No, Parr. That's not my point. Can your shields take a blast at this range?"

"Guess it depends on the blast," Parr said. "Aurrie here was built for speed."

"Great," Ren replied under her breath, but loud enough for Parr to hear it. "Maybe we can outrun him in an enclosed hangar."

Parr typed a series of commands into the ship's nav and pulled the *Dreadnet* up on visuals. His hand hovered over a blinking button.

"What are you doing?" Ren asked.

"It's OK," Parr said. "I got this."

Parr wanted to put on a good show for Ren, but he was worried. He'd been in plenty of rough scrapes before, but not at this range. He wondered if the *Aurora*'s shields would hold.

The klaxon sounded.

Please, Parr thought. His finger hovered over the blinking button.

Boom!

A black singe mark smoked on the far side of the hangar. Norfung had fired and missed. Parr's preprogrammed maneuver had worked.

"See?" Parr said. "Fast."

The tordaver's voice cut in. "Das enuff now, innit? Norfung, mate, I let you in 'ere ta do a job, not so yous could shoot up me place o' business. Is right disrepekfuw, it is."

The station agent wasn't about to do Parr any favors, but no one liked having their place of business shot up, and the tordaver was no exception.

"Did it—*blehp*," Norfung said. "Did it take both brains to come up with that stream of hot garbage you call words?"

"Right, ven. 'Ave it yoh way, mate."

What does that mean?

Parr looked up at the console's screen to see what was going on behind him in the hangar. The floor and ceiling shot toward each other and pinned the *Dreadnet* in an enormous vise. A purple-blue field sprang to life, trapping Norfung inside.

"Glogs and—nope, still can't do it—*blehp*. Come on aboard, tordaver; I have a surprise for both of you."

"I bet," Ren said off comm. "Can you imagine the state of that ship's interior right now?"

Parr could, actually. It made him queasy. "I don't think that's what he meant. You're sure about these nav cords?"

Ren held her palms up and returned his look with wide-eyed bewilderment. "Are you really questioning—"

"Yeah, OK, let's go." Parr took advantage of the fracas behind him and jammed the accelerator forward on his console. He tapped the panel. "Come on, Aurrie, let's show Ren what you got."

CHAPTER 15

The *Aurora* shot out of the hangar at full speed and, in no time, rocketed past the atmosphere of the tiny station and into the star-speckled freedom of open space. The ship's control panel moved from blue to green as the nav system kicked in, and the Fano-class cruiser's engines whined as they poured on speed and the ship entered the swirling blue embrace of the rift.

They were away and clear.

Parr unclinched his sweaty hand from the throttle, punched the button for auto, and leaned back in his seat. He exhaled a deep breath and pinched the bridge of his nose. "I can't figure out how he keeps finding me."

"I have to admit," Ren said, "I didn't quite believe the part about getting away from Norfung Gortn so many times, but it appears as though you may have."

Parr's pride swelled with each loop of the crystal around his finger. She'd just watched him slip the grasp of one of the most dangerous creatures in all the Sixteen and outer reaches combined. He imagined it had to be pretty impressive to see him in action.

It reminded him of the night back in the marketplace on Bilena where he'd palmed a beautiful jeweled necklace for Jessaba. How impressed she was when she didn't detect his grift despite standing beside him.

The night of their first kiss.

It felt like a carbon copy of that point in time, and Ren looked just like her—even in front of the blinking lights of the tiny bridge. There was definitely something brewing between them; he could feel it. All he needed to do now was play it cool, he thought.

He grinned and turned to face her. "I have my moments."

"'I have my moments,' he says." She threw up her arms as she rolled her eyes. "Yeah, sure, you have your moments against a food-poisoned Norfung Gortn who is already fighting with two arms tied behind his back."

"He was only food-poisoned this one time, and I think, traditionally, the saying is *one* arm tied behind—"

"I know how the saying goes. I'm illustrating a point."

Parr squinted. "Yeah, OK."

"Do you even know what it is that you twirl back and forth around your finger?"

"Yeah, it's my favorite thing."

"And your favorite thing is called … , " she almost sang as she lifted her eyebrows, awaiting a response from him.

"I don't know; I didn't name it. I just like the way it looks and feels—it's my little good luck charm."

"It's groppodite," she said. "The name of the "charm"—she made air quotes—"is groppodite."

"OK, it's called groppodite." Parr pulled the jewel on the gold chain curled around his finger up to his face. "You're called groppodite, did you know that?" he said like he was talking to a pet or a young child. "No, you didn't—ah, no you didn't." He gave it a kiss and turned his attention back to Ren. "So what?"

Ren strode across the bridge, put both hands on the edge of Parr's chair, and leaned close. "For the love of all that is—you don't know what groppodite is? It is impossibly rare. A source of energy that could power a planetary system for hundreds of years and a single planet for millennia."

"Did you hear that?" Parr whispered to the stone. "I always believed in you."

"It's also highly unstable," Ren said.

"Look who's talking," Parr said out of the corner of his mouth to the little jewel while hooking a thumb back at Ren.

She pushed away from his armrests and began to pace the room. "That's why Norfung is afraid to fire on you; that's why you keep slipping away so easily."

"Easily? I'm not sure if you were paying attention back there—"

"Oh, you're not? You think I was distracted while my place of business exploded? I saw you coming for farlongs. I spent years looking for the perfect mark while I wasted away on that grumhole of a station with that piece-of-grunk tordaver—well, one side of him wasn't so bad, but the other . . . " She shivered as she tried to shake off the memory.

"So, you *are* the missus he referred to."

"It wasn't like that," she said. "We weren't married; it was just a term of endearment. And he was a means to an end."

"Sounds gross," Parr said.

"Does it, Parr? Does it sound gross? Welcome to the galaxy, my friend. Some of us do what we have to do to get by out here."

"I'm just saying—"

"Be quiet. You know, I could not find anything about your upbringing, so I don't know where you come from or how you were raised. But not all of us can fall backward into a ship like the *Aurora*."

"Hold on, I traded—"

"And I *certainly* would not be dumb enough to haul cargo in a Fano-class cruiser. For the love of—do you understand how much money you would have made if you'd just stayed in the Corpulon Valvente?"

"Yeah," Parr said. "But they have all these rules, and you have to wear a uniform—"

"Oh, you have to wear a uniform? I did not know that—how awful for you. Let me ask you a question, Parr. Have you ever done one thing that you did not want to do?"

"No, isn't that the point of life?" Parr asked.

"So, that's who you are. I wondered," she said. "Were you a rising comet of talent from the void or a thoughtless son of industry? 'Point of life.' What point is there? Eat. Sleep. Survive. Yes? If only I had the luxury of pondering the point of this existence. We're born into this world wailing and gasping for breath, not smiling and laughing."

No one had ever talked to Parr like that, but now that someone had, he could recognize some of the hidden internal conversations behind the looks in other creatures' eyes. They looked at him the same way Ren was looking at him at that moment.

What must Jessaba have thought of him during all those nights together? He'd seen her give him a similar look from time to time—especially in the market. While a prince stole from his people to identify with someone who'd acquired the same skill out of necessity.

Had Jessaba ever really loved him? Had he ever really loved her? Why did he accept her fate so easily—because she'd stolen from him? His family? Their mantle? He couldn't even remember what it was she'd taken, but he remembered he hadn't cared one way or the other—even at that moment.

Who was he, really? Did he truly care about his people? After all, what did he know of them? Maybe Ren was right; he was playing at understanding life outside the royal bubble.

No one he'd interacted with since he'd left Bilena had had any type of plan B to their life, only the moment they lived in and maybe a tiny bit of the future. Maybe he was just a charlatan, pretending to understand the every-creature.

Ren's words seared deep into his soul, and he brooded as they sizzled.

CHAPTER 16

Parr woke early the next morning with a crick in his neck from an uncomfortable sleep on the floor of his personal quarters. Fano-class cruisers were built to accommodate a small crew, and the *Aurora*'s single pilot package had suited him just fine up until that point. That morning, however—not so much. Ren quietly snored in Parr's bunk close by.

He rolled onto his back and stared at the ceiling in the dark. The sting of their argument had faded after a night's rest, but the dull ache of truth remained. Ren had given him plenty to think about. Unfortunately for Parr, they were things he didn't particularly want to think about. Nevertheless, there he was in the dark with his thoughts, trying not to wake his guest, who was peacefully sleeping just a few feet away.

Before long, Parr padded to the bridge to escape his thoughts and practice some scales on the Skelly before transitioning to a few of his favorite songs. He even took some time to try to pick out the notes to Xonk and Shook's "Hail You Later," one of the top hits of the season. After an hour or so, he heard Ren bumping around and decided to invite her to breakfast in the *Aurora*'s small galley.

"How long have you been playing?" Ren asked. She held her arms close around her and squinted through sleepy eyes.

"Oh," Parr said. "Sorry if that woke you, I disengaged the resonator to keep it as quiet as possible." Parr moved about the galley grabbing a couple of bowls and spoons, cereal, and milk.

"I suppose there are worse ways to wake up," she said. "Was that Xonk and Shook's new song?"

"My approximation of it, I guess."

He set the modest table and poured cereal into both bowls before sliding one over to Ren. She tipped the milk container and underserved herself. Parr wondered if the pour was a result of habit. Forced conservation under restricted circumstances … or maybe she just liked a crunchier flake. He drowned his flakes in milk like he always did.

"You're pretty good," Ren said. "And it's a nice Skelly. Never seen one in that color before, where'd you get it?"

Parr recalled his encounter with Norfung back at the marketplace after parting ways with Manc. "Just something I picked up along the way."

She nodded and stared at him from across the table, quietly chewing. "I'm sorry about last night."

Maybe the light was softer in the galley, or maybe it was just the way her hair looked in the morning, loose and a little frazzled. He wasn't sure, but something was different—like all the sharp edges were gone. "Don't worry about it," he said. "I deserved it. Besides, you were right about a lot of things. You gave me a lot to think about."

"I mean, of course I was right." She smiled. "But, I … could have been more tactful."

"Same here, probably," Parr said before spooning cold flakes into his mouth.

Ren poked around her bowl with a spoon and eyed her scruffy new companion. Parr wondered if she was as unfamiliar with apologies as he was. It was nice—a little uncomfortable, but nice.

"You want to know how Norfung keeps finding you?" she asked.

"Spill it," Parr said. He was eager to transition from their previous conversation.

"It's the groppodite," she said. "Throws off an energy field as large as a planet. A totally unique signature that makes it easy to track, and therefore makes you easy to track."

Parr dropped his spoon. *It couldn't be that easy,* he thought. "Are you sure?"

"Of course. Now pay attention," she said, and pointed her spoon at him before dipping it back into the bowl. "That's how he finds you in *space*. What I want to know is how he finds you once you're on-planet."

"What do you mean?"

"The energy is larger than that of most inhabitable worlds, so once you're on-planet, it would just look like a giant glob to any scanner. It's like identifying the haystack, not the needle. So, the question remains, how is he finding that needle? How does he keep tracking you down?"

"I don't know, maybe that's why he's such a good bounty hunter," Parr said.

She slowly crunched a spoonful of flakes while looking up at the ceiling. Her eyes wandered past Parr to the display of tchotchkes and bric-a-brac he'd accumulated over a multitude of deals and marketplaces. "Maybe," she said. "Tell me, Parr, are you a creature of habit?"

"What do you mean?"

"Like, do you get up at the same time every morning? Stay at the same types of hostels and shop at the same places?"

Shop at the same places, what does that have to do with anything? Parr thought. He remembered the last few times he'd encountered Norfung while on-world somewhere. They'd all been in packed marketplaces—but in front of a different type of vendor each time. What was the common denominator?

He couldn't figure it out.

"Nope, can't say I do."

"OK," she said, and seemed to take her time to think some more before changing the subject. "I will handle the communications with the hangar at Versit. We'll need to disguise the *Aurora*'s manifest when we dock. Maybe that's how he finds you; I don't know. Plus, I wouldn't be surprised if the left side of that sweaty pink tordaver tries to make life difficult for you at check-in from here on out."

"OK, thanks," Parr said through crunches. "So, what's the deal between you two?"

"Three."

"You three, sorry."

"Oh, you know, the typical story. Dashing explorer plucks young girl from obscurity for a life of travel and indentured servitude with an impossible buyout. Girl learns things from port to port and becomes a woman who puts a little away here and there until she finds the perfect rube to double her life savings in one fell swoop and buys her way out of an impossible situation."

"You think that tordaver is dashing?"

"That's your takeaway from everything I just said?"

"No, of course not," Parr said. "There's a creature out there for everyone."

Ren responded with a blank face and a blink or two for good measure.

"So, I'm a rube, then," Parr said.

Ren playfully looked Parr up and down. "The rubest, believe me. I've seen 'em come and go all over this galaxy and never seen one like you, friend-o." She pointed her spoon at him and spelled out loud, "R-U-B-E."

"So you're telling me you think a rube would pilot a bird like this? Bridge, single living quarters, cleaner, galley—cargo hold? It's practically a palace in the sky."

Ren cocked her head and grinned. "It's actually not so bad, this one." She looked up, then her eyes flashed. "She's sleek on the outside. Cozy and comfortable on the inside. The company isn't bad either."

Is she flirting with me? Parr thought.

"Yeah, well," Parr said, "I try to run a tight ship."

She rolled her eyes and squeezed his hand over the table. "Try harder. This place is kind of a dump; I was just being nice."

I think she's flirting with me, Parr thought.

He chuckled, and she got up to put her bowl and spoon in the galley cleaner.

CHAPTER 17

The overhead lights of the bridge thrummed a cool green as communications with the station were established. Ren sent the ship's coded and disguised manifest to the station's agent and awaited their reply.

Parr drummed his fingers along the edge of his captain's chair and thought that he and Ren might make a pretty good team. He let himself wonder what his life would've looked like had he met her sooner. Would he still be part of the Corpulon Valvente? Would they have explored new worlds and established new stations, or would they have gone off on their own in an even more successful smuggling endeavor?

The *Aurora*'s comm chirped to signal that the ship had been accepted, and Parr pulled up the display. *Welcome to Versit Station! Congratulations! You've been assigned to the A block in hangar WL-19, enjoy your visit!*

She must've booked the A block in case they needed to make a quick escape, Parr thought. He hadn't known Ren long, but he was pretty sure that she was the type to think about things like that.

Parr ran a quick diagnostic to ensure all systems were functioning properly. Satisfied with the readout, he brought visuals up to full screen.

The lights of Versit Station were beautiful from their vantage point.

He remembered his first visit to Versit. It had been his first stop after the escape from Bilena. He'd heard a thousand stories about it from all the pilots he'd trained with over the years and was thrilled to find out firsthand that most of the stories were true. The station had great food, fun clubs, an incredible market—everything he could ever want. He'd even traded the decommissioned ship he'd escaped in for the *Aurora* there, and it was where he'd met Manc for the first time. Well, there was one memory he wasn't so fond of, but no place was perfect.

"You still haven't told me where we're going," Parr said. "So …"

"So?" Ren replied.

"So, where are we going?"

"Just trust me," she said. "The less you know about my plan, the better. At least for now."

Parr didn't like her answer, but he didn't have time to dwell on it. The station's gravity required his full attention, and he dialed in his instruments to account for it. He carefully navigated his way through traffic, steering the vessel toward WL-19. The *Aurora* cut through the station's vapor barrier, and the panel beeped with coordinates for the final descent. A smaller cruiser cut across their path, and Parr banked the Fano-class hard and away from the errant vessel.

Ren braced herself against the console and cursed the pilot as he cruised off into the distance. "Stupid nummer almost killed us."

"Relax," Parr said. "I got this."

"Don't tell me to relax, it's condescending."

Parr didn't know what to do with that; he was just trying to put her at ease, but she had a point. "I—wasn't trying to condescend, I just—I'm sorry."

Ren cocked her head as though she didn't expect to hear the apology, and Parr wondered if she was surprised because it came from him or if she was just generally unaccustomed to them. He decided it was probably better not to ask.

Parr coaxed the *Aurora* back on course and took some time to soak in the sights of the station. Lights sparkled and beckoned from the largest off-world, creature-made settlement ever built—far away from the monarchy's long reach and the laws of the Sixteen. Versit Station, established long ago, had a code of its own.

Below, one of Versit's public transporters emitted a soothing glow while it moved creatures from one side of the station to the other at speeds unheard of for an on-grav transport and unique to this particular facility. The massive transporter slowed to a stop, and the tiny lights of smaller transports flitted about as they shuttled Versit's denizens to their specific destinations.

Parr directed the ship back within range of the auto-dock program and let the nav take over from there. He pulled up another display and scanned the surrounding area for any other would-be nummers that might cross their path, but luckily for them, it was smooth sailing the rest of the way.

The *Aurora* glided into the hangar and docked neatly into its allotted space in block A. Ren clapped him on the shoulder and gave him a slight nod before stepping away to prepare for disembarkation.

⌃

The hangar deck was awash with the noise of engines, overhead announcements, and the general chatter of hundreds of creatures. Ren worked with the hangar's officials to ensure everything was in order, while Parr dealt with the brown-chitined grounds crew that skittered their way toward his ship.

"I noticed something on your ship," the crew's leader said. "Let me show you and whatnot."

Parr couldn't believe he was about to entertain what was essentially a racket designed to scare people into spending good buldoons to avoid a disaster that would never come, but given his latest dust-up with Norfung, he thought he might give them a try.

The undercarriage of his ship was teeming with life as the crew crawled around to examine it. They were able to scurry into spaces that seemed too tight by half, and he was impressed by the speed with which they inspected the *Aurora*. Most of them were so fast, it was hard to keep up with them.

Their leader supervised their activity next to Parr; his long antennae twitched as he communicated with his crew. His large mandibles clacked while his forelegs cleaned one another, and he checked boxes along his display with another set of appendages.

An audible alarm went up from the ship's port side. The leader's antennae twitched back and forth in rapid succession before he slid his display closed and called his team back to him.

"We can't help," he said. "Sorry to bother you and whatnot."

"Whoa," Parr said. "Hold up. What did you find?"

The disturbance caught Ren's attention as well, and she wrapped up her business with the hangar official with brisk efficiency. "What's going on here?" she asked when she was far enough away from the official.

"I don't know, they won't tell me, but they obviously found something," Parr replied.

"No, we didn't. Everything looks fine and whatnot," the crew leader replied.

"Look," Ren said. "We just landed. It would be a shame to spend our first moments on Versit reporting your crew to the agent here. I've known her for quite some time, and she wouldn't be happy to hear your crew isn't providing the permitted service."

Permits for any type of hangar work were considered gold by most crews, and Versit was the gold mine to end all gold mines. No one would voluntarily risk losing their permit by refusing to perform their contracted service.

"You're bluffing and whatnot."

"I'm not," Ren said. "But lucky for you, I hate paperwork and would rather do anything but fill out the forms required to file a complaint. Why don't you just show us what you found and we'll . . . uh, how is it said on-world?" She looked to Parr as though he had the answer before turning back to the crew leader. "Ah, yes. We'll call it a day."

The crew leader's mandibles clacked, and his forearms cleaned themselves one over the other. "Fine," he said. "I'll show you what we found." His antennae twitched, and his crew rolled a portable lift forward. Parr, Ren, and the crew leader all stepped aboard before the crew raised it for a better view underneath the port side of the ship. The leader raised a large appendage and pointed inside a shadowy recess.

Parr squinted in the direction the leader was pointing in for a few seconds before he realized it wasn't his ship's lights glowing underneath, but two barnacle-like orbs emitting a greenish light. The orbs pulsed and swirled in what looked like clouds of energy behind glass.

"Multona drainers," Ren said under her breath. "Expensive, but usually worth the money. Must be what Norfung hit us with back there. One is enough to freeze a Tonko-class freighter, and two should be enough to take out all the ships in this hangar."

So that's what he hit us with, Parr thought. *And back at the port before that.*

"So how did we manage to bring our systems back up, much less make it all the way here?" Parr asked.

"I don't know," Ren said, but her eyes seemed to burn a hole through the pocket where Parr kept the groppodite gem.

Parr cleared his throat and nodded his head quickly to indicate he understood what she was getting at.

"I think we're good here," she said, turning her attention to the crew leader. "You didn't see anything, and we paid you for an assessment that found nothing."

"Do you one better and whatnot. We never even met, keep your money," the leader said, and signaled to his crew below to set them down.

Ren waited until the crew was far enough away before pulling Parr close. "The energy in those drainers is highly unstable; we need to get as far away as possible, as quickly as we can. Stay calm, and follow me."

"But my ship—"

Ren twisted his sleeve in her fist. "Our lives, Parr. Follow me."

CHAPTER 18

"If they're that dangerous, we should warn someone," Parr said.

"Come on," Ren said, and dragged him toward the well-lit corridor that led to the exit. White tiles lined the walls and the rounded arch of the ceiling. "They'll be fine as long as no one messes with them. That crew won't be back, and there's no need for a refuel given your little good luck charm."

Parr patted his pocket to make sure the jewel was right where it was supposed to be. It was.

"If those things are so unstable, why was Norfung firing on us from the *Dreadnet?*"

"Because you pissed him off."

Had he really pushed Norfung to the point where he'd risk all their lives as well as the lives of those in the hangar? The thought left Parr feeling pressured more than ever, like an outlander's noose was slowly tightening around his neck.

Parr chewed on the inside of his cheek as the two exited the hangar and stepped out into one of the station's busiest squares.

The lights of the city dotted the natural darkness. The station's creature-made atmosphere smelled like his homeworld after a rainstorm, only mixed with hints of garbage and fuel residue. He missed life on a big inhabitable like Versit and took in a deep breath that he let out with a sigh. This was real life. Not like the sterile streets of Palace City back in Bilena.

A multitude of animated ads bathed the streets in rich blues and vibrant purples, with an occassional burst of bright white from the flashy monitor displays. The projected image of a voluptuous orange and pink striped creature reclined along the red linen awning of a building across the street and beckoned to Parr with a curled finger as soon as he made a visual.

Ren jerked him forward and moved swiftly down the sidewalk, bumping slower-moving creatures out of their way in the process. Parr's comm buzzed with another ad for Moma Shando's delicious food. He shook his head, wiped it away, and tried to avoid the fallout from the collisions Ren was causing just ahead. He'd always ended up in some sort of altercation any time he'd crashed into a creature the way she was doing, and he felt a little short on luck at the moment.

Personal transports buzzed overhead as creatures leaned on the crossbars of their two-wheeled personals in the crowded streets. An arcade plinked and whirred beside them. He'd made his fair share of buldoons in a place almost exactly like it on his last trip out, and he was sure he could do it again. Parr grinned and tugged Ren's hand toward a lively establishment for a couple of quick games of chance.

She wouldn't be deterred, however, and pulled him onward. She was all business, which should have been sobering, but instead, Parr found it alluring. For him, there was nothing more attractive than watching someone perform the very thing in which they excelled. He actually wasn't even quite sure what it was she was doing, but she had a commanding presence, and he couldn't wait to see what was next.

What came next was an abrupt shove through the turnstiles that led to one of Versit's massive public transporters.

"Hey," Parr said. "Easy."

"Do I have your attention?"

"Well, yeah."

"Good. This isn't a pleasure trip, Parr. Keep your head down and move."

"But then, what if I start running into things?" He flashed one of his most practiced grins.

Ren hooked her arm in his, and not in a fun way. She ushered him down the well-lit but grubby tiled corridors until they reached a crowded platform—one of many at several levels. The platform's advertisement-covered walls met a dusty, dark ceiling. A group of wide-eyed youth brushed past them, all hard-edged squawks and chirps, eager for a big night out. A tall, skinny, blue-billed sconkovox dropped his hat on the ground, leaned against a wall, and began to play his quartolux for tips. It wasn't long before the puri began to clink in the makeshift receptacle below.

A whooshing noise soon displaced the music of the quartolux as the transporter arrived.

It was massive and full of sharp angles. The core itself was a series of structured tubes that housed hundreds of hexagonal prisms, or as most called them, hexes. The transporter carted creatures around the station and made stops to allow hexes to detach to take their occupants to their desired locations.

The massive vehicle slowed to a stop and buzzed as it magnetized itself to the platform for stability. Once docked, it seemed like part of the structure itself. The doors opened, and a few creatures exited.

Ren checked their surroundings one more time before pulling Parr from the flow of the crowd to an open door of the transporter. The door dinged pleasantly as they moved through, and Parr's comm buzzed to let him know he'd paid for public transportation.

The inside of the transport was mostly full. An old ad tracker ran across the top of the dull green walls. Light blue arrows appeared on the scuffed gray floor that indicated open hexagonal stations along either side. A hex lit up blue close to the entrance, and after one last check of their surroundings, Ren led them inside.

The blue light of the hex morphed into a pleasant gold after Ren tapped her wrist to the nav and informed it of their destination.

Parr watched behind the windows as others boarded and found their seats in hexes along the aisle. Most of the windows clouded into privacy mode as the engines of the transport rumbled to life. The growl transitioned to a gentle purr as the transport detached itself from the platform and began to glide forward toward its route.

"Couldn't help but notice—" Parr said.

"Shhh," Ren said. She flipped open her display and examined the space. She used it as a lens to inspect the tiny cabin. The screen blinked red in a concentrated area from the hex in front of them. She cursed under her breath. "I think someone is onto us."

"What?" Parr asked. "What do you mean? Why would someone be onto us? Who would care about—"

"Be quiet," Ren said.

Parr blinked back and wondered why Ren was so on edge.

"Stay here," she said. She opened the unit and discreetly stepped from the hex.

Parr peeked out into the aisle. It was clear both ways, with all the commuters content to stay in their hexes. There was a happy couple in a unit down the way, its windows transparent, but they were deep in conversation and oblivious to the world around them.

Ren knelt down to examine the handle of the hex immediately in front of them. She shot Parr a look that told him to get back inside.

He shook his head no and leaned a little further out into the shared space.

Ren let out a deep exhale before collecting herself and returning her focus to the task at hand. She pulled on a puzzle glove from her kit and held an open palm just over the handle.

"Why are you picking the lock to that door?" Parr asked in a whisper that was loud enough not to count as one.

Her jaw clenched, and she looked back to mouth something he couldn't understand.

"I can't understand you," he said, again in his loud whisper.

Ren responded with a rude hand gesture that was impossible to misinterpret.

There was a soft click, and the hex pulsed blue. Ren looked both ways before coolly opening the hexagonal compartment, then sprang into action. Fierce and graceful all at once, she disappeared into the hex, and Parr heard the report of two distinct thuds, like a butcher's hammer on meat.

There was a quiet rustling before she reappeared, holding a small drab rectangle in her fingers. She gave it a quick once-over before snapping it in half and letting it drop to the floor. She crushed the device with the heel of her boot as she pivoted her attention down the length of the transport.

The couple in the clear hex down the aisle looked up from their conversation, and she gave them a terse grin that inspired them to go back to whatever it was they were doing. They did their best to look toward the ad crawl in the distance before their hex slowly faded into the opaqueness of privacy mode.

Ren kicked the remnants of the device down either side of the aisle before she stepped back into the hex in front of them. Parr heard the beep of the hex's nav receiving coordinates as she returned to the corridor and closed it. The lights shifted from blue to gold. She attached something over the seam of the door and smoothed it over with her hands. Whatever it was, Parr was sure no one would be coming out of that pod at least for the rest of the trip, and probably longer.

Ren walked back to their hex and nodded for Parr to move over before she slumped into a seat. She reset their nav for a new destination, and the hex shifted to its opaque privacy mode once again.

"Are we being followed?" Parr asked.

"Not by those two," Ren said. "Not anymore, anyway."

"Sorry," Parr said. "Let me rephrase. *Why* are we being followed?"

"Don't ask," she said. "The less you know, the better. Let's just get where we need to go and get out."

"Where are we going, exactly?"

"Look, I promised I would get you back inside the gates of Bilena Epso Ach, and I will. I made a deal, and what we need is here on Versit."

The transport slowed to a stop to allow hexes to whir away to their various destinations and to wait for unoccupied or returning hexes to drop down and attach themselves as space became available. The hex in front of them hummed to life before careening off toward whatever destination Ren had coded for it, and it wasn't long before a new hex slid into its place. The transporter rumbled back to life and purred along its pathway once again.

"So, where are we—"

The question was arrested by an arched eyebrow and wag of her finger.

"Fine," Parr said. "But can we play a game or something? I'd like to do anything other than worry about my life for however long we have left in this thing."

Ren didn't quite relax but turned to face Parr. She brought her hands down and curled her fingers into fists to challenge Parr to a game of slice, cover, bash.

"Look," Ren said as she threw the slice symbol. "I'm sorry I'm on edge. It's just that this place is very dangerous for me."

"Versit?" Parr asked. He'd just thrown cover—he lost that round. "Don't worry, I've been here loads of times. Sure, there are some questionable creatures out and about, but it's mostly safe."

She dropped her hands and stopped the game. Ren closed her eyes and took a deep breath. "It's not just Versit. It's the particular venue. Remember, the less you know, the better for now. Will you trust me?"

Parr grinned and looked into her eyes. "Lady, I don't trust anyone."

Ren returned Parr's grin and gave his shoulder a playful punch. "Fella, it's time to expand your horizons."

The two locked gazes for longer than usual. Parr averted his eyes first, then refocused. "Alright, we'll see. Back to the game?"

"Back to the game," she said, and put down her fists again for another round.

He was surprised how much fun he was having, considering they weren't wagering on any of the matches, and the two played in relative silence for stop after stop until their hex finally whirred to life. A dashboard and windows appeared inside the personal hexagonal craft as it released itself from the transport and floated above a dark, deserted street.

No signs lit the sidewalks below. All was dark except for the occasional light peeking through the bars of personal dwellings high above the street-level shops, or at least the kicked-out windows and doors where shops used to be.

The hex whirred along block after block. Parr noticed creatures huddled in shadow here or there and wondered if they were settling in for a rest or crouching in wait for some unlucky passerby.

A busted sign tried in vain to spark itself to life above a shop that was closed for the night. Graffiti covered the locked and sealed metal barrier. Steam and vapor billowed out of grates in the middle of the street every few hundred feet or so. Places like these usually ran colder than others. There wasn't enough commerce in this area to support proper environmental control, so they had to deal with the lowest setting the station provided that still supported life. No one would freeze to death on the streets below, but they wouldn't exactly be comfortable out there either.

Ren's head was down and she was looking into her display, punching a message together with her fingers before sending it away with a flourish. She looked up with a small, dead smile past Parr to the scene outside.

Something was going on behind those eyes, Parr thought, and he was sure she didn't want to talk about it. So, instead, he looked down and pretended to find something of interest on his pant leg to scratch at. Eventually, the glow of lights in the distance caught his attention.

Blues, whites, and reds competed for attention in the shadows before the transport curled around the corner to reveal a brightly lit sign.

Moma Shando's, it read.

CHAPTER 19

A vast array of vehicles lined up the front of Moma Shando's brightly lit walk and curled out of sight around the block, sleek, shiny displays of luxury and affluence the elite carried in their cargo holds, so they didn't have to rent or take public transport once on-planet or -station. Valets hustled forward to open their doors and walk patrons down a velvet-roped, red-carpeted walkway. White and yellow lights flickered around the gaudy marquee, and the space above the oversized glass doors depicted scenes of legend from around the galaxy in exquisite inlay.

Ren and Parr's hex glided to a stop, and the door closest to the sidewalk opened automatically. Parr stepped out and offered a hand to Ren, which she ignored as she exited the small vehicle.

Parr's hand hung still in space, and he casually laughed as he eyed the area for whoever may have been watching. Ren didn't stop to wait, and Parr hurried to catch up to her.

In surprising contrast to the gold marquee and flickering lights, the inside of Moma Shando's was a humble seafood market. Aquatic life from across the Sixteen and outer reaches lay flat, displayed on ice, while creatures in formal wear took numbers and mingled with the riffraff of the neighborhood.

Ren strode past a number dispenser and put her wrist to a door. She motioned for Parr to keep up, and he joined her just before the door opened to reveal a massive, bustling dining area. Large horned glactons (not to be confused with their cousin the great horned glacton) met them at the door to the grand room. Their many well-muscled arms busted the seams of their formal wear as they welcomed the two travelers with grunts and nods.

"Hold here," one of them said as he scanned Ren. "Now you," he said to Parr. "Bring any weapons?"

"Why would I bring weapons to a fish market? Or whatever this place is."

"Scan him," the glacton said to his colleague.

The scanner dinged, and the glacton arched a scaly brow at Parr. He removed a blaster from Parr's coat.

Parr flashed an uneasy smile. "Forgot I left that in there."

"Wrist, please."

Parr raised his wrist, and the glacton bumped it.

"Your weapon will be waiting for you back on your ship. Enjoy Moma Shando's."

Ren seemed unfazed by the exchange and was already tracking a creature similar in appearance to Parr and Ren. He swanned toward them with a polite grace, his chin raised ever so slightly.

He was the maître d' of the establishment and carried himself with an air of borrowed affluence. His torso was rigid, while his extremities moved with the elegance of a swombid floating across a pristine lake on a summer day.

Ren leaned in to the maître d' to whisper a discreet message that was met with a tight smile. Kind of like when Parr would tell his sister rude jokes just out of earshot of anyone else at a crowded party or state-sponsored event.

"Right this way," the maître d' said before a fluid touch of the cuff of his sleeve. A golden pathway of ornate vines with beautiful, woven blooms appeared on the red carpet in front of them, and he beckoned them with a wave. Parr stayed close behind Ren as the pathway unfolded a few steps in front of her at a time. The maître d' followed behind them with clasped hands until they came to another door.

"Pardon me," he said as he walked past them and knocked in a clear, distinct pattern. Three sets of red eyes glowered through a slider as a creature behind the door sized the duo up.

Parr thought it might be a sharp-toothed fanctovax.

"Protocol Nine, please," the maître d' said with a twirl of his wrist that ended in an outstretched palm. "Cal will take it from here," he said to Ren and Parr. "Enjoy yourselves."

Ren looked down at the maître d's hand and over at Parr. Parr returned her gaze for a beat or two before the unspoken message sank in. He hated places like these. He'd never understood the point of a tip. He was used to getting something out of his money. Information, supplies, good service during a meal … anything. What had this guy done, taken them twenty yards?

Parr stared at the maître d', who stood poised and politely expectant. He wondered how much money he was really going to have to spend before he was able to get back to Bilena. Before long, he understood his hesitation had made things awkward and slid his wrist over the awaiting palm. A cheerful chirrup signaled the gratuity was successfully processed. "Thank you, sir, enjoy your time here at Moma Shando's."

The maître d' glided away before the door opened to reveal that the red-eyed creature behind it was, in fact, a sharp-toothed fanctovax. He beckoned them forward with a plump-fingered hand adorned with various rings. The pinky of his right hand was particularly stacked with gold jewelry indicating that he was a "made" creature in the reaches—untouchable, polished, and incredibly dangerous.

The smell of smoke hit Parr before he noticed the billowy wafts coming from the area below. Creatures gathered round and cheered at a green-felted blocca table close by as a dealer accepted a tip from a lucky winner. *That's more like it,* Parr thought. *A tip for luck—something.*

"Welcome to Moma Shando's," the fanctovax said. His voice sounded like warm butter poured over a bucket of gravel. "Name's Caldovan Peik, but you can call me Cal."

"I'm Parr, this is—"

"Someone who values privacy," Ren said.

"You look familiar," Cal said.

"I'm not," Ren replied.

Uncomfortable with the iciness of the moment, Parr let his eyes wander to the gambling floor below. The fanctovax put a hand on Parr's shoulder. "Care to try your luck before I take you back?"

"Don't mind if I—"

"No," Ren said. "Straight back, if you please."

Two of the fanctovax's three eyes smoldered before he responded. "You're the boss, miss. Right this way."

The room seemed to go on forever and was brimming with creatures in formal attire from various sections of the galaxy—everything from the stiff starched collars of Far Nglula to the flowing silks of Inner Eiber. Each one of the well-to-do creatures seemed more of a mark than the next. *How in the five suns did they pull this type of clientele? Especially with those terrible ads.*

Crystal chandeliers dripped from the ceiling, and servers buzzed from table to table in tight-fitting outfits, ensuring no guest saw the bottom of a glass. What Parr wouldn't have given just to spend an hour or so among them. There was nothing better than a wealthy mark looking to try their luck, and the room was full of them.

Wherever Ren was taking them had better be worth it, he thought.

Cal greeted staff and high rollers alike along the way. He seemed to know everyone in the joint, and anyone he didn't know knew him. Parr could tell there was something dangerous beneath Cal's polished image by the way some of the creatures avoided eye contact with the fanctovax.

It was inevitable that creatures racked up debt in a place like this, and Parr knew he wouldn't ever want to owe this house money or favors.

A server approached and offered drinks from a platter.

"No thanks, none for me," Cal said. "You two?"

"Yeah, sure—"

"No," Ren said. "None for us." She pulled Parr in. "You down even half the liquid in one of those glasses, and you won't be able to tell your foot from your hand—let alone sleep—for at least two cycles. Now get your act together and focus, you're embarrassing me."

The fanctovax grumbled a smoker's chuckle before muttering into the sleeve of his custom suit. He waved them forward. "This your first time at Moma Shando's?"

"Yes," Parr said. "Your ads are awful, how do you keep this place so packed?"

The fanctovax's eyes flashed along with the pointy teeth of his grin. "Our ads are targeted. We tailor them to the individual. Moma Shando's attracts a variety of clientele from the crème de la crème to the nastiest pirates, rogues, and smugglers the galaxy has to offer. It takes all kinds to run an establishment like this, and what your ad says speaks volumes about your character."

"Yeah," Parr said as he scanned the crowd and kept up with Cal and Ren. "I must have confused your ads with someone else's then, but I've definitely heard of the place."

"What about you?" Cal asked Ren. "Ever been to Moma Shando's before?"

Ren just eyed him and nodded.

"Of course," Cal said. "That makes sense. Protocol Nine and all." The fanctovax stopped and did a double take. "Katherine?"

She shook her head. "You must have me confused with someone else. Name's Ren."

"C'mon," Cal said. "It's been years. Where've you been?"

"You have me confused with someone else."

Cal narrowed his eyes. "I don't get confused, and I don't forget a face."

Parr wasn't sure what was going on, but he knew better than to cross a creature like Cal. Whatever Ren was playing at was a dangerous game, especially at a casino like this.

CHAPTER 20

"Protocol Nine," Ren said. "Now take us straight back. I won't ask you again."

Stars and fathers, Parr thought. *She's going to get us killed.*

Parr checked the room for escape options. He was no match for a fanctovax, but if he could get away from Norfung Gortn in a backwater marketplace, he could probably lose this guy in a crowded room.

"Fine. Like I said, you're the boss." Cal's face turned red, and he blew an aggressive exhale through his nostrils. "Have it your way."

Wait, that's it? That worked?

Cal stormed off, with Ren and Parr in tow. His friendly countenance replaced with a fiery glare that directed itself everywhere around the room except behind him as he escorted the pair across the casino floor.

"What is Protocol Nine?" Parr asked out of the side of his mouth.

Parr studied Ren's face, but she wouldn't return his gaze. She clenched her jaw and looked straight ahead.

"Why'd you lie about your name?" Parr asked in a whisper.

Ren hooked her arm around his and pulled him close. To most, it would have seemed an affectionate embrace. However, the pain from his pinched skin between her fingers let Parr know that it was anything but.

"Please. Be. Quiet," she said through a forced grin before letting go of his arm and continuing to stride ahead.

Cal led them forward, ignoring welcoming looks, open hands, and offered drinks, until they finally made it to the end of the casino floor and banked a hard left to follow a wall lined with tables, chairs, and synthetic plants. They came to a stop in front of an unremarkable length of wall, which, of course, made it remarkable to someone who knew better. Why else would there be twenty-odd feet of unused wall space in a place like this?

Cal turned to face the room with his back to the wall and scanned the area for looky-loos before stepping back and knocking a couple of heavily ringed knuckles against the middle of the open expanse of wall.

A tall, rectangular outline cracked into shape before becoming a door that slowly opened for the party. Parr took note of the difference in security protocol. It seemed a little more lax than the transition from the restaurant to the casino.

Parr wondered if this transition didn't require the security of the last stop because it led to a place no one wanted to go.

It was not a pleasant thought.

He couldn't help but think about the places that casinos used to disappear their debtors. He'd heard story after story of the shadowy hallways, the well-lit interrogation rooms with no edges, the threats— and worse, the deliveries on the threats. The lost appendages and the division of assets until the house was made whole while the debtor was made . . . less so.

"Through here," Cal said. He seemed to notice Parr's curiosity and added, "The casino is so heavily monitored, we don't need the peekaboo strip like before."

"Thanks," Parr said, and widened his eyes at Ren. "Because that's definitely the only thing I was wondering about."

Ren ignored Parr's unspoken communication and looked straight ahead with a determined mask and eyes like the blazing forges of Malf Leridian.

The door shut behind them and left him and Ren alone in a dark corridor. Lights hung from the ceiling between dully lit doors on either side of the hallway. The silence and lack of visual stimuli felt like whiplash in relation to the richly appointed buzzing environment of the casino floor.

A hanging light in the corridor flickered, and a door down the hall began to glow a soft blue. Ren nudged Parr's arm with an elbow. "Stop looking like that."

"Like what?" Parr said.

"Like a toddler in a morto tank."

"Why would a toddler be in a morto tank?"

"You know what I mean," Ren said. "We cannot show weakness in here."

"Whatever you say, Katherine," Parr drawled under his breath.

Ren pursed her lips and nudged him forward, and Parr shot her a glance before running his fingers through his hair. Judging by the the look of the hallway, Ren was right; it wasn't the place for weakness. But Parr didn't exactly do tough. He did, however, do a sort of haughty over-confidence just fine, and decided to lay it on thick for whoever might be watching behind a remote viewscreen. He scanned the corridor as though he were inspecting it before purchase.

Ren looked over and did a double take as they walked down the hall toward the blue door. "Why is your face like that?"

"No weakness," Parr replied. "Don't worry; I got this."

"Some weakness, then. Dial it back to the face of a toddler told about a morto tank as merely a jape."

"Merely a jape?" Parr said.

"It's a joke."

"I'd never joke about a morto tank, Ren. Relax, this isn't my first rango."

"What's a rango—"

The door hissed and rose to reveal a well-lit, perfectly round meeting room. No edges, no compartments—no place to hide things.

Most of the furniture was transparent and arranged around a large round table outfitted with a lazy susan on top that took up most of the space. Presumably for the transfer of small goods without close contact.

"Parr, you scruffy-looking, white-eyed shank of a dolker!"

No, Parr thought. *It couldn't be.*

Ren's eyes widened as she turned to face Parr. "You know Ludon Yelray?"

Parr gave her a confused look and hooked a thumb at the room's only other occupant. "No, but I know Manc."

"Please, ludon's just a title. Manc Yelray at your service, young lady. Yours too, I guess, you green-boned yorp of a noctor!" Manc said before pulling a mouthful of meat away from a shank of a benixton.

"How could you possibly know—" Ren said.

"Me and the lad go back quite a ways," Manc said between open-mouthed chews. Bits of food spilled out as he talked.

"That's right," Parr said. "He's the one who sold me the Grolen slak I offloaded at your station. Or was it Gorlem … I can't remember, can you, Manc?"

"C'mon, Parr; it's just business," Manc said before swallowing his mouthful of food. "Always check your receipts, son, and besides, I can't believe the napedes you traded were genuine Varulean. I was sure you were going to cheat me."

"Why would I cheat you? I always play it straight."

Ren and Manc eyed Parr pointedly.

"Fine," Parr said. "I mostly play it straight."

"Like the time you fleeced me out of the fastest ship in the galaxy, you slippery little ringolun?"

"I didn't fleece you out of anything," Parr said. "You straight-up traded me for the transport. Also, weren't you just bragging about fleecing me out of a badged and keyed vehicle back on Lobrow?"

"That was just for appearances, lad. But you knew that," Manc said. He held out the shank of benixton and narrowed his eyes. "You had to know. Somehow. You treacherous, beady-eyed—"

"*He* sold you the *Aurora*?" Ren asked.

"Aye," Manc said. "Worst deal of my life. Could have been me out there in the Corpulon Valvente. Of course, I had my time, but maybe I would have gone back for a bit with a ship like that. I don't know why you ever left it, Parr. With the way you fly, I thought you and the *Aurora* were a perfect fit for the Corpulon—a better fit than what you've been doing ever since, anyway."

"Right?" Ren said.

"No one hauls cargo in a Fano-class!" Manc and Ren said together.

Manc arched his back and showed his belly in a throaty guffaw. "I like her, boy. She's good creatures. How'd you get tangled up with this spindly veined wardelow?"

"Long story," Ren said.

"Ha, I'll bet," Manc said.

"How much?" Parr asked.

"How much? How about thirty—wait a minute." Manc squinted his eyes and pointed to Parr with the meaty bone in his hand. "You—I'll get to you later." Manc turned his attention back to Ren. "So, young lady, you came calling for the great Ludon Yelray, and now you have me. Let's get down to business; this place gives me the woolly marooleys. The sooner I'm out of here, the better."

Ren nodded and offered her wrist. "It's all here."

Manc set the meaty bone down on the table before wiping his hand on his pants and tapped her wrist to complete the transaction. His eyes seemed as hungry as his stomach as he watched her pull up the display, and he matched her grin for grin as she read over the information.

"Neat and tidy," she said, eyebrows raised. "Surprisingly tidy."

"Don't let the packaging fool you, girl. I'm a business-creature, first and foremost."

With one clean motion, Ren virtually slid the information to Parr. The comm on his wrist buzzed with her incoming message. Parr's face scrunched in a confused look as he pulled up the information on his display. It was a receipt for the sale of the decommissioned cruiser Parr traded Manc for the *Aurora*. According to the point of sale, it was worth fifty times the value Manc's "independent" assessor had quoted during their transaction.

Parr raised an eyebrow over the display, and Manc distracted himself with the bone from the shank of benixton and conspicuously looked off at the rounded blank walls of the room.

There were additional notes about the last known whereabouts of the ship. The most recent report showed it was on Anatone Seven, a dusty colony in the far outer reaches. The seventh and final settlement of failed developer Susoford Anatone, it was rumored to be home to Agrofor Telfo, a pirate's pirate. A pirate king, if there was that sort of thing. If Norfung Gortn was a folk hero, Agrofor Telfo was a folk legend. The pirate king's word was gold, but Telfo's unannounced presence meant certain doom.

"What is this?" Parr asked.

"Your way in," Ren said.

"Way into what?" Parr replied.

"Agrofor Telfo owns the ship," Ren said.

"I'm not going out there to meet with Telfo," Parr replied.

Manc's eyes followed the two as they verbally sparred. He vigorously chewed the benixton as though he were trying to keep up with the mounting tension in the room.

"All you need is that ship. It's badged, keyed, and ready to go. Bang, you're through the gates, safe as a babe after Walling's Day," Ren said.

"What gates?" Manc asked between chews.

"I don't like it," Parr said. "There's got to be another way."

"There may be, but that's the deal," Ren said. "Ludon—Manc, whatever, will take you the rest of the way."

"Hold on, that wasn't the deal," Parr said. "*You* get me inside the gates."

"The deal was to get you inside the gates, and *he* will."

"Which gates?" Manc asked again. "That wasn't our deal."

"That's when you collect the second half of the payment," Ren said.

"You said on delivery—ohh, I see," Mank yawped. "Tricky. I like this girl, Parr."

Parr turned to face Manc and held a hand out toward Ren. "How can she deliver payment if she's not there—"

Parr was interrupted by the hiss and release of the door to the room.

All three turned to face the silhouette of a creature similar in size and shape to Ren, accompanied by two lumpy bodyguards who stood just outside the door as a sandy-ridged sammakin slithered past to inspect the space.

The sammakin, as the name suggested, was a sandy speckled brown with a triangular head and six articulated, sticky toes attached to the same number of feet. They were known for their keen eye, even keener nose, and graceful speed. They were rare, coveted creatures that had to be coaxed rather than captured, which is probably why his father's guard had never had any luck with the blasted things.

The sammakin raced around the walls and then across the ceiling before returning to the floor, where it wriggled between furniture and the assembled group. It rose up on two feet and addressed the shadowy figure. "All is sssafe, misss."

"Wait outside," said the silhouette with a wave of her hand. Her voice was assertive but wavered with age. The sammakin returned to the floor and scuttled away on all six of its feet.

The creature with the assertive tone stepped out of the shadows. Her hands were hidden in opposite sleeves of a fine yellow silk robe embossed with electric blue and blood-red flourishes to match the heavy make-up that covered her face. Her hair was up and away from her face and adorned with pins and daggers that harkened back to an era long before the civility of the Sixteen Systems. "They told me you were here, but I dared not believe them."

"I can explain," Ren said.

"I'm sure you can, Katherine," Moma Shando replied.

CHAPTER 21

"Moma Shando," Manc said under his breath before dropping the shank of benixton to the table behind him and stooping into an artful bow. "It's an honor, ma'am, a true honor—"

"Quiet, Yelray," Moma Shando said in her wavering voice. Her lips were tight, her face as hard as the hull of an armored battle cruiser. "I've come to collect my daughter."

Parr wondered how old she was, it was hard to tell under all that make-up.

Manc seemed to shrink at her reprimand and gawped wide-eyed at Ren.

"You're her daughter?" Parr asked, confused. He turned to Ren. "What about the story of the handsome rogue?"

"Let me guess," Moma said. "She told you a story that melted your heart, made you feel sorry for her, then made some sort of deal that's led you here. That sound about right?"

She stared at Parr like the cave-dwelling mogrifer eyeing its prey into a hypnotic daze, but Parr did his best to mask his thoughts like a good cloaking program. Although he'd never heard of Moma Shando before he'd seen her ads, Manc's respect and the tense density of the air in the room told him not to give anything away.

Moma Shando chuckled under her breath and arched an eyebrow at her daughter, "The Victim's Gambit."

"Mother, stop," Ren said. "It's not like that." She turned to face Parr, her eyes like deep pools. "Parr, it's not like that."

"Poor little girl," Moma said. "Fending for herself on some backwater station, I'm sure she said. Didn't she?"

Parr glared at Ren. He had just started to trust her. He knew better.

"Ah," Moma said. "I taught her that technique. The story was mine … is mine. I rose from nothing to where I am today. Operating one of the, if not *the*, most profitable enterprises in the Sixteen and outer reaches. I taught her how to gather information and identify the perfect rube, and all the intricate mechanics of a profitable deal. It's how I built my empire. Moma Shando's, the largest establishment in the galaxy that no one's ever heard of.

"*You've* heard of us though, haven't you, Parr?"

Parr flinched. His name on her tongue stung like the gorbet's lash, and he couldn't stop his mind from wondering what other information she might have.

She looked down at her wrist, scrolling through data for a moment, before returning her gaze to him. "I see you received our 'Try Moma Shando's Delicious Food' promo." Moma cackled. "Nice catch here, Katherine."

"Parr. Wow," Ren said. "Actually, now that I think about it, that makes a lot of sense."

"What, why?" Parr asked.

"Yes, why!" Moma seemed to glide across the room, her feet invisible under her long silk robe. "The question I find myself asking is, why? Why you, Parr? Why has she arrived at my door, after all these years, with you, and the degenerate pirate Yelray?"

"Ay there, missy, I'm no pirate," Manc said. His eyes darted sideways. "OK, I hear it now."

Moma Shando eyed Manc for a moment before returning her attention to Parr. "So, I did a little digging, and you know what I found?"

Is this it? Parr thought. His worst fear in front of him? Had Moma Shando discovered she had Prince Parrtec, heir to the throne of the Sixteen Systems, held captive in the dark underbelly of her establishment?

And if so, how would she use him to her advantage?

Parr crossed his arms in such a way that he could grip the sleeves of his jacket to dry his sweaty palms. It beat wiping them on his pants, and he couldn't allow his mannerisms to give him away.

He wondered if she'd already reached out to Malista or if she had other plans for him. Plans so dark and nefarious, he dared not think about them. Except he couldn't help himself—he thought through a handful of scenarios, and none of them ended well for the young prince.

He was wrenched away from his thoughts by a stern but wavering voice.

"Nothing," Moma said. "I found nothing beyond a few years back." She eyed him up and down like a gambler on a final call. "I find that unusual, especially now."

Parr was relieved. She didn't know after all.

"What do you mean?" Parr said. "Why is that unusual now?"

"I've watched how you've carried yourself," Moma said. "A true outlander can't help but gawp at the ornate decorations, the gaudy display of riches, and the wealthy creatures they attract. You, however, seem right at home."

"I am," Parr said. "But it has more to do with the games. I'm more at home with the likes of Cal and Manc than the herd of vapid, high-class creatures you have milling about out there." It was a good cover, Parr thought. "See, I'm more interested in their money than their company."

"Perhaps," Moma said. "But how would a poor outlander come across a ship like the *Aurora*, much less learn to pilot it? And how would a mere station urchin come to learn of the Corpulon Valvente, much less make their ranks in their first trial?"

"Ha!" Manc said. "Like there's creatures out there ain't heard of the Corpulon."

Moma glared at Manc for a moment before returning her gaze to Parr.

"It's true, lady," Parr said. "I'd heard of the Corpulon my entire life; it was a dream come true to join their ranks."

"So why leave?" Moma asked.

"Growing up, I had to fend for myself," Parr said, and looked away out of the corner of his eye. "You know as well as I do that the galaxy doesn't just hand you anything. If I wanted something, I learned how to take it. And, over time, I got really good at taking things … just about everything but orders. Turns out, that's the one thing I can't take. So, I left."

Parr had meant to lie, but he couldn't help but find his own line of truth mixed up in the story. Moma Shando's questioning eyes looked Parr up and down before she gave him a loose nod.

"OK, that's enough, Mother," Ren said. Her face was flushed, and a vein bulged in her temple. Parr thought it would have been attractive if it weren't a little scary . . . *OK,* he thought, reconsidering, *it's both.*

Ren began to pace. "Typical Moma Shando. Say one thing, do another. You told us you were here to talk to me, but you've been talking about him this entire time. I'm here. If you want to talk, then let's talk."

Moma Shando's face dropped to a null expression before she tilted her head slightly toward the door. "Fine. Let us speak in private," she said, and held her arm out toward the corridor. "After you."

Ren stormed out the door, followed by Moma Shando. The door hissed to a close.

Manc hopped up and made a seat out of the table. He entertained himself by spinning around on the lazy susan while gnawing on the last of the benixton. "So," he said. "You and Ren." He waggled his eyebrows as he slowly spun. The two momentarily broke eye contact until the wheel brought him around the table again.

"Stop doing that," Parr said. "You're acting like a child."

"You're just jealous I'm on here and you're over there standing around like a little lost gwampus."

"I saw how much you made off our deal. Your guy undersold that ship's value."

"Ha!" Manc said. "Always have your own guy, Parr! Rule number one—know your value."

He was right, Parr should have known the value of the badged craft. Of course it would be of value, especially to an outlaw like Agrofor Telfo, who could use it to come and go through the gates of Bilena as he pleased. Who knew what kind of illicit affairs the pirate king would be able to set up with that kind of access?

Of course, Parr wouldn't trade the *Aurora* for anything, but the knowledge that he could have negotiated for more stuck in his craw like last night's mitchken.

"Then why do you think I got the better of the deal?" Parr asked.

"The *Aurora* is special, lad. Not sure what you did to her, but it's not every day you let the fastest ship in the Sixteen slip through your fingers. I have a feeling I could have traded you for anything with two bunks and an engine."

"Joke's on me then," Parr said. "The *Aurora* only has the one bunk."

Manc almost choked on his benixton as he wheeled around the table once more. His hybrid of coughing and laughter was cut short as the door to the room whooshed open and Ren stepped through.

Her hair was up in pins and daggers in the same style Moma Shando had worn earlier. She'd changed into similar robes as well. In fact, if Parr hadn't known any better, he would have sworn a younger Moma stood before him. The two would have looked identical given enough distance.

"We have to go, now," Ren said. Her eyes were wide, and she was breathing heavily.

CHAPTER 22

"C'mon, we don't have much time," Ren said. Her face was covered in make-up similar to Moma's. "Get a move on."

Manc brought the spinning lazy susan to a halt, dropped the meaty bone to the floor, and wiped his hands across the front of his pants as he wobbled toward the door. Parr sprang into action and gently gripped Ren's shoulder.

"Are you OK?" Parr asked.

"Yeah, I'm OK," she said. "Look, I'm sorry about what she said back there; it's not true. She's just trying to mess with our heads."

Parr thought about it for a moment. It's wasn't like he was unfamiliar with manipulative parents. Maybe he could trust her.

"Parr, get out here. You're not going to believe this," Manc called from the hallway.

Parr and Ren joined the old pirate in the corridor, where he was pointing at two security guards slumped awkwardly against a wall.

Manc's eyes narrowed as his gaze shifted to Ren. He circled a finger in the air toward her. "When did you have time to put all that on," he asked Ren.

"Doesn't take that long," Ren replied. "I used to do it all the time when I was younger."

"Looks good," Manc said.

"Does it?" Ren asked.

"Yeah," Parr said. "But you'd look good in anything."

Ren and Manc stared at Parr.

Parr's face flushed. "So," he said. "You were saying, Manc?"

"Right," Manc said. "You do this, girl?" He pointed to the floor, eyebrows raised.

"Yeah," Ren said.

Manc's face went red as he stifled laughter. He seemed to know better than to draw attention. "You sure are full of surprises," he said, and shook his head. "I hope we make it out of this alive."

Parr noticed that Moma Shando lay along the edge of the corridor as though she'd decided to lie down for a nap in the hallway. Either that or someone had knocked her out and gently set her down with care.

Her hair was loose around her face, and she was outfitted in the black leather of the Oowen-ra, the famed guild of skilled assassins.

"Ha ha," Parr fake-laughed. "Yeah, I hope we make it out of this alive too."

Five suns, Parr thought. A thousand different scenarios seemed to run through his mind, but he quickly distilled them down to two: stay with these two, or cut and run on his own. In his desperation to get back through the gates of Bilena Epso Ach, he'd put his trust in an outlander from a backwater station who'd turned out to be the daughter of what appeared to be a dangerous criminal underlord … who'd targeted him with terrible ads. He could tie his fate to her and that no-good pirate or figure out how to get back through the door and out to the casino on his own.

He could probably blend into the crowd long enough to find an exit to the street, but what then? Security details in a place like this were—pardon the pun—on their game. He doubted he could get past the first few blocca tables on his own.

He chewed the inside of his cheek and eyed Ren, who was excruciatingly attractive even in a situation like this. She seemed like the best option: smart, resourceful, and apparently familiar with their current environment. Plus, she smelled incredible. He wondered if that was a perfume or just a mixture of various products. He reminded himself to ask her about it later.

Parr took one last look at the feared Moma Shando lying on the floor.

"Interesting," Parr said. "The robes of high society over the leathers of—"

"No time," Ren interrupted. "Let's go," she said, and started down the hall.

Parr followed. "Where's the sammakin?" he asked. Sammakins creeped him out. You never knew where one might be hiding.

"It got away," Ren replied. "Slippery creatures, sammakins. Yelray, get a move on!"

Manc was still gawping at the floor. "Girl, what have you done? That's Moma Shando!" He ran a hand through his unruly mane. "That's Oowen-ra leather."

Ren came to a stop and looked back. Her eyes darkened as her eyebrows knitted together. "No time, Yelray." The hem of her robe flared. "Follow me."

"I like her, Parr," Manc said as he fell in behind Ren. "She just took out three creatures as quick as a broodlehos snatches a geck." His arms swung wildly to match his stride as he wobbled down the hallway. It wasn't long before they reached an unmarked door at the end of the hall. A beep chirped as Ren slid her wrist across a sensor, and they were quickly through to the other side.

Parr and Manc huddled behind Ren as she leaned over a console in the hallway.

"Just need to adjust a few things on our way out to give us some time," she said.

Ren furiously typed away before pressing a key with a final flourish and spun away toward a new destination down the dimly lit corridor.

One side of the hallway was lined with what Parr assumed to be the see-through side of one-way mirrors peeking in on rooms like the one they'd just left, with speaker boxes set up beside the glass. He heard snippets of heated arguments, hushed conspiratorial conversations, and one or two discussions in alien tongues or code he didn't recognize.

Wherever they were, and wherever they were going, the passage was built for secrets.

Meeting rooms gave way to views of private gambling alcoves, kitchens, and some sort of slithering scene in a darkened room that Parr was thankful he didn't have more time to observe. Gromorbian tentacles always gave him the woolly marooleys.

Ren stopped at another console at a fork in the corridor and typed away at its interface. Her face reflected a pulsing green light that slipped to red. She shook her head and cursed under her breath.

She slapped the side of the machine. "Come on, now. Take the code." She typed some more, only to yield the same result. She slammed the front of the console with her knee and looked up at the ceiling as though a cloud of ideas were floating just within reach.

"Let me see," Parr said.

"Please, Parr," Ren said. "Be my guest; I know how you're a master of decryption."

Parr took one step toward the console before Manc stuck a hand out. He shook his head. "I don't think now is the time, lad."

It took a moment for the old pirate's wisdom to kick in, but he was right. She wasn't asking for help, which was fine, because Parr wasn't quite sure he could.

A dimple quirked Ren's cheek before she rummaged around in the sleeve of her robe. Parr wondered what might have been sewn inside of Moma Shando's sleeves. No doubt the variety of tools and weapons that were the signature of the Oowen-ra. He recalled how coolly Moma Shando had appeared in the room—a hardened assassin inside the costume of a high-society creature.

"Aha, I knew it!" Ren said, and her hand emerged holding a round, black loop that looked to Parr like a loose personal identifier. He leaned forward. If it was, it was very rare; in fact, he'd never seen one that wasn't attached to a creature before.

"Is that a personal—" Parr started to ask.

"Yep," Ren replied.

Those are illegal in most outposts, he thought. Parr raised his eyebrows. *Nice.*

She manually scanned it into the console. "Mother likes a manual backup."

"I'm sure she does," Manc said with a chuckle.

Ren and Parr both glared at the old pirate.

"Sorry," he said, and straightened his furs. "What? C'mon, we're in a hurry."

Ren gave him one last glare and clenched her jaw.

Apparently, either the loop was an old one or the console was outdated, because the identifier wasn't a perfect fit. She knelt and stared at the monitor with a determined look while she finessed the hardware.

It reminded Parr of his father during the final spin of the sloom for the Galaxy Championships when he was ten. His father had always said he didn't believe in luck. He merely thought he could influence outcomes in his favor by sheer force of will.

Manc beamed over her shoulder like a proud father. It was the look Parr had always longed for from his own father. Approval. Joy in watching a child succeed. Something akin to the look Parrtec had caught out of the corner of his eye whenever his father observed him piloting a vessel.

However, Manc and his father couldn't have been more different. One had been a highborn creature of rational thought and discipline who believed he could impose his will on the world around him. The other was an outer-system castoff who lived by pure luck, chance, and opportunity and suspected his mere presence and desire for a positive outcome increased his and anyone else's odds for success.

There was just a fine line between the two beliefs when Parr gave some thought to it.

The side of the monitor lit up green and stayed that way until another door appeared in a wall tangled with wires and ducts.

The party slipped through and found themselves in almost complete darkness. Parr could barely make out Ren's hand feeling along the wall for something before she double-tapped to confirm. There was a soft click, and the floor of the hallway pulsed to life before glowing a steady blue.

Manc eyed Ren.

"What are you looking at?" she said. "Go!"

"This is too easy," Manc replied.

"Too easy?" Ren said. "No, this is what a good contingency plan looks like. Do you know what that word means, pirate?"

"Of course I do, I'm just saying this doesn't feel right, is all. Got my senses tingling something fierce." Manc flattened himself against the wall and held a hand out to relinquish the lead to Ren.

She brushed by him in the slim corridor. "That better be all that's tingling, Yelray."

"Ha! Good one," Manc said as she stalked down the pathway, then dropped his voice to speak to Parr. "You heard of that word before? What in the five suns is a contingency?"

"It's like a backup plan," Parr said.

"Right then," Manc said. "I have a few contingencies about how to get outta here."

Parr almost elaborated on the usage of the word, but they were in a hurry, and it was close enough to right.

Ren crouched in the corridor just ahead. She looked through a slider in what Parr could only imagine was another hidden door.

"What do you see?" Manc asked in a whisper.

"Four," Ren said.

"For?" Manc asked. "For information, I suppose? Just curious is all."

Ren slowly blinked before looking back at Manc. "No, four guards. The *number* four. How did you become a ludon, anyway?"

"Ooh," Manc said, then twisted back to wink at Parr. He wasn't dumb. He just liked to make dumb jokes. It didn't matter that the moment wasn't the most opportune.

"Let me handle this," Ren said, slamming the slider shut. "Parr, stay glued to Manc. Manc, give me a close but respectful distance."

"Aye. Just what's your contingency here, miss?"

Ren opened her mouth to answer but seemed to change her mind before the words came out. "Just keep a close but respectful distance, OK? Moma likes her security, but she also likes her space."

"Right, right," Manc said. His hand absentmindedly reached back behind him to find the hilt of a blaster underneath his coat.

Parr's thoughts were caught between awe at Manc's gall in bringing a weapon into Moma Shando's inner sanctum and awe at his ability to do so. He wasn't sure why he was even surprised at this point, though. The old pirate always seemed to have a trick up his sleeve.

"How far away are we from … wherever it is that we're going?" Parr asked.

"Close," Ren said. "Just bear with me."

"OK," Parr said. "Good. Good-good-good. Bearing with you. So, um, just real quick, how far are we from Anatone Seven?"

Manc shot Parr a look as if to say his line of questioning should soon come to an end. "It's not that close, lad."

"So, how are we getting there?" Parr asked.

"In your ship," Manc said.

"In his ship," Ren said at the same time, hooking a thumb at Manc. Ren rose from her crouch and smoothed the fine silk of her robes. She glared at Manc. "In *your* ship, pirate."

"Aye," Manc said. "That works for me."

Ren shook her arms to release any tension in them before clasping her hands and adopting a tall, wooden posture. "Now, get it together, you two. You're security, I'm Moma. Got it?"

Manc nodded.

"Good," she said. Ren took a deep breath and exhaled before grazing a hidden sensor with her wrist.

There was a quiet but solid click. The door released and lazily dangled a moment before she marched ahead. The room on the other side was barely more than a wider corridor and about a hundred feet long. Four guards stood under four lights, two across from each other. Parr couldn't see into the darkness beyond them.

She strode through the room with determination; her eyes focused straight ahead without acknowledging a soul in the area, as though she owned the place—which, as far as anyone else knew, she did.

Manc wobbled behind her, nodding to some guards as he passed while waggling his eyebrows at the others—all the while struggling to keep up at a respectful distance. Ren's demeanor reminded Parr of his mother on Andlas Day. The way she passed by her staff without a look while Parr and Malista kept pace behind, handing out tiny handmade or repurposed gifts to the creatures that had served them so well over the past year. The same creatures that lined the halls of their palace instead of sitting down with their families for Andlas lunch.

Parr adopted the face and posture of his father as he'd walked beside his mother on those days. Poised, disinterested, but discreetly aware of his surroundings.

The guards stood a little taller in the presumed presence of Moma Shando and kept their gaze on the wall across from them. One of them swallowed hard after Parr caught his eyes tracking Ren. The guard's cobalt eyes seemed to plead with him not to acknowledge the breach in protocol. The fear in them was intense.

Parr wondered what his father would do. Then he thought about a more compassionate response that still played to his strengths at the moment.

His father had never been in danger for a single moment in his life … at least until the last one. Parr decided to return the look with a haughty chuckle just under his breath and lazily turned his gaze toward the darkness ahead.

The lights above them made it hard for his eyes to adjust. Even so, he could see movement in the low light. Ren's posture changed ever so slightly. It was imperceptible (or hopefully so) to those who didn't know her better.

A fifth guard stepped forward out of the shadows with a face as blank as slate and twice as hard.

Where did he come from? Parr thought.

Have we been made?

CHAPTER 23

The guard was dressed differently than the others, his uniform more ornate. Not in a way that stood out at first glance. Black-on-black badges and stitching. A nod to the Oowen-ra, but certainly not one of the guild … at least not anymore.

His gaze tilted down to reduce the risk of eye contact. He opened a door for the party without a word.

We may get out of this yet, Parr thought.

They moved from room to room without a scrutinous eye falling on them or word said. Each space they passed through was just as interesting or mysterious as the last. One room sat nearly empty save for one little box on a pedestal in the middle, a button atop the piece. The next room was filled with glowing orbs that floated randomly about.

After that came a cargo hold filled high with crates, covered art pieces, and cages full of creatures Parr had only seen renderings of in old texts and questionable documentaries—like the woolly-toothed oripian. Which, as it turned out, wasn't woolly toothed at all. The tusks displayed were sharp, pointy, and all business.

The oripian was a tall, well-muscled biped, draped head to toe in a gauzy, flowing mane that floated gently in the breeze of the atmospheric conditioner. All four of the woolly-toothed oripian's glowing green eyes acknowledged the party as they entered but quickly scanned back to the guards as though it were silently plotting its rage-filled revenge.

It was the creature's eyes that made an impression on Parr. He wondered for a moment why they weren't called "ominous green-eyed oripians" but decided "woolly toothed" had a better ring to it regardless of its inaccuracy.

The group continued forward. Moma's guards bought the ruse and truly believed that Ren was Moma Shando. Confidence began to radiate among the three as they made their way toward the massive door to the cargo hold. Ren communicated a few coded messages with her hand, and the guard nearest to the door hit the oversized red button next to it.

Based on the size of the door, Parr expected there to be the loud crank of machinery or the piercing squeal of unoiled hinges. However, the motion was utterly silent, which made sense the more Parr thought about it. Moma Shando wouldn't want to call attention to a place built to hide valuables.

On the other side of the door was a tiered hangar for ground transport along with a wide berth to allow for offloading shipments of food and supplies. The various tiers were full of the black cars he remembered seeing out front, as well as a couple of smaller interstellar-class luxury vehicles.

A few ships stood out here and there, but one was particularly noticeable, and not in a good way. A mossy green number that looked like it had just been dragged out of a swamp. It was boxy for any type of vehicle, much less one that would need to travel through an atmosphere before it reached the vacuum of space, where aerodynamics wouldn't matter.

There was another, however, that caught Parr's attention. A sleek matte-black vessel—the color of deepest space, with all the hallmark devices an experienced smuggler would long for. Extra boosters, redundant cloaking devices on different parts of the ship. If Parr didn't already have the *Aurora*, he'd have done anything to get that one.

There weren't supposed to be private docks on this station, and Parr wondered if those ships were even on the books. Maybe another courtesy Moma extended to her clientele.

Between them and the hangar, though, stood a cadre of guards dressed all in black.

Ren pressed forward with all the confidence in the Sixteen.

"Good evening, ma'am," said one of the guards in a deep, dulcet tone. He stepped forward from the group and respectfully arrested Ren's progress. "Forgive me," he continued, "our itinerary has you in another section at this time. The hangar is not prepared for your presence."

"It is quite alright, Captain," Ren replied. Parr then noticed the braided leather epaulets on the guard's uniform. The Oowen-ra was rumored not to be a hierarchical organization outside of whoever led them at the moment, but Moma Shando had seemingly integrated them into a more traditional structure. "I was personally seeing our guests to their ship. They've had a very profitable stay with us."

"Of course, ma'am," the guard said. "Please, just a moment while we secure the area."

Parr took another glance over at the mossy green oddity and wondered who it belonged to. Why would someone utilizing a private hangar fly something so conspicuous? Whoever it was had parked in the section closest to the hangar doors. Probably in case they needed to make a fast exit. At least as fast as that hunk of scrap could go.

Something wasn't right, Parr thought. The guards weren't moving, but their captain was communicating something into his wrist. Ren's posture was like that of a catarnarn—a four-legged predator that always looked rigid and still. It held the same posture whether it was about to lie down for a nap or spring into a vicious attack. You never knew with those creatures.

"Thank you, Captain," Ren said. "I'm sure our standard protocol is fine, I'll take it from here."

The captain put his hand out flat and indicated for the group to halt. His other wrist was to his ear. "Just one moment, please, ma'am."

"I'm afraid we're out of moments," Ren said. "We do not treat guests like this."

A few dozen guards trotted into the hangar from several ship-lengths away.

"Nice to see you again, Ren," the captain said. "You're starting to look just like your mother."

"Wish I could say the same, Captain," Ren replied as she took her hands from her sleeves and rolled three spheres toward the assembled guards. "Run!"

"Where?" Parr shouted.

"That way," Ren shouted. "I'll catch up."

The spheres started to smoke and put up a visual barrier between the two groups.

Manc struggled to get his bearings, but once he'd turned, he was able to lean into a remarkably fast amble. "I don't think you look anything like her mother, Captain," he said over his shoulder. The old pirate could really move once he got going and even managed to beat Parr back through the sliding door.

Behind him, Parr heard a few barked orders amid the hissing sound and turned back to see Ren sprinting through the wall of vapor.

Once she was back in the warehouse, she turned the device on her wrist, and the massive doors slid shut with surprising speed.

"Go!" she said. "That's not going to hold them for long."

Manc was already on his way back toward the other side of the massive warehouse with Parr on his heels, and it didn't take long for Ren to catch up.

"Har har," Manc actually said instead of laughing. "I haven't had this much fun since I was a wee reed of a gilded wumper."

They flew by the stacks of crates holding various treasures, including the woolly-toothed oripian's cage. The monstrous biped's green eyes tracked them from where it stood. It seemed to come to life amid the commotion.

Parr looked over at the old pirate. "We're dead, you know."

"Har har," Manc replied. "If I had a skonk of Varulean napedes for every time I've been a surefire goner, I'd be retired."

"Retired?" Parr said with a laugh. "You could have a million buldoons and still figure out how to gamble them away, you old wharf rat."

"That hurts, Parr. I always thought of myself as a ship rat."

"Yeah, well. We're still going to die."

"Har har, maybe, Parr. May-be!"

Ren seemed to be holding something back. There were definite signs of concern but nowhere near the dread and panic Parr felt inside.

"You don't seem worried," Parr said to her.

"Why would I be?" she replied. "They're not going to kill me."

The door to the other side of the warehouse flew open, and a half dozen guards marched forward toward them with weapons raised. Ren and Parr came to a stop, while Manc, unable to maneuver as fluidly as the other two, tumbled into a stack of crates.

Luckily for Manc, the crates stood between him and the guards, but unfortunately for Ren and Parr, they were caught out in the open.

"Hands up," one of the guards said. "Slowly."

Parr glanced over at Ren. She exhaled a hissing breath through her teeth before a succinct curse.

"Do it now," the guard said.

"Slowly," another reiterated.

Manc chuckled to himself as he leaned against the crates out of the guards' field of vision. The old pirate seemed to be getting a kick out of their situation. He retrieved the blaster from his belt and held it up just to the side of his face. In fact, upon a closer look, Parr noticed him scratching his nose with it.

"Go ahead and raise your hands, Parr," Ren said.

He raised his hands slowly and wondered what was coming next. Were they going to throw him in some hidden room and work him over until he spilled all of his secrets? What would they do once they figured out who he was? Or would they just neatly and efficiently take him out because he'd dared to cross Moma Shando in her own house? Or worse, what if they decided to torture him to death to teach anyone else with similar ideas a lesson?

Parr grimaced as he imagined all the types of sharp and dull pain that awaited him.

Muffled chuckling pulled Parr from his thoughts and over to a red-faced, chortling Manc, who kept checking over the side of the crate to track the guards' progress. *What in the five suns could be funny about this situation?* Parr thought.

He also wondered what Ren thought about Manc's antics and noticed her hands were raised but suspiciously close to the sticks that tied her hair up above her head.

"Don't move," one of the guards said as they got closer to the two just on the other side of the crate from Manc. There were too many for him to do anything meaningful, even if he got the drop on them. So why was he still laughing?

Parr didn't have long to dwell on the thought as the group got close enough for Manc to spring his trap. A single blast into the open space, before he dropped the gun and skidded it across the floor just out of reach as the guards closed in.

"Sorry about that," Manc said with his hands raised. "Trigger is itchier than my bottom after a long day at the beaches of Webberwell."

"Disgusting," Ren said, shaking her head.

What was that shot? Parr mouthed.

"My contingency," Manc said. The old pirate waggled his eyebrows.

The guards surrounded the tiny group and started to move in.

A roar ricocheted around the walls of the warehouse, and the guards all froze in place.

Parr felt a wind behind him and turned just in time to see the woolly-toothed oripian lower its shoulder and send a cluster of guards flying. The beast started flinging others to various locations around the room.

Its feathery hair appeared to float lazily in the breeze, in stark contrast to the speed with which the creature moved. It screamed another roar and took off after another set of guards. The impressive display was more than that of a raging creature—the oripian moved methodically, as though it were herding the guards into small groups before picking them apart.

All of the stories Parr had heard about woolly-toothed oripians painted them as mindless, ferocious creatures meant only for zoos, menageries, and personal collections—except one: the story of Novie the Swift.

It was more of a tale than a story, really. One could never be sure of its authenticity. It claimed Novie the Swift was a captain in the Corpulon Valvente before he and his crew launched out on their own to pursue fortune and glory.

If the story was true, it meant oripians might be more than mindless murder machines—that maybe, just maybe, they were regular creatures just like anyone else.

At any rate, this one was at least a good distraction.

Manc slid over to his blaster and started opening fire. Parr hopped around on one foot as he tried to pull his own smuggled blaster out of his other boot. Manc wasn't the only one capable of sneaking a gun into Moma Shando's . . . even if his was bigger.

The guards were like sitting ducks on a pond.

Manc was able to pick them off at will as they focused on the oripian tearing around the room, dismembering its former captors. Soon, though, the former Oowen-ra couldn't help but take notice and started to return fire.

"Don't shoot to kill," Ren said.

"I would never," Manc said, then added in a lower voice, "Starting now."

Parr and Ren slid behind some crates for cover. Parr blasted toward the guards so that Manc could wobble his way over to join them.

Ren cursed as she looked down at her wrist device. "They're almost through the hangar door. I tried to code it, but they're figuring it out. We don't have long."

"Har har," Manc said between shots. "Might as well let them in, I'm sure our furry friend would be happy to see them."

"That's a pretty good idea," Parr said.

"Besides," Manc said, "our only way out is in that hangar. Did you see that beaut of a ship parked out there, Parr?"

Parr thought back to the matte-black number out in the hangar. "I did."

"What would you say if I told you she was mine?"

"I'd say that's the bit of luck we need."

"So, let me get this straight," Ren said. "Your idea is to open the doors and let in my mother's group of highly skilled assassins?"

"Former assassins, right?" Parr asked.

"Sure, former assassins, if that makes you feel better," Ren replied.

A shot blasted through the edge of a crate by their heads.

"Har har," Manc said. "You see any way out other than us leaving in the trustiest ship in all the Sixteen?"

"Second trustiest," Parr said.

"I said trustiest, not fastest, lad. Don't get your skivs in a bunch. Not everything has to be a contest."

"Fine," Ren said. "But I grew up with a lot of these guys, so let's try to keep the body count down. They're creatures of action, so I'm sure they'd respect some fallout, given the situation, but just keep in mind I'd like to come back here someday."

"You think they'll let us back after all this?" Parr asked.

"Not us," Ren said. "Me."

"Har har," Manc laughed between blasts. "Almost got me, you skinny runt of a voldocriper." He gave Ren a nudge. "It's now or never, girl! Open the door and move like you mean it to the mossy green beauty beyond."

"Mossy green?" Parr said. "Not the matte black? You mean to tell me that pile of welded-together shipping crates is your ship? Even if we make it out of here, we'll never outrun Moma Shando in that—even if she's on foot."

"That hurts, Parr," Manc said, "seeing as how I value your opinion and all. But I got myself a contingency."

"What's that, pirate?" Ren asked.

"It's like a back-up plan," Manc said.

Ren rolled her eyes. "What is *your* contigency?"

Manc pulled something from his pocket and hurled it across the room; it whizzed by the bridge of Ren's nose and missed her by the narrowest of margins. It made a loud clang that momentarily drew the guards' attention. "Follow me," he said, and sprint-wobbled toward the massive door.

Ren glared at Manc before turning toward Parr.

"What are you looking at me for?" Parr asked. "You're the one who hired him. Just open it before he gets himself killed."

"The men behind that door will kill us faster than anything in this room," she said. There was a dull thud close by, and a guard inchwormed over to a pile of crates using his one functioning limb. More collateral damage from the oripian. "OK, maybe not anything."

"I think he's on our side," Parr said.

"Let's hope so," Ren replied. "But I have my own contingency plan." She swirled a few motions to her wrists, and the massive door began to slide open.

Are they both going to keep saying "contingency"?

Blaster fire immediately filled the room. Manc rolled behind a pile of fallen crates for cover while Ren and Parr serpentined around stack after stack of boxes until they rejoined their friend—who still somehow managed to look pleased amid the blaster fire, and oblivious to a guard who was about to get the drop on him.

The guard crumpled silently to the ground, and Parr noticed Ren's hair fall loose past her shoulders. She twirled the one remaining dangerous-looking hairpin in her left hand. The other stuck neatly through the eye of the guard, who was still on the floor. Ren tossed a few more smoke emitters between the group and the former Oowen-ra and slid next to Manc behind the stack of crates.

"What now?" Parr asked through heaving breaths.

"What do you mean?" Ren asked.

"What's your contingency plan?" Parr replied.

"That was it," she said. "Those are the last of the smokes; we need to run."

"Then what are we doing here?" Manc asked.

"Deciding on a direction," Ren said. "We need to stick together through the mist."

"Har har," Manc said. "This way."

"Shouldn't Ren lead—" Parr began to say, but it was too late. He was off, with Ren falling in behind him. "The way." Parr shook his head before sprinting forward to join them.

The group grabbed on to each other's sleeves and darted into the fog of smoke and random blaster fire. The roar of the woolly-toothed oripian echoed throughout the warehouse and into the hangar.

The smoke dissipated sooner than Parr would have liked, but he was happy to find they'd put some significant distance between themselves and the guards. He could make out a few of their outlines through the haze. They were lost in the smoke, each setting out in their own direction, some with their hands out in front of them to stop them from stepping facefirst into something hard with sharp edges.

Parr fired a volley at a few clearly defined shadows.

"Nice going," Ren drawled. "You just gave away our position."

"I just tried—" Parr started to say before three reports sounded out in the hangar and one blast found its home in Parr's midsection. He fell to the floor and tried to roll back up but found he was unable given his injury. Manc continued on his way, seemingly unaware of his comrade's plight.

"Hey!" Ren yelled while throwing her remaining hair stick into the outline of the blasting perpetrator. "Parr's down, you bloody freebooter! Help me get him up."

Manc maintained his wonky momentum. "I'll just warm the ship up for us."

Parr gasped for air. Every inhalation felt like another blaster shot, or worse. "What did you think he was going to do?"

"No-good pirate," she said under her breath, and tried to pull Parr to his feet.

"Ow," Parr said with a wince before he sent another blast toward an outline in the smoke. "That hurt."

"There'll be plenty more where that came from if we don't get aboard that nice, warm ship."

"I'd rather not with an open wound," Parr said. "No telling what microscopic life-forms are lurking about inside that heap of health hazards. You think he spent good buldoons on a self-cleaning function or scrub bots?"

"Are you seriously trying to have this conversation right now?" she said, and with another effort, managed to help him to his feet. The two hobbled toward the mossy green garbage pile Manc called a ship. It didn't take long for Moma's guards to get their bearings.

Shots whizzed by their heads and bounced off the floor as well as adjacent ships in the area. *Who knew the Oowen-ra were such bad shots with blasters?* Parr thought. *Maybe they should have spent more time practicing with conventional weapons instead of just learning how to grab and throw each other around.*

Another blast ripped through Parr's torso, and Ren caught one to her thigh.

Parr regretted jinxing himself with his earlier internal monologue and made a mental note never to do it again.

Any and every movement made Parr want to scream. Somehow the two blasts had managed to hit him in the only nonlethal spot that seemed to connect with every other nerve and muscle in his body. The pain was overwhelming and made him want to retch.

Ren grimaced but was back on her feet quickly.

The blaster fire stopped.

"That's enough," the captain said coolly as he emerged from the vanishing smoke. "We've orders to take you all dead or alive, Ren. I'd rather it be alive."

"Let us go," Ren said.

"I don't understand," the captain said. "Why are you doing this? All this could be yours—where've you been?"

"Just let us go," she said.

"Orders are orders," the captain replied.

"I don't ever want to see her again."

"Fine," he said. "Have it your way. Blindfold her and take her to her mother; dispose of him discreetly."

"Hey," Parr said. "I'll see her mother again; I don't care."

The captain smiled as he raised his blaster for the kill.

CHAPTER 24

There was no report, however. No muzzle blast. In its place rose a sound unlike anything Parr had heard before. Like celebration bells or the roar of a cheering crowd, the cry of the woolly-toothed oripian broke through the wash of noise in the busy hangar.

The oripian leaped from the mist and took the captain down like a tumbling ball through a child's tower of blocks. It crouched close and roared into the captain's face before turning its attention to the rest of the guard.

Ren took the opportunity to drag Parr toward Manc's ship, which was already pulling away from its spot in the hangar.

Ren dropped Parr's arm and screamed into her wrist, "You don't get paid if we're not on board."

The ship arrested its progress, and the mossy green pile of incongruous blocks dropped its loading platform for the two to board.

Ren pulled Parr forward and managed to dodge the sporadic blasts from what was left of the Oowen-ra. She hit the button for ascent once they were safely on. Parr reached up and pushed the lift's button a few more times in the hopes that it would speed up the process even though he knew it probably wouldn't do any good.

"Why are you hitting it more? You know that doesn't do any good," Ren said.

"It feels like it does," Parr said.

Ren just looked down at him.

"Yeah, I know it doesn't," Parr said.

There was a hiss from below the sleek matte-black vessel as its quick-stair unfolded. Parr jealously searched the area for its pilot and noticed the woolly-toothed oripian hurtling toward it.

The huge biped took a sharp turn and darted up the matte-black vessel's steps but paused briefly to salute Ren and Parr with one massive gauzy paw above its four green eyes. It turned on its heel and disappeared inside along with the folding staircase.

Maybe the fable of Novie the Swift was more than just a bedtime story, Parr thought.

The lift on Manc's ship came to a halt with a crunch of grinding of gears. Once Parr's eyes adjusted to the light, he found himself in a musty cargo hold that, just as he'd suspected, hadn't seen any type of sanitation in ages.

Reinforced by massive beams, it was mostly empty save for a few boxes that were attached to the walls and floors, their latches loosely held together by shoddy patches of gray bonding tape. The creature-made light of the hangar poured through thin cracks around the seams of the lift—which indicated it wasn't closed all the way.

Which meant they couldn't leave the atmosphere.

Trustiest ship in the galaxy, he said. Parr opened his mouth to say something sarcastic but was silenced immediately by the pain caused by the inhale. He grimaced hard instead.

Parr's ragtag alliance may have momentarily defeated Moma Shando's security team, but they wouldn't be deterred long. There was no way they could allow the small group to escape. Moma Shando had a reputation to uphold.

They heard Manc's loud, unintelligible curse, along with the sound of what Parr guessed was a tin cup flying across a room further down the ship. Manc's wobbly footsteps approached the two. "Did one of you push the button more than once?"

Ren looked down at Parr. Parr looked back at a point in the hull far away from either of the other two.

"Uh, no," Parr said. "Why?"

"The lift won't shut, and I'll be a greasy square pornunculous if I can figure out why. Sometimes it sticks if the call button gets overloaded with signal."

"What does that mean?" Ren asked.

"Like when someone presses the button too many times," Manc replied.

Parr cleared his throat. "What would happen if that was the issue—how would you fix it?"

"I'd have to shut her down and re-fuse the connector."

"We don't have time for this," Ren said. "We have to get moving, Moma Shando's crew will be out in full force in no time."

Manc shook his head. "We can't make the jump with the lift in that condition. It's not making a seal, see?"

"How long would the fuse thing take?" Ren asked.

"Hour or so, I suppose," Manc replied.

"We don't have an hour!" Ren said. "We have to move now. Horizontal if not vertical—can you get us to the A block in WL-19?"

"Har har," Manc replied. "Does a three-toed gornorvor crap purple?"

Ren blinked. "I don't know. Yes, hopefully? Whatever it takes to get us moving."

Manc threw his head back and let out a deep belly laugh before he clapped Ren on the shoulder. "They do—big purple turds! High as the Fevalon Tower. Welcome aboard *Vanessa's Complaint*, folks. Med kit's across from you on that wall. Fix yourselves up and join me on the bridge as soon as you can."

Ren located the med kit and grabbed hold of one of the reinforced beams as *Vanessa's Complaint* came to life and surged forward. Parr was too busy wincing to grab hold of anything but his side, and as a result, he slid back until the cargo hold's rear wall brought him to a sudden stop.

"Ow."

After a quick patch and bubble, Ren was able to mend Parr's blaster wounds as well as her own, and the two rejoined Manc on the bridge of *Vanessa's Complaint*.

The room was just a shade less dingy than the cargo hold, outfitted with two chairs and what looked like a wet bar with all the appointments toward the back. Manc was in his captain's furs, leaning forward over his nav screen. "Traffic looks clean as a gollectoir's gazork up until the WK sector. Looking for a contingency or two after that."

"Perfect, we could use some good news," Ren said right before *Vanessa's Complaint* lurched sideways from a cannon blast.

Lights strobed red in the bridge, but no hailing signal came. There was no question as to who'd sent the blast, and it wasn't a good sign that they weren't even attempting to communicate, Parr thought.

Another blast sent the *Complaint* careening off in another direction. Manc roared a series of obscenities that Parr did not understand.

"How are the shields on this bird, Manc?" Parr asked.

"Tougher than a trinosed blale on a gobber's island, boy."

"Is that good?" Ren asked.

Parr shrugged.

"Har har, could be worse. Could be worse," Manc said before a cannon blast sent them hurtling off in a completely different direction. "See? Now we're heading toward my contingency. Har har!" Manc pressed a button built into his armrest, and a hissing noise ripped through the ship. "Let's see how they deal with the ol' cloak 'n' smoke."

Ren and Parr shared a look before turning their gaze to Manc.

"I just cloaked the ship and sent up a bunch of smoke. Makes it hard to find us that way, see?"

"Yeah, that tracks," Parr said.

"Now, what's in WL-19 if you don't mind me asking?" Manc queried.

"Parr's ship," Ren said.

"The *Aurora,* then?" Manc said. "Fine. Fine, indeed. Suppose it'll be hard to catch a crew in the fastest ship in all the Sixteen, right, Parr, my boy?" He wobbled around the bridge stuffing things into pockets before grabbing a bag and heading to the back.

"Where are you going?" Ren said.

"Not sure when I'll be back," Manc shouted from another room. "Thought I might grab a few things for safekeeping. You know, as a contingency."

As luck would have it, there was no way to avoid the traffic in WK-19, which one had to travel through to get to WL-19. *Vanessa's Complaint* came to almost a full hover in the maddening stop-and-go traffic.

"Rush hour," Ren said. "Why did this have to happen during rush hour?"

Crash. Boom!

Quick-pulsing amber lights flashed through the bridge as Manc cursed a new string of filth Parr was unfamiliar with.

"How did they find us cloaked?" Parr asked.

"They didn't," Ren said. "Did they?"

"Aye," Manc said. "I mean no, they didn't."

"What?" Parr asked.

"We just got rear-ended, Parr," Ren said. "Take her out of cloak, Manc. We can't risk the station guards coming after us too. Let's just trade policies with whoever—"

"Har har, I'd like to see 'em try," Manc said as he pulled *Vanessa's Complaint* out of traffic and into the restricted air space above it. The hailing comm blinked. There were usually auto-signals in the case of ships crashing, but Manc shut that down too. Parr couldn't help but laugh as he watched the old pirate in his element, weaving around, through, and above the various traffic patterns and altitudes. That crusty old ship rat really could pilot this hunk of hangar trash, Parr thought.

The bridge lights flashed blue and red.

"Brilliant," Ren said. "Station guards."

CHAPTER 25

Parr was ready for the entire ordeal to be over. The sooner they took possession of that old badged and keyed vessel on Anatone Seven, the sooner Manc would be on his way. However, that also meant his time with Ren would come to a close as well. Nothing was ever simple.

The hailing signal blinked.

"Don't be stupid, Yelray," Ren said. "Take the comm. Moma Shando's people can't do anything while we're in contact with the station guards, and they'll more than likely beat us to the A block after that stunt you just pulled. It's perfect."

"Don't trust guards," Manc said. "And I never have."

"Manc," Parr said. "She's right. Just set the *Complaint* down."

"*Vanessa's Complaint*. Show some respect, Parr."

"Sorry. Just, please listen to Ren, Manc."

Manc put his finger over the button to engage the comm. "Hold on to something," he said, and jammed the throttle forward instead. Ren lithely stepped back into the only open chair in the room, while Parr reached out, too late, to try to steady himself on the arm of Manc's captain's chair. The ship's sudden burst of speed sent him careening back toward the wet bar, which ultimately arrested his momentum.

"Ow."

Parr eyed the bar and thought about how good a quick drink would feel before rejoining the other two at the front of the bridge to take in the various views from the nav screens, but decided against it. The room continued to flash blue and red until Manc punched in a code that set the lighting back to its original drab yellow-brown.

"Why?" Ren said.

"Like you said," Manc replied before jerking the ship in another direction to avoid an aerial barricade. "Moma Shando's goons wouldn't dare show themselves while the station guards are around."

"There was an easier way," Ren said.

"Easier way, she says. Har! Trust me, girl, this is easier than talking to any station guard." Manc banked hard again to avoid another barricade and sent Parr flying once more.

"Are there emergency straps anywhere I may be missing?" Parr asked.

"Har har," Manc laughed. "Not for you. I used them to secure cargo in the back. Sorry about that, lad. You're just going have to find something else to hold on to."

The nav screens glowed orange, not from a hail but from a blast. The standard color of the pulsors that station guards used throughout the Sixteen.

"How many warning shots do guards fire on Versit?" Parr asked.

Manc shrugged. "I didn't know they fired warning shots here."

Parr inched his way forward through the cabin amid the jerks and speed changes. "How far away are we from the hangar?"

"Won't be long now," Manc said as *Vanessa's Complaint* violently shook.

She'd taken a direct hit from the guards in pursuit.

"Hoo, now. Guessing the answer to your question is one," Manc said, then began to sing, "One warning shot on Versit Station, one warning shot for me." He looked down at one of his nav screens, punched in a few keys, then read the results. "Two direct hits, and we're all deaders, two hits outta three."

"Are you serious?" Ren asked, then swiveled in her chair to face Parr. "Is he serious?"

Parr shrugged. "Manc, surely this bucket—I mean, ship, can withstand more than a couple of shots. She seems sturdy."

"*Vanessa's Complaint* is as sweet as they come. Sturdy as the day is long back on Cavalon Nine, but them pulsors in this environment with this grav—son, I *hope* we can take one more."

"So, what's your plan?" Ren asked.

"Fasterrr," Manc replied, pushed the throttle down hard, and leaned into a diving turn. Luckily, Parr saw the maneuver coming this time and was able to hook his arm around his chair. Although suspended in the air was a suboptimal position to find himself in, it beat hitting the back wall again, and it gave him a clear look at the nav screen. Manc's maneuver put some distance between them and the guards in pursuit.

"There's more coming—" Parr said.

"I see 'em, I see 'em," Manc replied between adjustments to the panel in front of him. "Like dozens of summer flies after you stir up their little nest. Don't worry. I got 'em right where I want 'em."

"I can see that," Ren said. "Everything is obviously going to plan."

The nav screen pulsed white, and the sounds of pulsors screamed by.

"Har har! See? They missed. Not as many angles when more people join the formation. Makes it harder to take a good shot."

"Wow," Ren said. "That actually makes sense."

That was the kind of thing Parr had heard about. The bravado, the maneuvers, it was all a part of Manc's reputation, and thankfully, the rumors were true. *This guy is amazing,* Parr thought.

Wham! Parr hooked his arm even tighter to the chair. *Vanessa's Complaint* had taken another direct hit.

Manc cursed and slammed his fist down on one of his nav screens.

"How are they even hitting us while we're cloaked?" Ren asked as she gripped the arms of her chair, holding on for dear life.

"Math, girl. I don't know," Manc said without looking away from his nav. "They have some sort of calculation that makes a guess based on trajectories or somesuch." He smiled as he signaled in a pattern. "Let's see how they like my crackling clusters."

The nav behind them displayed a half dome of smoke and fire just before a team of guard ships went spinning off in different directions.

"You've just gone from evading to firing on station guards. Are you crazy?" Ren said.

"Almost there now," Manc replied. "Don't you worry. Everything's under control."

"We're one hit away from the big deletion! I can't believe I let you talk me into this, Parr."

"Me?" Parr asked. "How are you blaming me for this?"

"Because it makes me feel better!" Ren exclaimed. "Can't you allow me one dying wish?"

"Har har, you should have wished for something great. Like an escape plan."

"I thought you had a plan!" Parr and Ren said at the same time.

"Of course I do, just having a little jape," Manc said with a chuckle. "Watch this."

"Watch what?" Ren said.

"When did everyone start saying 'jape' all of a sudden?" Parr asked.

Manc checked his nav screen with cheery eyes and a wide grin. That slowly dropped into a look of confusion.

"They didn't do the thing." Manc's voice was a little tighter than usual. He punched a few patterns into the nav screen, hit the side, and tried a few more patterns. "They usually do the thing."

"What thing?" Ren asked.

"The thing they do once you've fired on them," Manc replied. "The defensive-to-offensive maneuvers. The thing!"

"We're close to the A block now, I think," Parr said. "Just set her down."

"Yeah? And then what, Parr?" Ren asked. "Think they'll just let us walk away?"

Manc hit the nav screen with the meaty part of his palm. "Where in the five suns are they?"

"Just great, Parr," Ren said. "Some captain this guy turned out to be."

"What? This was—I just know him from before," Parr said. "This was your plan!"

"I told you," Ren said. "Let me have this one thing!"

"Har har!" Manc exclaimed. "There they are!" He beat a fist against the arm of his captain's chair. "They're doing the thing now." He rubbed his hands together before putting them back on the console. "Parr, grab something and hold on." He punched in another pattern and sent *Vanessa's Complaint* into a dive roll.

Parr's stomach tried to come up for a visit, but he was able to keep it in place. *At least he warned me this time.*

The nav screen showed pulsor fire all over the place, as well as a direct hit. Fortunately for them, this time it was one of the guards' ships. Manc's deployment of the crackling clusters coupled with the ship's maneuver forced the guards into a formation that created a crossfire and turned them against each other. Another two ships fired on each other for direct hits that sent them hurtling toward the surface of the station.

Manc leaned forward and frantically entered more patterns on the nav while checking several other screens, then rechecked his main for good measure. A button on the arm of his captain's chair pulsed red. "Hang on to your bottoms—here goes everything."

The display glowed white with the light of a pulsor headed straight toward them.

CHAPTER 26

Boom!

Another direct hit. The last one, according to the earlier assessment, that *Vanessa's Complaint* could take. Manc pressed the pulsing red button on the arm of his chair just as the missile met his ship, and Parr found himself spinning around the room almost as though he were in zero gravity. The sensation didn't last long, as he quickly found himself plastered against the back wall of the bridge.

"Ow."

Manc chuckled from above and punched a few more patterns into the nav. "Told you I had a contingency."

"What, to crash us?" Ren asked.

"Did you just spin us off?" Parr asked. He wasn't surprised that the kludged-together ship was so easily separated, but he was surprised that it was in good enough repair that the mechanism worked when called upon.

"Ha! See, you're not half as slow as the girl here says you are."

"Wait, so they think they hit us?" Ren asked.

"Yarp!" Manc said. "And they did. Just not the piece we're still in."

"And this part's still cloaked?" Ren asked.

"Har har, that's right."

"I knew I made the right decision, hiring you," she said. "You shouldn't have doubted him, Parr."

"Yeah—crazy, right?" Parr said, and gave Ren a sidelong look.

"Now," Manc said. "Let's get this old bird back upright and stealth in close to WL-19."

"Close?" Parr asked. Then he nodded. "Right, I guess we can't just fly this inside, cloaked or not."

"Why doesn't cloaking work as well on-world, or at least on-station?" Ren asked.

"More stuff to bounce signal off of," Parr said. "Easier to triangulate. Not much to bounce off of in space—that's why it's called space."

"Like I said, math," said Manc.

"I know why it's called space, Parr. You remedial," Ren said. "So, you're sure they're not looking for us?"

"No," Manc said. "They got the smoking wreckage they were hoping for, plus however many smoky hulls of their own. Should have their hands full for a while now."

Parr went and fixed himself a drink from the wet bar. He mixed a brown sepsidorian, his favorite, and passive-agressively ignored drink requests from his fellow passengers as they prepared to leave for the gates to hangar WL-19.

⌃

Once on the ground, the three packed up what they could carry from *Vanessa's Complaint*. Mainly the essentials—med kit, some rations from the wet bar, a change of clothes for the old pirate, and a box of rare gemstones Manc kept on hand since they were tiny, valuable, and easy to move.

Ren popped the emergency hatch and stood in the doorway. "Ready?"

Parr checked the straps on the pack he carried on his back. "Yeah."

"How do I look?" Ren asked.

"You look great," Parr replied.

"Think so, huh?" Ren asked. She looked Parr up and down and quirked a flirty grin.

Manc took one last look around and slowly toured the bridge, touching things as he went along as if to say goodbye. He gripped the arm of his captain's chair one last time before wiping his face with the arm of his sleeve. If Parr hadn't known any better, he'd have thought the old scoundrel was tearing up, but that would require feelings and sentiment—two things Manc Yelray wasn't exactly known for.

"Dust in my eye from the blown hatch," Manc said, and wiped a sleeve over his eyes. "Bye, now, Vanessa. Farewell, girl." He shot a look at Parr. "What're you standing around for? We're sitting ducks here."

"What's a duck?" Ren asked.

Manc rolled his eyes. "What's a duck, she says. It's like neither of the two of you has seen the galaxy. Let's go!"

The three of them piled out of what was left of the cloaked *Vanessa's Complaint* and onto the sidewalk of Versit Station. A couple of creatures who were out for a walk gave the trio sideways glances before hurrying along their way.

"Pedestrian gate to the hangar is up ahead," Ren said.

Parr and Manc followed her lead, and Parr did his best to enjoy the synthetic sunlight of the station one last time. He wasn't sure why smaller spacecraft weren't able to get it right, and being stuck without sun exposure for days and weeks on end in space sometimes could do a number on a creature—at least those that had evolved to crave light for half the day like Parr, Manc, and Ren.

There was a mercifully short line for the pedestrian entrance into the hangar. A guard in an ill-fitting uniform sat in front of an automated authenticator.

"Card, please," the guard said.

"How about a bracelet?" Ren replied.

"Of course, ma'am, just scan it there." The guard pointed to a flashing green-glassed scanner that would have been an obvious place to scan anything to any creature standing within sloom-flinging distance, Parr thought. Ren passed her bracelet by it and the machine made a satisfying chiming noise. The door whooshed open for the party.

"Right this way," the guard said.

"What in the five suns is that creature's purpose?" Manc said once they were out of earshot. "Could have done that all ourselves. 'Card, please'? Who still uses cards?"

"Security protocol," Ren replied. "Obviously."

"Har! Some security! We just took out half of Versit's guard ships in the sector, and they let us stroll in here and up to our trusty ship for a tidy escape."

"Say it louder, Manc," Parr said. "I don't think they heard you in the dispatch master's box."

"You're a dispatch master's box," Manc grumbled under his breath.

"Let's take a sled down to the *Aurora*," Ren said. "She's on the other side of the hangar closest to the doors, and I want to ship out as soon as possible. Plus, this bag is getting heavy. What did you pack in here, Manc?"

"Just essentials," Manc said.

"They better be," Ren said. "C'mon. Sleds are this way."

The three crossed what seemed to Parr like a fairly barren hangar. He'd expected a more lively scene for a station the size of Versit.

"Anyone think it's strange there aren't more creatures out?" Parr asked.

"No," Ren said. "Now focus. We're almost to the ship. The faster we can head out, the better."

They ducked under a small P-90–class midrange skiff on their way to join the surprisingly short queue for the sleds.

Everyone in line for the sleds wore the same uniform—save one: Moma Shando. She wore a similar robe to what Ren had on, only red.

"That's not good," Manc said.

"Is red an aggressive color?" Parr asked under his breath.

"Yes," Ren said. "But it's also an omen of good fortune."

Parr sighed, "Why do I have the feeling this isn't my lucky day?"

Upon further review, Parr knew their path on foot to the hangar was too easy with all the creatures on the lookout for them. He checked behind the group for an escape route, but a few dozen of Moma's guards had already stepped up to block their path. They were surrounded.

"This way, dears," Moma Shando said, and stretched out a robed arm toward a shadowy hallway. "You can pass your weapons along to Jortem, here." She signaled to a guard.

Parr evaluated their options, but there was no way out. She had them surrounded. Her cordial tone, however, gave Parr the hope of another option besides death. Quick eye contact between Manc and Ren sufficed for an extended conversation. They gave their weapons over to the guard.

"Your guys confiscated my blaster at Moma's," Parr said.

"What about the one in your boot?" Jortem replied.

"Oh yeah," Parr said. "Forgot about that one."

"That everything, Yelray?" Jortem asked.

"Does a rendecker swim in the salted sands?"

"I don't know, Yelray," Jortem said. "Just answer the question."

"That's everything."

"That will be all, Jortem. We are not to be disturbed," Moma Shando said with a smile that would have frosted over the windscreen of any suborbital vessel in the Sixteen. The guard bowed, turned on his heel, and left the party behind.

Parr eyed Ren for a sign of what lay in wait for them, but her face was a blank canvas.

"Now, please. No dawdling," Moma said.

Ren followed first, Manc wobbled behind, and Parr reluctantly joined them. He recalled the hidden rooms back at Moma Shando's. The punishment dealt to creatures that crossed the business—what would she do to those who crossed her personally?

He heard the soft padding of Moma's guards as they fell in behind them. Their boots didn't make the *click-clack* against the metal floor that one would expect, but then Moma's guards weren't your average hired guns.

Further down the hall, the sandy, speckled head of the sammakin emerged from an open door. Its beady black eyes blinked at the approaching party.

"All is sssafe, misss," he said as Moma approached.

"Thank you, pet," Moma said. "In here, please. Just these three and my consort. Everyone else stay outside unless you hear otherwise."

The sammakin hissed at Ren as she approached and scurried up the wall. Once they were all inside, it sealed the door behind them with a *thunk* and a low humming buzz.

"It's OK, dear," Moma said, and stroked the sammakin's pebbled, triangular head. "You know Ren. Remember?"

"Yesss." The sammakin glared at Ren while Moma sized up the room. Its tongue darted out to wipe both eyes before it scuttled to the ceiling to observe the meeting from above.

"Sammakins, right? Creepy," Parr whispered to Ren. She didn't acknowledge him.

"Quiet, lad," Manc whispered back. "This isn't the time."

Parr could tell that the old pirate was serious, and perhaps even nervous. It didn't matter that they'd just faced down most of Moma's elite guard; this somehow felt even more dangerous. Only this time, they didn't have a woolly-toothed oripian on their side.

The gunmetal-gray room was windowless, save for a head-sized port in the airlocked door. Parr recalled the two-way mirrors and the network of corridors that Moma used to spy within her property. Despite the handful of ways they could be observed and recorded, he felt as though they had complete and total privacy.

Moma motioned for them to have a seat at the table. Parr slid into the chair nearest to him and leaned back as he spun around to face their captor. His royal, political, and military training had taught him that regardless of how he felt, it was critical to show no fear in the face of dangerous situations.

Manc fell into the chair across from him but sat up as straight as possible in one of the few signs of respect Parr had ever seen the old scoundrel offer.

Ren pulled her chair out but stood beside it as she stared down Moma Shando. "Please, after you," Ren said. But the way she delivered the seemingly innocuous phrase made Parr's hands sweat. They had no leverage under their current circumstances, and Ren's posture looked as though she was prepared for a duel to the death.

Moma displayed a grin that looked like it had been rehearsed ten thousand times as she glided into her seat at the head of the table, keeping a noticeable distance between herself and the rest of the group. Ren eased into her chair without taking her eyes off her mother.

"You've been a busy little bug, haven't you?" Moma said.

"Isn't that what you wanted from me?" Ren asked. "To make something of myself? To scrape my way out from the bottom?"

"Yes, and here you are," Moma said. "Free and clear."

"Free and clear," Ren replied. "It doesn't feel like I'm free. Do you feel free, Yelray?"

Manc cleared his throat. "Locked in a heavily guarded room, feeling like a caged uramptus at a zoo? No, not really."

Moma arched an eyebrow at Manc.

"Company's nice, though, isn't it?" Manc said. His eyes darted around the room. "I'll just sit here and stop talking then."

"Wipe that off your face, dear," Moma said, and flung a cleaning cloth at Ren.

It landed softly on the table in front of her.

Ren glared at her mother and grabbed the cloth. She held the cloth over her face. Plumes of vapor puffed from underneath the cloth and Ren wiped at her face a few times before pulling up her image in her wrist device.

Ren examined her face from a few angles as she wiped away at the corners of her eyes and just below her nose. She blinked a few times and disengaged the view finder.

"Better?" Ren asked. Then tossed the cloth back at Moma.

It landed in an unceremonious crumple on the table in front of her. Moma's hand stretched from a silken sleeve and clutched the cloth. The two sleeves of her robe met as she stowed the cloth away in one of the sleeve's hidden pockets.

A decidedly unrehearsed dimple creased Moma's cheek. "I had to test you, Katherine," she said. "Just like my mother tested my sisters and me. A test of worthiness."

Ren cocked her head. "I don't have any aunts—"

"Exactly."

Ren's jaw clenched. "I'm your daughter, and you abandoned me—"

"I trained you," Moma interrupted. "Gave you every opportunity, every luxury. You were so close to spoiled, and I could not let that happen. I would not let that happen.

"There is no hunger in legacy. Generational wealth breeds complacency. My enterprise can only be run by someone who has trudged through a swamp of desperation, only to arrive at the sands of the desert of hopelessness—yet sees it all as an opportunity. Someone who can put down roots in the harshest climate. Someone who can build a bustling city in a barren wasteland."

Rather than take offense, Parr considered her point. He recalled the children of the rich and powerful he'd grown up alongside. How they filled their days with fashion and travel. They'd talked of the ordinary citizens of the Twelve as though they were a subspecies subordinate to them that existed simply for their entertainment and scrutiny. Their money worked for them, spawning more and more of itself as they sat idle and perused menus for the most fashionable drink of the season.

"What of Her Royal Highness?" Parr asked. "She comes from generations of wealth and power."

"Ah, yes. But Malista is not everyone, and even she experienced the loss of one she held dear. Her poor brother, Prince Parrtec."

"Her parents too," Parr reminded her.

"True, although, I think that may have been a different type of loss, don't you?"

"What do you mean?"

"Nothing, of course. Nothing." Moma Shando stared at Parr over tented fingers.

Ren cut in. "You left me on a street with nothing but the clothes on my back. No tools, no resources—"

"Wrong! I gave you your mind. I trained you in multiple arts—martial and otherwise. Gave you the best education money could buy. I gave you every tool and resource you needed—and here you are."

"No thanks to you. If it weren't for that tordaver—" Ren collected herself. "Even then, I was not my own."

"But you overcame," Moma said. "You were resourceful, unbent by circumstance. You've proven yourself worthy."

"We defeated your guards," Ren said.

"Just enough to earn their respect," Moma replied.

"I don't want to be around you or anything you built."

"You lie."

"I don't. You think I'll welcome you back into my life now that you're bribing me with legacy?"

"Of course you don't want to make good with me, child. However, you lie about the legacy. I know you covet power—even more so now that you've experienced a life in which it was stripped away from you. I can see it with my own eyes."

"You can see it in my fingers as well," Ren said, and made a rude gesture.

"Hold on, hold on," Parr said. "Look, Moma—I think what Ren is trying to say is—uh. What are we doing here?"

"You're bearing witness," Moma replied.

"Bearing witness to what?" Parr asked.

"Bearing witness to my generosity—you remain with your lives intact. Bearing witness to my resources—there is nowhere you can go where I will not find you. Bearing witness to a promise."

"What promise?" Parr asked.

"She wanted you to ask that," Ren said.

Moma Shando pursed her lips before she said, "A promise that all of this will be yours, Ren."

"Fine," Ren said. "Can we go?"

"Yes," Moma said.

"Yes?" Manc asked.

"Yes," Moma said.

"Yes?" Parr asked.

"By all the suns in all the systems," Ren said. "If someone else says yes again—"

"You did just then," Manc said.

"Enough," Moma said. "You're free to go as you please. Just know you don't have much more time to claim my enterprise for your own."

"Before the offer expires?" Ren asked. "Yes, I've learned how to sell, Mother—"

"Before *I* expire," she replied. "I don't have long left. You have a claim, but there are others who will likely find a way to take it for themselves in your absence."

"Is this where I'm supposed to cry?" Ren asked. "Oh, mother who left me for dead or worse, I'm so sorry you're about to die. Does that sound real?"

Manc shifted in his chair uncomfortably. "Er, maybe you shouldn't—"

"It's OK, Ludon Yelray," Moma said. She popped the cuffs of her sleeves and straightened herself in her chair. "It's more than OK, in fact. She is right. She is strong; she is without sentiment or pity. She is ready to lead my establishment."

"Great," Ren said. "Have Jortem send me a note once you've stopped breathing. Are we done here?"

"Almost," Moma said. "We were going to make some upgrades on your ship—"

Parr perked up. "What did you do to the *Aurora*? I swear, Moma—"

Moma raised a hand. "At ease, child. You're acting like a petulant little prince."

Parr's blood ran as cold as an iced brown sepsidorian. Did she know?

"I hate it when you say things like that, Mother. What did you do to his ship?"

"Nothing," Moma said. "No one will go near it with those multona drainers attached."

Ren looked to Parr. "I told you they're dangerous."

"So, we arranged other transport," Moma said.

"Oh no," Parr interrupted. "Nice try, but I'm not giving up my ship. Me and Aurrie have been through way too much."

"Who is Aurrie?" Moma asked.

"His ship," Ren said. "He has a fixation on material things that can't love him back. Can we go?"

Parr let go of the tiny gem he'd been clutching in his pocket. "Hey—" he said, but was cut off before he could continue.

"It's your life, child. I just hope you'll treat my legacy with less recklessness than you're showing today."

"I'm going to convert it all to low-cost housing and use your advertising channels to bring in families from the outer reaches."

"You wouldn't dare—"

"I think that's our cue," Parr said. "Thanks for the hospitality, Your Eminence."

"Don't call her that," Ren said.

Moma stood up and eyed Manc for a moment. "I thought you talked more." She moved to the outer wall and pressed the button to open the airlock. "Excellent ship placement in the hangar, daughter. Perfect for a hasty retreat."

"Is that a threat?" Ren asked.

"No," Moma said with a wave of her hand. "It is merely an observation. You have my protection to the outer boundaries of Versit Station."

"Guess that's my protection now," Ren said, "isn't it?"

Moma's eyes sparkled like the stars that made up Blankin's Belt in one of the strangest moments of pride Parr had ever witnessed. She stood and gave the group a graceful bow before she exited the room.

The sammakin wiped its jet-black tongue across its dark eyeball and blinked before clambering down the wall and out the door to rejoin Moma Shando.

"So, that's that?" Manc asked.

"I think so," Ren said.

"Can't be this easy," Parr said.

"Oh, has this been easy, boy?" Manc asked. "How's yer ship? Fine, yeah? Well mine's in two big pieces back there, and one of those pieces has pieces now, so I'm going to have to disagree on the level of difficulty here, you callused hoof of a wangderbloofen."

Ren slowly stood, her face as solemn as a funeral procession. "Let's go."

The three exited the tiny room to find their gear in three neat piles against the wall of the shadowy hallway. Parr had his gear right and tight before he noticed Ren helping Manc with his pack. She cinched his shoulder harness and made sure the buckles held.

"Thanks, girl. Hard for me to—"

"Let's go," Ren said as she grabbed her pack and slung it around her shoulder.

Parr searched up and down the bay, but Moma Shando and her detail were nowhere to be seen. No hangar crew hung about to track their position, and there were no sounds of any doors opening or closing.

He wouldn't have been surprised to learn Moma had her own passageways throughout the station, and his mind went back to his meeting with Ren in the tent on that podunk station out in the middle of nowhere. He remembered the tunnel she had dug below the market for a quick and easy escape.

"Hey, Manc, can you give us a minute?" Parr asked. "We'll catch up to you."

The old pirate arched an eyebrow and looked Parr up and down before glancing over at Ren. "Sure thing, son. Catch up when you can."

Parr waited until Manc wobbled out of earshot. "You're not her, you know."

Ren adjusted the straps on her pack and faced him head-on. It wasn't so much that the mask cracked, but she certainly softened. "Yeah, I know," was all she said.

"No, I mean it," he said. "You're not going to be like her."

Ren took a deep breath and exhaled slowly. Her eyes began to water, and she wiped at her face. "Why do you say that?"

"Because you don't want to be," Parr said. He swallowed what felt like a giant lump in his throat. "Just like I don't want to be my father. We're not destined to become our parents. We have a choice."

She closed the distance between them, threw her arms around him, and sobbed into his chest. Parr's eyes clouded with tears of his own as he pulled her close. The two embraced until the tears stopped coming.

Ren pulled back, wiping her sleeve across her face. "Thank you," she said. "I needed to hear that."

Parr did his best to dry his face with his hands. "Thank you," he replied. "I think I needed to say that out loud."

He meant it.

He needed to believe that.

He hadn't thought about the words; they'd slipped out naturally.

Parr's father had operated the way he did based on tradition. He'd felt obligated to act like his father and his father's father before him. Parr doubted his father had ever thought twice about it. Maybe if he had, their relationship would have been different. His life would have been different. The kingdom would have been different.

For better or for worse.

Parr suspected Moma had acted on similar instincts but with wildly different motivations. She was a survivor. Regardless of whether or not she needed to worry about where the next meal was coming from, she was constantly operating out of fear. What may have been necessary for her predecessors was not necessary for Ren. And he wanted her to realize that.

Because he cared about her. He realized that he genuinely cared for her well-being.

It was terrifying.

Maybe not terrifying, but it was certainly something he'd never felt before. So, at least off-putting.

"And if you tell Manc I cried, I'll blast you," Ren said. She flashed a grin and gave his shoulder a playful punch.

"It's OK to cry, you know," he said. "Neither of our parents would."

What is this? he wondered. *Why am I saying these things out loud?*

"Stop saying things that make me like you," she replied.

What's that, now?

"So, you like me," Parr said. "Like . . . like me, like me?"

She rubbed the top of his arm. "Never mind," she said. She exhaled and patted his shoulder. "You ruined it."

"Yeah, well," Parr said. "I do that sometimes. Ready to go?"

"Yeah," Ren said. "Let's see if the old pirate actually waited this time."

"I think he has to," Parr said. "He doesn't have a ship."

⌃

"Watch your step, sons and daughters," the kindly sled driver said. He was a tree grooben of the four-armed variety. His green and orange speckled face was ringed with dark eyes so blue they were almost black.

He helped ease the party into the sled with three of his long arms, his fourth leaning against the side of the sled for leverage. "Buckle in nice and tight," he said. "There you go. Slip ticket or bracelet?"

"Bracelet," Ren said in a soft voice that sounded like it wanted to break.

"Right here then, miss," the driver said, and offered his wrist for a bump. Ren obliged, and he waited, each eye blinking in a circular formation around his face, for the results to show.

Maybe this was when Moma Shando's trap would be sprung, Parr thought. Perhaps they'd been flagged as a threat, and all of Versit's guards would come screaming in from all directions toward them. Or maybe this was where Parr would find that the ship wasn't in the register—or worse, had already been picked up. Of course Moma Shando would want the *Aurora* for herself. The fastest ship in all the Sixteen.

"Fine and good, everything's in order, miss. I'll take you straight-away," the driver said.

Or maybe not. Parr almost relaxed but couldn't. Part of him felt like celebrating—it seemed like a victory. They'd faced down Moma Shando and her guard, as well as the Versit guard, and come out clean on the other side. His companions, on the other hand, seemed about as far away as Bilena Epso Ach. Their gazes in different directions focused on nothing in particular.

Not much was said along the short sled ride to the *Aurora*. Parr thought about the moment he'd shared with Ren in the hallway and wondered if he was getting attached, then realized he'd talked to her about his father.

What if she'd asked him more questions about his father? What did he mean that they could be different from their parents? He'd exposed himself, and mercifully gotten away with it—this time.

When they arrived at the ship, the driver accepted a tip and waved goodbye to his former passengers (one hand for each of them) before speeding off to rejoin the queue and await his next fare.

The three stood underneath the ship and waited for the *Aurora*'s landing pad to hit the metal floor of the hangar before stepping on. As the pad lifted them, Parr took one last look at the flickering, swirling light of the multona drainers and wondered if they were as dangerous as everyone seemed to think.

CHAPTER 27

"How long do you think he's going to be in there?" Ren asked. Her mood had lifted a bit, and she leaned against a console of multicolored blinking lights on the *Aurora's* bridge. She viewed the primary monitor and watched Versit shrink away to nothing as they journeyed toward Anatone Seven. Her fingers fidgeted with a small puzzle that Parr had left lying out.

"What, in the cleaner?" Parr replied. He punched a few patterns into his nav from his captain's chair and looked at the results. "As long as he needs, I hope. I don't know if you noticed, but *Vanessa's Complaint* didn't have one. I wonder if he only takes them on stations."

A thin smile spread across Ren's face. "I think I smelled him before I saw him back in that room at Moma's."

"You know what they say: she who smelt it, dealt it," Parr said.

"No, they don't, that is gross," Ren replied. "I'll never forgive you for saying that."

"What?" Parr asked.

She tossed the puzzle aside and shook her head. "Just like I'll never forgive that old pirate for taking so long in the cleaner," she said. "I need to use the bio-refuse evac. Why do you have both units in the same shared space?"

"Yeah, I didn't design this thing—easy cleanup, maybe? I don't know. The *Aurora* was built for speed, not for comfort."

"Sounds like you."

"Uh, what?" Parr asked.

"I'm just kidding," she said. "Relax."

"I'm relaxed," Parr said. He tapped his fingers along the arm of his chair. "Speaking of pirates, you sure we have to meet with Agrofor Telfo?"

"You scared?" she asked.

"Look, if you think you're going to goad me into going along with your plan by challenging my bravery, it's not going to work. Of course I'm afraid of Telfo, he's notorious."

"I don't buy it," Ren said.

"What?" Parr asked.

"Why would you be afraid of Telfo when you're not afraid of Norfung Gortn?" she said. "*He's* notorious."

"Is that what you think?" Parr replied. "Good." He chuckled. "It's just that Norfung has a code. I don't particularly like crossing him, but he's not Agrofor Telfo. Telfo is as ruthless as they come. It's healthy to fear someone like that. From what I hear, he'd cut you just as fast as he'd say hello. Anyway, you think he's really out on Anatone Seven?"

"For what I arranged to get the information? He better be."

"I can't believe I'm going to have to buy back the ship I sold to Manc. You sure this is the way?"

"Parr, it's a badged and keyed vessel. All you have to do is board it and fly through the gates. Simple as that."

"It's simple, alright. Except for the part where I have to pay for it. What if I don't have enough?"

"I'm sure you'll come up with a plan. You're bound to have something he wants."

"Maybe I can offer up a service."

"Or the fastest ship in the galaxy ..."

"Stop with that! She can hear you," Parr said. He leanded down toward the console. "My sweet baby Aurrie."

"She's not that kind of ship, Parr. She's not listening to us at all."

"Don't listen, girl," Parr said, and gave the arm of his captain's chair a little pat. "Ren's just jealous."

"What about the groppodite?" Ren asked.

Parr patted his pocket. The little crimson jewel had been his talisman, his good luck charm, all through this second life of his, and according to Ren, it was also some sort of major power source. If she was right and it was worth as much as she said it was, maybe that would be something worth letting go. He'd do anything to keep the *Aurora*. "Yeah, I think I could let the groppodite go for the right price."

"You really love this ship, huh."

"Fastest in all the Sixteen."

"You realize she's fast because of the groppo—"

"What do you think a pirate king wants with that dusty old colony?" Parr knew she was right about the groppodite, of course, but he also knew the *Aurora* was special. She'd been fast even before he'd picked up the gem.

"Maybe Agrofor doesn't see it as dusty," Ren said. "Besides, what do any of us want, Parr?" She looked down and kicked at the floor before bringing her gaze up to meet his.

"What?" Parr asked.

Ren rolled her eyes. "A home."

Parr nodded. *A home,* he thought. Of course; even dirty old pirates needed a place to call their own. Although most felt that way about their ship, some wanted something larger—a place to stretch their legs. Parr could relate to that, obviously, as it was the reason they were all there together to begin with—and at that moment, he felt for Ren.

Any of us, she'd said.

They were currently hurtling away from her home as fast as technology and good piloting could take them. Despite everything that they'd just been through and the complicated relationships she'd left behind, he could see that it hurt her to leave. The fact that she was there because he'd held her to a deal made him feel something he hadn't felt in quite some time, if ever—guilt.

He wasn't used to the feeling. Pain, yes, of course—like when a deal went sideways or when a trader had a good right cross. Sadness, like when something didn't go his way. But this. This was something else entirely. No wonder he'd spent years armoring himself against the universe. Emotions could be overwhelming.

If he felt this way now, what was it going to be like when he had to make decisions for all the citizens of the Sixteen?

He thought back to his father after the Decree of Dumphor. The law had created a new trade route through the Marzon belt, which adversely affected the inhabitants of the two moons of Crob. Parr remembered how quiet his father had been at the table that night.

"Ren, I'm sorry—"

"Cleaner is runnin' a little cold, I'm afraid," Manc said as he ambled onto the bridge wrapped in multiple towels. "Just put my kit in for a spin or two, then it'll be all free."

"I didn't realize you had work done," Ren said.

"What? This ol' leg?" Manc said, and rapped his knuckles on a smoky black and brass bionic prosthetic. "She's a real beaut, alright. From my shiny toes all the way up to my hip. Got it after a little misunderstanding on a station I don't care to return to any time soon."

Parr leaned back in his chair and looked up toward the old pirate. "Don't care to, or can't?"

Manc shrugged and waved off Parr before he wobbled over to lean against a control panel lit by a slowly pulsing purple light that illuminated several knobs and levers. "It's just a little ban. Besides, who would want to go back there, anyway? I hope it spins out of orbit." Manc adjusted the towel around his head. "We out of the boundaries of Versit yet?"

"Yeah," Ren said. "Have been for a while now."

Manc scrunched his face. "How long was I in there?"

"Judging by the grime on those towels," Parr said, "not long enough."

"It's jus' a little seasoning, lad," Manc said with a wink.

"Disgusting," Ren said.

"Stop winking at me," Parr said.

"You think this is bad, wait until we get to Anatone Seven. Place is full of the crustiest creatures in all the Sixteen and beyond," Manc said, then chuckled. "I love it!"

"And you're sure Agrofor Telfo is there," Ren said.

"As sure as my mam's name is Grace, my dear."

Parr spun his chair toward Ren and hooked a thumb back at Manc. "That's not a yes, you know."

"Aye, but it's a probably," Manc said. "Telfo's been rumored to hold court on the Seven for a while now—least in a few of the circles I run in."

"Your mother's name is probably Grace," Ren more confirmed than asked.

"Yes," Manc replied.

"OK, that's a lot to unpack, so I'll leave it," Ren said. "Better hope for your sake that it's better than a probably. This deal has turned out to be a lot costlier than anticipated."

Manc's face sank at the comment. Which was strange; Parr hadn't seen that emotion on him before. The Manc Yelray he knew was mostly either irritated or jolly, even in the face of fear. "I'm sorry, girl. If I had known—"

"It's fine," Ren said.

"It's just . . . ," Manc said. "If I'd known, I wouldn't have insisted we meet there."

Like tumblers in the great safe in the palace treasury, things slowly clicked into place for Parr. Of course; why would Ren return to Moma

Shando's the way she had? The meeting place hadn't been her idea at all, but instead, a terrible coincidence. Parr imagined Ren had a much different agenda in mind for her return. Revenge? Maybe. A mission to take the Shando legacy for herself? Possibly. Most likely a little bit of both.

"So, Moma Shando just let us leave?" Manc asked.

"Appears that way," Ren said.

"I've been checking for tails ever since we left. Nothing," Parr confirmed.

"Have you checked for viridium markers?" Manc asked.

"And trillium, and bio-seg-lofogant," Parr said. "This isn't my first rango, Manc."

"Ah, I remember my first rango, I—" Manc began, but Ren crossed the bridge toward the hallway.

"Sounds fascinating, I'm sure," she said on her way toward the bio-refuse evac.

"My clothes are still in there," Manc said.

"Don't worry, I'll throw them out on the floor for you," she replied.

"What's her issue?" Manc asked after Ren left the room.

Parr shrugged.

"That girl is a real puzzle—"

"Yeah, a real riddle, Manc," Parr said. "Or maybe, *maybe* she's just sorting through having a reunion with a mother who left her for dead, killing creatures she grew up with, and realizing that the aforementioned killing impressed her mother instead of repulsed her."

"Well," Manc said. "My mother, Grace … probably my mother, anyway—"

"Oh," Parr continued. "And all that back there is hers for the taking. Her mother is dying, and if she wants it, all she has to do is claim it, but instead, she's with us on a sketchy trip to the outlands and the home of a pirate king."

"So, this one time Grace—"

"Because I held her to a deal like some sort of—"

"Slimy, leaf-sticked gordo-lobber?"

"Yeah."

"Hey, what's this?" Manc asked. He held Parr's busted peg winder in his hand and clicked the button. The device spun out of control.

"It's a peg winder for my Skelly," Parr said.

"Sure it is," Manc replied with a wink.

"Seriously, stop winking at me. Especially in a towel. Look, it really is for my Skelly. It winds the strings. Now put it back."

"Sure, whatever you say," Manc said, and put the winder back where he'd found it. The two looked at each other for a few moments before Manc arched an eyebrow. "So … can I drive?"

Parr eyed Manc, who bobbed back and forth on his biological and bionic toes while swinging his arms. He waggled his eyebrows and barely managed to catch one of the towels he had wrapped around him before it hit the floor. "Maybe after you get some clothes on," Parr said. He tried not to imagine the wiping down of his seat after Manc drove for a bit but couldn't help himself. It was an unpleasant thought.

Still, the old captain was a good pilot, and Parr could use a nice steamy cleaning after everything they'd been through.

⌃

A fresh but damp Parr stood in the doorway to the bridge and watched Ren sift through the bags from *Vanessa's Complaint* while Manc ran a few patterns through the nav. Water dripped from Parr's hair onto his clean shirt. "I can't believe you used all the towels."

"Yeah, and I can't believe how much alcohol you packed, Manc," Ren chimed in.

"I left a dry towel," Manc replied. "And besides, I said I was packing mostly essentials."

"There are two more of us on this ship," Parr said.

"You smell fine," Manc said.

"Are you saying I didn't?" Ren asked. "Wait. Don't answer that. How long until we get to Anatone Seven?"

"There aren't any rifts to take," Parr said. "So we have to fly straight on. Shouldn't take more than a couple of days, though." He pulled out the tiny piece of groppodite and spun it around his finger. "Maybe less."

The lights in the room seemed to glow a bit brighter. Manc's eyes went wide as he checked and double-checked the readings on his nav. "I'll be a slick-nosed thornogrix! This ship has its secrets, Parr; we'll be there in no time."

"Great," Ren said. "I'm going to whip something up in the galley and get some sleep. You two take turns on watch. Wake me for the third."

Parr thought he saw the *Aurora*'s proximity alert light up in the nav screen closest to Manc. "Someone within range?"

Manc looked down at the screen and ran a pattern with his fingers. "Nah, all clear here, son. Why don't you go grab something to eat with Ren and maybe get some sleep. I'll wake you up when my watch is over."

"Are you sure?" Parr said. He strode toward the main nav and punched up a pattern of his own. There was a blip, but nothing solid. Maybe it was a comet passing just out of range or a hunk of jettisoned garbage. "Alright, well . . . just keep an eye out."

"Aye-aye, Captain," Manc replied, and made finger goggles over his eyes one at a time.

"I'm not a captain," Parr said, "and I'm too tired for puns."

⌃

Ren was sitting in the galley when Parr walked in. She saluted him with one of Manc's flasks and poured a clear liquid into a couple of glasses. "You trust him in there by himself?"

"Trust him?" Parr asked.

"You don't really trust anyone, do you?"

Parr squinted. "I don't know about anyone, but Manc? No, not really. I understand his motivation right now, though, so I can trust that."

"He doesn't get paid until we get what we're after?" Ren asked.

"Right." Parr grinned and slid into the chair across from her. "Not until I'm behind the controls of that old badged and keyed vessel. Does he get paid immediately or when I'm through?"

She slid a glass toward him. "He's paid once you're safely out of Anatone Seven's orbit."

"It's a pretty low-grav situation, I better hustle." He took the glass in front of him and lifted it in a toast. Ren obliged, clinked glasses, and downed the contents. Parr followed suit.

Whatever was in the flask tasted awful, like something he'd use to scrub the bio-evac unit if he had to do so manually. He coughed hard and fought for breath that wouldn't sting his lungs with the remnants of alcohol.

He heard Manc laughing from the other room. "Sounds like you got yourself into some real drink."

"Quiet, Yelray," Ren tilted her head back and shouted before returning her attention to Parr. "You OK, lightweight?" Ren shot him a playful grin, and crooked an eyebrow.

"What is this?" Parr asked. He picked up the flask, swirled it, and smelled its contents. It almost blew him back out of his chair, and he slapped his hand against the tabletop to keep himself from succumbing to another coughing outburst.

"Your guess is as good as mine. A lot of things ferment," Ren said. "I've had worse."

Parr grinned and looked down at the table. There weren't many creatures like Ren out there in the galaxy. Strong, smart, fearless. Moma Shando may have been a horrible mother, but she'd managed to raise a formidable daughter. Parr's mother had often said that the best leaders were born into their role, but he'd never fully bought into that. He could see Ren operating that enterprise.

Parr could see her running a lot of things.

"I haven't," Parr said. "That, right there, is the worst drink I've ever had. Bar none."

Ren retrieved the flask and poured another glass for herself. "Sorry to offend your delicate sensibilities. Anyway, this should help me sleep."

"Yeah, it should definitely do that," Parr said.

For the first time in a long time, the two let a silence hang between them. Parr found himself looking across the table into Ren's eyes. He wondered if he'd ever get used to the jolt of electricity he felt whenever he found himself locking gazes with someone he was attracted to. What was the appropriate amount of time—three seconds? Five? Whatever it was, it always felt longer.

Ren leaned forward and crooked an eyebrow. "You know what else would help me sleep?"

Parr grinned and leaned forward as well. "What's that?"

"A bedtime story."

"Oh yeah?" he asked. "What kind of bedtime story?"

She shot him a look and traced the rim of her glass with her finger. "Why don't you tell me why you want to get through those gates so bad?" She poured him another drink from the flask.

Well, that didn't go as I'd hoped.

Parr thought for a moment. What was the best non-answer to give that wasn't a total lie? "Thank you," he said, and raised his glass to her, downed the drink, and somehow managed to suppress another coughing fit. "I think I've done my time in the outer reaches." He stretched and reclined in his chair, "The way I see it, the opportunity is inside the gates of Bilena, not out here. It's time for me to go back to the big cities of the inner system."

Ren downed the contents of her glass and slammed it down to the table. Her eyes narrowed, and she leaned back in her chair. She stared at Parr for a few seconds before leaning forward and pointing her finger toward his chest. "You're a liar," she said, almost slurring. Her words were harsh, but her smile took the edge off. "I mean, I know you're technically telling me some sort of truth," she said. "But you're leaving a lot out." She sniffed the contents of the flask and recoiled. "What's your angle, Parr? Just tell me."

"My angle? I just told you. Opportunity, money—"

Ren waved a hand to cut Parr off. She cocked her head and looked in his eyes. "You know everything about me," she said. "You know my mother, my journey—all of it. Yet you hold everything about your story close inside. Too afraid to let anything seep out. You know exactly what I'm passing up to be here right now. What are you hiding? Just tell me."

"You made the deal—"

"Oh," Ren said. Her hand slid down her face as she shook her head. "Oh, I made the deal. So we're just business partners then. Is that what we are? Great, well let me treat you like a business partner—"

"I'm sorry," Parr said. "I'm sorry. That's not what I meant."

He wrestled with the thought. Should he tell her? The truth was that he didn't feel like they were just business partners anymore. He knew she could have put her foot down harder and had Manc guide him to Anatone Seven, but instead, she'd stayed with him to honor the deal—or maybe there was something more. She said he didn't trust anyone, and maybe he didn't. His father hadn't trusted anyone and had kept everyone he knew at arm's length. Look where that had gotten him—a son who faked his own death and a daughter who killed him for it.

Allegedly.

Maybe he could trust Ren. He'd like to trust her.

In fact, for the first time in a long time, Parr *wanted* to trust someone. He was exhausted from holding up the false front he'd spent years crafting. It would be such a relief to set it down and be vulnerable with someone for once.

Her eyes smoldered like coals across the table from him. He had to do it; he had to give her a chance.

Stars and fathers, what is in this drink?

"My secret," he said. "My secret is that I am Prince Parrtec, son of King Rab and Queen Mable, heir to the Twelve, and future ruler of Bilena Epso Ach."

It was the first time he'd said his true name out loud in a bromar's age. It felt good, it felt right, but most of all, it felt … terrifying.

Now that he'd said it, he worried that she would refuse to believe such an outrageous claim. Why would she? Who would believe he'd faked his own death to pursue a life of instability, danger, and purposelessness? Why would anyone leave a life of security and riches to scrap it out in the outer reaches?

"Finally," she said. She smacked the table and leaned back in her chair.

"Finally?" Parr asked.

She chuckled. "Moma told me as soon as she pulled me into the hall back on Versit. And it's Sixteen now, you know."

Relief passed through him like ions from a solar flare. "She did? And I know, but I was heir to the Twelve, technically."

"Of course she did," Ren said. "She didn't mean to, of course. She thought I was running some big con on you—and to be honest, I can't believe I wasn't. I mean, Prince Parrtec—Parr … it was sitting right there in front of my face."

"So why not sell me out?" Parr asked. "Why didn't you say something earlier?"

"I wanted to see if you would tell me," she said. She reached her hand across the table to take his. "I wanted to see if you trusted me." She squeezed his hand and let it go to lean back in her chair. "Besides," she said with a wink, "I still had time if you didn't come clean."

A lopsided smile spread over Parr's face.

Maybe it was something more than the deal. *Of course it's more than the deal,* he thought.

The two gazed at each other across the table. It was the first time Parr had trusted someone in a long time. Maybe the first time ever outside his immediate family. Ren had had everything to leverage against him, but she hadn't. She'd honored the deal.

He'd always enjoyed the low light of his galley. It felt warm to him, safe. And in that moment, the dark, cozy glow accentuated Ren's sultry features, and Parr's pulse began to quicken.

Her weight shifted, and before Parr knew it, she rose up and across the table to lean in for a kiss.

As she approached, a whisper of a scent accompanied her. It reminded him of something—a flower, but what flower? he wondered. Lavlabo? Yes, lavlabo, just like the ones in the fields on all those summer retreats.

He closed his eyes and tilted his head.

"What are you two whispering about?" Manc asked. He leaned against the door to the galley, gnawing away at a slippery hand fruit.

I am going to kill that old pirate.

Ren looked either enraged or embarrassed, it was hard to tell. "I'm going to sleep," she said. "One of you two can clear the crockery."

"Gimme my flask back," Manc said. He grabbed the flask off the table and waggled his eyebrows at Parr before wobbling back to the bridge.

But they hadn't been whispering, Parr thought. Had Manc just heard everything they'd said?

If so, what would it mean for him with the old scoundrel loose in a settlement full of pirates? Trust was something new for Parr, and this was a lot to take on all at once. He knew he could trust Ren, but he wasn't sure about Manc.

Alone in the kitchen, Parr found himself gazing at the spot where the old pirate had once stood.

CHAPTER 28

"Just give us a space in Bolton's Hangar, you squeaky-voiced, pole-haired marconet," Manc said before he stomped his leg down on the footrest of the captain's chair. His hands squeezed the ends of the arms.

The outburst roused Parr from his uncomfortable sleep underneath the back control panel of the bridge. "What?" Parr asked.

"What?" the voice replied over the comm.

"You heard me the first time, don't make me raise my voice," Manc said in a voice that was well beyond raised.

"Are we there?" Parr asked, and rubbed his eyes.

"Hangar's full, old-timer," the voice said. "But maybe we can find you a spot in Vana Rousalin's Bay."

"Vana Rousalin's Bay?!" Manc said as he rose from the chair and spun it out of frustration. "Vana Rousalin's Bay! Listen here, you prepubescent swattle-tailed purple pondiver: I ain't some fresh-faced, wide-eyed offworlder greenhorn! I'm Ludon Manc Yelray, of *Vanessa's Complaint*, and member in good standing of the Order of the Seven."

"Ludon?"

"Ludon."

"Ludon, right. Hold on, let me check."

Manc grumbled under his breath and took a moment to admire some of the flashing lights on one of the consoles along the wall. He ran a finger across a fairly dust-free wall mount, as though he were inspecting it for a report. The comm clicked, and voices could be heard outside the range of whoever he'd been talking to.

"Ludon Yelray, sir," the voice said. "My apologies. We have a spot in Bolton's Hangar, or you may prefer Virto's Keep. Our latest—"

"Bolton's Hangar will be fine," Manc said. "Sending you the particulars now." Manc squinted down at the captain's-chair nav and ran a pattern on it with his finger.

"Received, sir. The *Aurora*? Well done, sir, she has quite the reputation. How did you manage to take it off the kid who spurned the Corpulon Valvente? I heard he—"

"Still his ship, son. Still his ship."

So they've heard of me, Parr thought.

"But where is *Vanessa's Complaint,* sir?"

"Ain't none of your concern where Vanessa is. Just see us through." Manc's face seemed redder than usual. He spun the captain's chair and watched it a rotation before slumping down into it. He seemed surprised to see Parr standing at the far end of the bridge.

"How are we already at Anatone Seven?" Parr asked.

"Didn't know you were awake," Manc replied.

"You think I could sleep through that?"

"Don't worry about it, lad; you have yourself a top ship here. Never seen anything fly so fast since my wife left."

What in the five suns? Parr thought. That was a lot to just toss up in a throwaway comment. He knew the *Aurora* was fast, but Versit-to–Anatone Seven–in-like-half-a-cycle fast? That seemed almost impossible. Also, Manc had a wife? Interesting. He guessed that was the Vanessa from the *Complaint.*

"What is with the yelling?" Ren said. "I checked the systems from the cabin, and outside of fuel levels everything seems normal."

"What's wrong with the fuel settings?" Parr asked.

"They're full," Manc said. "Noticed that myself, Ren. No way we didn't use at least half our reserves on this trip—especially at the speeds we've been pushing. You should have the grounds crew take a look at the gauges when we dock, Parr."

"There's nothing wrong with the gauges," Ren said.

"Ren, maybe we—" Parr said.

"What do you mean?" Manc asked. "No ship is that efficient, especially a Fano-class as fast as this one."

Parr squeezed the groppodite gemstone held within his pocket, and Ren seemed to observe his anxiety about letting loose too much information around Manc. She checked her bracelet as though she'd just received new information.

"You're right," she said. "Couldn't hurt to have someone take a look at it in the hangar."

⋀

"I don't know if you noticed, but you have a few scratches on your hull and whatnot," the crew leader said to Parr as they stood on the platform of Bolton's Hangar. The creature's mandibles clacked as one set of clawed hands cleaned each other while the other set held a clipboard and stylus.

Bolton's Hangar looked like it was from another era, and although Anatone Seven wasn't exactly new, it certainly wasn't old enough to look as grand as this. The parts must have been shipped in from someplace else at great cost.

"Have them check your gauges, boy," Manc said as he ambled past. "Going to procure some accommodations for us. I'll message you later."

Manc's voice didn't reverberate the way it normally would have in most hangars. In fact, Parr noticed the place was almost noiseless, which was odd, especially for an active hangar. He could understand why Manc wanted this particular spot. Telfo must have poured more buldoons into this place than most stations spent on their entire build. The attention to detail spoke volumes about the pirate king.

The clacking of mandibles pulled Parr from his thoughts.

"We can do that and whatnot," the crew leader replied. "We can do a full scan of the hull and systems for next to nothing."

"Next to nothing, huh? Sure," Parr said, and looked down at the clipboard offered up by the crew chief, but after reading a few lines, he whipped his head toward Manc. "Wait, accommodations? How long are you planning on us being here? Hey!" But Manc was already out of earshot, or at least far enough away that it was plausible he didn't hear Parr's question.

"Definitely," the crew leader said, and pulled the clipboard back. "Compared to what you'd pay to repair something when it's already too late. We get into those dark places that crews on other stations won't bother checking. See where my guy is now?"

Parr looked in the direction in which the crew chief's clawed appendage was pointing and saw one of his team skittering into the shadows underneath the ship. It wasn't long before the creature dropped to the floor and skittered away, clicking and clacking excitedly.

"OK, so my guy says everything is good and whatnot. Check you later."

The multona drainers, Parr thought. *They saw the multona drainers.*

Ren bumped into his shoulder and leaned into his ear. "You know, you really ought to have those disposed of. Or get a new ship."

Parr laughed. "A new ship, good one."

"It's not a joke, Parr. I'm serious—they're dangerous. I hardly slept on the way over here."

"But you slept."

"What can I say, I'm gifted," she said, and cinched up a pack around her shoulders. "I brought some provisions, but I hope we're not here long."

"When do you think we'll get an audience with Telfo?" Parr asked.

Ren shrugged. "Might be a couple weeks for any creatures off the street."

Parr shot her a look.

A dimple creased her cheek. "But we're not just any creatures, are we?"

"Not for what I'm paying," Parr replied. He meant for it to be playful, but he wasn't sure if he'd said it with too much of an edge.

Ren rolled her eyes.

Good, Parr thought.

Ren stared at the ceiling like she did whenever she was thinking something through. "It could be anywhere from a few hours to a few days, depending on his connections."

"I have no idea what to do with this information," Parr said.

"If it were me," Ren replied, "I'd give it a day once I'd arrived. I wouldn't want whoever I was negotiating with to think I was too eager."

"But not wait long enough for them to think about it too much," he said.

Ren nodded.

"So," Parr said, his thoughts settling back to the unfinished business from the night before. "What should we do until Manc messages us?"

Ren grinned and shook her head before striding away. "Think I'd let that old pirate out on his own? I put a tracker on him. C'mon, let's see where it takes us."

It wasn't exactly where Parr had been heading with the question, but it was a solid option, nonetheless.

CHAPTER 29

The pair exited the hangar onto a dimly lit street, clear of traffic, save for a lonely transport that whirred by. The shops along either side were backlit in muted reds, greens, and purples with no facsimile of natural light anywhere to be seen. It took Parr a few moments before he realized the shops were teeming with life beyond the lights and into the shadows.

"This way," Ren said as she pulled his sleeve. Parr was tempted to grasp her hand in his but decided against it.

Parr got the feeling that the barren walkway closest to the street made them targets, and Ren must have felt the same way. She eased their path into the shadows of the storefronts where the actual bustle of the area took place. The walkway was filled with life from all corners of the galaxy and creatures in varied dress, from the dark leathers of the Cavliers to the blood-red robes of the Sebadol Order. Parr noticed the spindles of the conjoined porches had a grime-sledged patina from years of use and neglect, but the top bars and footrests gleamed brassily from years of finesse at the hands and claws of the outpost's countless patrons. He imagined the stories told leaning against the railings of the storefronts and what secrets the old façades held within.

"Leave it," Ren said, and swatted away a tentacle that encroached into Parr's proximity. She turned to the shadows. "Who was that? Was it you?"

Parr was snapped back into reality from his daydream to find Ren staring down a shadowy figure until the creature faded away into the dark. Once she was satisfied it was gone, she turned her attention back to Parr. "You have to watch yourself here, Parr. I thought you knew better than that."

"I saw it coming; he would have been in for a surprise."

"I'm sure he would," Ren said with a sarcastic smile. "Just keep your eyes active." She nodded down the street. "Look, Manc's just ahead."

"I see him. Is he talking to someone?"

"I can't tell," Ren said. "He doesn't normally move that slow."

"Yeah, it's like he's at half wobble."

"He just took that corner. Keep close and watch yourself."

Parr thought he'd rather keep an eye on Ren, but she was right; Anatone Seven was said to be one of the more dangerous places in the outer reaches—he needed to focus.

They caught up to the point where they'd last seen the old pirate as quickly as they could and turned the corner onto a desolate path. The way forward was barely lit by a storefront light quite a ways down the wood-slatted walk. Nevertheless, that was the direction Manc was headed in, so that was where they needed to be. After they'd put some distance between themselves and the busy street, Ren pulled up on full alert.

Thunk! Thunk! Thunk!

Three knives of uniform length thunked down in the walkway beyond them. Parr's adrenaline spiked, and it felt like every nerve ending in his body electrified all at once. Was it Norfung? Parr scanned the area and waited for a "Glogs and borlongs," but nothing came … other than an additional three *thunks*.

Three more knives embedded themselves in the railing beside them, and Ren quickly disappeared into the shadows. Parr reached for his blaster but found a tentacle held his wrist firmly in place.

He felt its suckers press and pull against his skin as he swatted at it with his free hand. "Stop it! Stop it, gross," he said instinctively, and immediately felt embarrassed at the words that escaped his mouth. "Show yourself." He tried to peel the appendage away from his arm, but another burst forth from the shadows and wrapped itself around his other hand.

Is this one creature? Where is it?

"Boo," said a graveled voice. Parr turned around and saw a mottled gray face framed by the high collar of a dark leather cloak. The face was pierced with rows of small metal loops along its cheeks, and its slimy neck bubbled in and out as it processed air from the artificial atmosphere. "Heard you might be carrying something mighty valuable. Now, you hold still, and tell your friend to come out nice and slow." Parr struggled against the tentacles and heard a snuffling rustle as another mucusy appendage wormed its way toward him.

"What friend?" Parr asked. His voice cracked at the end of the last word as another tentacle wrapped around his throat. Definitely not Norfung, but who was this guy, and what did he want?

"Cute," the creature drawled through a jagged-toothed smirk. "But don't test my patience."

Flikt!

The creature grunted. Parr breathed a little easier as the tentacle around his throat suddenly loosened. Parr craned his head to find the creature pulling one of Moma Shando's hair sticks from its neck.

Good, Parr thought. The hair stick to the neck forced the creature to let go of Parr's throat so he could take it out. *Now, if I can just spin out of this last tentacle.*

But it was too late.

It was only one hair stick, after all.

Additional tentacles tightened around both his wrists.

How many of these things does this guy have? And why wouldn't he use a different one to take the stick out? Do many-tentacled creatures have a dominant tentacle? Why is this important to me right now?

He watched as the tentacles changed color to match the area around them, and almost instantly, the appendages were practically invisible.

I don't like this. This can't be good. Parr tried to calm himself and evaluate the situation at hand. *At least she can still see his clothes.*

He chuckled to himself.

Classic invisible-guy error.

Parr watched the outline of a tentacle hit a button on the cloak, and the high collar around the creature's face went translucent as well. Just like that, the creature had become almost impossible to see.

Stars and fathers, he thought. *I cannot catch a break.*

He felt a tentacle return around his throat just as he was about to call for help.

"I'll either choke this kid to death or pierce his carotid if you don't come out to where I can see you."

Tiny spikes poked through the suckers of the tentacles and menaced the arteries around Parr's neck and wrists.

The gravelly voice whispered from an indeterminate distance away, "I'm going to let loose just enough for you to call out and let her know I'm serious. Nothing too loud, now, or these spikes get real familiar with what's below your skin."

"He's—" Parr fought for air as well as control of the timbre of his voice. "He's serious." The tentacle tightened around his neck once again and cut off his voice along with some of his air. Parr wondered if he could wiggle his wrist enough to get a proper lunge at his blaster, but then again, where would he shoot? The tentacles were constantly moving, and he couldn't get a good bead on where the creature was.

Ren didn't show herself, which was a smart move. It would only eliminate any leverage she had. As long as she remained hidden, there was a chance for her to either save Parr or escape on her own. Part of him wondered if she'd already done the latter.

There was a sudden whip of motion from the darkness, and Parr felt tiny pellets and fine granules spike against his skin. His eyes burned like the five suns.

"Ow!" Parr screamed. "What the, why—" he started to say before he realized he could talk again. His hands were free as well. He blinked through the pain, tried to wipe away whatever was in his eyes with his sleeves, and looked toward the sound of wheezing screams.

The creature was now fully visible, even through Parr's tear-filled eyes. It writhed on the ground in a bubbling, color-changing mess. Creatures began to emerge from the stores and shadows down the corridor to get a good look at the source of the commotion.

"This way," Ren said in Parr's ear as she pulled him into a run.

"What was that?" Parr asked.

"The rest of our salt for the trip," Ren said.

"Salt?"

"Yeah, salt. Good thing I packed provisions, huh?"

"Yeah, quick thinking, I never would have thought to incapacitate both the assailer and the assailant. Very unconventional."

"You are such an ass."

"Speaking of which, that salt is everywhere on me. And I do mean everywhere."

"So are eyes, Parr. Keep that groppodite somewhere safe."

She had a good point, as usual. He gripped the groppodite in his pocket. He decided it was safe enough there. He'd never had any trouble before, and what were the odds that someone would try for it there again?

Ren checked her wrist again and yanked at Parr's sleeve to pull him in the right direction. Her fingers grazed the palm of his hand, and once again, Parr resisted the urge to take her hand in his. Regardless of how close they were to the old badged and keyed vessel, he wished they were anywhere else in the galaxy at that moment. However, Anatone Seven was far too dangerous for public displays of affection—real affection, anyway.

Parr smiled to himself. For the first time in a long time—maybe ever—he wasn't afraid of opening himself to another creature. Which brought on a whole new wave of anxiety and insecurity he didn't have time for. He pushed those to the back of his mind for the moment, shoved his hands in his pockets, and kept walking.

CHAPTER 30

The two stood in front of a large metal door just off a side street on one of Anatone Seven's busier thoroughfares. Ren's eyebrows knitted together as she looked down at the device on her wrist and back up to the door.

"This it?" Parr asked.

"Yeah," she said. "I think so."

"So, what now?"

Ren felt the door for a latch or some sort of release to get in but couldn't find one. She scratched her head and glanced at Parr.

Slankt!

Startled, Ren looked back to discover a slat had opened in the door around eye level.

"Password," a deep, bubbly voice bellowed.

"Uh—" Ren started to say.

"Get out of here," Parr said.

"Why are you being such an ass?" Ren asked.

"What? It's the password," Parr replied.

Metal gears clinked and clanked as the heavy door slid open for the two to enter. A squat little creature climbed down a ladder attached to the sliding door, naked as the day it was born, save for a bright red vest festooned with a name tag that read "Nacer."

"Welcome to Mick's," Nacer said before trundling off to presumably resume the chore he'd been tasked with prior to letting them in.

Ren cocked her head. "Look at you, knowing things." A thin smile spread across her lips as she raised an eyebrow at Parr.

Mick's was a well-appointed inn of polished wood and glass. Stemware adorned with a jaunty script was arranged neatly on the tables in three parallel rows. The room was lit in a comfortable yellowish-white hue that reminded Parr of the fireplace in the lodge his family retreated to on certain holidays.

Mick's also had a fireplace. A cozy rarity in the outer reaches, and the signature feature in all of their establishments.

"How did you know the password?" Ren asked just above a whisper as she leaned into Parr. Her hair fell over his shoulder, and she grinned as though they were a happy couple celebrating an anniversary.

"You've never stayed at a Mick's? I love these places."

"You two have a reservation?" Nacer asked as he polished a table.

"Yes," Ren replied. "I think he's handling it." She motioned toward the front desk.

"Parr, you keen-eyed, two-wheeled, short-horned bobosorn! I was just about to message you two—how'd you find me?"

"We were in the neighborhood," Parr said.

"You put a tracker on me, eh?" Manc replied. "Or was it you?" He threw his head back with a deep belly laugh. "I bet it was you, Ren. You contingency-making whip of a gottermump!"

"What is a gotter—"

"We got ourselves two rooms," Manc said. "One for Parr and me, and one for you."

Parr considered rooming with the old pirate and then remembered the state of his towels after Manc got out of the cleaner on the *Aurora*. "I have some points with Mick's," Parr said. "I think I'll get my own room."

"Sold out," Nacer said as he walked behind Parr polishing a glass. "Your friend just booked the last two."

"We'll figure it out," Ren said with a glance toward Parr. Her face was as blank as a nav screen in the deepest parts of Galton's Expanse, but her eyes sparkled like sunlight on water.

The party retired upstairs to put away their things, and even though the choice seemed blatantly clear, Parr wrestled internally with the room assignments.

On the one hand, he was sure that he and Ren had a chemistry he'd like to explore further, but on the other, moving from flirty banter to sharing a room was a big jump.

He chewed on the inside of his cheek.

One thing was for sure: opening himself up to others was more than he'd bargained for. He didn't think he'd second-guessed himself this much in his entire life.

He ended up following Manc into a no-frills but stylish room with two beds side by side. Parr regretted the decision within a matter of seconds.

Manc was a sure hand behind the console of a ship, but he was a terrible bunkmate.

The code of the cosmos was significantly different from that on an inhabitable, and the many and varied sounds and smells of Manc emitted further reinforced Parr's desire to change rooms. Parr cursed his olfactory system and wished he had a cold … or nose plugs … anything to save him from this.

Parr sat on the edge of a bed and stared blankly at a piece of art on the wall. He wasn't going to have many more nights like this. In fact, he realized, this might be his last night as Parr. The next night, he might once again be Prince Parrtec, with all the responsibilities that came with that title.

Once he had the old military vessel, he'd be through the gates of Bilena Epso Ach in no time, and on his throne shortly thereafter.

What then?

What would happen to Ren? Would she go back to run Moma Shando's enterprise? Could he talk her into staying with him? Would his people allow it?

His people.

He was going to have start putting them first when it came to his decisions. But he was also not his father. He felt something for Ren, and if she'd agree to go back with him, she would be welcome in his court.

Manc hung up an extra pair of breeches from his pack, broke wind, and laughed to himself.

Manc, on the other hand . . . he could just go back to doing whatever he did after this, Parr thought.

"Parr," Manc said. "Did I ever tell you of the time I hauled this shipment of adorable little mupwocks?"

"Nope," Parr said. Manc had never told him the story, and he certainly wasn't interested in hearing it. All he could think about was Ren.

Sure, she's welcome in my court, he thought. *But as what?*

The old pirate sat on the edge of the other bed and started taking off his boots. "I have a strict rule," he said, and pointed a boot toward Parr for emphasis. "No transport of live creatures. But there I was, already three farlongs into a haul, when I heard them start to sing. Singing! Can you imagine? I had no idea they were even there—clueless as a pink-sided snorlbon!"

Parr sighed and scratched the back of his head. *I mean, why would Ren come with me, when she could go run her own empire?*

"So, naturally," Manc continued, "I put the *Complaint* on auto and go check out the ruckus."

What if that's what I really like about her? That she doesn't need me?

Manc had both boots off and was flexing his bionic toes. He leaned forward and gestured behind him. "By the time I'd gotten back there, they'd figured out how to let themselves out of the crates, and they were everywhere—and I mean everywhere." The old pirate began to wildly gesticulate. "Hanging from the ceiling, wasting all the tape from the med kit, sliding around on a whole month's worth of gelatin spheres as though they were skates."

Parr looked down at the floor. *What does that say about me? That I want someone who doesn't need me? Is that good or bad?*

"So I says to 'em, I says, 'Get back in there, the lot of you, or I'll have you up by your tiny little gizzards, you bright-eyed little shanks of dolkers.' And that's when it happened—are you listening?"

There was a brief silence before Parr realized Manc was waiting for an answer. "Yeah, I'm listening."

The old pirate was chewing on something.

When did he have time to—where did he get that hand fruit?

"You're never supposed to show mupwocks red lights."

Yeah, everyone knows that.

Parr looked back down at the floor and wondered what Ren was doing at that very moment. Was she thinking about him?

"Did you know that?" Manc asked with a mouth full of fruit. "You want to know how I know that?" Manc asked. "Parr, you know how I know?"

"What?" Parr asked.

"Well I'll tell you," Manc said. "Because I hit the emergency cutoff so they couldn't get to the bridge is how. So the red lights started flashing as a standard alert, and they just went bonkers. Whizzing this way and that."

Maybe it's because for the first time in my life, I've met someone without an angle. Her life would be fine without me. Well, maybe fine after some heavy therapy, but money, real money, isn't a motivator for her—or power, for that matter.

She had both, and none of the responsibilities of a monarch.

So, why does she like me?

Parr needed to know if Ren felt the same way about him, and he was running out of time. It was now or never.

"By this point," Manc said, "I'd had it."

"Hey," Parr said. "That's great, but I have to go."

"But I was just getting to the punch line," Manc said. His mouth was wide and full of food, and he held a finger up. "Just give me ten more minutes."

Parr stared at the old pirate.

The old pirate squinted back. "What?"

"No," Parr said. "Not a chance. I need to go downstairs and check on something."

It was a strange and unnecessary lie.

Manc winked at him. "See you in the morning, lad."

"Stop winking at me. You know I don't like it," Parr said.

He let the door shut behind him to the sound of Manc's booming laughter, a dirty joke at his expense, and his heartiest of well-wishes.

⌃

Ren opened the door.

"Hi," she said.

It was then Parr realized he had no idea what to do with his hands. Should he lean one against the door frame? No, that was ridiculous, he thought. No one should do that. Should he keep them at his sides? No, of course not. What kind of monster just hangs his arms loose at his sides? He decided to stuff them in his pockets.

"Hi," Parr replied.

A dimple quirked her cheek, and after a moment, she invited him in.

The room seemed to welcome him with the smell of Somvelian root incense and woodsmoke. A tiny plume wafted in front of the warmly backlit center console between the two beds in the room while the strings of a Varulean orchestra whispered through unseen speakers.

"Where did you get the incense?" Parr asked.

"I've had it," she said.

"You've had it this whole time we've been sharing the same enclosed space with Manc, and you're just now using it?"

"Are you really about to ask me why I didn't light something on fire inside a vessel in deep space?"

"You make a good point," he said.

"So," she said.

"So," Parr replied.

She arched an eyebrow.

"I wanted to continue our conversation from back in the galley," Parr said.

"Yeah?" she asked.

"Before Manc walked in."

"I'd like that," she said.

Parr was nervous. He'd been wondering what it would be like to have some time alone—truly alone—with Ren since they were in the galley together, and now they had it.

Parr wasn't inexperienced romantically, at least in the physical sense, but he'd never really been with someone he'd known or cared about more than a few cycles. Not since Jessaba, at least. What would it be like to share an intimate moment with someone he actually knew—and, maybe for the first time, someone who knew him. It was as terrifying as it was exciting.

Parr's hands began to sweat inside his pockets.

But what if this was a part of Ren's plan? What if he gave in to his feelings, only to have them betrayed?

Why do I do this to myself?

He thought back to his father's advice about how good rulers always kept their emotions at bay. It sounded like good advice at the time, and it had always served him well, but this seemed different. Ren was different—or maybe Parr was.

He wondered if what made for a good leader might also make for an incomplete creature. Maybe a more balanced creature could learn to trust and give in to their true emotions from time to time.

Plus, Ren was already in the process of undressing.

She cast a glance over her shoulder and beckoned him forward. Parr gave in to what he hoped was his better nature, crossed the room, and took her in his arms.

∧

Parr opened his eyes and stared for a moment at the back of Ren's head next to him. Her long, thick hair draped across her pillow.

She was as gorgeous as a Sordonian sunrise, and to his delight, she was still there with him.

Of course she's still here next to me, he thought. *It's her room.*

He was used to waking up alone after a night like they'd had. Either Parr or his partner made a perfectly believable excuse to leave before one of them fell asleep. Or one of them would wait for the other to fall into a slumber before they stole away quietly into the night.

It was a code he was used to, and one he usually found comfort in, but this was different. Even with Jessaba, he'd always found his way back to the palace at a decent hour, but not last night. Parr had spent years building intricately designed walls around his heart for protection. Strong, beautiful, masterfully constructed walls. Walls that most wouldn't even notice as a barrier—just something unique to look at, a quirk of his character, part of the overall charm he had to offer.

He was surprised to find that there was now an open gate in those walls. Maybe it was a new addition, built with help from Ren. And now she was inside.

What would she do now that she was there?

It was terrifying, but it was far too late to change course. He'd taken the chance, and there was no going back.

What's the worst that could happen? he wondered.

Betrayal, humiliation, despair, and possibly an agonizing death, he answered himself.

He traced the outline of her exposed shoulder with his finger.

"Stop," Ren said. Her voice was hoarse, and she rolled toward him. "Five more minutes." She said, and nestled her head on his chest. She hooked her leg over his.

Parr weighed the worst that could happen and decided it was worth the risk. He closed his eyes and went back to sleep with Ren in his arms.

⋀

A loud series of knocks woke them both. "Get up, you two!" Manc bellowed from behind the hotel door. "I got us a meeting with Agrofor Telfo. Stop acting like a couple of nesting bronodons and get yourselves together and presentable! We leave in twenty."

"Thirty," Parr raised his voice to reply.

"Twenty-five," Manc replied, and beat the door with a solid fist to drive the point home. Parr could hear him wobbling down the hallway but noted that the old pirate was all business in his tone.

This is it. I'm almost home.

"Thanks for the extra five," Ren said. "Hey, I want to talk to you about something."

Here it comes. See, this is why you don't sleep over. I should have gone back to Manc's room.

"Let me guess," he said. "You had a good time last night, but you don't want me to be confused."

"What?" Ren said. "No. No, is that what you think of me? I don't just sleep with someone—"

"Before the first date?"

"You stuck-up, elitist, insecure—"

"Hey, I'm sorry," Parr said. "I was scared you were—"

"Yeah, I know you're scared. That's life. Be an adult."

"I—"

"Just be quiet," she said. "I like you. I like you a lot, Parr. I'm scared too. If things go well with Telfo, you're on your way back to take the throne, and I just go back to being me. Sure, it's a version of me with the primary stake in one of the galaxy's leading establishments, with money, power, and influence—but I'd be alone."

Parr looked into her eyes. As if they were the healing pools of Lonverdun, he wished he could just get lost in them and stay in that moment forever.

"Why?" Parr asked.

"Why what?" Ren replied.

"Why do you like me?" It was at once both the craziest thing he could think to ask and also the most reasonable. Everyone he'd ever known as a prince had had an angle when they approached him. Proximity to money, power, parties—what was Ren's?

"I trust you," Ren said.

"You trust me," Parr replied. It wasn't the answer he'd been expecting.

"Growing up in Moma's shadow, I never knew if someone wanted to be my friend because they liked me or if they wanted something my mother could give them . . . then there was everyone I met after—" She tucked her hands around her elbows. "And you have good hair, that's why."

Her faced scrunched into a tiny laugh. Parr knew that laugh. That was the laugh of someone who'd said more than they'd intended. She'd just laid it all out there for him to see. Parr returned her laugh with the kindest smile he could muster.

"I like you too, Ren. A lot." Parr brushed her hair behind her ear with his fingers. "More than anyone I've ever known. I trust you too, you know."

She looked away for a moment before returning her gaze to him. "So, what happens to us?"

Parr scanned her face. He knew what he wanted to say was crazy, but he'd never live with himself if he didn't ask. "Come with me."

There was pounding at the door again, and Manc's muffled voice erupted from behind the wood and steel. "I don't hear no cleaner washing, but I do hear you two bickering like a couple of crested-beaked profoons."

"We're not bickering," Parr said.

"Where does he come up with that stuff?" Ren asked.

"I don't know, I was thinking the same thing," Parr replied.

"Do it now," Manc bellowed. "You have fifteen!"

"Come with you?" Ren asked.

"Yes!" Parr replied.

"If I come with you," Ren said, "I leave everything behind."

"Fifteen!" Manc reiterated through the door.

"It doesn't have to be that way," Parr said. "You can run Moma's from wherever you want. A queen can go wherever she pleases."

A queen? What am I saying?

It was crazy enough for him to think it, but now that he'd said it out loud, it sounded insane.

But did it? Who else would he ever trust more after everything they'd experienced together? Who else would he ever come across who would take him as he was? Parr, not Prince Parrtec. Not the king regent. Just some guy they happened to like that led to love.

Royal marriages weren't like that . . . but, then again, most royals didn't fake their own death either, so he might as well keep blazing new trails.

"A queen?" Ren asked.

"I mean, I'd be a king. You get how this works, right?"

"I can't run Moma's as a queen."

"So run it as an alias. You can trade your queen title for whatever Moma's is when you're there. See? I solve problems."

"That's actually not bad, Parr."

"Fourteen!" Manc yelled.

"I guess we should get ready," Parr said. "Just tell me you'll think about it."

"I will."

Parr quickly pressed a kiss to her lips.

It was like something was welling up in his chest. He'd felt the sensation before but always cut it off or shoved it back down. Emotion, love, whatever it was, felt like it wanted to move from his heart and over to hers as he pulled her close. So, he let it. He gave in.

And it felt good.

It wasn't scary at all. It was almost like relief.

Manc pounded on the door. "Ten!" he yelled.

Ren squinted. "I guess we should get going. Big day, huh?"

Parr slowly rolled out of bed. "I guess," he said. "I mean, if meeting the pirate king of Anatone Seven, then heading out to claim my birthright as sovereign of the galaxy is your idea of a big day, then sure."

"Parr, how much do you know about Agrofor Telfo?" Ren asked.

"What's to know? He's a pirate, he's a king. I'm familiar with both of those things."

"Parr, tell me you're joking."

"I'm joking," he said.

But he wasn't joking.

CHAPTER 31

The group mustered downstairs and checked their bags one last time before they set out into the dark streets of Anatone Seven. Manc wobbled down the dimly lit path with a nervous energy Parr hadn't seen from him before. His lips moved as he rehearsed a speech, with an occasional curse and repeated phrase.

Ren walked shoulder to shoulder with Parr. When her hand brushed against his, Parr found himself in the middle of a full-toothed, deep-dimpled grin and weaved his fingers between hers. He glanced over to see Ren's face had turned a deep shade of red even in the gloom. The two walked hand in hand down the shadowy thoroughfare as a couple for the first time.

It was a new experience for Parr. Sure, he'd taken home many a creature hand in hand this way before, but it had never meant anything to him—and it probably hadn't meant much to them either. At that moment, however, the small gesture meant everything in the Sixteen to Parr.

"Stop that," Manc snapped. "Are you two crazy?"

Parr blinked. "What?"

"Look, it's been as obvious to me as the nose on a blue-footed gaboo that you two have a thing for one another for a while, but I at least had to get to know the both of you first. You don't want to broadcast any attachments like that out here, lad. Drop the hands before someone sees you."

"Manc, who cares, I've—"

Ren dropped his hand like a freight runner cutting loose their cargo. "He's right, Parr. We're way off-world, no need to give anyone any additional leverage."

Parr glanced at her. Even when she was all business, he was into her. Maybe especially, who was to say?

He was. Obviously.

Manc checked his wrist and cursed under his breath. "Hurry it up. We're going to be late."

There was no morning, afternoon, or evening on Anatone Seven— just a constant dim, purplish light. Creatures stirred in the corners and in the shadows of the storefronts, just out of view. For a moment, Parr could have sworn he saw a familiar ruddy face, but it was gone just as soon as it appeared, and given Manc's hurried gait, there was no time to double-check.

Moreover, if it was who he thought it was, he wasn't that interested in a closer look.

Manc pulled the group through a tight-fitting alleyway and picked up the pace as though to elude anyone who might be following them. The alley twisted and turned in seemingly random patterns, but Manc was decisive in his movements.

It was as though they were traversing a maze—a fitting entrance to the home of Agrofor Telfo, the famed pirate king.

The group came to a stop at a grimy wooden door that somehow looked weathered even in the climate-controlled atmosphere. It had to have been imported from some far-flung outpost, given the crude but sturdy craftsmanship.

Manc whispered a password through a small steel-barred window. *Clunk.* The door slowly opened with a long creak, and the group passed by a hallway that teemed with glowing red eyes in the shadows beyond. More twists and turns followed through stone-block passageways. Parr felt as though they'd been transported from an off-world settlement to a planetary coastal castle hundreds of years old. The air even had a damp, musty smell to it. Lost in thought, he bumped into Manc as the old pirate came to a stop in front of another door.

"Watch where you're going, son," he said, and rapped the door with a series of musically timed knocks.

A pattern returned from the other side. Manc shook his head and spit before he replied with a furious series of knocks and scratches. It seemed more like a language than a passcode and reminded Parr of stories he'd heard of prisoners' learning means of communication while in solitary cells. There were rumors that an entire subculture had emerged based on the language—factions within detention facilities banding together to help each other survive.

The more Parr thought about it, the more he realized there was a lot about Manc that he didn't know.

Clunk. Thunk. Click. Clack.

Bolts and locks slid and twisted from the other side. The door opened on well-oiled hinges with just a few creaking noises from the door frame itself. A creature the size of an oripian loomed like a waxing moon on the other side. Clothed in a dark cloak with a hood covering most of its face, it stretched one of its oversized arms and directed the group inside. The gauzy fur that peeked out from the massive gloved paw indicated that the creature wasn't just the size of an oripian but most likely was, in fact, an oripian.

Parr marveled at the size of the creature and thought how strange it was that he'd gone most of his life without ever seeing one in person, and now he'd encountered two in such quick succession.

Manc ambled forward, followed quickly by Ren, with Parr at the back of the group, just ahead of the oripian. The walls of the stone-block tunnel transitioned from a deep blue glow to the warm orange of torchlight. After a while, it opened up into a massive cavern.

Anatone Seven was entirely creature-made, so either the room had been manufactured to look like natural rock, or it had all been transported in at great expense. A massive stone structure stood at the center of the room, surrounded by a vast moat.

Dozens of the galaxy's most wanted lounged in booths and at tables positioned around the moat on the other side of the stone structure. They gambled, plotted, and otherwise caroused.

A figure reclined in a great golden throne with one leg draped over the arm of the chair atop a steep rocky tower that was flat on top like a plateau. There was no mistaking the great Agrofor Telfo once you saw her.

Her, Parr thought.

Why did everyone refer to Agrofer Telfo as a him?

The graceful feline creature swiped away at the screen in front of her and ignored the small group that had just entered her space. Several creatures buzzed about on top of the rocky mound, while others operated consoles of bronze. Parr wondered what they could be monitoring.

"Ludon Yelray," Telfo purred. "I see you brought quarry. Well done, good and faithful servant."

Quarry? Parr thought. *Manc, you no-good, double-dealing son of a—*

CHAPTER 32

"I tease, of course," Telfo said. "Come forward, my heart. It's good to see you."

Parr couldn't tell if she was teasing. Maybe she was, and maybe she wasn't, but either way, it set him on edge.

The oripian gently nudged Parr and his group forward toward a wooden drawbridge adorned with metal chains on either side. The slack chains served as handrails and were neatly fastened through the rock on each end. The chains were sturdy but ornate. The whole thing was designed elegantly, making something beautiful out of the mundane.

But so what? Parr thought. *How hard would it be to swim that small distance if someone needed to?*

A ripple in the water immediately answered the question for him. Although he was unsure what was below the surface, he was confident that he didn't want to find out.

Once they were across the bridge, another creature appeared from a well-hidden space within the large mound. Perhaps it was a guard outpost or a tunnel to who knew where.

The creature stood tall, with an upright posture that could just as well have been a product of fused vertebrae as a posh upbringing. The creature's movements, however, were as fluid as the ripples in his long purple robes and impressive white beard. He looked down on them and patiently surveyed each of the members of the group. "Ludon," the creature said with a nod toward Manc.

"Cormorand, you stuffy old data sniffer. Long time."

Parr noticed Manc's truncated insult and took that as a sign of respect. Clearly, this wasn't a creature to be trifled with.

Cormorand's eyes flitted to Parr for a moment. He took a deep breath through his long nose and exhaled through his thin-lipped mouth. "Perhaps for some. Wait here while I announce your presence, Ludon."

Announce our presence? Parr thought. *She's already addressed us. What is this formality?*

Parr scanned the creature-made cavern and admired the way Telfo had merged technology into the rocky façade of the natural setting. He particularly liked the choice of brass handles and analog gauges as opposed to the white-enameled, multicolored blinking consoles to which he'd become accustomed. The lights of Telfo's consoles were off-white, orange, or red to indicate the status of whatever it was the gadgets monitored. He preferred the warmer, more lived-in feel of the space versus the stark, sterile interior design of the ships that made up his family's armada and the royal reception areas.

His family's armada, Parr thought. Soon he'd be back on the very ship that he'd used to escape his old life and all his overwhelming responsibilities. Before long, he'd be back within the palace walls in which he'd been raised. He'd see his sister for the first time in what seemed like a lifetime.

In fact, from a certain point of view, it was.

He wondered how Malista would react to seeing him for the first time and hoped that she would be overjoyed to see her brother after thinking him dead the last few years. He'd hug her and tell her what a wonderful job she'd done with the kingdom. Perhaps he should keep her on as high counselor for a while until he got the hang of the job.

Something nagged at the back of his mind, though.

How *would* she react to his return?

Probably not like that.

"This way," Cormorand said before a half dozen leather-clad guards emerged from behind him to escort the group up the rock mound. They each held one long spear just off the ground with such ease that Parr wondered if they had some sort of stabilizer in them. There was hardly a wobble as they marched forward.

Parr decided he would figure out the details of the reunion with his sister later and turned his attention toward the matter at hand: the legendary Agrofor Telfo, scourge of the Sixteen, pirate king, and patron saint of the lawless.

"Thank you, my hearts," Agrofor Telfo said as she dismissed the cadre of guards with a gentle wave of her paw.

The lithe creature slinked forward from her golden throne, layered in black leather and ringed metal. Her exposed fur was yellow with a pattern of black spots, while her deep green eyes seemed to glow like station beacons in the dimly lit space.

Telfo circled the group, stroking her long whiskers with an articulately clawed paw, and yawned wide, as though she were bored. Parr guessed it had less to do with a lack of sleep and more to do with nonchalantly displaying the long, dangerous canines that would otherwise stay hidden behind her smirking white muzzle.

"Manc Yelray," she said as she brushed up against him on her way past. The tip of her long tail embraced his shoulder for a moment before she walked it out of reach, then circled back toward him. "It's been a long time."

"That it has, Your Majesty," he said.

Parr noticed the straightforward reply. No colorful metaphor, no gruff rejoinder. Just a direct response, a hint of fear in his voice.

She smiled as she continued to circle him. "Please, Manc, you can drop the formality. We've got history, you and me."

"If it's all the same to you, Your Highness, I won't. There's not much I respect in this life, but I will never break the code. The code binds us."

"The code binds!" voices rang out from across the room.

"That it does, Ludon, that it does," she said. Her claws pulled at the shoulder of Manc's captain's furs as she continued to circle the old pirate. "Cormorand briefed me on why you've come. You're here for a badged and keyed vessel from the old Twelve."

"That's right, Your Majesty, the same one I sold you back in the day."

"Hmm. Now, why would you want a dusty old vessel like that thing? I just won a Corvin-class I think you'd rather like. Quite an upgrade from the *Complaint*."

"A Corvin," Manc said. "Really? What do you want for her?"

Telfo smiled a mouthful of daggers. "That's what I like about you, Yelray. Most would ask how much."

Manc cleared his throat. "I know favors are as good as currency for you, Your Highness. It's like you said, we got history."

"Why don't we retire to my quarters to discuss the details," Telfo said.

"If it's all the same to you, Your Majesty, I'd like to discuss it here."

"It's not all the same to me, Ludon. But have it your way. I understand you arrived in a Fano-class with your friends here," she said with a twirl of her paw and a twinkle in her eye. If Parr didn't know any better, he'd have thought she'd winked at him.

"That's right," Manc said. "Nice ship, in a pinch."

"Are you in a pinch, Ludon?" she asked. "Why? Did something happen to the *Complaint*?"

Manc's hand covered his face as though he were swiping away the rage before it took control of his countenance. The old pirate managed a chuckle and scuffed his prosthetic against the lair's rocky ground. "Nothing I can't recoup, Highness."

"So the reports that *Vanessa's Complaint* is strewn about in pieces on Versit Station are erroneous?"

"Wouldn't be the first time I pieced it together from a yard."

Telfo chuckled. "Maybe the first time you've encountered someone as vindictive and well connected as Moma, though. I don't think there's anything left for you to put back together."

Manc looked visibly disturbed. Parr noticed small beads of sweat starting to gather around the old pirate's temples.

"Eh. Maybe so," Manc said. "But back to business, Your Majesty. I'm here for the old battle cruiser."

"Yes. The one you sold me. Slow as a herd of lommoxes on the sludgy wastelands of Rafilda. Barely room for two on a long haul and absolutely no room for cargo … and you're looking to replace the *Complaint*. Very curious, Ludon.

"Now, normally, I'd take a double return on my investment and be done with it, but the keys and badges can slip me into the Sixteen whenever I want. Hard to put a price on that."

"I'll pay you three times what he sold it for," Parr interjected.

Telfo and Manc stared at Parr, Manc wide-eyed, while Telfo's eyelids hovered at half-mast. Her teeth were on full display. She drummed her claws on Manc's shoulders as her tail swished in the air. "I like the boy, Manc. Full of moxie, and a head for business."

"I'm leading the negotiation here if you don't mind, Your Highness," Manc said. "Pipe down, lad, you don't know what you're doing."

Telfo slinked toward Parr but found her progress arrested when Ren stepped between the pirate king and the soon-to-be ruler of the Sixteen.

Telfo looked down on Ren with bemused admiration as she redirected her progress. "Please, your money is no good here, boy," she said. "If you want the vessel, I'm sure we can come to an arrangement."

Parr felt a wave of relief wash over him. He wasn't sure his account could cover what he'd blurted out, and he was always up for a challenge. So why did Manc suddenly look more anxious than before?

"You're the captain of the *Aurora*, yes?" Telfo said.

Parr felt a wave of emotion overtake him. And just like a wave, when one washes over you, another one comes behind it. The one you're not ready for. In this case, one that crashed over you and held you down to the ocean floor until your lungs burned for air. One that carried hundreds of tiny stinging creatures.

"I am," Parr said.

"She's a fast ship, my boy," Telfo replied.

"She's alright."

"Come now, Parr, let's drop the pretense. Fastest in all of the Corpulon Valvente—one of the select few to have ever evaded Norfung Gortn, am I correct?"

"We may have outrun Gortn a time or two," Parr replied. He couldn't help himself. The encounters with Norfung had just as much to do with his skill as the *Aurora*'s speed, and he wanted everyone else in the room to know it. Parr shook his head as though he were trying to shake the grin loose from his face. His pride wouldn't allow him to just let something like that pass by.

"So, the rumors are true," Telfo said. "Everyone says the *Aurora* is the fastest ship in the galaxy by a farlong."

"Maybe when I'm flying her," Parr replied.

"Fine," she said, her paw squeezed into a fist as she turned away from Parr and stalked toward Manc. "I'll take it."

"No!" Parr exclaimed. "She's not for sale."

"Don't be a fool, Parr," Ren whispered through gritted teeth. "It's just a ship."

"She's my ship," Parr whispered back.

"The ship isn't fast," Ren whispered. It's the . . ." She made a twirling motion with her finger, indicating that it was, in fact, the groppodite that made the *Aurora* so fast. She continued, "Any ship is going to be fast as long as you have it on board."

"I've been through too much with her," Parr whispered.

"How would you even get it back through?" Ren asked. "It's not badged or keyed. This is the perfect scenario."

Parr thought about it and quickly came up with a solution. "We captured her."

"What?" Ren asked.

"We captured her, and we're bringing her through."

"So, you want to have a conversation with the guard command of the Sixteen? Are you out of your mind?"

"Ludon, is there a problem?" Telfo said with a pointy-toothed smile. "Your comrades seem to be distracted."

Manc looked to Parr and Ren with his eyebrows raised and palms out to signal a question: *Do we have a deal or what?*

"No issues here," Ren said. "Sounds like a good deal, right, Parr?"

Parr's eyes burned like twin engines before a jump. The *Aurora* was just as much a part of him as anything else. She symbolized everything he'd left his royal past to attain. Freedom, adventure … home. He couldn't imagine life without her.

But he was going to leave this part of his life behind, regardless. Maybe Telfo would put Aurrie to proper use, flying a covert mission or leading a vast pirate armada . . . and maybe he could still figure out a way to keep her between now and their departure. Ren was right; it made the most sense.

"Fine," Parr said. "You have a deal, but I need to get some of my stuff out first."

Ren elbowed him in the ribs, while Manc chuckled to himself. Telfo's tail twitched at its end.

"Deal," Manc said, and grasped Telfo's paw to seal the transaction.

"Fine and well," Telfo said. "Deal. We'll retire to my quarters to sort the particulars. Cormorand, I expect you can handle things here while I'm away?"

"Certainly, ma'am."

"Thank you, my heart. Right this way," Telfo said, and made a quick series of motions with her hands. A door emerged and split into two from the rock wall behind her throne.

Manc wobbled forward with what Parr could easily tell was feigned confidence. He'd never seen the old pirate inside his head this much before, and it made him uneasy. Ren, however, seemed cool and aloof—which made him even more anxious.

CHAPTER 33

The pirate king's quarters had a pleasant smell like citrusy furniture polish and were mostly carved heartwood from a tree Parr didn't recognize. Luxurious red curtains adorned the windowless room with gold filigree here and there, along with hand-carved built-in cabinets. A single round table stood in the middle of the room, hand-carved of the same heartwood.

Agrofor Telfo poured four drinks in crystal goblets inlaid with gold. Parr had seen similar sets in one of his father's admirals' quarters growing up. The goblets were meant to be a nod to the old explorers, and if he were in any other dwelling, he'd have wondered how his host had been able to acquire them. Given his present company, he was somewhat curious but not surprised to see them.

"Your Highness," Manc said as he received a goblet from Telfo. She passed them around the group from an oblong tray. "My colleagues and I have traveled far and overcome a great deal to be here. Your reputation and grace have—"

Parr could tell it was the speech he'd been practicing under his breath on the way over, but she cut him off before he could get going. It was one of the few times he'd seen the old pirate visibly shaken.

"*Colleagues*," she said with a snort. "Well, well, well, this certainly isn't the Manc Yelray I remember."

"Creatures change, Your Majesty."

"Creatures never change, Manc. They only think they do. You were a scared gutter punk scamming tourists on the streets when we met, and you still are. Only now you have a title. Of course, I might be a little nervous too, were I a ludon without a ship."

"How did you know—"

"How did I know?" she said. "I always know, Yelray. You know that. Your friends may not, but you do. Young Shando, for example, do you think she knows who I am?"

"Your legend cannot be contained within the Sixteen, Your Highness," Ren said.

"The Sixteen?" The rings around Telfo's cuff jingled as she smoothed the fur around her ear. "Girl, who cares a wampler's bump about the Sixteen? Do you think I built this for the Sixteen? A kingdom built on the backs of creatures stuck in a system that benefits one family over all others? A system where the rich keep getting richer while the poor stay poor?

"I doubt I'm much known in the Sixteen, dear. Outside a few strategically greased palms, anyway, and that's just the way I like it." She slinked around the room, swirling the drink in her glass. "I joined a meritocracy here, made my way up through hard work and just the right amount of skullduggery. My own kingdom, built outside the lines, outside the reach of the royal family and its twisted, ruthless queen."

Parr didn't like listening to someone talk about his sister that way. Even if they had a point. He was used to hearing creatures criticize his parents, but it bothered him to hear someone criticize Malista.

"I see that, Your Highness," Ren said. "You and my mother share much in common."

"That we do, Ren, that we do. We've done business in the past, you know. I admire her. I've heard stories, but I've never really gotten to know her in person." The pad of Telfo's clawed finger circled the rim of the glass. "Tell you what, let's you and I get to know each other. I'll tell you my story, and you tell me yours."

Ren took a sip from her goblet, winced, and then smiled like a crack in the windshield of a speeder. "This is good stuff," she said. Parr knew Ren could hold her drink and wondered if the wince was from the alcohol or the moment.

"We like to live well here," Telfo said. "You know, where I grew up, we lived well too. Nothing as extravagant as Anatone Seven, but we had a natural sun and plenty of food and drink. It was a wonderful settlement outside of the Eleven, as it was referred to at the time. A bustling little city on one small continent so lush and verdant that it would support any type of life.

"Creatures came from all over to mine its resources. From the deepest parts of its oceans to the highest mountains. In harsh climates, far removed from the idyllic settlement where we lived."

Telfo's tail twitched as she leaned against the counter from one of the room's built-in cabinets and looked down at the floor. "My friends and their families settled from all over—castoffs from the Eleven along with some of the lesser moons in between.

"Every home was unique inside. Décor from all over the galaxy. Different sounds, different smells—music playing while cauldrons bubbled and ovens hummed. It was incredible. You never knew what you were going to have for lunch. Only that it was going to be delicious.

"Until one of the mining operations made a lucrative discovery." The claws in Telfo's free hand dug into the counter. "Suddenly, everything changed. More ships started to appear—types and classes we'd never seen before. Beautiful, gleaming wonders that purred as they passed by, as though they were consistently maintained—or perhaps they were so well put together that they didn't need any upkeep.

"Soon, a smattering of my friends had money. Their clothes changed; they moved to a different part of town where tall towers had been flown in and bolted down. They started participating in sports we could not afford and took elocution lessons to speak in an accent much different than what we'd grown up with.

"More ships came in. Creatures poured in from all over the Eleven, offering us money for our house, which my mother gladly took. However, we had to move further away from where I grew up. Soon, more creatures came to inhabit that area as well.

"Our planet was annexed, and the Eleven became the Twelve."

"Sounds like the Twelve gave the people of your planet upward mobility. What's the problem?" Parr asked.

Telfo and Ren both glared at Parr. Telfo's eyes reflected light in a way that made them look like they glowed orange. Manc shifted his weight from one leg to another and fumbled with the drink in his hands.

"What?" Parr asked. "What did I say?"

Telfo straightened herself up and stalked toward Parr, brushing against his shoulder as she walked past. She ignored his question. "Before long I did not recognize our city, and worse, it didn't recognize me. Creatures began to stare at us on the streets. They would recoil when they heard us speak and tell us to go back where we came from. It didn't matter that we were there before them.

"Eventually, every resident had to present their identification as a citizen of the Twelve. Only, my mother did not have any, and the process to get it was lengthy and confusing.

"One night, we were roused from our sleep by a banging at the door. Officers from the Twelve were there to check identification, and when my mother failed to produce any, they removed us from our house. They took us to a large dock, along with myriad other terrified families, and sent us all to different ships.

"I never saw my mother again."

"That is awful," Ren said.

Parr hadn't ever heard that side of annexation before. He'd only heard his father and his top economists speak of growth, development, and upward mobility. They even had a saying: *Better together, prosper forever.*

Were those lies or just convenient parts of the story? Parr resolved to look into this when he assumed power again. His kingdom would uphold the original ideals of the system.

"The only thing worse than growing up on the streets," Telfo said, "is remembering a time in which it was not necessary to take someone's valuables in order to eat that night." Her maw curled in what looked like a friendly grin as she caught Manc's eye. "But hey, I met our friend here shortly after, and here we all are, right?

"I've added to my kingdom, outside of the one ruled by a cruel family of callous, inbred monsters. I'm glad they're mostly dead now, aren't you?" She eyed Parr with a look that reminded him of a blaster's glow moments before it fired.

Manc cleared his throat. "So, down to business?"

"But I haven't heard Ren's story yet," she said.

"I don't know that my story is that interesting," Ren replied.

"No?" Telfo said. "Your mother tossed you out at a young age to fend for yourself to see if you had what it took to run her enterprise. You worked as an—ahem—indentured servant until you were able to pay off your debt. A feat so rare that if it were served in a restaurant, few could even stomach it. Then, after all of that—*all of that*—you go back and deny your chance to claim what is yours.

"You're right, that is so boring." Telfo winked at Ren. "Perhaps you and I have more in common than your mother, girl."

"So, about the Corvin," Manc began.

"Did he tell you about us?" Telfo asked. She turned her attention to Parr and Ren and her back to Manc.

Ren's posture relaxed, and she shifted her hips as she set her goblet down on the table. "Us? No, he hasn't said much about you two. Mostly just strange metaphors."

"We used to be lovers," she said, and closed her eyes as if she were savoring a fine wine. "We had a good time back then, eh, Yelray?"

Ugh, Parr thought. He hated it when creatures used the term "lovers."

Manc bounced on the balls of his feet, and his face turned a dark shade of scarlet. "That we did, Your Highness."

"Before Vanessa, anyway," Telfo said.

Manc turned a different shade of red at the mention of her name.

"She took my lover and my ludon." Telfo's claws clinked along the edges of the goblet she held in her hand. "I wonder what ever happened to her."

Manc gripped his goblet so tight Parr wondered if the thing would shatter into a thousand pieces.

"But you're right," Telfo said. "Down to business."

It was a masterful move, Parr thought. She'd put everyone in the room on edge. Which he'd learned long ago was a terrible state in which to do business. She had them all right where she wanted them—except him. She hadn't targeted him. All Parr needed to do was keep his cool, get the ship, and return to Bilena.

"Let's work out the details," Manc said. "What do we need to finalize this deal?"

"And don't forget, I need to get some stuff out first," Parr chimed in.

Telfo glanced over at Parr before returning her gaze to Manc. "The fastest ship in the galaxy for an out-of-date combat ship that never left the dock. I'm not even sure it operates, to be honest. I'd be a fool to say no."

"You're nobody's fool, Your Highness," Manc said.

"That's right, and I asked you to stop calling me that, Yelray."

"My apologies, Agrofor."

"Nobody's fool, you say." Telfo slipped off the table she'd been leaning against and swirled her drink in the goblet. "Now, it would be foolish to hold on to an investment when such a prize is on the line, but I have to ask myself why.

"Why would you need that ship? Why are we even talking about it after I told you I have a Corvin in need of a captain? I find that interesting, don't you?"

"I don't," Manc said. "I don't find it interesting in the least."

"Hmm," she said.

"Hmm," he repeated.

She really had him there, Parr thought.

"You know," she said, "one could posit that one could use that ship for easy entry into the Sixteen, but one could also gain access if one had the right good to trade or service to provide."

"One could, I suppose," Manc replied.

"Yes. Well, anyway. I don't like the deal anymore; I require more."

Manc rolled his eyes. "Of course. How much more do you want? I can offer up a few points."

She waved him off. Her claws clicked together with the motion, and Parr wasn't sure that was unintentional. "No, I tease, of course; we had a deal, and you lived up to it." She held her wrist out to seal the transaction, and Manc bumped it.

Manc bumped it.

Why did Manc bump it? Parr thought. *I should be doing the bumping.*

"I've even thrown in the ship. I think you'll enjoy the Corvin, Yelray," Telfo said. "Cleanest I've ever seen, not that *you* care about that. Fast too. I can't believe I'm letting it go, but you'll need something to pilot if you want to stay in my reserves."

Her reserves? Parr thought. *Manc still serves her.*

Ren set her drink down and stood up straight. Not rigid, not tense, but balanced. She took a step back toward Parr and stumbled into him, catching herself around his pockets. It seemed a little graceless for her, but she recovered well before whipping her attention to a door that had just opened in a spot in the room where a door shouldn't have been.

"Glogs and borlongs! I have you at last."

CHAPTER 34

Norfung Gortn ducked his head and squeezed through the door frame into the room. The rustling sound of myriad items tucked away in various pockets and the flexing of leather harnesses seemed like a klaxon call in the sudden silence.

The door shut without the slightest whir and replaced itself seamlessly into the wood-paneled wall. "No sudden moves," Norfung said. "I'm just here for the boy . . . and this." A wide grin spread across his face. His arm extended, and Telfo slinked toward him. He pulled her close for a deep, lingering kiss.

Parr didn't like it.

The feeling of being trapped and betrayed by one of his best friends, or whatever Manc was—it was complicated. Parr imagined what torture awaited him, and perhaps, ultimately, an untimely death. But mostly, and certainly intensely . . . he did not like the sight of the famed bounty hunter deep-tonguing the pirate king of Anatone Seven right in front of him.

It was truly disgusting.

Ren stepped between Parr and Norfung as subtly as an absentee bidding at an auction on Inner Gemonton. Not subtly enough, however, to escape the attention of Manc. "Stand down, girl," he said under his breath, as though he were talking his daughter down from the ledge of the tallest tower in Palace City. "There's nothing to be done here. No point in a fight, there's no escape."

"No point, he says," Ren scoffed in a voice considerably louder. "No surprise there, you jiggling mound of self-obsessed lordo droppings."

Parr was more taken aback at the edge in her voice rather than her volume, but perhaps mostly at how much Manc had influenced her vocabulary. Whatever was happening, his betrayal seemed to have hit her just as hard as anything else.

Norfung didn't seem bothered by Ren's play, but the same could not be said for Telfo. The pirate king's tail stood at attention, and its tip swished back and forth like a twitchy metronome.

Parr scanned the room for anything he could use to his advantage. He'd been in tight spots before and always found a way out. It was just a matter of opportunity meeting preparedness … or desperation.

It was then he realized that outside of a few glasses, a table, and a couple of chairs, there wasn't anything in the room he could use. The doors were both closed and locked, and if he and Ren weren't outmatched, they were certainly outnumbered—although he wasn't quite sure what Manc would do if things got rough. The old pirate wasn't a physical threat per se, but he knew how to fight, and it was usually dirty.

Parr was sure he was no match for Norfung in a physical confrontation, but as usual, he had the confidence in himself to try to figure something out.

As skilled as she was, he wasn't quite sure how Ren would fare in a fight against someone who had risen from nothing to become the king of all pirates, but after seeing her in action a few times, he liked her odds better than his.

Still, something was holding him back.

He quickly cycled through a few scenarios in his head and settled on the one with the best odds for success. There were three obstacles between him and freedom, and he had a plan for each. He could wing a glass at Telfo, and she'd probably duck to avoid it. However, it would distract her just long enough for him to throw a chair at Norfung. Knowing the bounty hunter like he did, Parr thought Norfung might catch it, dodge it, or kick it to pieces—it didn't matter, any of the three would buy Parr a few more precious seconds. Finally, while Norfung was doing whatever it was he would do, Parr would kick another chair toward Manc. The old pirate would probably just take the full brunt of the projectile, and if Parr was lucky, Manc would fall over and become another impediment for Telfo and Norfung to dodge. After everyone else was distracted, or at least on their back foot, Parr would make his break toward the door. Easy as that.

Parr chewed on the inside of his cheek.

He realized it wasn't just him he had to worry about. If Parr did something stupid, Ren could get hurt—or worse.

It was then that he understood his time as a freewheeling loner was done. He'd known it would be over soon anyway; he'd just assumed it would come after he ascended the throne of the Sixteen.

But Ren was more important to him than some symbolic chair. Maybe if he gave himself up, they'd let her go.

"It's OK, Ren," Parr said as he stepped forward and put a hand on her shoulder. He hoped it was true even though he was pretty sure it wasn't. He leaned in and whispered in her ear, "It's going to be OK."

It was a lie, but it was one she needed to hear.

Norfung peered down on him with something resembling pity. His handsome brow scrunched into a wad. "You've been a worthy adversary, Parr, but I always get my bounty." He bound Parr's wrists in restraints behind his back. Parr felt the cold metal buzz and heard a whisper of energy before he felt them tighten.

Manc wobbled forward to give Ren a fatherly embrace rather than merely hold her back. She shrugged him off. "No," she said. He persisted, and she eventually melted into a crying heap on his shoulder. "Why?" she asked, and pounded her fists against him. "How could you?"

Telfo slinked forward. "Pull yourself together, dear, you mustn't let others see you this way. What would your mother say?"

Ren glared at Telfo with red, tear-stung eyes. "Probably the same as you," she sniffed, and wiped her face with the cuff of her sleeve. Her jaw knotted. "Something about pushing back the emotion … and settling old scores at the appropriate time."

A growl bubbled inside Telfo's chest before she was able to catch herself. She nimbly transformed it into a haughty laugh. "You're right, of course, and lucky she arranged for your safe return after an unvarnished threat like that. Moma and I have a history, after all. But you and I have a future."

"On this, we agree," Ren replied.

Norfung began to pat Parr down from wrist to shoulder and neck to nethers.

"You think I'd smuggle weapons inside Agrofor Telfo's inner sanctum?" Parr asked as though he were chatting up a creature from a spaceport shoe-shine.

The small blaster he'd concealed clattered to the floor as Norfung shook his pant leg and raised an eyebrow at Parr.

"I said 'weapons' with an 'S.' Plural. Of course, I'd carry in at least one. I'm not crazy."

Norfung chuckle-grunted under his breath and began the search all over from back to front. "Glogs and borlongs, boy," he said in a conversational tone. "Where is it?"

"Where's what?"

"Don't play games, Parr. I'm a professional, we can keep this clean. Where's the groppodite?"

The groppodite? Really? After all this? Parr thought. On second thought, of course it was the groppodite. Parr kicked himself for palming the shiny object way back when.

He'd just liked the way it looked; he hadn't realized the real value of the tiny crimson gem. But of course the clean, efficient, and immensely powerful energy source would have a considerable price tag associated with it.

Why was he surprised someone would come looking for it?

Because he'd never considered the value of energy because it was always available for him? Yeah, probably. Because energy acquisition was always handled by the kingdom's administration and military? Also yes.

Of course it was Telfo who'd hired Norfung. Someone who could afford the initial price tag of the groppodite could certainly afford to pay the most successful bounty hunter in the galaxy to track it down.

Ren had a strange expression on her face as she met Parr's gaze.

Tricky, he thought. *Nicely done.*

There was a reason Norfung couldn't find the groppodite on him.

If he were in any other situation, he might have laughed. That was why Ren had stumbled into him earlier. It was the look in her eyes. Instead of showing shock or embarrassment from the stumble, she'd had a fierce, clear-eyed expression. Now that he thought about it, he realized he'd felt the misdirection with one hand and the lift with the other. The way her face had softened—it wasn't that she'd regained her balance; it was that she'd had the jewel safely in hand.

It was quick thinking, expertly executed.

She had picked his pocket and now had the crimson charm on her somewhere. Ren seemed to have a sixth sense for danger and was always one step ahead.

Parr needed a plan. Maybe he could pull the group apart and give Ren a better chance of escape, or maybe—just maybe—he could figure out a way to get himself back on the *Aurora*. Behind the controls, he'd either make his escape or meet his end in a glorious, multona-boosted explosion in the cosmos. He didn't like his odds one way or another, but he'd have a fighting chance back on his ship.

He remembered "the code binds" and decided to put it to the test. *Let's see if this king follows her own laws.*

"You think I would bring it here with me?" Parr asked. "It's locked away safely back on the *Aurora*. Why do you think I negotiated to keep my stuff in front of everyone?"

The hair stood up on the back of Telfo's neck before it slowly laid itself back down. She hissed out a staccato chuckle. "Quick thinking, boy. I wondered about that, but your reputation for collecting trophies and trinkets preceded you, and I just chalked it up to that. A miscalculation on my part. I suppose you can show me around my new ship while we retrieve the groppodite."

Parr hadn't made that calculation at the time, of course, but was thankful to have it as leverage. It looked as though his gamble was going to pay off.

"Why don't you just send someone to retrieve it?" Norfung asked.

Stars and fathers, Norf, be quiet.

"Appearances, my love. Appearances. I made a deal, and I'm a creature of my word."

Parr closed his eyes and quietly exhaled.

"Glogs and borlongs, Agrofor. He's shifty." Norfung scratched his head. "Be careful."

"You forget yourself, my love," Telfo said. She gently scraped a claw across the side of his face. The gesture was seemingly playful, but with a hint of menace, like a full-bellied predator toying with prey that would otherwise find itself to be a meal. "I'm always two steps ahead." Her claws retracted, and she patted him with the pads of her paw. "Don't forget how I built your reputation. My intel is impeccable and my resources even more so. You're the one with the execution issues." She seemed to stare him down despite the difference in height. "My love."

What does she mean she built his reputation? Parr thought.

Telfo turned on her heel and faced Manc. "Our business is done here, Ludon. Take Shando back to her mother, along with my warmest regards."

Good, she's going to let her go, Parr thought. Now, if he could just get himself out of the restraints, he'd be in business. Fortunately for him, the group seemed to have forgotten a key component of why they were gathered together in the first place.

"Whoa, whoa, whoa," Parr said. "We're not done here. The *Aurora* is still mine since we haven't concluded our business."

Telfo let out a sigh. "Very well, a deal is a deal, and my word is my bond. Enjoy ownership of a vessel you'll never step foot in."

"I'll just need you to let me out of these restraints," Parr said.

"Not going to happen, I'm afraid," Norfung replied.

"Seems we're at an impasse," Telfo said.

"Are we?" Parr asked. "The way I see it is that you made a deal in front of all your people, and as you said, your word is your bond."

"Don't overplay your already-bound hand, dear."

"You didn't think this through, did you?" Parr shot Ren a look with a lopsided grin. He didn't like his long-term prospects, but at least he was winning the moment. Ren did not return his gaze, however. Her attention seemed to be elsewhere, like she was halfway through her journey to a plan. Parr's heart dropped; he hoped she wasn't about to do something to put herself at risk.

Telfo opened her mouth to display her large canines and hissed a curse before regaining her composure. "I could say our negotiations went south and we couldn't agree on a deal, and then just impound the *Aurora* once you're taken away and have stopped paying docking fees."

Parr fought to control his body's urge to shake at the threat. It was very real, of course. If he got out of this in one piece, he was going to have to learn to control his mouth. The king of the Sixteen couldn't just spout off at foreign dignitaries. Especially hostile ones. "You could, but that's not what's happening. Your code wouldn't allow for it. The code binds, remember?"

"You don't know that," Telfo replied. Her muzzle twitched.

"I know your reputation," Parr said, and suddenly had an idea. What would he say to a hostile foreign dignitary? He'd play to their ego, play to what they believed was their strength. "Moreover, I believe your reputation."

Telfo seemed to relax. "My reputation," she said as she stubbed at something on the floor with a clawed toe. "My code." She began to circle Parr. "What do you know of code, reputation, or honor?"

"I didn't say anything about honor," Parr drawled.

Why in the five suns am I still talking? he thought as he immediately regretted his outburst.

"What could you say about honor, Parr?" she replied. Telfo rounded closer, her tail curling around him. "Parrtec," she almost whispered in his ear, the last syllable catching in her throat like the release in a dagger's hilt. "Clever disguise. Shortening your name by three letters … who could have ever guessed?"

"Like Prince Parrtec?" Manc asked, his eyelids at half-mast, as though he were crunching a complex calculation.

"Yes. Just like that," Telfo said as she continued to circle, her tail curling around his neck. "Isn't that right, Your Highness?"

"No?" Parr said.

"Of course, no," Telfo said. "Why would the heir to the throne fake his own death and live in the outer reaches with the rest of us common folk?"

"Exactly," Parr said.

"Certainly not to escape any type of responsibility. Put his flight education to use by joining up with the Corpulon Valvente. Put his economic education to use in the negotiation of trade. Not to mention his access to vast resources that he could sock away before he hatched his little plan."

Economic education, Parr thought. *Ha! She obviously hasn't seen my cash balance.*

"Leading a life of adventure," she continued. "Taking whatever he can—beholden to no one."

"Why would a prince do that when they could just live out their days on some beautiful island far away from the worries of the system?" Parr asked.

"Duty wouldn't allow for it, would it?" Telfo said, her tail tightening around his neck. "Tradition wouldn't allow. Heavy is the head that wears the crown, am I right, young Parrtec?"

She's good, Parr thought. However, he couldn't let her see that she had him. He put his training in negotiation to work and used his best grin to mask any anxiety. "So do we have a deal, or what?"

"A deal for a vessel to take you back to the system, no questions asked, to reclaim your throne and rule the Sixteen for the rest of your days?" She purred as she slinked. "It was a solid plan, truth be told, though I could think of a few other ways in."

"Like how?" Parr asked. "You know, just in case this doesn't work."

"I almost admire your resolve in the face of adversity," she said. She patted his cheek in time with the last few words. "You still believe there's hope."

"So, I'm confused, what are we doing here? You have valuable information, but you're letting Norfung take me to someone with a grudge on a petty lift? Aren't I worth more as a ransom?"

"You think your sister would pay a ransom, do you?" Telfo asked.

"For the sake of this conversation," Parr said, "yes."

"You think she would just welcome you home, hand over everything she's worked on, and disappear into the shadows?"

"She wouldn't have to disappear," Parr said.

"Parrtec," Telfo said. "Drop the act. Do you think your sister would save you? Or pay me double to eliminate you?"

Parr thought about it. Face-to-face, they were family; they could work something out. But way out in the outer reaches, where he was just a word on a screen, it was an easy cost/benefit play. Money wasn't an object, and for that matter, neither was he. He was just a theory, an intangible.

"Probably eliminate," he said.

"Now, why would you say that about your sister, Parr?" Telfo asked.

"I don't get it," Parr said. "Isn't that the answer you wanted?"

"Truth be told, I don't care one way or the other. I'm just curious. Why would you think that?"

"She killed our parents, allegedly. What's one more family member?"

"How?" Telfo asked.

"What do you mean how? Everyone knows how."

"How?" Telfo repeated.

"She had them tossed off the side of a bridge."

"And they plunged to their deaths below."

Parr struggled against his restraints. They were uncomfortable, but not anywhere near the level of discomfort he felt imagining his parents' death. Regardless of how cold his father had been to him, he was still his father.

"Yes," Telfo said. "Seems a lot of her rivals find themselves flung off the sides of high places, don't you think?"

"Yeah, yeah, she's a sick, twisted creature. Fine. We agree."

"Yes, we agree, but I think you're missing the point, and I'm not surprised you can't see something that's right in front of your face. It's like you're incapable of understanding anything that's not a cost/benefit play. Have you no emotional faculty?" She continued to circle him. Parr felt like prey just before the attack. "How did she lose her brother?"

"She didn't; I'm here."

"How does she *think* she lost her brother?"

Like the last tumbler in a sequence, it finally clicked in Parr's mind. What had he done? Their parents, her rivals, all had fallen to their deaths—just the same way his sister believed she'd lost her brother.

"Ah, there it is," Telfo said, her mouth a perfect O shape as her eyes grew wide. "There-it-is." Her face settled back into a haughty smirk. "Guilt from a royal?" Her claws dug into his skin as she grabbed both his shoulders and leaned into his ear. "Your sister loved you, Parrtec."

Of course she'd loved him—in her own way. Despite their rivalry, Parr was the only one she was ever able to talk to without an angle. Every other relationship she'd cultivated had a purpose for her, something to be gained, but not with him. She could always be her authentic self with him.

Telfo continued, "From what I've gathered, you may be the only thing she's ever loved—other than power. Your death simultaneously snapped whatever tether she had to sentimentality and set her on a course to seize that power. I'd actually admire her if I didn't hate everything she stands for—everything you both stand for.

"So no, I don't think I'll ransom you. I'm not sure that would be good for me or my hearts, but the information that you faked it all and left her behind . . . now, *that* could come in handy someday."

CHAPTER 35

The tension in the room was as thick as the hull of a battle-class destroyer. No one spoke for an uncomfortable amount of time.

"I thought of a contingency," Manc said. He held up a finger and cleared his throat. "Seeing as the lad can't access his wrist nav."

Parr was annoyed that Manc kept using that word, but then he wondered: was it a signal? From the look on Ren's face, she seemed to be doing the same calculation.

"Go on," Telfo said.

"I've seen Ren access devices before," Manc said. "I'm sure she could crack into Parr's and complete the transaction so that everything is by the book."

"Is this true, young Shando?" Telfo said.

Ren eyed Parr as though to ask permission. Considering he was all out of ideas, he shrugged back.

"I think I can manage it," she said, and knelt behind Parr to access the device around his wrist. Parr knew she'd crack it within a few moments. Wrist devices were secure, but he'd seen her break into a system that had been built to keep out the worst of the worst. Still, it was taking much longer than he'd anticipated.

She jerked his wrist, sighed, and seemed to start a new range of motions. If he hadn't known any better, he'd have thought she was working on two separate transactions. "Ready," she said, and pulled Parr's wrists up toward Telfo.

Parr winced. "Ow," he said. "I have shoulder sockets, Ren."

Telfo grinned and bumped wrists with Parr. A chime rang out with a slight echo, and the figures in the room were set into motion. Manc gently took Ren by the arm and escorted her toward the door. She quickly slipped his grasp and turned Parr around by his shoulders.

"It's going to be OK," she said before she pulled him close and kissed him with the burning intensity of a dying sun—the final flash before a supernova.

That's the lie I need to hear, Parr thought.

"Alright, that's enough," Telfo said. She cocked an eye at Norfung. "Time to move him, my love."

Norfung firmly gripped Parr's arm. "Only business, kid," he said, and led him toward the door.

"Goodbye and good luck, Ludon Yelray," Telfo said. Her clawed paws gently gripped the back of his neck and she touched her forehead to his. "Enjoy the Corvin." A claw traced down his nose, then she patted his cheek. "Always good to see you, my heart."

"My pleasure, as always, Your Highness," Manc said, rocking back and forth on his heels.

There was a loud thunk followed by a jingle as slight as a breeze. He anchored a magnetic tether to a metallic wall mount and a cuff to Ren's wrist. She looked back at him in shock as he casually thwarted her last-ditch effort to save the creature she loved.

Manc refused to look her in the eye but gently pulled her aside to make room for the pirate king as she slunk toward the doorway to join Norfung and his quarry.

"Parr!" Ren screamed.

The sound of her voice faded as they moved through the halls of Agrofor Telfo's inner sanctum, and Parr wondered if it would be the last time he heard it.

⌃

The *Aurora* stood proud among the other vessels on the dock. She wasn't much to look at to the casual observer—she was weathered and worn some—but she was beautiful and true to Parr. She would always be more than just a ship to him. She'd been a stock Fano-class when he'd acquired her, but he'd made it a point to customize the ship to his specifications over time. An upgraded part here and there, changes to software as needed—or desired.

She'd changed along with him over time, and they deserved all the notoriety they'd accrued over the years. Her: a better version than what had left the factory; him: a creature made by word and deed rather than birthright. They'd earned their reputation together.

She was home. More than any palace ever was or would be. Only now she belonged to someone else. Soon, someone else's key sequence would bring down the sled. Someone else would ease forward the throttle from the captain's chair he'd sat in for so many hours, days, and years.

As he approached her for the last time, he didn't care that he was the one in restraints about to be handed over to a fate as bad as or worse than death. He was preoccupied with her future and his soul-heavy dread of saying goodbye. It felt like someone had attached a weight that dragged down the inside of his chest, and his eyes filled with tears.

"Are you crying?" Norfung asked, and shoved him forward. He tilted his head as he examined his prisoner and turned to the pirate king. "I think he's crying."

"The prince cries for an object that cannot love him back. How appropriate," Telfo said.

Parr was surprised to find himself in a melancholy grin as he blinked away tears. He was crying.

He was actually crying.

Parr had thought he'd lost the ability to cry years ago, but there he was manifesting the appropriate response to what he felt at the moment.

He didn't try to push the feelings away, didn't deflect with a sarcastic comment; instead, he just allowed himself to feel.

What a time for an emotional breakthrough, he thought. But it wasn't just because he was seeing the *Aurora* for the last time; it was more than that. Much more. It was that he had more than likely seen the last of Ren as well.

And, strangely, it was that he would miss Manc, too. At least the idea of his relationship with Manc before he'd double-crossed Parr and Ren.

Manc was a scoundrel to be sure, but the old pirate had a heart. Whatever they'd been through, he believed Manc cared about Ren too. Parr was sure that by now, both Manc and Ren were aboard the Corvin-class cruiser, on their way back to Moma Shando's. There she'd be safe and sound with the groppodite smuggled away and well out of the reach of the pirate king.

He just needed to waste as much of Norfung and Telfo's time as he could before they discovered the groppodite was gone. And maybe, if he got lucky, he could pull off one last surprise.

He just needed to figure out a way to get his hands free, and he was pretty sure an opportunity would present itself soon.

Telfo traced a pattern into her device in order to summon the boarding sled, but instead of the gratifying chime of release, she received the splatty sound of a rejected code. She hit the side of the device and traced the series again with the same effect.

Parr chuckled. "Ahem," he said.

Telfo's green eyes peeked up at him over her wrist, and Parr responded with a well-practiced, perfectly pedigreed royal grin. "Just as a fail-safe, I put in my own security protocol."

"Punch in the code, Parr," Norfung said.

"I can't," Parr replied, and turned to show the bounty hunter his wrists. "Not while you have me in these restraints."

Norfung cursed. "We shouldn't have let the girl leave like that. She could have been useful at least one more time. Why did you let her go?"

Telfo's ears twitched. "Do you want Moma Shando and what's left of the Oowen-ra descending on this place?" she asked. "I tell you the truth, my love. I'd rather face the principalities and all the armadas of the Sixteen before I'd even entertain the thought of crossing *that* creature."

Norfung chose to look up at the *Aurora* instead of looking back at the scolding countenance of his partner. Parr watched his eyes dart to the underside of the craft. Norfung squinted and strained his neck forward before running a trembling hand through his jet-black mane of hair. "The multona drainers hit," he said. "They hit and are still in place." He looked at Parr, then back at the ship. "How?" He turned to face Telfo. "Maybe we should wait until you get a team out here to dispose of them."

"Drainers," Telfo seemed to confirm more than ask. She looked up and took notice of the swirling colors inside the deadly orbs. "No wonder none of the chittery service crews are anywhere to be seen. I'll have a word with their spindly little chieftain about this." She spat on the ground. "I'll flay his guts on the flight deck." Telfo rounded on Parr. The intense green of her eyes seemed to swirl almost as violently as the energy in the drainers themselves. "How were you able to fly with these?"

"How *were* we able to fly with them?" Parr arched an eyebrow. He didn't know, and sometimes when he didn't know the answer to a question, he would just repeat it back to the person who'd asked it. Sometimes it gave the impression that he knew more than he did. He hoped this was one of those times.

"I can stop the drainers from pulling any more power," Norfung said as he punched commands into the device on his wrist. "But they still need to be removed. I don't even want to walk onto this bird for fear of a reaction." His fingers bloomed to mimic an explosion for Telfo, who seemed unmoved.

That solves that, Parr thought. *How dangerous could these things be? We've been flying with them without a problem. Unless . . . yes, of course. The groppodite probably stabilized them like it does everything else.*

Highly optimized energy. Parr wasn't sure of the science, but it seemed right.

Telfo punched in a message on her nav. "I have a crew on their way to remove the drainers."

Norfung exhaled. "Good. What should we do with the boy until then?"

Telfo cocked her head. "Have him take us on a tour of my ship, of course."

Norfung's chest heaved as he prepared for a response, but he was cut short by Telfo's raised paw. She peered down at Parr. "Well?"

Parr displayed his bound hands as best as he could, given his position. "Let me out, and I'll let us in."

⌃

The *Aurora* welcomed Parr back one last time. What some would call dim lighting, Parr considered cozy. He ran his unbound hands along the walls of the interior on his way to the bridge.

"No sudden movements," Norfung said in a voice like the warning growl of a Gordivan mumfort.

"We'll have to work on the smell," Telfo said as she gazed around the room.

What smell? Parr thought. He didn't smell anything. Parr tried to imagine his ship smelling like Telfo's personal quarters—the scent of citrusy furniture polish—and although he didn't hate it, it was still kind of depressing to imagine.

Parr squinted at the pirate king; she seemed different here.

Her gait had a certain bounce to it. Her shoulders had loosened, and a smile displayed all of her front teeth instead of just her canines, like a Gordivan mumfort ready to go outside for a walk.

Parr couldn't help but raise his eyebrows, however subtly, as comprehension settled over him—he'd felt the exact same as he rocketed away from home in that old battle cruiser.

Telfo was just a captain again, not the leader of many, not a chief administrator—merely a creature taking charge of a vessel.

She ran the pad of a finger along the display case full of trinkets from scores gone by and kept exploring the ship. "But I like what you've done with the Fano, Parr. I never liked how they shipped these out with the stark white interior—always felt like a lab instead of a vessel."

One trinket, in particular, caught Parr's attention as he stopped to admire his meticulously curated collection. He eyed the tiny figurine he'd acquired on Bostrap. His first trophy from his first big-ticket haul. The shiny golden hat gleamed in the tiny spotlights of the display case, and he couldn't help but grin at the rustically carved little creature.

"It's in there, is it?" Norfung asked.

Telfo turned on her heel with the grace of a dancer and rejoined the other two.

Parr shook his head. "No," he said. "I wouldn't keep it someplace so obvious."

"Move it along then, kid," Norfung said. "Every footstep here is a risk."

So what if it was, Parr thought. He wondered what would happen if he started stomping around the cabin. Would that be enough to set off the drainers? With both Norfung and Telfo aboard, his chance of escape was lower than that of a comet crashing toward a sun. He'd need to come up with a new plan now.

The sound of Telfo's claw along the glass of the case pulled Parr from his thoughts. "Mostly junk," she said. "But I see your eye through this. You have taste. I may keep some of these for myself."

Before he could offer a reply, Norfung's forearm caught Parr squarely between his shoulder blades and set him shuffling off toward the bridge. His captain's chair sat like a throne. Only here, it was in a room filled with blinking lights rather than a grand hall filled with the smiles of admirers. Parr certainly preferred the former to the latter. For all intents and purposes, that chair *had* been his throne for the best few years of his life. And from that chair, he'd ruled over whatever air and space he happened to be flying through. In his mind, there was no better pilot in the galaxy, and certainly no better ship. Together, they were unbeatable.

Telfo circled the chair with the wide eyes of a child about to open her Andlas Day gifts. She gently spun the chair, eased into it while it was in motion, and gracefully stopped to pore over the console. "I like this setup, Parr. No frills," she said, and started analyzing the layout on her device. "Advanced settings disabled to give you more control. Interesting.

"Ah, clever boost here, I wouldn't have thought to redirect power from that system." She looked up at him with a canine-revealing smirk. "You're really not as dumb as you look. We could use you if you weren't—you."

I'm not going to miss her, Parr thought. He had a new plan in mind; all he needed now was a short window of opportunity. *Go ahead, keep smiling. I can't wait to wipe that smug look off your muzzle.*

Telfo's smirk drooped when she saw at what sat next to the chair.

That was fast; what is she looking at?

"What is this?" she asked.

"What is what?" Norfung replied.

"This looks like the Skelly I gave you, my love." Telfo gazed at Norfung. "To celebrate our time together. To remember those poems you put to song for me during our trip to Hasan Nau."

Wow, Parr thought. *She's the one who gave him the Skelly? Bad move, Norf.*

"You fixed it," Norfung said. He glanced at Parr before he picked up the instrument like a craftsman would pick up a tool. He ran through a scale with an alacrity that caught Parr off guard before setting it back down.

Norfung must have seen the look on his face. "Lot of free time between sites, and I don't have to tell you, it can get lonely out in the great expanse."

Telfo grabbed the neck of the Skelly with force, and one of the strings sprang out and fell away at the touch of her razor-sharp claws. Her intense gaze drew Norfung in as she leaned forward from the chair. "Why is it here?"

Parr wondered if he should fan the flame of discord between the couple. Anything to buy Ren and Manc more time. Corvins were among the fastest ships out there, but better safe than sorry—who knew what kind of vessels the pirate king might have at her disposal.

"I picked it up at a market," Parr said, then added with as much smarm as he could manage, "Incredible price too; the guy said he got it for next to nothing."

"Next to nothing?" Telfo asked. The hackles on the back of her neck rose. "He picked it up at a market?" Her voice clicked at the end of each word. "How would he pick it up at a market?" She bounced up from the chair and began to circle Norfung as though her legs were coiled springs. "Perhaps you laid a trap for the boy? A trophy for his case?"

That would never fit in the case, Parr thought. It would have been funny to voice that out loud, but he figured it would be better to let the two argue without distraction.

"I tell you the truth, Agrofor; it was broken. I had no use for it. There's no room on the *Dreadnet* for broken things."

This guy, Parr thought, and chuckled to himself.

"No room for broken things? I don't even know why I'm surprised—"

"I see what I have done," Norfung said. "I am sorry. Parr, do you have another string so I may play my love a song?"

"I am prepared for just such a contingency," Parr said, and winced. Now *he* was saying the word.

It was just the distraction he needed. The lovers' quarrel would give him all sorts of time and opportunity. He hit the release for a storage compartment and pulled out a string wrapped in a packet as well as the broken peg winder. He passed them both to Norfung and discreetly palmed an additional string packet before he shut the compartment.

Norfung acknowledged Parr with a slight nod but kept his attention on Telfo, a smile as soft as a mumfort pup's ears set on his ruddy face. He skillfully put the string in place and through the peg on the end. Telfo returned his gaze with admiration for the skill he showed in attending to the instrument. A crease cracked across the bounty hunter's cheek as he put the peg winder to the peg.

Doink!

The string broke almost instantaneously as the broken peg winder sped through the winding process and jerked the string to its breaking point.

"Glogs and borlongs!" Norfung's eyes burned through Parr like the active volcanoes of Gallas.

It took all Parr's training, focus, and will to live to keep from laughing. He couldn't risk bringing attention to himself. Instead, he held out the palmed string packet to the bounty hunter. "Forgot to mention the winder is a little tricky."

The bounty hunter flung the winder at Parr, and to both their surprise, Parr caught it. For a moment, Norfung seemed even angrier, until the pad of Telfo's paw caressed his cheek. "Don't worry, my love. You know what's coming to the boy. I want to hear our song."

We'll see, Parr thought, and absentmindedly placed the winder into his jacket pocket.

Norfung sighed and began to manually wind the instrument's peg. *This is it, now's the time.*

He eased back toward the console and leaned against it as though he were preparing himself to enjoy a show. His hand felt underneath the console of blinking lights for a release he'd hoped he'd never have to use.

Auto-destruct.

Norfung wound the string into tune and tested it before giving the instrument a few strums. Telfo curled her tail around him and pulled herself close as he began to play a few bars of descending notes.

Parr's fingers found purchase and gently gripped the release he was looking for.

Norfung's song was beautiful. Nothing he'd expected to hear from the galaxy's most dangerous bounty hunter, and nothing he could have heard from the palace court's most skilled musician. There was heartbreak in his tone, there was hope on top of the heartbreak, there was a life unmatched and unknown inside the Sixteen in its composition.

It was a song worthy of this room, worthy of the *Aurora,* and worthy of the moment. The last thing he'd ever hear.

Parr depressed the button. In a moment, it would all be over. A moment the galaxy would speak of forever. The moment where the prince defeated the pirate king within her own kingdom. A death worthy of lore, and more than he'd ever hoped for.

He released the button and his hold on life in one last, desperate act.

CHAPTER 36

Everything was dark. Just as Parr had always imagined death to be. However, he'd always hoped it would be like the time before he was born. He'd be nonexistent, or maybe resting so peacefully that there was nothing to think about or remember. Yet there he was, thinking about his predicament. Perhaps he could sleep. Drift off for eons as stars formed, grew, and died. As the Sixteen expanded, shrank, relocated, or collapsed.

He'd never have to eat again, never have to worry about his next score—he'd never have to worry about anything anymore, just float there in the dark.

So why did it feel heavy? Why did it still feel like he had mass?

The reserve lights hummed to life, a dim orange brown.

He was still on the ship.

How am I still on the Aurora?

Parr ran through all the modifications he'd made—software hacks, a circuit replacement here, a module there—but couldn't remember ever messing with auto-destruct. So, what was it?

He pinched the bridge of his nose and shook his head.

Of course, Parr thought. There wasn't enough fuel for the self-destruct. The groppodite had kept the fuel reserve full, but with the gem gone, the drainers must have finally been able to do their work properly and had started to empty the cells.

The system had required too much power, and when it couldn't access it, it had just shut down. Of course, it wouldn't have been a problem if he hadn't coded the software in such a way as to divert certain systems to another for a more powerful and efficient engine thrust.

Telfo held out a clawed finger. "Treachery."

His last hope dashed, Parr's shoulders crumpled. His head felt like it weighed as much as a grint of Gorlem slak. It hung low as he gazed down at the floor, and he barely took notice as Norfung tackled him to the deck and replaced his restraints, and added some new ones around his legs.

Parr lay on the floor staring blankly at his captors' ankles and almost grinned at his predicament. There he was, on the floor of his ship, with no hope of escape from two of the most dangerous creatures in the galaxy. It was literally the lowest point of his life.

"Where is the gem?" Telfo asked, looking down on him. Her pointed teeth gnashed as though she was coming for his throat—and maybe she was.

Parr chuckled. It wasn't a put-on; it was just all he could do.

Norfung stung his jaw with a blow from his forearm. "Tell her."

Telfo knelt beside Parr and gripped his throat. The tips of her claws unsheathed around his neck with the promise of a swift end. That sobered him up—for a moment.

"It's not here," Parr said. His mouth filled with a salty copper taste; he leaned to his side and spat out blood. "You just sent it off to the one place even you wouldn't try to retrieve it from."

Telfo seemed confused for a moment, then let out a string of curses fit for the mantle of pirate king. It was so loud, vile, and poetically creative that Parr momentarily forgot the danger he was in and appreciated the verbal artistry on display.

"The girl . . . the stumble . . . the catch . . . of course," she said.

"Glogs and borlongs! Someone tell me what's going on."

"The girl is taking the gem back to Moma Shando's." The pirate king pulled up her device and started a whirl of motions, no doubt pulling information and sending out directives. "Maybe Ludon Yelray can bring her back to us."

Parr hoped he'd read the old pirate correctly. Still, his hands began to sweat.

"I love the food there," Norfung said.

"Yeah, I've heard it's great," Parr replied.

"Silence him," Telfo said as she continued to scan and fidget with the controls on her wrist.

Norfung reached down and grabbed Parr by the collar before bashing his head against the floor.

"Ow," Parr said. "Shame about the groppodite. Guess that puts us all in a bind, right, guys?"

He immediately regretted saying it.

The bounty hunter hardly struggled to pull Parr's full dead weight up off the floor before throwing him against the console and roughing him up with an elbow to the jaw.

It didn't matter. Parr didn't care what happened to him anymore. All hope was lost. At least Ren had made it out, and that was all he cared about. He was almost pleased when one of Norfung's blows finally knocked him unconscious.

⋀

The sound of bickering roused Parr from his blunt-force-trauma–induced nap. His vision returned to him around the edges, then slowly came back to full view. He was being dragged through the hangar by his collar.

The *Aurora* stood proud in the hangar among the other ships. But from Parr's point of view, her ports looked down on him as though she didn't want him to see him go. She would be fine, he thought. Telfo would take good care of her. Maybe even make her the flagship of her fleet. Telfo's crew were already at work carefully removing the drainers.

Goodbye, Aurrie.

Tears filled his eyes and sinuses, and eventually, he couldn't help but sniff. A signal to his captors that he was back with them.

"I won't apologize for my methods, there was too much at stake—he's awake," Telfo said. He couldn't see her, but her presence loomed large. One did not attempt to destroy the pirate king of Anatone Seven without inciting her wrath.

"Treachery voids the last of the deal, Parrtec," Telfo said. She was clipping the ends of her words again. "You leave with nothing, and I've upheld the code."

"The code that binds," Parr said in a punch-drunk singsong voice.

Norfung flung him down by his collar roughly and bounced his head against the floor of the hangar. "Ow," Parr said with almost a chuckle. "Good one there, Norf." Parr cleared his throat. "It's not like I was ever leaving, though. Right, Telfo?"

"Clever," Telfo said. "When did you work it out?"

The truth was, he hadn't really—not consciously. It had just kind of spilled out in the moment. It seemed like he was onto something, though, so he thought he'd let it play out. "Back on the ship, when I tried to blow us all up," Parr said. "Remember?"

"Hit him again," Telfo replied.

"Whoa, whoa," Parr said. "Hold on."

"Show me your powers of deduction, Your Highness," Telfo said. "Dazzle me."

"I don't know about dazzle," Parr said, "but I'll tell you what I think." *Maybe I can keep them talking and find a way out.* "See … ," Parr said, and then the realization dawned on him. Now that he really thought about it, it all made sense. "The guy I lifted the gem from didn't strike me as any type of mastermind. He talked a little too much, acted too mysterious, but I didn't buy his act. Seemed like he'd been a lifer on that station, and anyone stuck out on that outpost certainly wasn't someone with the means to hold something of value like what you and Ren have described. That's why I didn't think twice about taking it from him in the first place."

"Go on," Telfo said.

"Of course it was you, all along," Parr said. "There is no way that guy could afford Norfung." He wished he could see their faces. "Maybe that's why I never figured out exactly why you were after me, Norf."

The bounty hunter grunted.

"Anyway," Parr said, "I figure he was just holding the groppodite for you, and when you sent someone to retrieve it, it was gone."

The pirate king chuckled. "I didn't even have to pay," Telfo said. "Not with coin, anyway."

Parr couldn't see her face, but it sounded like she said it to Norfung with a sultry grin, and it grossed him out.

"I never put you two together," Parr said, "you and Norfung, but now that I see it—it makes sense. The galaxy's most feared bounty hunter supplied by the galaxy's feared pirate king—with knowledge of every shady deal in the most questionable of outposts anywhere outside of the Sixteen. How long have you been supplying him with information?"

"Quite some time," Telfo responded.

"He's been playing with a loaded deck all along," Parr said to himself, but out loud.

Norfung casually banged Parr's head onto the deck again.

"Ow," Parr said, and rubbed the back of his head. "What doesn't track, though, is why you remained so personally involved. You could have just given him access to your information."

"She does that so we have a reason to talk," Norfung said. "That said, I didn't know the gem was yours all along."

"Oh, so you don't like talking to your lover?" Telfo replied.

"No, I do—I do."

"So first of all," Parr said, "ew. 'Lover.' You know that's gross, right?" Norfung kicked at him, but Parr was able to move his head out of the way. "Secondly, that's adorable—you two seem to communicate well."

"My patience is fading," Telfo said.

"Thirdly, I didn't consider any of it at all, I was just spitballing. Total lucky guess, like one in a million."

But the two ignored him.

"You should have just told me," Norfung said. "You can trust me. If you weren't just seizing an opportunity, what are your plans for the groppodite?"

"I do trust you, my love, but I can't have that type of information out there. With the gem in hand, we can finally mobilize like a real army. No more operating at the fringes."

Parr couldn't see what was happening above him, but he could hear Telfo whispering something to Norfung.

"Maybe we can work out a deal," Parr said. "These handcuffs for my freedom. They look expensive, I bet you could get a pretty coin out of them."

The couple ignored him, and Norfung urgently whispered something back to Telfo.

"We're good at the fringes, my love," Norfung said, and slowed to a stop. Parr could feel the two pull close even if he couldn't see them.

"We could be better," Telfo said.

"You couldn't be any better, my love," Norfung replied.

Parr was thankful he couldn't see the kisses and wished he couldn't hear them. The smacking, deep-throated groans, hungry noises, and weird purring. Fortunately for Parr, Telfo's wrist device buzzed and mercifully brought the exchange to an end.

"The energy signature is massive," Telfo said. "She's still here."

No, Parr thought. Why didn't Ren leave? What was she up to, but maybe more important, what was *Manc* up to?

"How could that be possible?" Telfo continued. "The ludon hasn't returned my communication, and he should have left with young Shando long ago. With the groppodite aboard the Corvin, they should almost be halfway there by now."

It was then that the ringing in Parr's ears from the multiple blows to the head was replaced by the thrum of the engines of two vessels closing in on them from either side of the hangar.

CHAPTER 37

The golden nose of a Corvin-class cruiser descended directly in front of Parr's field of vision. He turned his head around in the opposite direction to find the no-frills outline of the military ship that had facilitated his escape all those years ago coming to rest.

His chest swelled with excitement, and he allowed himself the spark of hope that maybe he could escape on that ship one more time.

The noise from the exhaust ports of the Corvin's landing gear caught Parr's attention. Slowly, out of the mist, stepped a large figure dressed in wrapped leather, similar to Agrofor Telfo's attire. A gauzy, flowing mane whipped around furiously in a wash of wind. The creature grinned and casually rested a blaster the size of a floor cannon on his shoulder.

Another oripian? Parr thought. Or was it the same oripian as the one in the tunnels? How was it he'd gone his whole life without seeing one, and now they were popping up left, right, and center?

"Novie the Swift," Telfo drawled.

So the stories are true, Parr thought.

"I thought I was rid of you," Telfo continued. "Didn't you eliminate him, my love?"

"I delivered the package," Norfung replied. "Last I heard, he was being held at Shando's for final delivery. No one escapes Moma Shando."

"Yet, there he stands," Telfo said.

There's no way, Parr thought. The famed captain of the Corpulon Valvente turned infamous pirate. *He* was the one in the cage back at Moma's?

The oripian brought the business end of his blaster down from his shoulder and aimed it at the small group as he shifted his weight in a swaggering lean. "So, that's how you deal with a political rival, eh, Telfo?"

"Sometimes," Telfo replied. "Others, more personally."

"But you needed cover," Novie said. "And to embarrass me with capture."

"Glogs and borlongs! It's no embarrassment to be awashed in the *Dreadnet*."

"No offense, Norfung," Novie said. "You're a formidable creature. I just never understood how you found me."

"They're working together," Parr said.

"Yes, I know," Novie said. "Thank you, Your Highness, I'll take it from here."

Your Highness, Parr thought. *Does everyone know? Why did I even bother faking my own death?*

"You seem to have a lot of information," Telfo said. "I have more if you'd like to retire back to my quarters."

Novie chuckled. "Thank you, but no. You can't be trusted. You broke the code."

"The code that binds us," Parr said in a singsong whisper.

"You broke the code and left me for dead," Novie said. "A miscalculation that will cost you. My old crew has a long memory, and with a few well-placed buldoons, it didn't take much to get close. That's when I ran into an old friend of ours."

"Told you I had a contingency," Manc said.

Manc? Parr thought. "I knew I could count on you," he said.

Truth be told, Parr hadn't known he could count on the old pirate, but he was certainly relieved to hear his voice again.

Parr whipped his head around just in time to see Manc wobble to a stop. A blaster and a cutlass pointed toward Norfung and Telfo, respectively. Parr couldn't help but wonder why Manc would be holding a cutlass, of all things, but he had more important things on his mind. Like, where was Ren?

"Where's Ren?" Parr asked.

"It's going to be OK." Ren's voice boomed through the speakers of the military vessel. The speakers on board were built not only to communicate but to disperse crowds in a pinch. As a result, the sound made everyone in the hangar jump.

Parr exhaled through a joyous grin. Things really were going to be OK.

Telfo took that moment to grab Parr by the throat with yet another promise of a bloody end.

Or maybe not.

Novie the Swift drew a cutlass of his own and pointed it directly at her. "You may ignore the challenge of a ludon, but you cannot ignore mine. The code compels you."

Parr decided that it wasn't the time to cut in with a jaunty "the code that binds" rejoinder. The mood in the hangar was somehow even more tense than it had been when only the blasters had been drawn.

The cutlasses were some sort of ritual challenge, Parr thought. *Did Manc really just make a play for pirate king?*

"I am the code," Telfo replied. "The code is what I will it to be."

"Glogs and borlongs, love."

"We're nothing without the code," Novie replied. The oripian's countenance changed, as if he were a child learning St. Corundian wasn't real. "Without it, everything unravels."

"Blasters away, or the young prince here meets his doom," Telfo said, and squeezed Parr's neck tighter.

"Grrk!" Parr exclaimed.

"I owe him my life," Novie said, and nodded toward Manc. "And he's traded in his favor for the safe return of the boy. You and I settle this now, Agrofor."

"I'll take the bounty hunter, you take Telfo," Manc said.

"That's what I just said," replied Novie.

"Glogs and borlongs, Novie! Don't be a fool."

"No sudden moves," Novie said. "I find you an honorable chap, Norfung. This is between her and me."

"It doesn't have to be this way, Manc," Telfo said. "You have the Corvin; you could be my Sword."

"And risk the wrath of Novie's crew?" Manc asked. "No, I don't think so, Agrofor."

"They'd come to heel," Telfo said. "They always do."

"I made my deal, Agrofor," Manc replied. "The code still means something to me."

"Seems we're at an impasse," Telfo said. "Or are we?"

"A deal can always be struck," Novie said.

"Our lives for the boy, then?" Telfo asked.

"For now," Novie replied. "But you and I have unfinished business."

"Naturally," Telfo replied. "I'd expect nothing less."

"So, it's a deal?" Manc asked.

Telfo released Parr's throat. "Unlock the restraints."

Novie returned the cutlass to its enormous sheath but kept the floor cannon trained on the couple.

Norfung released the foot and wrist restraints without ceremony. Parr glared at Telfo as he rubbed his wrists where the restraints had bound him.

"Good luck, young prince," Telfo said. "You'll need it."

Parr shook his head and started to pivot to the old military vessel but paused for a moment when he locked eyes with Norfung.

In their previous encounters, he'd only imagined what Norfung had looked like when he was outmaneuvered in their dogfight. The look on his face as Parr relayed a pithy one-liner before pulling away into the safety of a rift.

However, it was nothing like the eyes he stared into now. The look of fear.

He recognized it.

Not fear for oneself, but fear for the very thing one lived for. The thing you truly loved more than anything. The Norfung Gortn he'd come to know would easily meet death with all the vim and vigor of a true warrior. This Norfung, however, would do anything to keep his loved one alive. Parr didn't like to see it, even from Norfung, and felt compelled to avert his gaze.

Novie, who naturally towered over the rest of the party, eyed Manc for the next move.

"The boy goes with us," Manc said. "As discussed."

Telfo tracked Parr like the apex predator she was as he fell in with Manc.

"Your Highness," Parr said.

"Majesty," Telfo replied.

Manc looked like his old self again to Parr. Dodgy, but trustworthy in his own way. His eyes seemed to say it all. An apology for the elaborate ruse necessary to get to the promised result. Manc's eyeline shifted from Parr to Novie. "I want her back in one piece."

"Farewell," Novie replied. "I hope if we see each other again, it will be under better circumstances."

"Hope? No, I mean it," Manc yelled. "One piece!" He clapped Parr on the shoulder and whispered under his breath, "That furry-headed mound of teeth better have my Corvin when we're on the other side of this, or by the five suns—"

Parr felt the mood change before he heard it.

"Run, lad," Manc said. "Run!"

"Where?!" Parr shouted.

"What do you mean, where?" Manc replied. "To the ship! Let's get out of here and get you home, bumble-forked wisp of an arvo."

The floor was moving, he thought. No, only parts of the floor were moving—the hangar's defenses had been triggered. He took a last look over his shoulder as he boarded the old military vessel to see a wildly grinning Agrofor Telfo, one hand raised, wrist at her maw.

"Avast, my hearts," her voice boomed over Anatone Seven's public address system. "To Bolton's Bay!"

CHAPTER 38

The retired vessel smelled of dust and oil. Its interior was stark and gray, with one main cabin, a small hold, and a couple of spartan latrines.

Parr felt Ren's tear-streaked cheek against his as she pulled him close in a tight embrace. "I was afraid I'd lost you," she said.

"You should have left when you had the chance," Parr said. He leaned his forehead against hers and brushed her hair behind her ear. "But I'm glad you didn't." He kissed her, then pulled back to gaze into her eyes. "Thank you."

The two bounced sideways when Manc caught them with a shoulder as he wobbled by. "There's no time for that," he said as he pulled up the ship's controls. "We only have a few moments before those cannons are up and operational."

Ren kissed Parr's cheek and, with a shove, sent him toward a gunner's seat as she strapped into one of her own. The cabin was lined with them on either side. Manc found his perch in the captain's chair and began to fidget with the controls. He accidentally brought up the monitor in front of the first mate's seat, which sat empty.

The lights on the console in front of Parr shone red, yellow, or white if they were on at all. He pulled up the old monitor and tested the gun's responses. Everything worked as it should. Manc cursed and hit the console in front of him. "Go, you fat-bellied wardo stuck in second-autumn muck." He looked back at his tiny crew. "We're like a brick in a swamp here. I can't get the system to respond."

Parr eyed Ren.

"I flew us here," she said. "I managed to hack your device so that Telfo sold the ship to both of us instead of just to you."

"So, you had access to all the ship's systems," Parr said.

"So I had access," Ren said with a grin.

Parr unstrapped and headed toward the front. "Switch with me," he said to Manc. "Hurry."

Manc rolled out of the seat and went back toward the row of gunner seats across from Ren. Parr strapped in and brought up all the systems. Everything operated as it should. He was more familiar with the layout than Manc was, since he'd learned to fly on military vehicles. The monitors showed the rising defense system from the hangar floor was almost online. After a quick series of commands to the console, the ship grumbled to life and was on its way.

"Take out those cannons," Parr barked. It felt good to be in control again.

He was back in his element, back behind the console of a ship. Soon, he'd be home to collect what was his by birthright; all he had to do was find a way to escape one last time. *No problem,* he thought. *Just have to escape the galaxy's most feared bounty hunter and the pirate king of Anatone Seven in her fortified hold.*

Most creatures would have been terrified in this type of situation, but Parr had never felt more alive. He steered the heavily armored hulk toward the exit. The old bird wasn't the sleek, elegant ship he was used to piloting, but then again, she was never designed to do the things Aurrie did.

All that said, the ship had strengths of its own. Significant strengths. Like a hull as tough as a rindocline's back and cannons that could blast through a civilian craft's shields like a hot knife slicing through butter.

A civilian craft like a Fano-class cruiser, for example.

"One last mission, old girl," he said under his breath with a gentle pat along the ship's console. "Just get us home in one piece."

Ren and Manc began to take out the cannons rising from Bolton's Hangar with a mix of clinical efficiency and swashbuckling panache.

"Har har," Manc said as he took out the last of them.

Parr jammed the throttle forward and gave the hangar one final look. A sprinting Norfung Gortn was the last thing he saw as the ship left port. He was dashing straight toward the *Dreadnet*.

Parr tried to bring the pilot's cannon online in time, but it was too late. The *Dreadnet* was at an impossible angle, and he couldn't risk turning around for a clean shot. There wasn't any time.

He cursed under his breath as he took the ship out toward the great expanse.

"Why are we on this heading?" Ren asked. "This is taking us toward Ursine Minor."

"Grav sling," Parr and Manc said at the same time.

They both knew that they were going to need as much speed as they could possibly get, and the small moon was the only thing with enough gravity in the area to get them to where they wanted to go.

"We'll ride the gravity from Ursine Minor Seven and shoot out toward the rift to the Sixteen. We're going to need every advantage we can find to outrun the *Dreadnet,* and who knows what else they'll be throwing our way," Parr said.

"Say, for example, an advantage like this," Ren said. The crimson gem swung to and fro on its golden chain below Ren's outstretched hand. She grinned and tossed it to Parr. He caught it, kissed it, and gave it a nimble spin around his finger.

"Bring me luck one last time, baby." Parr gripped the gem and kissed his hand.

"It's not luck," Ren said. "It's science."

"And luck," Parr said.

Ren rolled her eyes. *Science,* she mouthed.

The old ship hummed with new life thanks to the groppodite. Parr pulled up the systems log and watched the fuel supply charge to full. He pulled up a few schematics and started to check for quick hacks he could make to push more power to the thrusters. He found a few, made the changes, and hooted in victory as the ship poured on speed. They hurtled through space like a chunk of unrefined ore, but as his old teacher said, "You don't need aerodynamics in a vacuum, only velocity."

"Talk to me, Manc," Parr said. "What do we have coming our way?"

"Not much," Manc said as he maneuvered the instrument panel in front of him. "Aside from every available ship and battle-hardened crew on Anatone Seven."

"Anything we should be worried about?" Parr asked.

"Outside of the aforementioned assured death?" Manc replied. "Just the volley of missiles headed our way."

Parr saw it on his screen and deployed an anti-attack barrage to draw their trajectory. "Good looking out there, Ludon."

"Don't call me that," Manc said. "Not no more, anyway," he mumbled under his breath.

A lopsided grin spread across Parr's face as he went back to the panel to see where he could find more thrust. He made a couple of quick adjustments and rerouted some of the systems protocols.

"Looks like they're all taking the direct route toward the Sixteen," Ren said.

"No, they're going to form a blockade in front of the rift," Manc said.

"Don't worry, I got this," Parr said as he adjusted some of the instruments above him. "Wait, what's that?" He turned his focus to the chart ahead. Sure enough, among the myriad ships that were launching and lining up from Anatone Seven, one in particular with a familiar signature blew past the rest.

The *Aurora*.

Parr guessed Telfo was piloting Aurrie. Parr had always wondered what it would be like to see the *Aurora* in action from that angle, but he'd never thought it would feel this way. It hurt to see her hurtling through space without him. *Don't be too hard on the controls, Telfo,* he thought.

His ship was a sight to behold as she rocketed toward them at breakneck speed. Parr nervously twirled the tiny crimson gem and hoped the sling would be enough to get old vessel past her.

Of more critical importance at the moment, though, was the ship that was streaking to intercept them before they could even get to Ursine Minor Seven, and it wanted to talk.

The comms blinked orange.

"You got Parr, go," he said.

"Glogs and turf-ridden borlongs, Parr."

"Norfung, buddy," Parr said. "We got to stop meeting like this."

"I'm not your buddy, kid. Power it down, give me the gem, and walk away clean."

"Don't think I'll be doing any walking out here, Norf," Parr said. "Bad for the lungs."

"Listen to me, you impudent little—"

"Look, Norf, I don't even know what kind of adapter we'd need for a safe boarding. Honestly, I'd just as soon keep my heading and make my way through the rift before you get your little blockade established."

"I'm a creature of my word, Parrtec," Norfung said. "Please."

Please? Norfung Gortn never said "please."

"Norfung, there's no doubt you're a creature of your word. Telfo, on the other hand—"

"Parr," Ren said. "We're not going to outrun him at this rate. We need more speed. Spin the gem faster or something."

She was right, Parr thought. Norfung would be within range soon and would cut them off before they got a chance to grav-sling if they didn't outrun him. Parr checked his systems for any little boost of power but couldn't find anything else. He spun the little crimson gem around the chain and pounded the arm of his chair with joy as the ship began to pour on speed.

"Glogs and borlongs! This is your last chance, Parr. I must have the groppodite."

"Couldn't hear that last part, buddy, you're cutting out—oh, no—" Parr said with a sarcastic grin and a wink at Ren.

"Goodbye, Parrtec," Norfung said. "I tried."

Parr dropped the grin immediately and sat up straight in his chair.

It was a masterstroke, he had to admit. He didn't see it coming. The blast enveloped the ship in a blinding white light and rattled them all like ice cubes in a shaker. Norfung must have fired the missile when the conversation began but only just now activated it, when Parr had exhausted the last of his goodwill.

Thankfully, the old vessel was built to take a few punches from even the most powerful cannons. It might have been old and slow, but it was built to last. At least for a few more hits. He wondered what lethal weapons the *Dreadnet* possessed within her hold. So far, he'd only escaped Norfung's nonlethal variety.

"Not so cocky now, are you, boy?" Norfung said. "I can't wait to see the look on your face once I've sorted your remains from the floating debris."

"Someone needs to tell him that's not how it works," Manc said as he frantically checked and double-checked the gauges in front of him.

The console alerted the crew that the *Dreadnet* had fired another round. The monitor marked the volley as critical.

"Heads up, lad," Manc said. "Incoming."

"I see it," Parr said.

Norfung was done playing, and Parr was no longer a bounty. As tiny as it was, they could eventually find the groppodite through its energy signature. It would be time-consuming, but it was a better option than letting it slip away inside the Sixteen.

"Coming in fast," Ren said.

"Let me see what tricks this old bird has up its sleeves," Parr said.

Parr checked his inventory and, to his horror, found he was low on anti-attack packages. He made a couple of quick calculations in his head. If they were able to get past Gortn, they'd still have to sling past an armada's worth of ships regardless of whether or not they'd been able to successfully set up a blockade.

"Everything alright over there?" Ren asked.

"Yep," Parr said. He punched a few maneuvers into his nav and grabbed the manual drive. He was going to need to draw on his skill, the ship's computer, and a whole lot of luck. "Everything is going to be OK."

Hopefully.

CHAPTER 39

Parr pulled back on the throttle to let the first missile pass, then punched it forward and twisted the ship into a maneuver to avoid the second and third. The ship's computer assisted with the fourth and fifth, and Parr pulled back hard to avoid the final missile on their path toward the small moon.

"Five suns, Parr," Ren cursed. "You couldn't have used an anti-attack package?"

Manc hooted and hollered, "That's flying, lad!"

"We only have a couple left, Ren. I'm doing what I can."

"Spin the gem faster," she said. "Or anything to agitate it further. He's on course to intercept."

"I'm spinning," Parr said.

Agitate it? Parr thought. *What could agitate it? Or how could I spin it faster?*

The *Dreadnet* was closing in, but there was a chance Parr could get his ship into position first. If they could slip by, they'd have enough speed to get past the blockade before it formed. Then he'd just have to worry about Norfung's gaining ground and the *Aurora*, wherever it was.

Another barrage headed their way, and Parr rechecked his inventory. To the suns with scarcity; he couldn't risk losing momentum. He engaged the second-to-last anti-attack package and watched in relief as it successfully drew Norfung's attack away.

"Are you two going to return fire, or what?" Parr shouted.

"What do you think we've been doing?" Manc yelled over his shoulder. "That ruddy-looking shank of a dolker is slipperier than a greased prooter through a Gruvnav's wheel well."

"It's going to be OK, Parr," Ren said. "You've got this."

"That's right," Parr said to himself. "I got this." He pulled up the ship's schematics again and looked for anything else he could tweak. Luckily, he found just the thing. A few reroutes, and they'd be able to push enough power to get them past the *Dreadnet* and into a grav sling.

Initializing, the monitor pop-up said.

Initializing?! Parr thought.

He cursed under his breath. The ship was old and needed some time to establish the new protocol. Unfortunately, Norfung had just unleashed a new barrage, and Parr had a choice to make: use the last anti-attack package, or hope the protocol established itself in time.

He looked at Ren through the reflection in the monitor. She was head-down at her console, looking for any and every angle that could give them an edge. Parr wanted to kick himself for thinking about how beautiful she was at that moment, but he couldn't help it. He'd never met anyone like her before.

He loved her.

If it were just him, he might have left it to chance, but it wasn't. He decided he couldn't risk it and pressed the button to release the last package.

It did what it was designed to do and drew the attack away. The protocol clicked into place, and the ship pushed forward into the grav sling. Whatever happened from that point on would be all speed and shields with a little bit of luck mixed in.

Parr wasn't sure how much the shields could take, but one thing he knew for sure was that their speed wasn't anywhere near what he could get out of the *Aurora.*

Parr felt his stomach drop as the gravity of Ursine Minor Seven took hold. He navigated the ship along the line between orbit and an early release. The line he'd been taught about all those years ago, the perfect trajectory he had a knack for instinctively choosing every time. He loved the feeling and prayed that the maneuver would be worth the gambit.

The tiny moon's gravity pulled them in and released them at just the right moment to put them on a collision course with the only nearby rift to the Sixteen. They would be nearly impossible to track at the speed they were going, and the volley of fire from the incomplete blockade missed every mark they set to hit the vessel.

Manc pounded his console. "Nice work, Parr." He slapped his hands together, then rubbed them. "You really do know how to fly."

"We're not out of the woods yet," Ren said. "There's one ship between us and the rift."

One ship. He knew it without looking. "Aurrie."

"Parr," Ren said. "How do you know it's—"

"I know," Parr replied. "You know it too."

"It's just a ship, Parr," Ren said.

How could she say that? "It's not. You know it's not."

"Telfo's not going to just let us pass like a brundle through a breeskin," Manc said.

"What makes you think Telfo's flying the *Aurora?*" Ren asked.

"She wants to take you out with your own vessel," Manc said. "You're a flashy pilot, lad. It will only add to her legend, and she needs that political capital every bit as much as she needs that groppodite for whatever weapon she's putting together. Novie will be back to challenge her, and he'll use the violation of the code against her."

Parr brought up the old tank's design one last time and looked for any other advantage he could find. Maybe there was a tractor beam he could use to pull the *Aurora* along with them. The sudden movement would catch Telfo off guard. He could activate the code for a captured ship and keep the *Aurora* after all.

There it is.

This old vessel had it—only he'd already redirected its functionality and put it toward the thruster. If he had enough time, maybe he could direct it back, but it would cost them speed.

There had to be another way, he thought.

Manc wobbled out of his seat and leaned in over Parr's shoulder. "I see what you're doing there, son." His voice was deep and rich, like a whisper through honeyed gravel. "It's a good idea, but you're not going to catch Agrofor sleeping."

"Besides," Ren said, "I'm not sure what that beam would do to the multona drainers. They'd likely explode, and you'd pull that reaction in toward us."

"Telfo had them removed," Parr said.

"Are you sure?" Ren asked. "When did she have time—"

"I saw her crew when I was back in the hangar. I don't think she'd even have been able to launch with the drainers attached. This thing was the only thing keeping us flying." Parr lifted the gem as it spun.

"What's plan B?" Ren asked.

Parr searched the ship's systems for everything he could think of, and he was running out of options fast. They were on a path to intercept, and he could see from the screen that the weapons system on the *Aurora* was up . . . only the weapon was something he didn't recognize. He wasn't sure how, but Telfo had managed to outfit Aurrie with a weapon he hadn't seen before.

"Fire even a glancing blow with one of these cannons," Manc said, "and the *Aurora* would be in pieces."

"Even at full shields, the *Aurora* won't be able to withstand the blast," Ren added. "Not from these charges."

Parr looked back as though her words were a slap . . . and they were. Who was she to say that about his Aurrie?

"Sorry," Ren said. "It's just a fact. I didn't mean anything by it."

Who was *she?*

She was the creature that Parr loved . . . and she loved him back . . . probably. She was almost everything to him now, more important than any chair inside a throne room, that was for sure. Even more important than the one place he truly considered home.

"It's OK," he said. "I know what I have to do."

He locked eyes with Ren for a moment before her attention was quickly pulled away. "More bad news," she said. "Norfung is approaching fast from behind."

"We have to do it now, lad," Manc said.

The ship's comms buzzed with static noise. He'd left them open after his exchange with Norfung earlier. "Don't do it, Parr," Norfung said. "I can stop her. Please, just give me the gem—I'll escort you personally."

Just pass the gem off, and I'm back through, Parr thought. It seemed like a good option. He chewed at the inside of his cheek.

"She'll never agree to it, Parr," Manc said. "He's desperate."

Parr manically tapped at the cold steel handle of the ship's throttle. Manc was right, of course, and Parr could understand where Norfung was coming from. In fact, he'd never identified with the bounty hunter more than he did at that moment. He'd say or do anything to save the one he loved.

Parr cut the comms and turned his attention to the nav screen.

His systems showed the *Aurora's* weapons were charged and ready, but the old military vessel had the edge in firing range. Aurrie may have been built for speed, but this thing was built for war.

Parr's eyes welled with tears as he thought back to the warm interior of the bridge and the grimy cabin of the Fano-class cruiser as though the answer might be on one of its dingy walls. The blue, green, and orange lights . . . their comforting rhythm and the soothing hum of the atmosphere unit. His beautiful angel, his home.

"I don't have the angle from here, Manc," Ren said. "Do it for him."

Manc shook his head. "Let him, dear. He needs to be the one."

"I've got this," Parr said. "It should be me."

Ren had always said it was just a ship. That it wasn't even as fast a ship as it got credit for and it was mainly the groppodite all along. But Parr knew better. He hadn't always had the gem with him, and they'd accomplished mission after successful mission together. Score after score. They were a team. Creatures knew him because of the *Aurora*, and maybe some knew her because of him—but they were linked. Together, forever.

Until that moment.

Parr pulled up his cannon and zeroed in.

"Goodbye, Aurrie," he said.

And pulled the trigger.

The blast did exactly what he thought it would. The *Aurora*'s shields were no match for the ship's cannons. The Fano-class cruiser exploded like a tiny supernova, bright, wondrous, and the end of something beautiful.

At that moment, the Parr whom the outer reaches had known died with her. The Parrtec of the Sixteen would soon rise in his place.

CHAPTER 40

The swirling blue lights of the rift embraced them.

"I'm sorry, lad," Manc said. He gripped Parr's shoulder. "I know what it's like."

Parr wiped at his eyes with one swipe from his sleeve. "It's alright. I'm alright."

Parr wasn't alright, though. He'd just lost his companion, his symbol of freedom—his home. And he was the one who'd put her down. He had done something that, for once, he couldn't undo.

The cabin fell silent aside from the whir of the oxygen unit and a few clanks of the vessel's machinery.

Parr looked at the outline of Ren's reflection in his nav and smiled. He knew he'd do it all again if it meant he could be with her. He had everything he needed right there in the outdated vessel. Still, something nagged at the back of his mind.

"Manc," Parr said, "why'd you come back for me? Why'd you save Ren?"

Manc stroked his beard and slowly exhaled. He paced around the cabin a few times before returning to clap his hand on Parr's shoulder. "Son, I'm at an age where . . . well—" The old pirate stopped and collected himself. He fidgeted with his fingers. "See, I've acquired all sorts of treasure over the years. Sometimes for the thrill, sometimes out of necessity. To be honest, most times out of fear for what the future may hold, you know?"

Fear, Parr thought. Fear was an unrelenting motivator. If what Telfo had said was true, Manc had come up fighting for every scrap life threw his way, constantly wondering where his next meal would come from.

"You saved money?" Parr asked.

Manc chuckled and waved him off. "I'm trying to say something sentimental here, lad."

"Sorry," Parr said. "Go ahead."

"It was hard to lose *Vanessa's Complaint.* Just like it was hard for you to lose the *Aurora.*"

Parr nodded.

"It was harder to lose Vanessa, though."

"Why was it harder to lose your ship than mine?" Parr asked.

"Not the ship, lad," Manc said. "Not the ship. Vanessa. She was the only family I ever really had. Until now, that is."

"Are you saying that sometimes life is its own treasure?" Ren asked.

"No," Manc said, his face pinched in disgust. "I don't think I'd ever say that."

Ren rolled her eyes and shook her head.

Manc shot her a wink. "I guess what I'm trying to say is that I'd rather spend time with the both of you than keep floating through space on my own looking for the next score. You're like family to me. Like a son."

Parr saw it. In fact, he'd seen it for a while. In a way, Parr had always trusted the old pirate, even if he had played a little fast and loose with their deals. After all, Manc had taken him under his wing at Versit all those years ago. Walked him through what ship might be right for him in the outer reaches before the two settled on the trade for the *Aurora.*

Moreover, Manc had stuck his neck out for him, and he wasn't sure if his father would have done the same . . . and now he'd never know.

"Uncle, maybe," Parr said, "or like a way older fourth cousin."

Manc's face dropped.

"Manc," Parr said. "I'm kidding. You're as family as anything I've ever known."

Ren walked over to put her arm around the old pirate. "For all I know, you could actually be my father," she said.

⌂

They found themselves on the other side of the rift, and even though they were hurtling along at the exact same speed at which they'd entered, all felt quiet.

Parr brought the nav full-screen so that it took up the expanse of the bow side of the craft. The massive wall that encompassed Bilena Epso Ach was visible on the monitor. It wouldn't be long now.

The comms blinked red, and Parr knew who it was before he answered. Who else could it be? As much as he loved Aurrie, Ren was right—she was just a ship.

There had been a pilot in that ship, however. A pilot who had a life, a history, and someone who loved her. A partner who'd planned to be with her for the rest of her life, and now that creature was gone.

"Don't," Ren said. "He's almost within range."

"We're almost to the gates of Bilena Epso Ach, Parr," Manc said. "You're almost home."

Parr flipped the comms. "I'm sorry, Norf—"

"Glogs and borlongs," said the voice over the speakers. Not a hero's declaration or the bounty hunter's expression of exasperation that Parr had become accustomed to, but the brittle lament of a broken soul. "Why couldn't you have just taken my offer?"

Parr didn't have the words. Ren muted their side. "Parr, he's on course to intercept, we're not fast enough."

"I'll end you here and now, Parrtec," Norfung said. "And if not now, soon. I'll come for you and all of your people. I'll never stop."

"Spin the gem, Parr, do something," Ren said.

Parr spun the tiny crimson gem on the slight golden chain as fast as he could. The vessel poured on speed, but it wasn't enough to put any distance between the two vessels.

"Do you hear me, Parr? I'll never stop. Today, or someday soon, I'll kill you."

"Manc, do you see anything we can do?" Ren asked. "Parr, snap out of it! We need you."

"I'll kill her," Norfung growled. "While you watch."

That was enough to sharpen Parr's focus. He'd exhausted every hack he knew. He looked down at the tiny crimson gem he'd once thought of as a trinket of good luck as it spun back and forth across his finger as fast as it could go, but his finger could only spin it so much. He eyed the groppodite and hoped it would give him inspiration one last time.

It did.

What if he could spin it faster?

He felt his jacket pocket and was pleased to find the glitchy little peg winder still in place. "Manc," he said. "Take over for me." He slapped an invitation to join him on the cushion of the copilot's seat. The old pirate shot up, wobbled over, and strapped in. "Ren, give us cover fire," Parr said. "Something for him to dodge."

"Aye-aye, Cap," she said. He couldn't tell if she was being sarcastic.

He took a look at the winder and found to his delight that the gem fit inside it, albeit loosely. He'd need something to secure it. There had to be something on board.

Parr searched the room for anything he could use, but nothing jumped out at him. He scanned the various labels for the storage compartments, most of which had been looted over the years in dock.

Fire of the five suns! he thought. *The labels!*

He carefully peeled off one of the longer labels above one of the compartments closest to him and tested to see if the back was still sticky to the touch.

It was.

"Parr," Ren said. "He's closing. We need to do something fast."

Parr jammed the gem into place inside the winder, using the little gold chain to wedge it in tight, and wrapped the label around to keep it from flying out once it got going. He tested the device, and sure enough, it spun wildly, just like it had the time it broke both his and Norfung's strings.

"Weapons hot from his side," Ren reported.

"I can see the gates of Bilena Epso Ach on the viewfinder, Parr," Manc said. "Defenses armed and aimed, although I can't tell at whom."

Did he just say "at whom"? Parr thought. Manc really was full of surprises.

"Incoming signal from the gates," Manc said. "Wants to know what's going on."

"Guess we're about to see whether or not the badges and keys still work," Parr said. "Don't reply. If we bring up a communication, they may redirect, and I don't feel like giving that armada behind us a chance to catch up. Norfung is bad enough on his own. The keys in this vehicle allow for situations where comms may be down; we can talk to them once we're inside."

"OK," Manc said. "Maybe not how I would handle it, but shutting down comms."

"Is he kidding?" Ren asked. "We're hitting the gates at full speed?"

Manc's laughter filled the room. "Unless you have a better idea, lady," he said. "Either way, it's been a pleasure to fly alongside the both of you."

Parr hopped back into his seat as the peg winder spun the groppodite like a tiny little centrifuge, faster than he ever could. By its nature, the gem made the device more efficient, and to Parr's relief, he found that meant it spun even faster than its factory-set top speed.

"Parr," Ren said. "We got a hull integrity warning."

"Ship's not made to fly these speeds, lad," Manc said. "She's about to come apart."

"What?" Parr said. "That makes no sense, there's no air resistance in space!" He eyed Ren. "Tell him."

Ren opened her mouth to say something, but Manc cut through. "Engines are humming away at a vibration that's loosening the panels. I can't explain it."

"Parr," Ren said. "He's right, this ship isn't engineered to fly like this. We have to slow down or risk a breach."

Parr checked the nav and found that they were pulling away from Norfung.

"We can't slow down," Parr said.

Now, if only the keys worked on the gates at this speed, they'd be golden.

"He just fired something big," Ren said.

Parr wasn't sure what it could be, much less whether or not their shields would withstand it. One thing was for sure: they were going to either scream through the shields of Bilena Epso Ach or shatter into a billion little pieces scattered along its width.

"Major hull integrity warning, lad," Manc said. "We're all the way red."

One way or another, it would all be over soon.

Parr jammed the throttle as far forward as it would go and looked back at Ren. He couldn't imagine a better sight to behold as the last thing he'd ever see.

CHAPTER 41

Parr blinked. Ren was still there. They were through!

The stern-side nav screen showed the distorted ripple from whatever it was that Norfung had fired from his ship. The blast wave rolled across the shield that protected the Sixteen from the outer reaches. Parr had never seen anything like the explosion before and had no idea the planetary system's shield had that type of malleability. He'd never seen the seemingly immovable wall ripple before.

The *Dreadnet* pulled up short of the gates and hung in space like a deadly promise—one Parr knew he'd have to deal with someday, but for now, he was back home … or at least back in his home system. *We did it,* he thought. They'd escaped by the narrowest of margins.

He leaped from his seat, and Ren met him soon after. A deep kiss and a long embrace with her meant more to him than any coronation ever would.

Manc stared up at the ceiling from his gunner's seat and exhaled. His lips made a raspberry sound that turned into a minor coughing fit.

The old military vessel cruised at a speed more to its liking, and the hull integrity warnings faded. Parr checked the systems log to find no permanent damage had been done. He sent a hail to the guards at Western Gate Command, and soon they responded with a blinking blue light. He cursed under his breath; he couldn't believe that after all this, they'd put him on auto-hold. He made a few motions on his nav to try to override the protocol.

^

"Parr," the voice from Western Gate Command said over the comm. "Let me make sure I have this straight—you faked your death, assumed a new identity, and that new identity is essentially a shortened version of your actual name."

It sounded ridiculous when the station guard said it like that.

"Affirmative, control," Parrtec said. "I need clear passage back so that I can claim my place as ruler of the galaxy."

The comm line went mute before the voice returned. "And how did you get access to this line again?"

"I told you," Parrtec said. "I'm Prince Parrtec, rightful heir to the throne. Of course I know how to access the secure line."

"I see," the voice said. "Can you hold for a moment while I alert my superior?"

"Of course," Parrtec said, and folded his hands behind his head as he leaned back in the pilot's chair. He spun slowly around to see Ren and Manc staring back with open mouths. "Don't worry," he said. "I got this."

He took a last look around the spartan cabin of the old military ship and caught his reflection in one of the monitors. He put a hand through his shaggy, dark brown hair and checked it out from a couple of angles. He'd need to step into one of the latrines and have a shave before disembarking the vessel—yet another thing he would miss, a scruff.

Oh well, the things you do for your people, he thought.

He was almost home now, fresh from the far side of the outer reaches and inside the gates of Bilena Epso Ach, the two-planet, eight-moon system and capital of the sixteen-system intergalactic kingdom he'd soon rule, just like his father before him, and his father before him—all through the generations to the time before the wall that encapsulated the system.

It had never made sense to him that they called the grand translucent sphere a wall—it kept people out and all, sure, but "wall" seemed like such an inelegant term.

The comm link clicked, and Parrtec could hear what sounded like trailing laughter. "Your Worship?" a new voice from command asked.

"Please, Parrtec will do fine for now," Parrtec replied, and arched an eyebrow at Ren. He'd save the honorifics until after the crowning ceremony.

"Of course, sir," the voice replied. If Parrtec hadn't known any better, he would have thought she was smiling on the other end of the link.

"So sorry about your parents," the new voice said. "Such a tragic accident."

Tragic accident, Parrtec thought. He'd need to have a conversation with Malista once he got through.

"Your Majesty?" the new voice said.

"Oh yes," Parrtec said. "A tragedy, to be sure."

"And now here you are, a handful of years later, behind our gates—to claim your throne," the voice said.

"Affirmative," Parrtec said.

"I see," the voice said. "I'll need to alert my superior. Hold, please."

"Now, hang on a—" Parrtec began, but it was too late; the line muted out for the hold. He leaned forward in his chair. His fingers drummed the armrest, and he crossed and uncrossed his legs. Parrtec was starting to think the officials on the other end of the comm didn't believe him.

Manc's chest heaved as he tried to stifle his laughter. "I don't think they believe you, lad."

"I could be running my own empire right now," Ren said. "Maybe you could work for me."

Parrtec squinted at her and searched the depths of his mind for the appropriate sarcastic comment.

"Sorry, we're back," the voice from before said.

He grinned at Ren and held up a finger of hope.

"Yeah, we're here again," the original voice said. "OK. Tell us one more time who you are and why you're here."

Parrtec told them the story once again, with renewed enthusiasm for his new audience, playing up the story with a bit more liveliness than before. He even added a couple of adventures for good measure. He talked about how his skill as a pilot was enough to earn him the top spot in the Corpulon Valvente. How he'd breezed through the time trials on Zebulon Quarto, and how they'd just escaped the clutches of Norfung Gortn, Agrofor Telfo, and the quasi-armada of Anatone Seven.

He finished the last bit with all the polish and flair he could muster, drawing from years of personal tutoring from the galaxy's most celebrated public speakers. Parrtec leaned back in his seat, winked at Ren, and gave the peg winder a couple of last spins for good measure.

The voices on the other end of the comm erupted in laughter.

"Norfung Gortn," a lower, entirely new voice from command said. "Oh! That's good, that's very good. 'Oh! Oh! I'm Prince Parrtec, back from the grave! Listen to my brave, improbable stories.' Nice one," he said. "Thanks, you two. Thank you for alerting me."

Parrtec straightened in his chair, "Now, listen—"

"I told you, sir, it's one of the better ones we've heard," said the second voice.

The laughter began to trail off, and Parr quickly changed tack. "Got a shipment of Varulean napedes you might like," he said. "Finest in the Sixteen . . . "

He didn't, of course, but he was desperate.

"Oh, valk off. Get that ship in traction and the crew to med bay for psych eval," the chuckling voices replied just before he lost contact.

Really? Parr thought.

"Really?" Ren said.

"Really!" Manc said, and exploded in laughter. "All this, and we're headed to the brig for a mind shrink. Classic, lad. Classic!"

Parr remembered a tiny town beside the beach on the third moon of Kaweehan. Low security, plenty of naturally occurring instrument interference, and very few questions asked by locals. A couple of grav slings and they'd be there in no time.

"It's OK," Parr said. "I got this."

ACKNOWLEDGMENTS

Writing this book was a bright spot for me during tumultuous times, and I couldn't have done it without the help of a lot of great people. Thanks to my writing group (Tornado House) for all your help, this book wouldn't be the same without you. Kristin Luna, Shannon Fox, and Tyler West—y'all are the best!

Thanks to Blair Thornburgh, Aja Pollock, Emily Mullen, Kendall Davis, Jonathan Isaacs, and Jessica Reed for their guidance and expertise throughout the process. You're all fantastic!

To Ellen Lampl, for the incredible Electric Fern logo. I'm so proud of it, thank you for being there for me, I appreciate you!

Thanks to my family and friends for all your support.

And to the reader, thank you! I hope you enjoyed the book.

www.ingramcontent.com/pod-product-compliance
Lightning Source LLC
Chambersburg PA
CBHW070103120726
47909CB00002B/485